"Camille!"

She knew the voi
where she stood,
along with her he
face of the man –

For long moments it was as if time – the forest, the wind itself – became still. Which, then, was the mask? The bizarre leather, which was crafted in the form of a beast? Or this, the face of humanity, far more shocking than she had ever imagined, with its ruggedly hewn, arresting features, so classic in form they might have belonged to a distant god.

"Camille, please, for the love of God. Come with me. Come with me now."

Even as he spoke, she heard footsteps coming from behind her. She spun quickly, staring as the other man burst through trees and brush.

"Touch her and you're a dead man," growled the man she had known as "the beast."

"He's going to kill you, Camille. You know he's a murderer. For the love of God, Camille, the man is a monster!" the other softly intoned.

She looked from one man to the other, unable to hide the torment that stormed within her. Yes, one of them was a murderer. And the other was her salvation. But which one was which?

SHANNON DRAKE

Wicked

M&B

*M&B™ and M&B™ with the Rose Device
are trademarks of the publisher.*

*First published in paperback in 2005.
This edition 2006
by Harlequin Mills & Boon Limited, Eton House,
18-24 Paradise Road,
Richmond, Surrey TW9 1SR*

© Heather Graham Pozzessere 2005

*ISBN-13: 978 0 263 85084 0
ISBN-10: 0 263 85084 6*

136-0806

*Printed and bound in Spain
by Litografia Rosés S.A., Barcelona*

For Franci Naulin, with all the love,
thanks and best wishes in the world

PROLOGUE

Unmasked

THERE WAS NOTHING TO DO but run. And pray, because that was her only salvation!

Surely the police would come. There had been a death! Yes, dear God. Surely, the police would come.

No, she was grasping at straws. The death had not happened here, so they would not come to the castle. But if Camille let that fact rule her mind too sharply, she would panic. And she needed her wits about her now, because she was running. *And because she didn't even know the face of the evil that followed her.*

She was far from the great castle of Carlyle itself, and she could hear her own labored breathing. It was like a fierce wind, driving her along. At last she had to stop. Yet when she did, she knew that it was not just her own desperate lungs creating the sound she had heard. The wind had risen. It was playing through the trees, the great canopy overhead. She was glad, hopeful that the anger of the elements would continue to force away the fog that always seemed to linger in these woods, so close to the barren shrub of the moors.

There was a full moon tonight, as well. If the fog dissipated, she could see more clearly. But so could those pursuing her.

Indeed, it meant that she could be seen, as well.

She gasped in deep breaths, and when she thought she could move again, she spun slowly in a circle, trying to get her bearings. The fragile lace tie on the bustle of her skirt caught upon a twig, and she wrenched it free, heedless of the elegance she so readily destroyed. Her mind was strictly upon escape and self-preservation.

The road was to the east. The road to London, to civilization, to sanity, was to the east. There had to be a coach upon it, bringing visitors back to the city. If she could just make it to the road before…the killer came upon her.

She was certain this game had been played long enough, certain he was coming to destroy her, to make sure that she never told what she knew. To make sure she never gave away the secrets of Carlyle Castle.

In the darkness and the mist that swirled with the growing fury of the coming wind, she heard the eerie sound of the howling. Wolves, restless as she, were crying out to the heavens. Yet, at this moment, she hadn't the least fear of the wolves of Carlyle. Because she knew the real danger. Call it a beast, but it came in the form of a man.

A rustle in the foliage warned her that someone was near. She straightened, praying that instinct would give her a hint, a way in which to run…. But the rustling was near, too near.

Run!

The command screamed in her mind. But even as she gathered her strength, it was too late. From the brush, he burst upon her.

"Camille!"

She knew the voice, all too well. She froze where she stood, breath caught in her throat, along with her heart. And she stared at the face of the man—*the face beneath the mask!*

Once she had known him only by touch, seen him only

in fleeting moments of abandon. His was a striking face, rugged but aesthetic, with a strong chin, the nose fine and straight. And the eyes…

She had seen the eyes clearly, always. They had challenged, disdained and assessed her. They had fallen upon her with a startling blue tenderness.

For long moments, it was as if time—the forest, the wind itself—became still. She stared, seeing his face now. Which, then, was the mask? The bizarre leather, which was crafted in the form of a beast? Or this, the face of humanity, far more shocking than she had ever imagined, with its ruggedly hewn, arresting features, so classic in form they might have belonged to a distant god.

What was real? The predatory menace of the beast or the righteous strength of the man?

"Camille, please, for the love of God. Come with me. Come with me now."

Even as he spoke, she heard the footsteps coming from behind her. Someone else? A savior? Or someone with a far more classic and customary facade? One of the others who purported to be her champions, yet all of them entangled in the mysteries and riches of the past? Lord Wimbly himself, Hunter, Aubrey, Alex…oh, God, Sir John.

She spun quickly, staring as the other man burst from an overgrown trail through trees and brush.

"Camille! Thank God!"

He came toward her.

"Touch her and you're a dead man," growled the man she had known as "the beast."

"He's going to kill you, Camille," the other said softly.

"Never," the beast intoned softly.

"You know he's a murderer!" the other charged.

"You know that one of us is a murderer," the beast said calmly.

"For the love of God, Camille, the man is a monster. It's been proven!"

She looked from one man to the other, unable to hide the torment that stormed within her. Yes, one of them was a murderer.

And the other one was her salvation. But which one was which?

"Camille, quickly, carefully…come to me," said the one.

The man she had known as the beast caught her eyes. "Think carefully, my love. Think of all that you have seen and learned…and felt. Think back, Camille, and ask yourself which man here is the monster."

Think back? To when? Rumor and lies? Or to the day when she had first come to this forest, first heard the howling and…the sound of his voice.

The day she had met the beast.

CHAPTER ONE

"GOOD LORD, what has he done *now?*" Camille asked with dismay, looking at Ralph, Tristan's valet, man's man and—unfortunately, most often—his cohort in crime.

"Nothing!" Ralph said indignantly.

"Nothing? I am left to wonder why you are standing in front of me, breathless, looking as if I'm about to be called to once again come to the aid of my guardian and rescue him from some jail cell, brothel or other place of ill repute!"

She knew that she sounded indignant and angry. Tristan was incapable of staying out of trouble. She also sounded as if she would let him stew in his pot of problems, which she would not. Ralph knew it, and she knew it.

Tristan Montgomery was not much of a respectable figure as far as guardians went, despite the fact that fate had provided him with a certain status, this being a time when a man's title meant far more than his true situation or character.

But twelve years ago he had rescued her from a workhouse or a worse fate. She shivered, thinking of other penniless orphans who had been left to fend for themselves. Tristan's means of support had never been what one would call acceptable, but from the day he had first seen her, alone with her mother's still-warm body, he had given his heart and his means—whatever they might be—to her. And she would never give him less.

However, she had been striving valiantly for several years now to give him more—stability! An honest place in society. A home. A far more decent life....

Luckily, Ralph had met her discreetly at the corner, rather than coming into the British Museum, where his disheveled appearance and anxious whispers might have cost her the job she had at long last acquired. She knew more about ancient Egypt than most of the men who had been on excavations, but even Sir John Matthews had hemmed and hawed about the idea of bringing in a woman. And with Sir Hunter MacDonald in on the decision, it had certainly not been an easy road. Hunter actually liked her very much, but the fact that he admired her might well have worked against her. He thought himself something of a seasoned explorer and adventurer—one who apparently gave no credence to the new breed of women suffragettes and sincerely thought that the fairer breed belonged at home. At least Alex Mittleman, Aubrey Sizemore and even Lord Wimbly seemed to accept her presence without much ado. Thankfully, Lord Wimbly and Sir John mattered the most.

Yet the trials and tribulations of her work could not be of much import at this moment. Tristan was in trouble. But on Monday evening! Just at the start of the workweek.

"I swear, Tristan did nothing." Ralph flushed. He was a little man, no more than five feet five inches, but he was spry. He could move with the speed of a lynx, and just as supplely and secretively, as well.

Camille was aware that although Tristan might not have done anything, he had certainly been *planning* something illegal when he arrived in whatever his current—and dire—situation might be.

Camille turned, looking back. The scholarly curators of

the museum were now exiting the grand and beautiful building, and might stumble upon her at any second. Suddenly Alex Mittleman, Sir John's next in command, appeared. If he saw her, he'd want to talk, to escort her to the trains. She had to move, and fast.

She caught Ralph's elbow, hurrying him down the street. As she did so, the wind expelled a mighty breath, making the nip in the air more like a true bite of ice. Maybe it wasn't just the wind. Perhaps it was a premonition of fear that snaked so cruelly along her spine.

"Come along, speak to me and speak quickly!" Camille warned. She was already worried, very worried. Tristan was smart, incredibly well-read, with a street education to match that he had procured at the hands of a multitude of tutors when a young man. He had taught her so very much—language, reading, art, history, theater… And also the fact that perception was nine tenths of the law—the *social* law. If she spoke like an impoverished but genteel lady, and dressed as such, that is what people would believe her to be.

He could be so amazingly perceptive regarding so much around him. And yet, at times, it seemed as if he had no common sense whatsoever!

"Dougray's is ahead," Ralph said, referring to a pub.

"You do not need a quota of gin!" Camille remonstrated.

"Aye, but I do!" the little man moaned softly.

She sighed. Dougray's was known as a working class establishment and was of a better repute than many a place both Ralph and Tristan had frequented. The pub was also not averse to serving women, particularly the growing sisterhood within the clerical office force in the country.

Camille always dressed carefully to maintain her station as assistant to Sir John Matthews, associate curator for the burgeoning department of Egyptian Antiquities. Her skirt was a somber gray with a small bustle, and her blouse, with an attractive, tailored look that primly ringed her neck, was in a similar but lighter color. Her cloak was of good quality and appropriate. Once it had belonged to a lady of class who had presumably let it go to the Salvation Army when she had acquired one of more recent style. Skeins of rich sable-brown hair—which Camille considered to be her one beauty—were dutifully pinned atop her head. She wore no jewelry or ornamentation other than the plain gold band that Tristan had found on her mother's person, and which she had worn ever since—on a chain when she was a child, and now upon her finger.

She didn't think they were particularly noticed when they entered the pub.

"We're hiding?" Ralph whispered.

"Please, let's just move to the back."

"If you're trying to be nondescript, Camie, you should be aware that every fellow in this place has turned to look at you."

"Don't be ridiculous."

"It's your eyes," he told her.

"They are an ordinary brown," she said impatiently.

"No, lass, they're gold, pure gold. And sometimes they have a touch of the old Emerald Isle. Quite remarkable. I'm afraid that men do watch you, the proper ones—and them that aren't so proper!" he said, looking around with a flash of anger.

"I'm not under attack, Ralph. Please, move!"

She quickly urged Ralph into the smoky rear of the establishment, ordering him a gin and herself a cup of tea. "Now," she commanded, "talk!"

So he did.

"Tristan loves you dearly, child. You know that," Ralph began.

"As I love him. And I am hardly a child any longer, thank the good Lord!" Camille retorted. "Now tell me, immediately, what mess I must rescue him from this time!"

Ralph muttered into his glass of gin.

"Ralph!" she remonstrated, showing backbone and temper.

"He's in the hands of the Earl of Carlyle."

Camille gasped. Of all the things she might have expected, it was not this. And though she didn't have the story as yet, already she was dismayed.

The Earl of Carlyle was known to be a monster. Not just in his dealings with workmen, servants and society, but in truth. His parents, wealthy beyond comprehension through dual inheritances, had considered themselves scholars, great antiquarians and archeologists. The fervor regarding anything from ancient Egypt had taken root in their hearts, and they had lived their adult lives in Cairo. Their only child had been sent back to England for a proper education and university, but he had joined them immediately after.

Then, according to newspaper reports, the family had fallen victim to a deadly curse. They had discovered the tomb of an ancient priest, filled with precious artifacts. Among those artifacts was a canopic jar containing the heart of the priest's most beloved concubine. The concubine was supposedly a witch. Naturally, stealing away the canopic jar cast a serious curse upon the family. It was reported that one of the Egyptian diggers began to rant, pointing to the heavens, declaring that the selfishness and cruelty in stealing the heart of another would bring about disaster. The earl and his countess merely laughed at the man, which was a serious mistake, apparently, as they died themselves quite mysteriously—and horrendously—within days.

Their son, the present earl, had been with Her Majesty's troops, putting down insurrectionists in India at the time. Upon hearing the news, he had gone quite insane in battle and turned the tide in a skirmish in which Her Majesty's troops had been seriously outnumbered. He had prevailed, but not without injuries so serious that he was hideously scarred. And embittered. And saddled with a family curse, as well, one so dire that, despite the fortune he had inherited, it kept him from seeking a wife during any season in London.

According to rumor, the man was beyond vile. Hideous in face and form, he was as gnarled, blackened and evil as the heart that had come to Carlyle Castle in the canopic jar.

It was said that the relic had then disappeared, and many believed that the heart had become one with that of the now evil Lord of the Castle. He simply hated everyone. A hermit living at his overgrown and massive estate, he prosecuted any trespassers—at least, those he did not shoot—to the utmost degree of the law.

This much, Camille knew. If she hadn't read about it in the papers, she would have heard the story anyway—embellished she was certain—as it was always a subject of discussion in the Egyptian Antiquities section of the museum.

Ralph didn't need to say another word for her heart to be filled with dread.

She remained impassive and forced her voice to an even level as she asked Ralph, "Just how did Tristan manage to run afoul of the Earl of Carlyle?"

Ralph finished his gin with a shudder, sat back and looked at Camille. "He had it in him to…well, to waylay a carriage from the north."

Camille sucked in air, staring at him with dismay. "He

meant to rob someone, like an ordinary highwayman? He might have gotten himself shot—or hanged!"

Ralph squirmed uncomfortably. "Well, you see, that wouldn't have happened. We never got that far."

Hurt, as well as dismay, suddenly filled her. She had a job now! A perfectly respectable job. Work that filled her with fascination and paid quite decently. She could support the two of them—and Ralph—decently, if not in the lap of luxury, without his resorting to any criminal trickery.

"Pray, tell me, what prevented the two of you from getting your fool selves killed?" she demanded.

He squirmed in the badly upholstered seat once again. "Carlyle Castle," he said, his eyes downcast.

"Do go on!" she said.

His lashes flickered and he said defensively, "It's because Tristan does dote on you so, Camie, that he seeks another way to set you up properly in society."

Camille stared at him, anger growing in her heart, then dissipating. There was simply no way to explain to Ralph that she would never be a part of "society." Perhaps her father had been a nobleman; perhaps the fellow had even married her mother in some secret ceremony. The ring she had worn had been testament to a man regarding her mother with at least enough affection to invest in a fine piece of jewelry.

The world believed that Camille was the child of a distant relative of Tristan's, a man knighted for his gallantry in Her Majesty's Service in the Sudan. But it wasn't the truth. And there would never be such a thing as a socially prominent marriage, or a season or anything resembling the like. And if she pushed too hard, the truth would be discovered.

The truth was not attractive in the least. Her mother had

been a prostitute; she had died in Whitechapel. Once upon a time, she had surely had dreams of a different life. But she had fallen in love and been discarded in London's East End, disinherited and penniless. Whoever Camille's father was, he had long disappeared by the time she was nine years old. And Tess Jardinelle died in the same streets she had worked. If Tristan hadn't come along that day…

"Ralph," she said with a heavy sigh, "please, just explain."

"The gates were ajar," he said simply.

"They were ajar?" she demanded.

"All right…they were locked. But there is a break in the wall, and it seemed quite tempting to an adventurer such as Tristan."

"Adventurer!"

Ralph flushed but did not revise his adjective. "There were no dogs about. It was early evening. There are stories about the wolves that prowl the forest, but you know Tristan. He thought that we should just venture in."

"I see. Just to enjoy the grounds and the moonlight?"

Ralph shrugged uncomfortably. "All right. Tristan believed there might be some trinket…just to be found on the ground, which might fetch a fortune if sold to the right people, in the right places. That's all. It was nothing heinous or evil. He believed he might find something that wouldn't even be missed by one so great as the Earl of Carlyle, and that might still bring about a great deal of money when sold—properly."

"Black market!"

"He wants the best for you. And there is that young man at the museum who has shown such an interest!"

Camille could not help but roll her eyes. He was referring to Sir Hunter MacDonald, a "consultant" to Lord David Wimbly and the titular head of the Antiquities section, due to his experience at Egyptian digs and, no doubt, the vast amounts of money he had contributed to the museum.

Hunter was attractive. He was quite dashing, really. And he'd earned his knighthood in the service, as well. Tall, charming, well-spoken and broad shouldered. Yet, though she did enjoy his company, she was careful. Despite his allure, his continued flattery and attempts at something closer, she never forgot the circumstances of her birth. Many times she had imagined her mother, alone and beautiful, trusting in just such a man, her heart outweighing and denying all logic and reality.

She knew Hunter was interested in her, but there was no future there. No matter what his compliments and kind words, she was certain that she was not the type such a man would bring home to his mama.

In her life, she would accept no less than a real commitment. There could be no such thing as falling head over heels in love, or letting passion rule her mind. And Camille meant to keep her pride, dignity—and position—at all costs. The thought of losing her employment at the museum was one she refused to entertain, and it was why she was determined to be so careful now.

"I want no young man, Ralph, who is not interested in me for myself."

"That's well and good, Camille. But we are living in a society that seeks pedigrees and riches."

She nearly groaned aloud. "A record of arrest and time served, or a guardian with an address such as Newgate, would not give me riches or a pedigree, Ralph."

"Oh, come. Please, Camille, we intended nothing really evil! Outlaws and highwaymen have become quite famous and revered in legend for stealing from the rich and giving to the poor. We just happen to be the poor."

"And outlaws and highwaymen have dangled from

ropes far too many times!" she reminded him, eyes flashing. "I have been trying, with the patience of a saint, one might say, to explain to you both that stealing is not just considered to be evil, it's illegal!"

"Ah, Camie girl!" Ralph said miserably. His eyes fell to the table again. "Might I have another gin?"

"Certainly not!" Camille said. "You've got to keep your wits about you, and finish this story so that I know what can be done! Where is Tristan now? Has he been taken before a magistrate? What on earth will I ever be able to do? And if Tristan was caught…?"

"He pushed me back behind the trees and allowed himself to be taken," Ralph said.

"So he has been arrested?" she said.

Ralph shook his head. He bit his lip and told her, "He's at Carlyle Castle. At least, I think he's still there. I came as quickly as I could."

"Oh, dear God! They've surely had him taken to some jail by now!" she exclaimed.

To her surprise, he shook his head once again. "No, you see, I heard the beast."

"Pardon?"

"He was there. The Earl of Carlyle was there, riding this massive, black, very evil-looking steed! Huge, it were! And he was shouting to his men, telling them that the trespasser must be held, and that…"

"And that what?"

"He could never be allowed to say what he had seen."

She stared at him, confused, the cold that had once trickled at her neck now an icicle driving brutally into her flesh.

"What did you see?" she asked.

He shook his head. "Nothing! Honestly, nothing. But there were men with Carlyle. And they dragged Tristan to the castle with them."

"How did you know that it was Carlyle—the beast?" she asked.

Ralph shuddered. "The mask!" he said softly.

"He wears a mask?"

"Oh, yes. The man is a monster. Surely, you've heard."

"He is crippled, bent over *and* wears a mask?"

"No, no, he is huge. Well, very tall in his saddle. And he wears a mask. In leather, I believe, but it has the visage of a beast. Part lion, perhaps. Or wolf. Or dragon. It is horrid, that's all I can say. His voice is like thunder, deep…as if he is indeed cursed of the devil himself! But it was him. Aye, it was him!"

She stared at Ralph.

Ralph shook his head in misery. "Tristan would strangle me if he knew that he'd sacrificed himself just so that I would worry you, but…he can't be left there. Even if the police suspect him of being a robber…"

Yes, that would be better. If only Tristan had been hauled back to London to face accusation and trial, she could somehow pay for his legal defense. She could go before the magistrate herself and plead that he was going mad, that age had been stealing his senses. She could have… God knew what she could have done.

But, according to Ralph, Tristan was still at Carlyle Castle, held prisoner by a man with a reputation for merciless brutality. She rose.

"What are you going to do?" Ralph demanded.

"What else?" she demanded with a weary sigh. "I am going to Carlyle Castle."

Ralph shuddered. "I have done the wrong thing. Tristan would not want you throwing yourself into danger."

She felt a great pang of sorrow for Ralph, yet, what had he expected?

"I will not be in danger," she assured him, smiling wearily. "He did teach me something about being a con artist, Ralph. I will go in all innocence and naiveté, and they will return my guardian to me. You'll see."

He rose quickly. "You cannot go alone!"

"I don't intend to," she assured him dryly. "We must head home first, and I must change. And you, too, must change."

"Me?"

"Indeed!"

"Change?"

"Perception is everything, Ralph," she told him sagely. He looked puzzled. "Never mind. Come along. I think we need to hurry." She froze suddenly, turning back on him. "Ralph, no one knows, right? No one knows that the Earl of Carlyle has Tristan?"

"No one but me. And you now, of course."

She felt a cold clutch of bony fingers encircling her heart, reaching into her throat. Good God, no matter what kind of a beast he was considered to be, the Earl of Carlyle couldn't simply…murder a man.

"Ralph, we must move, and quickly!" she said, catching his arm and dragging him along.

"THE GENTLEMAN is resting nicely," Evelyn Prior said, coming into the den. She fell into one of the huge upholstered wingback chairs that sat before the fire. Beside her, the master of the house had taken a position in the matching chair, brooding as he stared into the flames and scratched the huge head of his Irish wolfhound, Ajax.

Brian Stirling, Earl of Carlyle, looked over at her, brows knitted, deep in thought. After a moment, he said, "How badly is he hurt?"

"Oh, not badly, I dare say. The physician said that he was merely shaken and sore, and he didn't believe the man had broken any bones, though he did acquire some bruising from climbing the walls, then falling. But I think he'll be fine in a few days' time."

"He will not be crawling about the house in the night?"

Evelyn smiled. "Good heavens, no. Corwin is on guard in the hallway. And as you know, we keep the crypts locked tight. Only you and I have keys to the gates below. Even if he were to wander, there would be nothing he could find. And he won't wander. Since he was in some pain, he has been given a good dose of laudanum."

"He won't wander. Corwin will see to that," Brian said with certainty. His staff at Carlyle Castle was small, far too small for the upkeep of such a property. Everyone here was not just in service, but considered a friend. And each man and woman was loyal to the core—far more than appearances would imply.

"You are right, of course. Corwin will be entirely diligent," Evelyn agreed.

"What do you think possessed the man to do such a thing?" Brian asked. He turned his gaze from the flames to Evelyn once again. "The grounds themselves are so overgrown, a veritable jungle. It's amazing he would risk a trek through them."

"And the estate was so beautifully kept when your parents were alive!" she murmured.

"A year of English rain, my dear, can do wonders," Brian said. "So we have a jungle and wildlife! What would make him risk it?"

"The promise of great riches to be stolen," she said.

"You don't believe that the man is working for someone, do you?" he asked sharply.

She lifted her hands helplessly. "Honestly? No, I believe he came to steal something of value, and nothing more. Yet, is it possible that he's working for someone, seeking to find out what you have and what you know? Yes, it's possible."

"I'll find out tomorrow," Brian said. He knew the sound of his voice was chilling. He hadn't meant for it to be so, but as far as Carlyle Castle and his current activities went, he did feel a certain ruthlessness. He was embittered, he admitted, feeling a strong right to be so. There was more than the problem of the past to be solved. There was the future.

Evelyn looked at him anxiously, worried about his tone. "He has said that his name is Tristan Montgomery. And he swears that he was acting alone, though you already know that, since you were with Corwin and Shelby when he was found."

"Yes, I know. He also claimed to have merely 'stumbled' onto the castle grounds. How one stumbles over a nine-foot wall, I don't know. Since he is claiming that he is innocent of any evil intent, he is naturally claiming innocence in any kind of a conspiracy. But we shall see. Shelby will go down to the city tomorrow and see what he can discover about the man. Naturally, he will remain our guest until his real intentions can be discovered."

"Should I ride down on a shopping excursion, as well?" Evelyn suggested.

"Perhaps," Brian mused. He sighed deeply. "And perhaps it's time I began to accept a few of the invitations that have come my way."

Evelyn laughed. "Indeed, I've been telling you that you should. But think of the fear in the hearts of many a debutante's mama!"

"Yes, that's a thought."

"It's a pity you haven't a fiancée or wife to stand charmingly by your side. Proof, of course, that there is no curse upon the house, and that you are not a beast, just a man, wounded by a great family tragedy."

"That's true, as well," he murmured, gazing at her as he considered her reply.

"Oh, good heavens, don't look at me!" Evelyn said with a laugh. "I'm way too old, Your Grace!"

He had to grin at that. Evelyn was a beautiful woman. Her green eyes were filled with deep intelligence, and though nearing forty, she still possessed a face with such fine lines that she would be beautiful until the age of one hundred, should God grant such a life span.

"Ah, Evelyn! You know my heart as no other woman could or ever will, and yet, you're quite right." His face hardened. "And if I were to know a proper young marital prospect, I'd not bring her in on this charade. God knows what danger she could face."

"Surely no one would drag an innocent into this tangled web of evil!" Evelyn murmured. "A lass could not be in danger."

"My mother is dead, is she not?" he inquired tightly.

"Your dear mother was unusual, and that you must know. In her knowledge, in her pursuits, in her courage," Evelyn said. "You will not find another woman like her."

"No," Brian agreed. "And still, that the fiends should have slain a woman turns my heart to stone, though I agree that I would have pursued this with no less resolve had it been my father alone who was so cruelly killed." He hesitated a moment. "Ah, Evelyn, I am not happy that *you* are involved."

Evelyn smiled. "I was involved before you were, actually," she reminded him softly. "And I am more than willing to risk my life and all that I have. Still, I don't believe that I'm in any danger. I haven't the knowledge or the skill your mother possessed. And I don't really believe that a young woman—a powder puff of a trophy on your arm—would actually be in danger, either. You are the one targeted, if there is to be any danger. Any enemy will know you will not let the dead lie buried until they do so in peace."

"I am the one cursed," he reminded her.

"And do you believe in curses?" she asked, somewhat amused.

"It depends on how one sees a curse. Cursed? Yes. I live in hell. Can the curse be lifted? Certainly. But I must find the cure, in all that I do," he said solemnly.

Evelyn shook her head. "See? A lovely young woman, claiming to love you despite the hideousness of your face and all that has occurred in the past, does much to change the appearance of Carlyle—man and castle, if you will. Perhaps there is someone we could…hire."

"You're serious!" he said.

"I am. Honestly, what you need is someone quite beautiful at your side. Someone to accompany you into the rooms of society, someone to prove you human."

"And I've worked so hard to create my image of bountiful kindness already!" he said sardonically.

"Yes, and that was necessary," Evelyn agreed. "We've had no intruders at the castle—until now."

"None that we know about," he said sharply.

"Brian! It's time for a change."

"I cannot change my course until I have come to the end."

"You may never come to an end."

"You're wrong. I will."

She sighed. "Fine, then see it my way. Add a layer to your charade, Brian. You've done what can be done from the shadows, and you will continue to do so. But I really believe it's time that you must reenter society. There is the invitation to the fund-raiser. You are certain we are dealing with members of scholarly organizations, and that is certainly a valid supposition. And who better than those who shared your parents' love and fascination with the wonders of an ancient world? You've told me that you actually have your list of suspects narrowed down."

He rose restlessly, paced before the fire. Ajax, nervous, sensing his master's mood, whined. Brian took a moment to reassure the dog. "It's all right, boy," he said, then gave his attention to Evelyn once again. "Yes, we are seeking someone with a deep knowledge of the field. That is a given. But we are also seeking someone capable of murder, the kind of cunning and malicious premeditation that killed my parents."

Evelyn was silent for a minute. Despite the year that had now gone by, it was impossible to remember how the late earl and his countess had died without feeling a terrible sense of pain and horror.

Brian walked to the occasional table behind the chairs, poured a portion of brandy into a snifter, swallowed it down and then looked at Evelyn. "Forgive my manners," he said. "My dear, would you like a brandy?"

"Yes, actually," she said, smiling. He poured some into her snifter first, then refilled his own.

Lifting his glass to her, he said dryly, "To the night. To darkness and shadows."

"No, to the day and the light," she said firmly.

He grimaced.

"It's time, I'm telling you," Evelyn insisted. "We must somehow find you a delightful young woman. Not incredibly wealthy or titled. That would be too absurd, considering…well, with your reputation, no one would believe it. Still, there would have to be just the right circumstances, the right someone. She should be young enough, beautiful, compassionate and possessing a certain charm, as well. With the right woman by your side, you'd be able to continue your investigations without worrying about desperate mothers ready to sacrifice their daughters to the beast, all for the sake of the wealth of Carlyle."

"And where do I acquire this charming beauty?" he asked, grinning. "She must have a certain intelligence—and the charm of which you speak—otherwise having her at my side would do no good. The concept of searching the streets to *hire* such a woman would not work, either. I can promise you that we will not find such a sweet, well-spoken beauty in such a quest. So there is little hope. It's most unlikely that such a perfect candidate will come knocking at the door!"

It was precisely then that a tapping did sound, firm upon the door to the den.

Shelby, in his footman's attire—a little bizarre, but certainly imposing upon a man of his great size and musculature—cracked open the door when bidden to do so.

"There's a young woman to see you, Lord Brian." He seemed quite baffled.

"A young woman?" Brian repeated, frowning.

Shelby nodded. "Actually, a very beautiful young woman, waiting down at the gates."

"A young woman!" Evelyn exclaimed, staring at Brian.

"Yes, yes, we've established that," Brian said. "What is her name? Why has she come?"

"What does it matter?" Evelyn said. "You must invite her in and find out what it is that she needs or wants."

"Evelyn, certainly it matters. She must be a fool, to be coming here. Or she's working for someone," Brian said.

Evelyn waved a hand in the air. "Shelby, you must bring her in. Immediately. Oh, Brian! Please, you mustn't always be so suspicious."

He arched a brow.

"Brian, please! We haven't had an actual visitor here since…in years!" she finished with a flush. "I can serve a delightful meal. It's actually quite exciting!"

"Exciting," Brian said dryly. He lifted his hands. "Shelby, do invite the young woman in." He looked at Evelyn. "For, indeed, she has come tapping at our door."

CHAPTER TWO

CAMILLE HAD BEEN QUITE CAREFUL regarding every move she made, including their conveyance and their appearances. Ralph was handsomely decked out in one of Tristan's day suits with a proper cap, giving the impression of a properly clean and dignified individual, but one in service. She had drawn out her best gown, a feminine concoction in deep maroon, the bodice neither too high nor too low, the bustle of a medium size, the overskirt in satin, with lace bordering the underskirt, showing through the delicate scallops at the hem. It was an outfit, she had determined, that dressed a young respectable woman who did not possess a great fortune, yet had the most respectable means to see one through life.

She definitely begrudged the money she had to pay the hansom cab to bring them so far out of the city, but the driver was courteous, glad of the fare and quick to assure her that he was willing to wait to return them to London. So it was that she stood at the massive gates to Carlyle Castle, staring at the massive structure of wrought iron that prevented them from entering, and turned to Ralph in disbelief.

"You two determined that you must scale *this* wall?" she said.

He shrugged unhappily. "Well, if you follow the wall itself around a bit, there's a damaged area. It was actually quite easy to get a foothold, and then…well, I boosted Tristan and he dragged me. Really, I might have broken bones escaping, since I had to depart the same way, and by that time there was some kind of very large hound after me. Unless, in fact, he does raise wolves…but no matter. I did escape, and I do swear I wasn't seen."

Ralph blushed, aware that she hadn't in the least appreciated his story.

She had already pulled upon the massive cord that presumably rang a bell somewhere in the castle.

"Tristan is within," she murmured.

"Camie, honestly, I'd not have deserted, ever!" Ralph protested. "But I didn't know what else to do, other than come to you."

"I know that you wouldn't have deserted him," she said softly, then added, "Hush! Someone is coming."

They heard a pounding of horse's hooves, and a man on top of a huge steed appeared behind the gate. When he dismounted, Camille could very well understand the huge horse, for the fellow was a giant. He stood many inches over six feet, and his shoulders seemed to have the breadth of a doorway. He was no lad, but neither was he ancient. She thought his age to be, perhaps, midthirties. Muscled and tense, he made his way to peer through the gate.

"Yes?"

"Good evening," Camille said, flustered despite herself by the fellow's size and foreboding tone. "Excuse the late hour and the unannounced call, I beg you. It's imperative that I see the master of the house, the Earl of Carlyle, on a matter of utmost urgency."

She had expected questions; she received none. The man stared at her from beneath dark, bushy brows, then turned.

"Excuse me!" she cried.

"I will see if the master is available," he called over his shoulder. He leaped atop the huge horse once again, and the sound of the animal's lope disappeared into the darkness of the trail that led to the castle.

"He won't be available," Ralph said pessimistically.

"He must be. I will refuse to leave until he sees me," Camille assured Ralph.

"To most men, the thought of a lady waiting at the gates in the darkness would be distressing. But we are dealing with the Beast of Carlyle," Ralph reminded her.

"He will see me," Camille insisted.

She paced before the gate.

"No one is coming back," Ralph said, growing distressed.

"Ralph, our hansom is waiting, but I will not leave without Tristan. If no one appears soon, I will ring that bell until they are all half-mad from the sound," Camille said.

She stood still, arms crossed over her chest.

Ralph began to pace. "No one is coming," he repeated.

"Ralph, it is some distance to the castle. The man surely had to go to it, find his master and then return to us."

"We will sleep out here," Ralph warned.

"Well, you do know how to break back in to the property," Camille reminded him.

"We should start now, then."

"We should wait," she said firmly.

She began to fear that Ralph was right, that she would be ignored, left to wait at the gates with no leave to enter and no refusal sending her away. But then, just when she had nearly despaired, she heard the sound of hooves once again and the clacking of wheels.

A small wagon, handsomely roofed in leather and fringe, appeared with the huge man at the reins. He hopped down from the driver's seat and came to the gate, using a large key to open the padlock braced around it, then swinging the gate open.

"If you'll please accompany me?" he said, the words polite, his tone as dour as ever.

Camille flashed an encouraging smile at Ralph and followed. Ralph came along, as well. The big man hoisted Camille into the rear seat of the conveyance, and Ralph hopped up behind her.

The small carriage took them down a long and winding path. The darkness on either side of the road seemed to be deep and endless. By day, Camille was certain, they would have seen massive trees and an overgrown forest flanking the path. The master of Carlyle liked his environs secluded, to the point of it all appearing to be like some godforsaken no-man's-land. As they trotted along, it seemed to Camille that the forest breathed, that indeed it was an overbearing entity ready to suck in the unwary, entangle the soul.

"And you two thought you might begin to *find* some treasure here?" she whispered to Ralph.

"You've not seen the castle yet," he whispered back.

"You're both mad! I should leave Tristan here," she murmured. "This is the greatest foolishness I have ever seen."

Then the castle loomed before her. Mammoth. It retained a moat over which lay a great drawbridge, permanently down now, Camille imagined, since armies were unlikely to come and besiege the place. Yet, it appeared quite certain that no one could simply slip into the place, since the castle walls themselves were staunch and windowless to a great height, and only narrow slits could be seen.

She looked at Ralph, angrier and more distraught the closer they came. What had the two been thinking?

The carriage clattered over the bridge. They came to a great courtyard and she saw just what Tristan might have known—the area was covered with antiquities, fascinating statues and pieces of art. An ancient bathtub—Greco-Roman, she thought—had been handsomely altered to act as a contemporary watering trough. There were various sarcophagi lining an area of the outer wall, and numerous other treasures were laid closer to the path that led to a great door. The castle had obviously seen some construction work to bring it into the nineteenth century. The doorway was rounded handsomely, and from the turret atop it, boxes of vines spilled over, offering a tiny bit of welcome to a visitor.

She continued to survey the courtyard as the huge man came to help her from the carriage. The artifacts belonged in the museum, she thought indignantly. But she was well aware that many things she would consider precious were ordinary to rich world travelers. She'd heard, as well, that mummies were so plentiful, they were often sold as fodder for fireplaces and heat. Still, there were many stunning examples of Egyptian art here—two giant ibises, a few statues of Isis and a number of others that were surely lesser pharaohs.

"Come," the big man said.

They followed him up the path to the door. It opened to a circular reception area, where once, it was planned that the enemy should be bottled and trapped, were they to get this far. Now, the area was a mudroom.

"If I may?"

The man took her cape. Ralph held tightly to his overcoat. The big man shrugged.

"Come."

They passed through a second door to an outstanding hall. Here, modernization had definitely been in effect. In fact, the room was actually gracious. The stone stairway curved to an upper level and balcony, and the stairs were covered in a warm, royal-blue runner. Weapons lined ceilings and part of the walls, but they were interspersed by beautiful oils, some of them portraits, others medieval and pastoral scenes. She was certain that many were the works of great masters.

A fire crackled in a massive hearth. The furniture surrounding the hearth was in deep brown leather, yet not austere in the least. Rather, it offered a plush and welcoming comfort.

"You, wait here," the man told Ralph. "You, come with me," he said to Camille.

Ralph stared at her like a frightened puppy being left behind in a ditch. She inclined her head to let him know that it was quite all right, and followed the man up the curving stairs.

He led her into a room with a massive desk and endless shelves of books. Her heart leaped at the sight of them. So many! And the subject matter on one wall was that near and dear to her heart. *Ancient Egypt* was a massive tome aligned next to *The Path of Alexander the Great*.

"The master will be with you shortly," the big man said, closing the door behind him as he left.

Standing alone in the large room, Camille was first aware of silence. Then, bit by bit, those little noises that intruded upon the night. From somewhere, she heard the plaintive, chilling call of a wolf. Then, as if to alleviate that chill, the snap of a fire burning brightly in the hearth to the left of the entry.

A crystal decanter of brandy, surrounded by fragile snifters, sat on a small brown table. She was tempted to run to it, seize up the elegant crystal and imbibe the brandy until it was gone.

Turning again, she noted a large and beautiful painting behind the great desk. The woman within it wore clothing of perhaps a decade earlier. She had lovely light hair and a smile that seemed to illuminate. Her deep blue eyes, almost a sapphire, were the most alluring aspect of the painting. Fascinated, Camille moved closer.

"My mother, Lady Abigail of Carlyle," she heard, the tone deep, richly masculine, yet somehow harsh and menacing.

She spun around, startled, not having heard the door open. Despite herself, she was afraid that she gaped, as well, for the face she saw upon the fellow who had entered the room was that of a beast.

He wore a leather mask, she realized, molded to face and features. And though not really unattractive—and certainly artistic—it was still somehow frightening. And in the back of her mind, she wondered if it hadn't been crafted to be so.

She wondered, as well, just how long he had watched her before speaking.

"It's a beautiful painting," she managed to say at last, praying that the time she had stared at him, mouth open, was less than she feared. She tried hard not to let her voice waver, though she couldn't tell if she succeeded.

"Yes, thank you."

"A very beautiful woman," she added, the compliment sincere.

She was aware of the eyes behind the mask, watching her. And she noticed, because the mouth was somewhat visible beneath the edge of the facade, that there was a mocking amusement to him, as if he was accustomed to gratuitous compliments.

"She was, indeed, beautiful," he said, and came closer, his strides long, one hand clamped around a wrist behind his back as he neared her. "So, who are you, and what are you doing here?"

She smiled and extended a hand graciously, hating the fact that she was playing at the social butterfly—which she was not and never would be.

"Camille Montgomery," she said. "And I am here on a desperate quest. My uncle, my guardian, is lost, and he was last seen upon the road before this very castle."

He looked at her hand a long time before deciding to bow to courtesy and accept it, bending over it. The lips beneath the mask were searing as they touched her flesh, yet he released her instantly, as if it were he who had touched hot coals.

"Ah," he said simply, walking past her.

Though not so tall as the giant who had come to the gate, he was certainly a few inches over six feet, and his shoulders were very broad beneath his handsome smoking jacket. His stature was trim, his waist quite narrow, his legs long and powerful. He appeared both strong and agile, whatever the condition of his face. A beast? Perhaps, for she could too easily recall the heat of his lips against her flesh, the length of his fingers, the power in his hand.

He didn't speak; his back was to her as he, too, surveyed the painting above the desk.

At last, she cleared her throat. "Lord Stirling, I do apologize with the greatest regret for intruding upon you at this hour and without inquiry. But I am, as you can well imagine, distressed beyond all measure. The dear man who raised me is missing, and there are so many dangers in the woods. Cutthroats, wolves…all manner of creature might be about in the night. I am so very worried, and therefore I pray that I may turn to a man of such high position as Your Lordship."

He turned, once again very amused.

"Oh, come, my dear! All of London has surely heard of my reputation!"

"Reputation, sir?" she said, feigning innocence. It was a mistake.

"Ah, yes, the misbegotten beast! Were I simply the Earl of Carlyle and recognized as such with a modicum of respect and dignity rather than fear, dear woman, you'd not have come to the gates with the least hope of being received by me."

His tone was flat and harsh, allowing no quarter for a pretense of ignorance. In fact, she nearly took a step back, but refused to allow herself to do so—for Tristan's sake.

"Tristan Montgomery is here, somewhere, sir. He was traveling with a companion and disappeared outside your gates. I want him given into my care, immediately."

"So you are related to the loathsome rascal who crawled my walls like the most common of thieves this evening," he said, unperturbed.

"Tristan is no loathsome rascal," she denied hotly, although she refrained from declaring that he was certainly not a thief. "Sir, I believe he is in this castle, and I will not leave without him."

"I hope then that you are prepared to stay," he said flatly.

"So, he *is* here!" she claimed.

"Oh, yes. He took a bit of a fall in his attempt to relieve me of my possessions."

She swallowed, trying to maintain her composure. She had never expected the man to be so blunt, or to hear a tone that could be both flat and entirely ruthless all in one. A new fear was also triggered within her.

"He is hurt? Badly?" she inquired.

"He will live," he said dryly.

"But I must be taken to him. At once!"

"In good time," he said simply. "You'll excuse me for a moment?" It wasn't really a question; he meant to depart the room and leave her again, and he didn't give a damn if she did or didn't excuse his rudeness. He strode toward the door.

"Wait!" she cried. "I must see Tristan. Immediately."

"I repeat, you may see him. In good time."

He departed, leaving her alone once again. She stared after him, confused and angry. Why would he agree to see her, only to disappear after a few minutes' worth of heated conversation?

She walked around the room, trying to calm herself, studying the titles of books as she bided whatever time she was to wait. Yet the titles did nothing but swim before her eyes, so she found a seat before the fire.

He'd admitted that Tristan was here. Hurt! Caught in the act of thievery.

Good God! No one could expect her to sit still while her guardian lay somewhere, perhaps in pain, perhaps even direly injured!

She jumped up anxiously and started for the door, but after throwing it open, she stood frozen. There was a dog there. Massive. It was merely sitting there, but its head came above her waist! Then the animal growled softly; a warning sound.

She closed the door and paced back to the fire, furious yet afraid. Was the animal trained to rip anyone to shreds who tried to move about the place on their own? Fueled by anger, she walked back to the door. But before she could reach it, it opened.

It wasn't the return of the Earl of Carlyle, as she had hoped. Instead, a woman entered the room. She was an attractive, older woman with dancing eyes and a quick smile. She was in a lovely dove-gray gown with a cast of silver to it, and the warm curl of her lips was more than startling under the circumstance.

"Good evening, Miss Montgomery," she said pleasantly.

"Thank you," Camille replied, "except that, I'm afraid, for me, it isn't a good evening at all. My guardian is being held hostage here, and it seems that I am likewise imprisoned in this room."

"Imprisoned!" the woman exclaimed.

"There is a dog—or a fanged monster, one might say—on the other side of the door," Camille said.

The woman's smile deepened. "Ajax. Pay him no mind. He is a big lover, once you get to know him. Really."

"I'm not so sure that I'm eager to make his close acquaintance," Camille murmured. "Madam, please, I'm most desperate to see my guardian."

"Indeed, and so you will. But first things first. Will you have some brandy? I've arranged a light supper for you and the earl, and it will be served quite soon. I'm Evelyn Prior, the earl's housekeeper. He's asked me to see that a room be prepared for you, as well."

"A room?" she said, distressed. "Mrs. Prior, please, I've come to take Tristan home. Whatever care he needs, I can give it to him."

"Well, Miss Montgomery," Mrs. Prior said, her tone sad, "I'm afraid that the earl was considering filing charges against your guardian."

Camille winced, looking downward. "Please. I don't believe he intended any harm."

"I'm afraid the master doesn't believe that he merely fell over the gate," the woman said lightly. "But…well, the two of you must talk."

Evelyn Prior seemed far too lovely, rational and sane for the environment here, that was certain. All about the castle seemed dark and menacing; she was as light and lovely as the summer air. Yet she, too, seemed to have very resolute objections to Camille simply gathering up Tristan and leaving.

She swallowed hard. "I am willing to make reparation for—"

"Miss Montgomery, I'm not the one with whom you must discuss the matter of your guardian's guilt or innocence, or any form of reparation. If you'll accompany me now, I'll see you to the master's quarters dining area. In time, you may see your guardian, and then your own chamber for the evening."

"Oh, we cannot stay!" Camille protested.

"I'm afraid you must stay. The physician has said that your guardian must not be moved this evening. He is sore, indeed."

"I can take care of him," Camille swore.

"He will not be traveling this evening. We cannot keep you here, of course, but I'm afraid that your guardian will not be leaving our hospitality as of yet."

Despite the woman's courtesy and easy smile, Camille felt chills erupt at the base of her spine. *Stay here?* Surrounded by the deepest, darkest forest she had ever seen? With the man in the mask, the imposing, brooding, harsh and seemingly indomitable *beast* of the castle?

"I...I..."

"Truly!" the woman said with a laugh. "We may well enjoy our solitude here, but we are not so crass or without comfort as you might imagine. You will be quite fine if you stay. Whatever His Lordship's reputation, he is the Earl of Carlyle, you know. He has responsibilities to the Crown itself, and is trusted by her most gracious Majesty, Victoria."

Camille lowered her lashes, trying to conceal the flush that came to her cheeks. Mrs. Prior had read her every thought.

"I have come with a servant. He has been left waiting in the great hall," Camille said.

"Well then, we shall see that he is comfortably bedded down for the evening, as well, Miss Montgomery. Do come along now."

Camille offered a weak smile and did so, having little choice.

In the hall, the dog waited. He looked at Camille with as much suspicion as had his master. Even the dog's eyes seemed to be hooded.

"Good boy!" Mrs. Prior said, stroking the great head. The monster hound wagged its tail.

Camille remained close at Mrs. Prior's heels. They traversed the long hall, coming to the far end of the eastern wing of the castle. The door was center at that end of the wing, and Mrs. Prior pushed it open. The lord of the castle awaited her.

Here, in the reception area for his private quarters, there were great pocket doors that rolled back to allow a scenic view of the darkness and the deep jungle of forest that helped create it. There must have been something out there, however, for he looked out at the expanse before him, hands clasped behind his back, legs firmly set, shoulders squared, as Mrs. Prior led Camille in.

There was a table set with an exquisite white cloth, fine bone china—the main plates covered with silver heating domes—shining silverware and crystal-stemmed glasses. Two chairs awaited.

Mrs. Prior cleared her throat, but Camille was certain that the Earl of Carlyle knew they were there. He simply hadn't chosen to turn.

"Miss Montgomery, sir," she said. "I will leave you two."

Camille was ushered in and the door closed behind her. The master turned at last.

He lifted a hand, indicating the table, then walked forward, pulling back a chair for her to sit. She hesitated.

"Ah. I'm sorry. Is the idea of dining with a scarred man in a mask far too loathsome a concept for you, my dear?"

The words were gently spoken, but they weren't filled with compassion. They might have been a challenge. Or a test?

"I believe you've chosen a rather bizarre mask, sir, but certainly it's your right. There is little that disturbs my appetite, and nothing *of appearance* that can disturb me regarding a fellow human being."

She thought she saw again, below the leather edge of the mask, a faint smile, both mocking and amused.

"How very honorable, Miss Montgomery! Yet is such a credo true in your heart, or simply what I might wish to hear?"

"I believe, sir, that any answer might be as dubious in your mind as the words already spoken. Suffice it to say, I had not realized my own hunger, and I am happy to share a meal while discussing the situation regarding my guardian."

"Then, my dear…?" He swept his arm toward the chair. She sat.

He walked around the table, took his own seat and lifted the silver cover from her plate. The aroma, just hinted at in the night air thus far, struck her heavily then, and it was delicious. The plate came with fluffy potatoes, a slice of roast that was mouthwatering and artful little carrots. She hadn't had a bite since her break at ten that morning, and then she had barely bothered with a muffin and jam.

"Does it meet with your approval, Miss Montgomery? Rather mundane, I'm afraid, but quickly achieved," he said.

"It seems exceptional, under such very timely circumstances, indeed," she said politely. She realized that he was waiting for her to begin, so she picked up her fork and knife and delicately chiseled off a piece of meat. It was as delicious as the aroma had promised.

"Excellent," she assured him.

"I'm so glad you approve," he murmured.

"As to my guardian," she began.

"The thief, yes."

She sighed. "My Lord, Tristan is not a thief. I can't begin to imagine what brought him into these walls, but there would be no reason for him to steal."

"Quite well-off, are you, then?" he inquired.

"We are certainly in able circumstances," she said.

"So he did not come to steal for small profit, but sought instead a certain treasure."

"Not at all!" she protested, realizing that it had some-how made him angrier and more suspicious when she suggested that they didn't need money. Small sums, at any rate.

"Lord Stirling," she said, trying to put forth a de-meanor of indignation, irritation and assurance. "You really have no right to suppose that my guardian was here to rob you. He—"

"According to him, he arrived accidentally upon the property. You saw the gate and the wall. It's rather diffi-cult to pass by accidentally, don't you agree?"

Despite the mask, he had impeccable manners. The bot-tom of the visage was cut so that it covered the cheeks and the bridge of the nose, but left the mouth free. She sud-denly wondered what his appearance was like beneath the mask, and just how badly he had been facially scarred to wear the leather over his features.

He was casual as he spoke, and she was almost lulled by his tone.

"I haven't seen Tristan as yet. You haven't allowed me to do so," she reminded him. "I have no idea what could have brought him onto the estate. I know only that I must take him home very soon, and that I can swear to you, there would be no reason on earth for him to steal."

"You are in possession of a great fortune of your own?"

"That would surprise you, sir?"

He set his fork and knife down, eyes assessing her. "Yes. Your gown is quite lovely and you wear it well, but I would estimate that it is several years out of date. You did not arrive in your own conveyance, but in a hansom cab, which, by the way, has been sent on back to London."

She tensed, ruing the morrow. She would have to get Tristan out of here quickly, else chance losing the job she so dearly needed and desired.

She set her own fork and knife down. "Perhaps I do not possess a huge fortune of my own, sir. Not as you see it. But I am fortunate, very able and far more than capable. I work, sir, and receive payment each week."

Dark lashes narrowed over his blue eyes. She gasped, realizing that he was imagining a far different employment from that to which she referred.

"How dare you, sir!" she sputtered.

"How dare I what?"

"I do not!"

"You do not what?"

"Do what you're thinking that I do!"

"Then just what do you do?" he inquired.

"You are no mythical creature, My Lord, just a boor!" she informed him, getting ready to toss her napkin down and rise, Tristan forgotten for a moment in her agitation.

He set a hand upon hers, preventing her from rising. He was close over the table, and she was aware of his tension, a strange, erratic heat, and the power of his hold.

"Miss Montgomery, we are discussing an important issue here, that of whether or not I shall have your guardian arrested. If you find seeking the truth to be offensive, you will simply have to take offense then. I repeat, just what do you do?"

She felt the surge of her own temper, but she was determined to stare him down and not wrench away to free herself, not when such a fight would be futile.

"I work, sir, for the museum, for the department of Egyptian Antiquities!" she hissed.

If she had flatly told him that she was a prostitute, she would not have gotten such a stunned and angry response, she was certain.

"You what?"

The words were a pure roar. Stunned by his reaction, she frowned and repeated herself. "I enunciate quite clearly, I believe. I work for the museum, for the department of Egyptian Antiquities."

He rose so suddenly that he knocked his chair over backward.

"It is a perfectly legitimate job, and I assure you, I am qualified for my position!" she expounded.

To her absolute amazement, he walked around the table with the same violence with which he had risen.

"My Lord Stirling!" she protested, standing, but his hands were on her shoulders, and he was staring at her with such loathing that she was afraid for her person.

"And you claim you came here for nothing!" he said.

She gasped. "You think that *I* have come here for anything other than the return of a human being I *love?* I am dearly sorry, sir, but your noble position in life does not excuse you from this outrageous display of bad manners—and violence!"

His hands dropped from her shoulders and he stepped

back. But his eyes remained blue flames of an intensity that pierced her very soul.

"Should I discover, Miss Montgomery, that your words are a lie, I do assure you, you have not begun to realize the state to which my *bad manners* and *violence* might rise."

He turned as if the sight of her were so repulsive he couldn't bear it any longer. He strode to the door and exited. The reverberation created as the door slammed in his wake seemed to shake the entire castle.

Trembling, Camille remained on her feet, staring at the door, long after he had gone.

"You are truly a wretched creature!" she cried then, certain that he was far beyond earshot.

The door opened. She tensed.

It was Mrs. Prior. "You poor dear!" she exclaimed. "He does have such a ferocious temper. I try constantly to make him see it, but…quite honestly, he can be charming and kind."

"I must see my guardian. And I must take him from this place," Camille said, fighting for what dignity she might summon. "Away from that monster."

"Oh, dear!" Mrs. Prior said. "Truly, he's not such a monster. It's just that…well, it is quite shocking that you work for the museum, dear."

"It's an honorable position!" she said.

"Yes. Well…" Mrs. Prior cast her head at an angle, studying Camille. Perhaps she, at least, approved of what she saw. She lowered her voice. "It's just that your employers—well, the group dealing with your department—were all there when…"

"When what?"

"When his lordship's parents were murdered," Mrs. Prior said. "It's not your fault, dear, but still…. Do come along, then, please. I'll bring you to your guardian." She paused, looking back. "Honestly, dear, he may look a bit beastly, and perhaps his behavior thus far has been horrid, but there is that dire fact of those terrible murders having completely changed his life."

CHAPTER THREE

CAMILLE HURRIED ALONG after Evelyn. "Wait, please. I've heard the rumors, of course. Everyone in London has heard the rumors. Perhaps if I understood more about what happened, I could even be—"

The word *helpful* never left her lips because Evelyn, who had been moving rapidly before her, came to a dead stop, throwing open a door. Camille, in her hurry to keep up, nearly plowed into Evelyn's back. Then Evelyn spoke as if she hadn't been listening to a word that Camille had said. "Here, child. Your guardian."

Thoughts concerning her host and his wretched behavior flew from her mind as she looked into the darkened room and blinked. A fire burned at the hearth, but all was cast into shadow. She felt her heart skip a beat as her eyes at last fell upon the figure on the bed. Still. Dead still.

"Oh, dear God!" she exhaled, trembling, her knees going wobbly.

Evelyn spun around, catching her by the arms, offering support before she buckled completely.

"No, no, dear! He was so restless that we gave him laudanum. He isn't at all dead. Well, I guess you can't actually be partially dead... Here I am, making no sense. He's all right. He probably won't be coherent, not that I seem to be doing much of a job in that direction." Evelyn, who had appeared such a composed woman, apparently did have a sense of sympathy, and was therefore flustered by Camille's heartfelt and terrified show of emotion. "Dear girl!" Evelyn continued. "Run on over, give him a hug. He may wake enough to recognize you."

Not dead, not dead, not dead! That was all that registered in Camille's mind. Then Evelyn's words sank in and she found the strength to tear across the room to the bed. Once there, she saw that there was color in Tristan's face and that he was breathing deeply.

In fact, as she hovered just above him, afraid for a moment to touch, he let out the most winded snort she had heard in the whole of her life. Flushing, she turned back to the door where Evelyn Prior remained.

"See, he is quite alive," Evelyn assured her softy again.

Camille nodded, then looked down at her guardian. He was dressed in a handsome linen nightgown—something he had never possessed in all his life, she was certain. He'd been cared for and well tended, that was obvious. The monster of Carlyle wanted his prisoners to be in decent shape when he saw them prosecuted, so it appeared.

She fell to her knees by Tristan's side, clutching his shoulders in a gentle hug, laying her head against his chest. "Tristan!" she whispered softly, tears springing to her eyes. Whatever sins he had committed in his life, he had surely redeemed himself when he had saved her, when he had given up his goods—ill-gotten and by other means—to feed a number of the street urchins they had known in their days together. But why now, when she had come to a point in her life where she could take care of them…?

"You sorry son of a sailor!" she muttered, lifting her head, angrily wiping tears from her cheeks. "Tristan, what on earth were you doing?" she whispered fervently.

He inhaled on another snort, blinked and met her eyes. Tenderness came to his, the gentleness that really was the crux of the man. "Camille, moppet! Camille...." He frowned, as if aware that she shouldn't be there. But the effort was too much. He blinked again, but his eyes closed, and she heard only the depth of his breathing once again.

"You see?" Evelyn called from the doorway. "The man has been quite decently tended. Now, come along, dear. I'll show you where you may sleep tonight."

She rose, kissed Tristan on the forehead, adjusted his covers and then turned to follow Evelyn. The woman led her out, closed the door firmly but silently and started down the hall again at a brisk speed.

"Mrs. Prior," Camille began, racing after her, "I can see that no harm has been done to my guardian, but, as you can understand, I'm anxious to get him home."

"I'm sorry, dear, but I do believe that Brian intends to prosecute."

"Brian?" she murmured, puzzled.

"The Earl of Carlyle," Mrs. Prior said patiently.

"Oh, but he can't! He mustn't!"

"Perhaps you'll be able to talk him out of it in the morning. Oh, dear! If only you hadn't worked for the museum!"

"To the very best of my knowledge, Mrs. Prior, many people have fallen prey to Egyptian asps. It is a danger of the desert region."

Mrs. Prior stared at her in a way that made her feel severely uncomfortable, as if she had, until that point, been deemed an intelligent young woman.

"This is your door, Miss Montgomery. The castle is large and winding, started with the Norman Conquest and built on ever since, not always with the best architectural eye! I suggest you refrain from roaming in the night. There is a quite modern bath connected to this guest room, I do say with some pride. Night clothing and toiletries have been left at your disposal. In the morning, dear, this situation will be solved, one way or the other."

"Yes…thank you. But wait! Perhaps, if I understood more—"

"The earl is awaiting me, Miss Montgomery. Sleep well."

"Oh! But Ralph, our valet—"

"Has been seen to!" Mrs. Prior called back over her shoulder. She disappeared around a corner.

Somewhat aggravated by her dismissal, Camille stepped into the hallway, debating the course of simply running after the woman and demanding more answers.

But just as easily as Evelyn Prior had disappeared, the hound from hell reappeared. It sat in the hallway and stared at her. She had never known before that dogs could actually sneer and dare someone, but that was exactly what this hound was doing.

She pointed at the animal. "You, sir, will get yours one day!" she vowed.

The dog growled.

Camille stepped quickly into the room she had been assigned and closed the door. Leaning against it, she closed her eyes with a beating heart, conflicting emotions racing through her. Then she opened her eyes and gasped.

The room was quite incredible. The bed was handsomely canopied, topped with a rich, embroidered ivory quilt and numerous pillows. The rest of the furnishings were…Egyptian.

Startled, she walked across to the dressing table and realized that certain pieces from antiquity had been copied for the decor and combined with current Victorian detail to create something of a fantasy. A dressing table with smooth, stark lines was topped with a three-fold mirror, carved with a symbol of the god Horus, wings spread, in a typical manner of protection. A large trunk was covered with hieroglyphs, as was the tall standing wardrobe. Chairs that stood before draperies were carved with the great protective wings of Horus, as well.

She turned and was startled by a large statue of a pharaoh. Walking toward it, she narrowed her eyes. The statue was real. Hatshepsut, she thought, the female pharaoh who had herself displayed with a beard, showing her world that she was a woman, but one with the power of a man.

The statue was surely priceless. And set here, in a guest room? It was a museum piece, she thought angrily.

On the other side of the door, she discovered another life-size statue, this one of the goddess Anat. A war goddess, Anat was supposed to protect the pharaoh in battle. She was usually sculpted or drawn with a shield, a lance and a battle-ax. This statue was slightly damaged. Still, a great find. A priceless relic! And here, in a guest room!

Camille stepped back, wondering if she had purposely been given this room. The statues might well unnerve most women. In fact, she was certain that many a young respectable woman—the type preparing for her season before society—might well awake in the night terrified and screaming bloody murder, certain the curse of the castle had awakened the statues, that they had become real and were seeking her in the night…. In the firelight, they were decidedly eerie, Camille admitted.

"But I'm not afraid!" she said aloud, then winced. It was as if she were assuring some long-dead or mythical creature that she was beyond its control. "Nonsense!" she whispered to herself.

Two lamps burned on stark little tables on either side of the bed. They, too, were in Egyptian motifs. And rather shockingly, both depicted the fertility god Min with his huge, erect phallus and double-plumed headdress. Camille hardly thought herself prudish, but really…!

Shaking her head, she had a feeling that she would not have been assigned to this room if she hadn't tempted the earl's fury with her assertion of the truth—that she worked for the museum. She had been sent here, she was certain, with a sense of vengeance. With that thought, she smiled. Fine.

She ventured more fully into the room, pulling back the draperies behind the chairs. There were, indeed, windows there. At one time, she was certain, they had not held panes, nor had they been quite so large. They showed the width of the castle stone, and in that they were far more startling than the Egyptian artifacts. At one time, these walls had been made for protection. Castle Carlyle had once defied the swords and arrows of the enemy, just as surely as the earl now defended himself from English society behind his bastion of stone and strength.

She let out a sigh, itching to race back to Tristan's room and give him a thorough tongue-lashing, even if he couldn't hear her. But she knew that the hellhound would be beyond her door, keeping watch. So she shook her head, walked to the bed and picked up the linen gown left for her, determined to find the bath.

Toiletries had been provided as promised, and the bath was quite modern with a tub, commode and running water. The earl might have his wicked sense of justice wherein he thought ancient artifacts might disturb a body's sleep, but at least the room came with niceties far beyond those to which she was accustomed.

A candle burned in the bath, and by it was a tray with brandy and glasses. Without hesitation, she drew hot water into the massive tub, then stripped, poured herself brandy and settled in.

How strange! The night was quite a disaster, yet here

she was, luxuriating in a hot bath, sipping brandy. Frowning, she reminded herself that the situation was extremely dire.

She felt herself tense and wasn't at all sure why she did so. A sixth sense gave her warning of something being not right. She held very still and thought that she heard something. Movement. Not a rustling. Not footsteps. Just…as if stone had shifted against stone.

She waited, but the sound didn't come again. Had she imagined it? Then, from outside the bedroom door, she suddenly heard a furious barking. Whatever had seeped into her senses, the dog had heard it, too.

She nearly threw her brandy down, but managed to set it upon the throw rug on the floor. She leaped out of the tub and into a heavy brocade dressing gown that hung on the bathroom door. It occurred to her that perhaps she should be locking herself into the room, but instinct sent panic into her veins, and she knew she had to find the source of the noise that had given rise to such a state of distress.

As she burst out into the bedroom, she heard herself being called.

"Miss Montgomery!" It was the Earl of Carlyle himself, shouting her name.

She ran forward as the door burst open. There they were, staring at one another. He, blue eyes sharp behind the beast of the mask, she, most startled and feeling terribly vulnerable, hair wild about her face, robe not at all decently closed.

She caught at the edges, seeking the tie.

The dog rushed into the room. He was no longer barking, but standing by its master's legs, sniffing the air, rigid.

"Ahem." The beast actually cleared his throat. "You're quite all right?" he asked.

She couldn't find her voice at first, so she nodded.

"Did you hear anything?" he demanded.

"I…don't know."

He let out an oath of impatience. "Miss Montgomery, either you did or didn't hear something. Was someone here?" He frowned, as if sincerely doubting the possibility of such a situation but determined he must ask.

"No!"

"You didn't hear anything?"

"I…don't believe so."

"You don't believe? Then why do you appear to have bolted from the bath as if chased by demons from hell?"

"There seemed to be…I don't know," she said, lifting her chin. "A scraping sound from somewhere." She squared her shoulders. "But as you—and your creature—can surely see, there is no one here. I assume that ancient places such as this might well creak."

"Mmm," he murmured.

She hated the mask. It hid all but his eyes, leaving her feeling as if she were continually dueling without all the weapons she needed in her corner. She stiffened again, determined on dignity. "Do you mind, My Lord? I am an unwilling guest at best, and as so, would prefer my own company at this hour."

To her surprise, he seemed reluctant to leave.

"You do not find the room…disturbing?"

"No. Did you intend that I should?"

He waved a hand in the air. "I am not referring to the decor," he said.

"Then…?"

"The creaking, or whatever it is that you—and my monster dog—apparently heard."

She shook her head, thinking on the one hand that she was a fool. *Yes! I want out of the room,* an inner voice cried.

But she wouldn't let this man know that she could be frightened. Not in any way.

"I'm quite content to remain here," she told him.

He studied her, and she thought that he might well insist that she do so. He didn't. Instead he said, "I will leave the dog, then."

"What?"

"I promise, you will be safe from creaks and groans, no matter what, with Ajax in attendance."

"Ajax hates me!" she said.

"Don't be ridiculous. Come. Give him a pat on the head."

She just stared at the man incredulously.

She was amazed to realize that he was actually smiling. "You're afraid of the dog?"

"You, sir, must not be ridiculous. I merely respect such a creature."

"Come. You'll have nothing to fear when he knows I wish him to look out for you."

She moved forward, once again determined not to betray fear. Yet, even as she did so, her heart was pounding. But it wasn't the dog. It was proximity to the man, she knew.

As she came near, he gripped her hand, not with any cruelty, just simple impatience. He laid it atop the dog's head. The animal whined and thumped its tail.

She felt the size of the Earl of Carlyle, his height, his very vital touch. Like a coiled snake, he seemed mercurial with energy, with something explosive within. It was hypnotic, like the heat of a fire. She stepped back, staring at him. "I'm really not afraid here. I'm sure that your dog—"

"He likes you."

"How nice," she murmured.

"Yes, actually, it is. He is a sound judge of character. He is most wary of your guardian."

She forced a grim smile. "Is that a reminder, My Lord, that we are prisoners here? That we are being...bribed, perhaps?"

She expected anger, something other than the dry laugh of amusement she received in return. "Perhaps. I will leave Ajax and rest assured myself that you will be safe and well throughout the hours of darkness. Good night, Miss Montgomery."

"Now wait!" she began.

"Good night," he repeated. He turned and was gone, closing the door behind him in a way that brooked no objection.

Camille stared after him, incredulous and angry. Had he left the dog because he thought she might be up to something? Or because he thought she might be in danger? Was she being watched, or guarded?

Ajax, staring at her, whined and thumped his tail. He padded over to her, still wagging his tail. She petted him on the head again. Huge eyes looked up at her. They seemed adoring now.

"You are really such a fine and handsome fellow," she told him. "What is it with you and that sneer and your growling? Is it all a facade?" A facade. Like the mask his master wore?

It was all quite ridiculous. And yet, it seemed that the lamps flickered suddenly when there should have been no breeze. Deep in his throat, Ajax let out a warning sound.

"What is it, boy?" she whispered. Despite herself, she felt a deep unease. But the statues were unmoving. The room was empty.

"I think, my fine fellow, that I'm going to finish my brandy. And I must admit, I'm glad to have your company."

Ajax must have believed her. When she finally doused the lamps—all but one, which she kept by her side—he leaped up on the foot of the bed. Thank God that it was a large bed. Still, she was glad to have him there, sitting sentinel through the night.

IN THE MORNING, she congratulated herself on befriending the dog. Now she could move about the castle as she chose.

She was determined to head straight to Tristan's room and have it out with the fellow before having to face the master of the castle again. If she knew exactly what Tristan had done and what had transpired, she'd be better able to stand up for him. But the minute she walked out the door, the giant who had brought her in the night before greeted her. Had he just been standing around in the hall all morning, waiting? It appeared to be so.

"His lordship is waiting for you in the solarium," the man told her gravely.

"Ah, what a surprise," she murmured. "Lead on, please."

Ajax trotted at her side as the man led her along the hallway, across the landing from the lower floor and into the next wing of the sprawling castle. Here, one giant room, a ballroom perhaps, led into another. Glass lined much of the ceiling, and it was actually quite beautiful, with the morning sun casting bright rays through to light the marble flooring and elegantly papered walls.

The earl was there, not seated but standing, hands clasped behind his back, at one of the long windows overlooking a central garden.

"Good morning, Miss Montgomery," he said, turning to greet her. Due to the mask, she was ever more aware of the sharp blue color and piercing quality of his eyes.

"Indeed, it seems fine enough."

"Were you able to sleep well enough after the disturbance?" he inquired politely, as if she were certainly a welcome guest.

"I slept just fine, thank you."

"Ajax was no trouble?"

"Ajax is a lamb, just as Mrs. Prior informed me."

"Usually," he agreed pleasantly enough. "Well, you must join me for some breakfast, Miss Montgomery. I hope we have something that you might desire. Omelettes, oatmeal, toast, jam, bacon, fish…?"

"I seldom eat heavily in the morning, Lord Stirling, but I do thank you for your generous hospitality. However, I hate to take advantage of it."

He smiled, quite grimly, she was certain.

"Hospitality is easily afforded here."

"Too easily," she said sharply.

"I do apologize for my lack of manners last night, but you did take me quite by surprise. So you work for the museum?"

She sighed deeply. "I am quite knowledgeable, I assure you. And yes, I work for the museum."

He walked to the table that had been set with shimmering silver, a snowy cloth and chafing dishes. From an urn he poured a cup of coffee. "Tea, Miss Montgomery? Or do you prefer coffee?"

"Tea will be lovely, thank you," she murmured.

"How long have you worked for the museum?" he asked.

"About six months."

"And your work for the museum had nothing to do with your guardian's appearance here?" he asked.

The words were politely spoken but they had a frightening edge. She decided that she liked him better when he was angry. There was something quite unnerving about the ease of his movement and the pleasantness of his tone.

She accepted the cup of tea he offered to her, and with little choice, also took a seat in the chair he pulled out for her convenience. He sat next to her, close, his chair at an angle, his knee nearly touching hers.

"Lord Stirling, I do assure you, Tristan is in no way involved with my work!" She didn't add that she kept her guardian as far from the museum as she could at all times. "I swear to you, I gained my position there through knowledge, work and dogged determination! And I'm terribly afraid that I am going to lose that position," she added bitterly. "Sir John has no tolerance for tardiness."

"Sir John?"

"Sir John Matthews. He is my immediate superior."

"The department is run by David, Lord Wimbly," he said sharply.

"Yes, yes. But Lord Wimbly seldom…" She refrained from saying that the man seldom actually worked! "He has many functions to attend. His work is seldom at the museum itself. Sir John sees to the actual care and study of the exhibitions. He works closely with two men who have been on many excavations themselves, Alex Mittleman and Aubrey Sizemore. When there is a new exhibit, Lord Wimbly is present, and with Sir Hunter MacDonald, they make the arrangements. They also choose what purchases shall be made for the galleries, and they are in charge of seeing who receives grants for study and further expeditions."

"Where do you fit in?" he demanded.

She flushed slightly. "I read hieroglyphics. And naturally, loving the subject as I do, I have the patience and care to work with artifacts."

"How did you get the job?" he demanded.

"I was there one day when Sir John happened to be working alone. I had come to view a new exhibit of artifacts from the New Kingdom, when a box arrived. Sir John could not find his glasses, and I was able to decipher the information he needed from a stone within. He needed someone. There was a meeting and I was hired."

He had been staring at her steadily all the while. She

continued to feel ill at ease, aware that she had seldom been watched quite so intensely.

She set her cup down. "I don't know why on earth you believe that I'm lying or making any of this up. You are free to ask any of the men involved, and you'll learn that I'm telling the truth. However, this job is important to me." She hesitated. "My guardian…well, his past has not always been the most pure. I am doing all that I can, My Lord, to see that we are respectable. I'm deeply distressed that Tristan fell over your wall—"

He interrupted her with a choked sound of laughter. "Imagine! And I had been about to believe your every word!" he exclaimed.

She felt her anger rising, and also her color, for he had every right to laugh. She stood. "I'm afraid, Lord Stirling, that you are doing nothing but seeking revenge upon me as well as Tristan, and that there is nothing I can say or do that will stop you from pressing charges. I can tell you only that my work is very important to me, that Tristan is often foolish and misled but never evil, and that, if you're going to press charges, you must just go ahead and do so. If I don't appear at work soon, I will surely be fired. That may not matter, because I would never deny my association with Tristan, and once you file charges, word will get out and I will lose my job anyway."

"Oh, do sit down, Miss Montgomery," he said, suddenly sounding weary. "I admit that as yet I'm still feeling a bit…wary, shall we say? Regarding you both. However, for the moment, I suggest that you take a chance. Play along with me. If you're ready, we'll get you into work right now, and I'll see to it personally that you receive no reprimands for tardiness."

Stunned, she sat in silence.

"Sit. Finish your tea."

She sat, a frown creasing her brow. "But—"

"I haven't been to the museum in quite a while. I wasn't even aware of how the hierarchy in your department worked. I think a journey in will be quite appropriate for me at this time." He rose. "If you'll be so good as to be at the front door in five minutes…?"

"But what about Tristan?"

"He needs the day in bed."

"I have barely even seen him. I must get him home."

"Not today, Miss Montgomery. Shelby will have the carriage at the museum doors at closing time."

"But—?"

"Yes, what haven't I covered?"

"I…must go home. And then, there's Ralph."

"Ralph can tend to your guardian today. He won't be leaving. I've seen to it that he has lodgings in the metal smith's place in the courtyard."

"Really, Lord Stirling, you can't just keep people prisoner."

"Actually, I can. I rather think they'll be more comfortable here than in jail, don't you?"

"You are bribing me! Blackmailing me!" she choked. "You are toying with me, playing some kind of game!"

"Yes, but you're a smart young woman, and therefore, you should play this game my way."

He turned to leave, perfectly aware that she would do as he had suggested. Ajax might have decided that he liked her, but certainly no more than his master. The giant hound trotted out in Lord Stirling's wake.

When they were both gone, she jumped to her feet. "I will not be made a pawn!" she swore aloud. But then she sank back into the chair again, staring across the expanse of the long hall. Yes, she would be made a pawn. She really had no choice at this minute.

She finished her tea, angry. And when she was done, she made her way from the wing to the great stairway. The Earl of Carlyle was waiting for her at the bottom.

She stopped before him, chin raised, shoulders squared. "There must be some agreement between us, Lord Stirling."

"Oh?"

"You must promise not to prosecute."

"Because I'm bringing you into London, to work?" he inquired.

"You are using me somehow, sir."

"Then let's just see how useful you prove to be, shall we?"

He opened the door. "You are buying a great deal of time, and since you arrived out here of your own accord last evening, I think it's rather chivalrous of me to see to it that you maintain your employment."

Her lashes fell and she walked past him.

The carriage, with the man, Shelby, driving, was waiting for them at the door. She was so angry that she jerked her arm away when the beast of the castle would have helped her in. She nearly careened off the step, but, thank God, saved herself. She somewhat crashed into the forward seat of the carriage, but that didn't matter since she was able to rectify her position before he joined her, sitting on the opposite side. He carried a silver-knobbed walking stick, and he tapped it against the top of the carriage.

As they started out, she fixed her eyes on the view.

"What is going on in that devious little mind, Miss Montgomery?" he inquired.

She turned to him. "I was thinking, My Lord, that you need a new gardener."

He laughed, the sound oddly pleasant. "Ah, but I like my deep, dark woods and the tangle of vines within them!"

She didn't reply, but once again stared out the window.

"You don't approve?"

She looked at him. "I'm sorry for what you've suffered," she said. "But I'm equally sorry that a man of your position should hide himself away because of that suffering when you could be doing so very much for so many people."

"I am not at fault for the ills of the world."

"The world is better when the life of one man, or one woman, is improved, sir."

He lowered his head slightly. For a moment, she couldn't even see the sardonic curl of his lips or the intense blue of his eyes.

"What would you have me do?"

"There are dozens of things you could do!" she informed him. "With this property."

"Shall I cut it into tiny lots and divvy it out?" he asked.

She shook her head impatiently. "No, but...you could bring the children from orphanages out here, let them have just a day with a lovely picnic! You could hire many more people, have beautiful grounds, give employment to some who desperately need it. Not that it will change all the ills in society, but—"

She broke off as he leaned forward. "How do you know, Miss Montgomery, that I don't contribute to the welfare of others?"

He was very close to her. She didn't think she had ever seen anything quite so intense, so silencing, so commanding and condemning as his eyes. She found that she wasn't even breathing.

"I don't," she managed to say at last.

He sat back.

"But!" she said. "I know what I have heard about you. And you are one of the most powerful men in our kingdom. I've heard that the Queen and your parents were devoted friends. I've heard that you are one of the—"

"One of the what?"

She looked out the window again, afraid that she was being quite crass. But then again, she was the daughter of an East End prostitute.

"That you are one of the richest men in the country. And since you were so blessed at birth, you should be thankful. Other men have lost their families, and they cannot all be bitter."

"Really?"

She had angered him.

"Tell me, Miss Montgomery, should murderers go free?"

"Of course not! But if I understand correctly, your parents were killed by snakes! Egyptian cobras. Again, I am sorry, but there is no man to blame for that!"

He didn't answer then, choosing to look out the window instead. She realized then that, far more than the mask itself, he had managed to build an emotional wall around himself. He didn't intend to speak with her anymore, she knew. And despite herself, she couldn't force the point.

She, too, gazed out the window until they came into the bustle and jog of London and then to the museum itself. He didn't allow her to refuse his help when stepping out of the carriage, and neither did he release her elbow as they headed for the building. Before the door, however, he suddenly came to a halt, turning her to face him.

"Believe me, Miss Montgomery, there is a murderer who brought about the death of my parents. I believe that the killer is someone we both know, perhaps even someone you see nearly every day."

A chill enwrapped her heart. She didn't believe his words, but she believed the fever in his eyes.

"Come along," he said then, walking once again. Almost casually he added, "Whatever I say or do, you will go along with, Miss Montgomery."

"Lord Stirling, perhaps I can't—"

"But you will!" he said firmly, and she fell silent, for they had reached the great doors to her place of employment.

CHAPTER FOUR

LORD STIRLING knew his way.

Employees and visitors alike seemed to know him or of him, for many greeted him—all trying not to stare at the mask—with respect and a bit of awe. Perhaps it was his size, his height and the breadth of his shoulders, the casual and handsome way he wore his clothing. Or the way he carried himself. Or the mere fact of who he was.

"I work in a back room on the—"

"Second floor, of course," he murmured.

They came to the section, and he immediately headed her toward the door that led to the rooms that were not open to the public. She pulled free then, nervously hurrying before him. Inside the first office, they came first upon Sir John Matthews, who was seated behind the entry desk, papers piled in disarray before him.

"There you are, at last! My dear Miss Montgomery! You know my opinion of those who cannot manage to arrive in a timely manner. I—" He broke off, seeing the Earl of Carlyle coming behind her. "Lord Stirling!" he exclaimed, astonished.

"John, my good fellow. How are you doing?"

"I…I…quite well!" Sir John said, still appearing somewhat in shock. "Brian, I'm stunned, pleased, delighted! Does your appearance here mean that you'll be…"

Brian Stirling laughed pleasantly. "Contributing to the Egyptology department again?" he queried.

Sir John flushed a rose hue, bright against his white whiskers and hair. "Dear me, that's not what I meant at all, really. You're family...you...well, all were so learned in the field. To have your enthusiasm involved here again would be quite fantastic!"

Camille could see Lord Stirling's lips curl and pleasantly so. She wondered if he might have felt a modicum of affection for Sir John at some time in his life.

"That's kind of you, John. Actually, I was considering attending your fund-raiser this weekend."

"Good God!" Sir John exclaimed. "Really?"

He looked from Camille to Lord Stirling, then back again, completely baffled. He shook his head, as if trying to clear it, as if their appearance together should perhaps make sense, but certainly didn't in any way.

Stirling stared at Camille. "You will be attending—correct, Miss Montgomery?"

"Oh, no!" she said quickly. She felt a flush rise to her own cheeks. "I'm not a senior member of the staff," she murmured.

"Miss Montgomery has not been with us long," Sir John murmured.

"Ah, but of course you will attend, Miss Montgomery, as my escort back into a world where I might feel quite lost were you not with me."

He wasn't making a request. And simply because of his tone, she longed to refuse. But she was being bribed or blackmailed, whichever word fit the situation better.

Sir John stood staring at her, eyes narrowed, still at a loss as to how she had come to be in the company of such a man as the earl.

"Camille, if the Earl of Carlyle would be more comfortable attending in your company, you will be here."

Stirling walked across the few steps that brought him before Camille, reaching for her hands, taking them into his own. "John!" he said, looking at Camille even as he addressed the man. "Please! You mustn't make it sound as if you're threatening the lass!"

Those sharp blue eyes of his focused on her with some humor. There was no need at all for Sir John to threaten her. She already knew that she was being threatened. Yet, along with whatever other skills he had acquired through the years, he was an excellent actor, for it appeared that he was being pleasant, as courteous and correct as his breeding should merit.

She tried to pull her hands away casually, but his grip was firm. She forced a smile. "How very kind of you, Lord Stirling. I'm afraid I should be a rather humble choice for such an evening."

"Nonsense. We are living in the age of enlightenment. What better choice for an evening's companion than a young woman who is not just beautiful, but intelligent and so very well versed on the subject of the evening's passion."

"Camille!" Sir John murmured, prodding her.

Stirling's smile was a bit grim, and definitely amused. She longed to jerk hard on her hands. In fact, she longed to tell him that she'd rather spend the evening in an opium den with hoods and thieves.

"It's not…the mask, is it?" he queried.

Oh, what a tone! The man was playing upon pathos now! "No," she said sweetly. "This is the age of enlightenment, My Lord, as you have said. No man, or woman, should ever be judged by appearance."

"Bravo!" Sir John complimented.

Apparently her tormenter decided that he wasn't going to wait for her actual agreement. "Then, indeed, yes, John, I will attend the upcoming fund-raiser. And you may be assured that both my interest and my income are returned full score to the pursuit of our educational ideals. Well, you've work to do, and I caused Miss Montgomery's tardiness. And now, I fear, I am taking more time. John, it is, indeed, a pleasure to see you so well—a bit disarrayed as ever in your studies and intents, but looking hale and hearty. Miss Montgomery, Shelby will be here with the carriage to attend to you at…six, is it?"

"It's usually at least six-thirty," she murmured, aware that Sir John was now staring at them both, gaping.

Stirling decided to let him out of his curiosity, a feeling so strong it was surely about to tear Sir John into pieces. "This dear young woman's guardian had quite an accident on the highway last night—imagine, if you will, right at my property. Naturally, he is my guest. And quite naturally, Miss Montgomery came in haste and fear to tend to him. To my great delight, Castle Carlyle is hosting guests once again. So good day, then, to you both."

"G-good day, Brian!" Sir John stuttered, still staring at Stirling as he turned about, exiting casually, yet with the natural dignity of a man born to position.

He was gone for several moments before Sir John— who stared blankly after him long after he disappeared from sight—turned to Camille, amazed.

"Good God!" he said.

She could offer only a grimace and a shrug.

"This is quite amazing!"

"I'm afraid I wouldn't know," she murmured. "I… merely went out to tend to my guardian."

"An accident?" Sir John said, frowning. "He's going to be all right?"

Sir John was a decent fellow. He seemed disturbed to realize that events had made him completely forget to ask after the welfare of a fellow human being.

"Yes, yes, thank you. We believe he has suffered some bruises, but nothing serious."

"These hansom and carriage drivers!" Sir John said with a sniff. "They can be so careless and reckless. Then again, it doesn't take much to set a fellow up driving!" He seemed quite disgusted that there was no training necessary for drivers, despite the fact that many a rich man, and probably several of his peers, had invested in such cabs, heedless of who might be driving.

She smiled, refraining from informing him that the "accident" had not involved a cab or, indeed, a conveyance of any kind.

He still stared at her troubled. "Quite remarkable," he said.

"Well," she murmured, lowering her eyes. "If you're pleased, then…"

"Pleased!" Sir John exclaimed. "My dear girl, Lord Stirling's parents were such patrons of this museum, you cannot imagine. And more! They were deeply devoted to the people of Egypt, anxious that, with foreign powers lending aid, the people should not suffer. And the work they did!" He studied her a moment longer, then seemed to make a decision. "Come with me, Camille dear, and I'll show you a bit of their legacy."

She was startled. So far, her work had entailed exactly what they chose to hand her—usually the most tedious work—and nothing more. But now Sir John intended to take her into the vaults, the storage facilities of the museum.

She was fascinated to realize that she had her threatening host to thank for this possibility. She hated feeling that she owed him any thanks whatsoever, but she wasn't about to miss this opportunity.

"Thank you, Sir John," she said.

He acquired a set of keys from his desk and brought her out of the offices, down stairs and through hallways, and then down once again. Here, the corridors were dark and the rooms were filled with wooden crates, some items unpacked, some in stages of being opened. They passed by a number of boxes that had come from Turkey and Greece and onward, until they reached a section shrouded in shadow. Some of the crates here were open. Smaller crates had been removed, and there was a row of sarcophagi still nestled in larger coffinlike boxes, cradled by their packing material.

"Here!" Sir John said, sweeping his arms to indicate the array of treasures.

Camille looked around slowly. There were definitely many riches here.

"Only half, of course. Many of the artifacts went to the castle," Sir John said. A scowl furrowed his brow. "Then there were several boxes that simply went missing."

"Perhaps they're at the castle, as well."

"I don't think so," Sir John murmured. "But, of course, transporting these goods…ah, who knows! Still, Lord and Lady Stirling were always tremendously detailed about their work. Everything written down…" He paused, looking abashed. "I believe the boxes did arrive. But no matter. Their last find was so rich, we've not managed to begin to study and catalogue what we've got."

"These were discovered by Lord Stirling's parents just before they died, I assume," Camille said.

Sir John nodded. "The small pieces and reliefs you are translating are from the same find," he explained. "A glorious, glorious find." He shook his head sadly. "Such a marvelous couple! Very aware of their responsibility to the Queen, but both devoted to study! It was quite amazing that Lord Stirling found a woman such as he did. Ah, Lady Stirling! I remember her well. No woman could so gracefully and kindly greet a room of friends, old or new. She was a stunning woman, simply beautiful. And yet, she could crawl into the dirt, work with a shovel or a brush, study texts, seek the answers to mysteries…" His voice faded. "Such a loss…"

Sir John's white hair glimmered in the pale gaslight of the museum depths as he shook his head once again. But then he grimaced sadly. "I had feared that Brian would hole up forever at that castle of his, tangled now with overgrowth, ever dark and forbidding, believing that his parents had been killed. But it appears he may at last be coming to terms with the past and dealing with his grief. And, my dear girl, if you have had anything to do with this magnificent rebirth of interest, you are perhaps the most valuable asset I have brought into the museum."

"Well, Sir John, thank you. But I hardly think that I've had much of an influence upon the man. We're not at all well acquainted."

"But he wishes you to attend the gala fund-raiser with him!"

"Yes," she murmured. She refrained from telling Sir John that it had nothing to do with the fact that he looked forward to her company.

Sir John frowned. "Camille, are you aware that this man is the *Earl of Carlyle?* Frankly, I'm flabbergasted that a man with such a pedigree would deign to ask a commoner anywhere. No insult intended, my child. It's just that…well, we English do have our society."

"Hmm. Well, as we've all agreed, it is the age of enlightenment, is it not?"

"An *earl,* Miss Montgomery. Even with his face hideously scarred, such a thing is unheard of!"

The man was not intentionally being cruel, but he continued to stare at her, and she felt as if she had grown some strange appendage. She was in no position to explain that she sincerely doubted the Earl of Carlyle had revitalized his interest in the museum, aside from continuing his quest to find the presumed murderer of his parents. And it didn't matter a whit to him whether she was noble or as common as dirt, as long as she served his purpose.

"Are you afraid of the man? Because of the scarring, or even his reputation?" Sir John demanded.

"No."

"You are not repulsed."

"A man's manner and conviction in life can be far uglier than his face, Sir John."

"Well-spoken, Camille!" he applauded, beaming. "Come along, then! We've work to do. As you are transcribing, I'll be happy to tell you more about the find they made. Naturally, the tombs of pharaohs are thought to have been the most magnificent. But sadly, most of those were plundered long ago. The very great thing about the Stirlings' discovery of the tomb of Nefershut is that, though the man was a high priest, he was regarded with awe, was wealthier than Midas, and his tomb had not been disturbed. And so many were buried with the man. The Egyptians did not require that a great man's wives and concubines be buried with him, yet look at this array of sarcophagi! And then there was the matter of the curse." He waved a hand impatiently in the air. "Apparently, according to popular belief, no tomb discovered can be without a curse. A love of the mysterious, perhaps. We have opened many tombs with no severe warnings at the entry. But in this particular instance—as in some others—there was a curse just inside the tomb. 'Let he who disturbs the New Life of the blessed one be cursed upon this earth.' And sadly, the Lord and Lady Stirling died."

"Did anyone else associated with the dig die?" Camille asked.

Sir John slowly arched a brow with something of a troubled countenance. "I…I don't know. Certainly no one of the renown of the Stirlings."

Camille started to turn, thinking she had heard a scraping sound just behind her, where the mummies and their sarcophagi lay.

"Camille! Are you listening to me?" Sir John demanded.

She was amazed that she had been so easily distracted. And it was evident that Sir John hadn't heard any kind of noise. She was afraid that she was beginning to hear things—taking the small-scale drama that had suddenly invaded her life to greater heights. She loved ancient Egyptian history and all the stories that went with it, but thus far, she had never fallen victim to silly romanticism. She didn't believe that mummies would rise from their tombs to stalk the living.

"I'm sorry. I thought I heard something."

"Camille. We're in a museum. Many people are walking over our heads."

She smiled. "No, I thought I heard someone in here."

He sighed with exasperation. "Do you see anyone?"

"No. I just—"

"There are others with keys to the vaults, Camille. We are not the only department in the museum!"

He sounded indignant, and she realized that he was angry he didn't have her full attention on a very important topic.

"Asps! Camille. Dangerous creatures. Anyone who ventures into Egypt is aware of certain dangers. Though heaven knows, the common tourist is forever traveling down the Nile these days."

She smiled and refrained from suggesting that everyone had the right to travel, to study, to marvel at the wonders of an ancient world. Even commoners.

"But," Camille pointed out, "if someone saw to it that the asps were in Lord and Lady Stirling's apartments, wouldn't that suggest murder?"

Sir John appeared alarmed. His frown deepened and he looked around quickly, as if afraid they had been followed. He shook his head. "Don't even think such an idea!" he warned.

"Surely, that is what the current earl must believe."

He shook his head vehemently. "No! And you mustn't spread such a suggestion. You mustn't ever speak such a horrible idea aloud again, Camille. Ever!" He really appeared unnerved. He turned, heading out, but when she didn't follow quickly enough, he looked back. "Come, come. We've used up quite enough time!"

She followed him, sorry that she had voiced her opinion. But one thing was quite certain. She'd be giving her work more painstaking care in the future, now that she knew more about the man, the curse and the find.

"Hurry!" Sir John said, looking back impatiently to assure himself that she was close behind.

"Yes, of course, Sir John," she replied, hastening her steps.

The museum was already filled with people. She heard different accents—British, Irish and from farther afield— and she was delighted, as always, to see that the museum was well visited.

She loved the museum. It was, she thought, a crowning jewel of England. It had opened to the public on January 15, 1859. At the time, it had been an entirely new

kind of institution, governed by a body of trustees responsible to Parliament, with its vast collections belonging to
the people. Admission was free, thus, it had been a place
she had come as a small child, her hand held safely in the
gentle clasp of her mother's fingers. Her own department
was now known as the Department of Egyptian and Assyr-
ian Antiquities, and they had Napoleon Bonaparte to thank
for some of their finest pieces, since he, in his attempt at
world conquest, had been the first to go into Egypt with
scholars and historians. The British defeat of Napoleon had
brought the majority of his collections to the British Museum.

As they walked, they passed the Rosetta Stone, the incredible find that had allowed for the translation of the ancient Egyptian hieroglyphs.

Continuing through one of the Egyptian halls, she heard
a young boy ask his father, "Papa, why do they do it? I
don't understand why it's all right to dig up the dead, just
because they've been dead a long time. Aren't the people
afraid when they dig up mummies?"

"Yes, dear, why is it all right to dig up the dead?" the
boy's mother asked. She was pretty, dressed in a handsome
muslin day dress and wearing a pert and fashionable bon-
net.

"Darling, we've moved many of our own, far more recent dead!" the husband replied. He, too, was in high fashion with his gray hat and jacket. "Honestly! The church
cemeteries throughout much of our country are defiled in
my opinion! Restoration! That's what they call the proj-
ects. Why, in the 'restoration' of Salisbury Cathedral all of
the gravestones were moved. It's indecent, I say. Restoration! Bah. But these fellows…the mummies, well, they
weren't of the church, son," the father replied.

Though she agreed with the man that much of the current "restoration" of historical sites seemed sadly careless of those who had gone before them in their own country, Camille was tempted to stay behind and offer the boy a far different answer regarding the fact that they should respect all countries and beliefs. She might have told the boy about the brilliance of ancient Egyptian engineering, but her duties did not include acting as a tour guide. Pity! She did so enjoy her subject, and would dearly love to be a guide if she were allowed to do so. Then again, she wasn't a scholar, had never been on a dig and was rather certain she was lucky to be tolerated as it was.

Sir John cast her a warning glare, and she kept walking, offering him a weak smile.

"To work now," Sir John said firmly. He returned to his desk, instantly lowering his head over his papers. She had a feeling that he was deep in thought, worried perhaps, but not about to show her his concern.

She went for her apron, hanging on a hook in the rear of the room, then entered the little cubicle where she was working on a section of a relief. Lain out on a long worktable, the stone was approximately three feet in height, two in width and three inches thick. The piece was very heavy, crowned with the Egyptian cobra, denoting that the words—the warning, as it were—had been given the blessing of a pharaoh. Each symbol had been beautifully, painstakingly chiseled into the stone, and each was small, thus the reason the tedious task had been given to her. The hierarchy here was also certain that this tablet did no more than reiterate other warnings that had been left around the tomb.

The man buried here had been beloved and revered. Now that Camille was aware of the number of people who had been buried with him, she was ever more fascinated as to exactly why. Had his many wives or concubines been killed to go into the eternal afterlife with him?

She sat down and studied the symbols in whole. She knew that Nefershut had been a high priest, but according to what she had already transcribed, he had been more, perhaps something of a magician for his day. She glanced at the words she had already written. *Know all who come here that they have entered the most sacred ground. Disturb not the priest, for he goes into the next life demanding all that was his in this, his time on our earth, as we know it. In his honor, disturb him not. For Nefershut could rule the air, the water. His hand dealt the whisper of the gods, and at his table sat Hethre. His life is blessed beyond this life. His power extends as she sits at his right hand.*

"Hethre," she murmured aloud. "Hethre…who were you exactly, and why is it you are the one mentioned, though you are not mentioned as his wife?"

"The fellow must have had some powerful magic, eh?"

Startled, Camille looked up. She hadn't heard the arrival of Sir Hunter MacDonald. She straightened, aware of her apron and a lock of hair that had escaped her pins. Certainly, her appearance must display a definite dishabille.

Sir Hunter was striking. Tall, well dressed, with rich, dark hair and eyes. She was aware that among the elite he had a reputation for daring, adventure and charm. And naturally, a reputation for attracting feminine enchantment. Though he might have been something of a rake, it did him no ill, for he was neither married nor even engaged. The mamas and papas among the wealthy and equally as elite could reason that such a young man should certainly sow his wild oats. Therefore, he remained prized as a possible catch in the marriage arena.

Camille could well understand his attraction, for he had always been courteous and charming to her. She was no fool, however, and neither did she intend to live the life that had brought her mother to such a tragic and dismal end.

With a certain dry humor she could appreciate the fact that she held an appeal to Hunter, as well. She was hardly among the class from which he would choose a wife, but neither was she one he could seduce for the mere value of entertainment. She would not allow it, and had always made that fact perfectly, if tacitly, clear. It did not prevent him from his continued attempts at charm, however, since he was also a man of enough ego to believe that if he really chose, he would eventually have his way.

"Ah, my dear Miss Montgomery!" Hunter continued, coming to her side. "Ever our glorious scholar, beauty hidden away in a tiny room in a musky old smock!" He leaned upon the table, eyes sparkling. "Alas! You must take care, my darling Camille. The years will pass! You will have spent them, becoming steadily more myopic into your old age, forgetting all about the wonders of the modern world."

She laughed softly. "Ah, wonders such as yourself, Sir Hunter?"

He grinned ruefully. "Well, I would be happy to escort you about London, you know."

"I fear the scandal," she told him.

"One must live a bit recklessly."

"Easy enough for you, Sir Hunter," she told him primly. "And I love my work! If I'm to grow old, gray and myopic, there is no better place."

"But the waste of such youth and beauty is a true tragedy!" he told her.

"You're most charming, and you know it," she informed him.

His smile faded and he grew serious. "I'm quite concerned."

"You are? Why?" she inquired.

He came around and stood by her side, and a bit too tenderly smoothed back a stray lock of her hair. "I've just heard that you've spent an extraordinary evening—and morning."

"Oh! The accident," she murmured.

"You slept last night at Castle Carlyle?" he demanded.

"My guardian was hurt. There was no choice."

"May I speak bluntly, Camille?" he asked, eyes gentle and serious.

"If that's what you wish."

"I fear for you! You mustn't ever be deceived. The Earl of Carlyle is a monster. He chose his mask as close to his heart as he might. Sir John has told me that he brought you into the museum today and is insisting that you attend the fund-raiser on his arm. Camille, he is dangerous."

She arched a brow. "Forgive me if I'm wrong, Hunter, but aren't you continually attempting to be just as…dangerous?"

Gravely, he shook his head. "My attempts are merely upon your virtue. The Earl of Carlyle is very nearly insane. I fear for your life and health. Apparently, he has fixated upon you, Camille. You entered his world, where he allows very few these days." He cleared his throat. "Camille, I'd not hurt your feelings for the world. Surely, though, you are aware that we remain a horribly class-conscious society. There's rumor, of course, that the earl prowls the alleys of London at night, seeking diverse entertainments, since he no longer appears, scarred and mutilated, in the drawing rooms of the gentle misses he might otherwise have sought. I fear that he is truly toying with you in the most cruel and heinous manner."

That was exactly what the earl was doing, but hardly in the manner that Sir Hunter imagined.

"Please, don't worry about me," she told him. "I'm quite able to handle myself." She offered him a rueful smile. "Surely you're aware of that. If I'm not mistaken, sir, you have been trying…well, to bring the wonders of the modern world to my doorstep since I came."

"I've not been a wretch, surely!" he protested.

"No, because I am quite capable of handling myself."

"I know how to settle this in the most courteous manner!" Hunter exclaimed. "We can say that you had already agreed to come with me."

"Hunter, how very kind," she told him, setting an arm on his shoulder, because she did believe that he was concerned. "But think of the scandal. In fact, I imagine that I could be in tremendous danger then, for dozens of highborn ladies would be after my throat if they imagined that a woman such as myself was after you!" She was teasing, but there was a grain of truth to her words.

He took both her hands, his eyes intense as they delved into hers. "Camille, really, it would not be a bad thing to let the Earl of Carlyle believe that there was something quite serious between us. And I am a humble 'sir.' He is an earl. A different matter altogether."

"Hunter, is that a proposal?" she teased.

He hesitated. She withdrew her hands.

"Hunter, please believe me. You have been ever kind to me, and I, like all those others, have not been immune. But, Hunter, if I were to engage in a small liaison with you, I would not be just common, but I believe many a common word would be added when my name was spoken."

"Ah, Camille, the temptation you stir in my heart to cast all else to the wind…"

"Would be foolish," she told him firmly. "I believe that I will be quite all right. You, of all men, should be aware that I know my class, my position, and that I therefore avoid anything *serious* with men of greater means."

He frowned, still intense. "Camille, you know, you do enchant…and more."

"Hunter, it is the very fact that I am unattainable that enchants you."

He shook his head. "No, Camille. You are aware, surely, that you have eyes of magic, green and gold, as alluring as those of a tigress. You are, unless you are without sight and reason, aware that you are graced with a form like many a classic statue that charms every man who enters here. You are alive and vital and intelligent. Yes, you could so beguile a man that he would be willing to do anything to acquire your hand."

She was startled by the passion of his speech. "You're implying that I believe I could withhold my company from a man such as the earl and gain…marriage?" she said, somewhat incredulous. She had been touched before but was suddenly angry.

"Camille! Please, I speak out of love. My admiration and care for you are deep, indeed."

She shook her head. "Hunter—"

"Is that it? Do you want marriage? Camille…yes, I would give you a proposal."

Again shocked, she said, "Hunter, you would hate me. You would deplore the scandal. And say you were really willing to cast sanity to the wind and marry me. In no time, I would no longer be so charming, because I would no longer be unattainable."

"Camille, you wound me."

"Hunter, you are worrying where you need not," she assured him.

"Is that the game you think you could play with Lord Stirling? After all, he is an earl, and even kings have married commoners. But, Camille, you must remember the fate of a certain commoner who married a king."

"Hunter—"

"History, my dear girl, history! Think of Anne Boleyn.

She forced Henry's hand by being unattainable. And when he was ready to move on, she lost her head!"

She couldn't help but laugh. "Hunter, I swear, I should be deeply, deeply offended. Indeed, if I were a fine young lady, raised to the best finishing schools, I think I should be required to slap you quite hard. But I'm afraid I lost my parents at far too early an age to have attended such a school, and as a mere commoner with an incredible thirst for knowledge, I believe I'm allowed to refrain from violence!"

"You're laughing at me, and I'm sincere."

"Oh, Hunter, this is terribly sweet of you. But, no, I'd never marry you—not that you aren't handsome and charming and so kind to even make such a suggestion."

"Am I not in the least seductive?" he demanded.

"Far too seductive, and truly kind with your proposal. Which I know you can't really mean." When he started to protest, she raised a hand to stop him and continued. "Please, Hunter! I don't want you to believe that you've made an offer, and that, by honor, you can't renege. Seriously, I do know that you would wind up despising me. And in the same vein the Earl of Carlyle cannot seduce me, because I do have one of those qualities you afforded me—intelligence. I'll be fine. I'm staying at the castle until I can safely move my guardian. I will attend the fund-raiser because I believe that he feels he can enter such a gathering, masked as he must be due to his scars, quite safely with a museum employee at his side. We will be here, Hunter, right here in the museum, and I will be surrounded by you, Alex and Sir John. And Lord Wimbly, of course, a protector of equal peerage."

The door opened again before Hunter could reply.

"Camille! I just heard that—" Alex Mittleman began. He stopped abruptly, seeing that she already had company in the small workroom. "Hunter," he said.

"Alex."

Alex, a slighter man and appearing more so since his hair was flaxen and his eyes were powder blue, coloring that gave him the appearance more of a handsome youth than of a mature man, flashed a frown in Camille's direction. The two men usually respected one another, though Alex complained often enough that Hunter was too much a rich dandy and not nearly enough a true scholar. Alex also considered himself a far more appropriate confidant for Camille, since he was more of an honest workingman. Just as she was an honest workingwoman.

Alex cleared his throat, then gave his head a little shake, as if deciding he might as well speak, since Hunter was apparently aware of the subject he meant to bring up. Hunter beat him to it.

"You arrived here this morning with Brian Stirling, the *Earl of Carlyle?*"

She sighed softly. "Tristan had an accident last night near the earl's gates. He was taken into the castle because he was injured. As it happens, he was shaken and bruised, yet suffered no worse trauma. Naturally, I went to his side. And so…well, there it is."

Both men stared at her, then at one another.

"Have you told her that he's…"

"A dangerous man and perhaps not fully sane," Hunter finished. "Not so bluntly until this exact minute, but, yes, I've tried to get that across."

"Camille, you really must be very careful around him," Alex said, still frowning. He looked very worried. "I'm rather shocked to say that Sir John is…well, frankly, pleased!"

"The Earl of Carlyle is a wealthy man," Hunter said harshly. "His grounds abound with treasures Sir John would love to see in the museum."

Alex swallowed suddenly. "I will go with you, Camille. I will go with you when the workday is over. We can hire a carriage and get your guardian home safely—"

"Alex, I certainly am better fixed to arrange a carriage, since I do have my own," Hunter interrupted firmly. "But you are right. We must get Camille and her guardian home quickly and safely, and away from that dreadful castle."

She watched the two of them, amazed. It wasn't that they hadn't shown her kindness or friendship before, but now they were truly vying for her attention. And both seemed most eager to get her away from Carlyle Castle.

Alex lifted his chin slightly, as if willing to be self-sacrificing for her greater good. "Fine. Hunter has his own carriage. However you are rescued from that dastardly place will suffice, as long as you are rescued."

"Alex, Hunter," she said softly, but before she could continue, the door burst open again.

Aubrey Sizemore had arrived. He was the last of the division's main employees, a man who was not quite so knowledgeable, yet, despite his lack of education on the subject, passionate about Egyptology, and he was certainly hardworking and determined. He was a large fellow of perhaps thirtysomething years, bald as a billiard ball and well muscled. He could easily move the heaviest boxes, yet had an incredibly gentle touch when it came to the finer and more delicate parts of excavation.

He stared at Camille as though she were an artifact that had suddenly proven to be the most bizarre find of the century.

"You came here with the Earl of Carlyle?" he demanded.

She sighed, weary of explaining, and said simply, "Yes."

"So he's out of the castle again!"

"Yes, so it seems."

"Well!" he said. "Well, good. We should have a great deal more money pouring in if he has come to acceptance. Indeed! He could plan a new excavation. There is nothing like real work, you know, in the desert sands."

"He isn't planning any expeditions as of yet," Hunter said sharply.

"But..." Aubrey murmured, watching Camille.

"Is there something else you wanted, Aubrey?" Hunter asked.

Aubrey scowled. "That old fellow, the stooped gray-beard we just acquired from Asian Antiquities. Have you seen him?"

They all looked at him blankly. "That fellow. He's been working for us now a few hours here and there. Arboc, that's his name! Old Jim Arboc, have you seen him?"

"No, we haven't seen him," Hunter said irritably. He didn't like Aubrey, but Aubrey had all the right assets to work in the department—raw muscle definitely being one of them.

"I've told Sir John time and time again that we must have a fellow in full time!" Aubrey said. "I don't mind the labor, it's the sweeping up that must be done. It's time-consuming!"

"Then perhaps you shouldn't waste so much time," Hunter suggested.

Aubrey almost growled in his direction, but smiled at Camille. "Excellent work, Camille, bringing back such an illustrious patron! Even if he has acquired something of an evil reputation. Perhaps the fellow is cursed." He winked at her, then went on out.

As he did so, Sir John arrived. "Whatever is going on in here?" he demanded, a rough, impatient note in his voice. "Alex, I believe that Camille is quite capable of working on this relief herself. Hunter, you may be a board member, but your role is not to take up the time of my employees. Lord Wimbly is on his way in, and I will not have my department appearing to be busy with nothing more than an afternoon tea social!"

Alex stiffened. Hunter shrugged laconically. "Camille, we'll speak later," he said, and strode toward the door. He opened it, ready to saunter out. But he paused.

Looking back, dark eyes raking quickly over the three of them, then landing on Camille, he said, "It appears that someone else is coming...for tea."

"Who?" Alex demanded.

"Brian Stirling, the Earl of Carlyle," Hunter said, his eyes resting on Camille. "We must, indeed, beware, for the monster comes this way!"

CHAPTER FIVE

DESPITE THE HUSH with which the others spoke, Brian could hear their startled and, he mused, somewhat *alarmed* whispers.

"Lord Stirling?" Sir John said, stunned.

"I thought he'd left." The frantic comment came from Alex Mittleman.

"Well, he hasn't. And I'm warning all of you…" That, from Sir John, who didn't finish the sentence, but came out into the hall, speaking more forcefully and with what sounded like good cheer and welcome. "Brian! We are, indeed, honored! Haven't seen you in forever, and today… well, we are honored!"

"Please, Sir John, you make me feel quite self-conscious," he replied, taking the man's hand.

"So…he never left!" Hunter mused softly, whispering into the ear of Camille Montgomery.

Brian saw her eyes. She was looking wary, thinking the same.

The little workroom where they had all gathered was apparently hers. She stood close to Hunter MacDonald. Alex hovered like a frightened rooster, determined somehow to defend his domain. Even Sir John had taken a stance that was defensive. Yet, Brian thought with a certain humor, he seemed ready—albeit reluctantly—to turn his lovely young ingénue over to Brian if that was what was required to pull him back in. Interesting.

Hunter stepped forward. "Brian, you old devil! We've missed you."

Again, the words were spoken with enthusiasm and apparent good cheer. They'd been in the military together and had known one another well. Indeed, they'd done a bit of pub hopping together. They might even have been called friends. Hunter liked to be thought of as a great world traveler, a tremendous adventurer, and he guarded his reputation as a ladies' man. He enjoyed women—of all sizes, shapes and social strata.

Was it the natural distrust for a man that might well be a murderer that caused Brian to watch him with so great a distrust now? Or was it the way he stood by Camille? Brian couldn't help the surge of curiosity that sprang forward in his mind, yet it was goaded by something far more instinctual. He wanted to wrench the woman from the man's side. Was she aware of Hunter and his reputation, hard earned and well deserved. *Were they already lovers?*

He'd known her but a night. And his distrust of her remained strong. After all, she had arrived at his house. And she worked at the museum. But was it simple distrust or something else? He had determined on his path. And she was part of it. But as he stood there, watching her, he realized the extraordinary depth of her beauty, the color of her hair, the crystal electricity in her eyes. Indeed, even in her work apron, with strands of hair escaping pins, she exuded a rare grace and dignity, even…sensuality.

He didn't trust her proximity to Hunter. And worse, he just didn't…like it.

"Lord Stirling!" Alex exclaimed, coming forward.

Though Alex might well appear hesitant and benign, he was no less dangerous.

"Lord Stirling!" he repeated, tentatively offering a hand.

Brian shook it. "Alex, old fellow. Good to see you." He cast his eyes upon Camille. "And I see here the hardest worker among the sorry lot of you!" he teased.

Camille wasn't at all flattered by his words. She forced a smile. "Lord Stirling. It is good to see your interest so well revived today."

"I've spent too long shut away," he said softly. "Amazing, isn't it? Days, months go by. A year comes and goes. One wanders in a fog. And then circumstance brings a chance meeting. Imagine, an accident in front of my castle, and it turns out to be a man who has, as his ward, the one true object of beauty associated with the museum and its department of antiquities! It is as if I have been…reawakened!"

He almost laughed out loud. Even Sir John, willing to sacrifice the fair maiden in his pursuit of the past, took a step closer to Camille.

"Camille is, indeed, the truest form of beauty we've discovered here," Hunter said, speaking carefully. "And truly cherished."

He saw a strange flash in Camille's eyes and knew her thoughts. *Hmm. Newly cherished. He knew this gentlemen's club. She was lucky to have gotten the work, lucky to be here. Unless she had actually acquired the position through her beauty and charms rather than through her knowledge….*

Anger filled him, and no matter how he told himself it was entirely unreasonable, there was no stopping it. The tension suddenly seemed palpable. He had no hold on the woman, other than threats and bribery. She might have been telling him the truth or she might have been lying boldly through her teeth. But his sudden proprietary feelings for her were nearly overwhelming. It was as if they were siding off for a fierce game of rugby and she was the ball between them all.

Sir John suddenly cleared his throat. "Were you interested in seeing some of the work being done?"

"There's time for that. I saw Lord Wimbly downstairs. We are meeting for lunch later. He is working with caterers down below right now, preparing for the fund-raiser."

"Yes, he does like to take charge of this type of thing himself."

"Little has changed, I see," Brian said. He frowned. "I don't see Aubrey."

"Well, he's working, of course!" Sir John said.

"Of course. Well, give him my regards." Brian looked at Camille again. "So, Miss Montgomery. You're working on finds that my parents sent to the museum."

He didn't think he had said the words as an accusation, but her eyes widened and hardened.

"Indeed. I believe Sir John invited you to see the work?"

"So nice to have the invitation," he murmured, and he saw her flush as she realized that he needed none, if he chose to make demands. "I have promised Lord Wimbly to meet him by the new Perseus, so I will just have to come back. Thank you."

He turned to leave and nearly smiled, well aware of the eyes focused on his back. "Miss Montgomery, my carriage will await," he told her.

"Goodness!" came another voice, deep and rumbling. They all turned.

Lord Wimbly himself had arrived.

"My entire staff, standing about!" he said, yet he smiled. Lord Wimbly was a man of indeterminate age—he looked quite the same as he had when Brian was a child, with a thick head of snow-white hair, and direct, piercing gray eyes. He was tall, slender, and looked every inch a lord.

"My fault, I'm afraid," Brian said. "Frightfully rude of me, being gone so long, then barging in and taking up so much time."

"Ah, but you've barged and we're so pleased!" Sir John said.

"Indeed," Hunter murmured dryly. His dark eyes met Brian's and there might have been a little friendly rivalry there. "High time you're back with us," he said. "You are the Earl of Carlyle, after all, and you're incredibly important to our efforts."

"Thank you."

Lord Wimbly clapped him hard on the back. "Yes, yes, my boy. Injury be damned, though your choice of mask—"

"Lord Wimbly!" Sir John interrupted, aghast.

Brian laughed out loud. "I like my mask."

"But, my boy, they whisper and call you the *beast!*" Lord Wimbly expounded.

There they were, the pack of them. Sir John, Hunter, Alex and now Lord Wimbly. The four who had been in Egypt, working with his parents. There to see much of the discovery. There to see his parents die. And now, seeming so pleased at his renewed interest. Offering enthusiasm, olive branches of understanding and friendship, all of them scholars. Yet, one of them was a murderer.

"I rather enjoy my fearsome reputation," he said, staring at Camille. "But perhaps you're all right. It's high time I honor the memory of my parents by returning to their work."

"Right, indeed!" Sir John said. "You must dust off the pain and solitude of the past and take your rightful place in society—at the head of a peerage that must see to knowledge…and education."

"And the poor," Camille murmured. Then her lashes fell quickly, hiding the brilliant, marbled, tiger coloring of her eyes.

They all stared at her, perplexed. Brian didn't think that these fellows cared anything about the poverty ravishing London. They had all been given a rather sharp slap in the face during the recent Ripper murders, but they were scholars. The pursuit of knowledge, of ancient Egypt in particular, was their driving goal in life.

That, or the riches and glory such study could bring.

"Yes, yes, the state of our poor masses," Lord Wimbly murmured. "Much to be done, eh, Brian?" Again, he slammed a hand against Brian's back. "Well, my boy, shall we?" he asked.

He nodded, looking around the group, smiling beneath the mask. "Gentlemen, I shall see you soon. Camille, I shall be deeply graced to see you later this evening."

"Of course, my deepest thanks," she murmured. "With any luck, however, my guardian will be well enough to leave your ever-so-kind and gracious hospitality."

"Ah, we mustn't rush his recovery!" Brian said.

"You are really far too kind."

"Not at all. As I said, Castle Carlyle is indeed graced by your presence. Lord Wimbly? At your leisure."

"Sir John, I'll be in bright and early tomorrow to inform you about the last of the arrangements. Ah, it should be a splendid affair! Simply splendid! All for a worthy cause, I say. I believe Lord Carnarvon will be joining us and that fellow he's getting such an interest in…Carver, Carter, something of the like."

"Carter. Howard Carter," Alex supplied.

"Yes, yes, that's the fellow! All manner of the tremendously supportive and dedicated will be among us, not to mention some society strictly interested in investing from afar. Now remember, we will be conducting some private tours. The place will be immaculate—right, Sir John?"

"Immaculate," Sir John said a little blankly.

"Goodbye, then, and keep at it," Lord Wimbly said.

Brian inclined his head and turned to follow Lord Wimbly. Again, he could feel the stares knifing into his back. He was well aware that tongues would wag the minute he and Lord Wimbly were out of range. Ah, to be a fly on the wall! Then again, that was something he was actually now managing to be rather well.

"TO WORK, the lot of you!" Sir John said, disallowing for conversation.

Camille was glad, anxious to retreat into her little work area without the fussy concern of either Hunter or Alex.

"Really, sir—" Alex began, but Sir John cut him off.

"Work! We're nearly out of time. Alex, get on to the storage facility, we've packing everywhere. We'll have to see about straightening all that without giving any threat to our artifacts. Hunter, if you'll join me at my desk?"

Sir John was all business. Both Alex and Hunter looked at Camille, their eyes conveying their deepened worry and that they were loath to leave her. She gave them a brittle smile in return, then went back into her room and closed the door.

Her heart was racing. Someone had been in the storage vaults when she had gone down with Sir John. And she was certain whoever had been there had come to listen in on their conversation. Someone had been down there specifically to spy on the two of them.

Could Brian Stirling, the Beast of Carlyle, have been silently stalking the vaults earlier, listening as she and Sir John discussed the death of his parents?

She turned to her table, to her work, and her skin began to crawl. *There, the curse!*

She didn't believe in curses, but knew that men could

be cursed with envy and greed. And if that was the case, maybe the earl had every right to be seeking out that evil.

She closed her eyes, her thoughts still running rampant. No, he had to be mad. She thought of the men in the circle of friends—or at least professional acquaintances—that had just come together. Lord Wimbly? Good heavens, no! Sir John? Never. Hunter? He was a charming womanizer, but a murderer? Certainly not! And Alex, gentle Alex…

It was all too insane. With irritation, she went back to work. The beliefs of the ancient Egyptians were beginning to appear far more normal and rational than anything she had heard that morning from learned men of the age of enlightenment!

TRISTAN MONTGOMERY AWOKE in a spacious—no, sumptuous!—bed in Carlyle Castle. The bed was big and soft, the sheets were pure heaven, and his blankets were fine and warm.

Then a little shiver went through him when he remembered that they were guests of that *monster.* And the man was an ogre, no mistake about it, grilling Tristan as if they were back in the days of the Spanish Inquisition. If the earl so wanted it, Tristan could rot in prison for all the wretched days of his life to remain!

There was a tap on his door.

"Aye?" he said tentatively.

The door opened. The woman was there, the one who seemed to actually be in charge of the household, though she deferred to the Earl of Carlyle with every word.

Tristan pulled his covers a bit more tightly about himself, wondering why she was capable of making him feel so uncomfortable. Ashamed! Well, perhaps he should have been ashamed. But there had been too many years when he'd had to make his way with the cleverness of his mind alone. And helping himself to a wee bit of another man's riches here and there, where possible. He wasn't entirely selfish or evil with his ill-gotten gains! Once he'd discovered Camille crying over her mother's body, he'd had a child to raise. There was Ralph to take care of. And too many times, a tired out, pathetic doxy in the streets—usually one so ugly and toothless he couldn't even imagine the most rotten old bugger enjoying a poke from the back— had been about to try her luck when the old Ripper had been at work. Tristan had seen to it to find the old whore a few pence doss money. So he was actually something of a regular old Robin Hood, stealing from the rich, giving to the poor. He just wasn't receiving the same appreciation. No, not in the least!

"Mr. Montgomery," the woman said smoothly. Prior, that was her name. She moved with a whisper of silk and a whiff of perfume, always stately, and always with those eyes that looked upon him as if he were…well, worse than he should be!

"Aye?" he asked, covers now beneath his chin.

"How are you feeling?"

Quite well, actually, he thought. He groaned aloud anyway. "Sore, lass, as if me bones aren't quite in the right as yet." He hesitated. "My girl, my Camille…she was here." He sat up suddenly, all thought of feigning tremendous pain wiped from his mind as he suddenly felt a deep and terrible worry. "She was here! Camille was here. Why, if that monster has done her the least foul, I'll…I'll rip his heart out, I will!" he finished bravely.

The woman lowered her head quickly. He bristled, quite certain she was laughing at him.

"If the man has harmed my lass in any way—!"

"Come, come, Mr. Montgomery. The Earl of Carlyle is not a beast, whatever rumor might hold."

"Aye? Well, the bloke might have fooled me," Tristan murmured. "Where is she?"

"Still at work, I believe."

Tristan frowned. "She was here?"

"Indeed, she was. And she will return."

"Here?" He frowned again.

"Well, of course. She will come back to the castle as long as you are here, Mr. Montgomery. You're quite lucky. She thinks the world of you." The woman walked into the room, drawing back the drapes, allowing the fine chamber to flood with daylight. Tristan shrank farther into the bed, aware that his cheeks were unshaven and that he probably looked like an old drunken sot. Which, upon occasion he was, but...

"Though heaven knows why she holds you in such high esteem!" the woman said, nearer to him now, seeing him in bright daylight.

Tristan arched a brow. "Does the Earl of Carlyle send you in for a more subtle form of torture when he's engaged elsewhere?"

She laughed softly. It was an oddly pleasant sound. "Sir, you scaled the man's walls like a common thief."

"I swear I fell over. No more."

"Amazing! What dexterity you must possess."

He smiled, suddenly himself. "Agile as a cat, ma'am. Truly. In many ways."

"But still in pain now."

"In pain and confused." He sighed suddenly. "If the earl wishes to call in the police, he should go ahead and do so. I might prefer a night in the clink to another night of being grilled alive by a man such as he! Dear God! You'd have thought I was after the Crown jewels!"

"If you'd been after the Crown jewels, he'd not have been half so angry," Mrs. Prior mused.

"Oh, good Lord! I happen to know a good Egyptian piece or two because of me ward. The girl knows all about this dynasty and that, though they all seem to me a bunch of pretty pathetic corpses, hanging on to worthless gold when the time in life to make use of it has passed them by. Truth be told, I'm aware that the right small piece can fetch a fine sum, but you would have thought I was in on conspiracy to commit murder!"

"Something like that," Mrs. Prior murmured, moving away. "Well, it's my belief that the earl has no desire to file charges, especially since you remain in such pain. You are in pain, correct?"

He frowned. She wasn't asking him, she was telling him. And the place *was* delightful. He'd never slept in such a comfortable bed in all his days, even when he was younger, even when he had been knighted for his bravery in Her Majesty's Service in India. And the food here...

He studied Mrs. Prior. She was an intelligent woman, he knew, and far more than a housekeeper. As long as he was injured or ill, he stayed. And she wanted him to stay.

His heart quickened and his rational thought trod heavily upon it. Maybe, long ago, there had been a time when such a woman might have been his. Ah, long ago. Now, he was certain, she would have no more respect for him than she would a sewer rat. Still...

He sat up, straight and proud. "I would die for that girl. I will not allow her to stand before a beast in my stead!" he vowed.

To his amazement, the woman came and sat at the foot of his bed. She was serious when she told him, "His temper is quick, I'll warrant you. But I swear upon my life, he would not hurt your ward. He is not a beast. He would merely flush one out. Strangely enough, Sir Tristan, you might have done us a good deed, *falling* over that nine-foot wall."

"I will not put her into danger."

"She is a beauty, Sir Tristan. With heart and soul and strength. Would it be putting her in danger merely to see her beautifully clothed and attending a ball on the arm of one of the country's most powerful men?"

"Power and riches do not matter, if that man is a beast."

"Appearances can be deceiving."

"Well, he yells like a tiger."

Again, Mrs. Prior smiled. Then, to his amazement, it seemed that she was pleading with him.

"Give me a few days' time. Just a few days," she asked.

He studied her, eyebrows knitted.

"I swear to you, I would lie down and die before setting her in the path of danger," the woman told him.

That gentle scent of hers seemed to come to him on a light and gentle whiff of air. Her eyes held his.

"So...Camille will return here," he said carefully. "What of my man, Ralph? Is he being held in some medieval dungeon within the grounds?"

"Don't be ridiculous."

"There is no medieval dungeon?"

"Of course there's a medieval dungeon. This is quite a historic castle, but we're not holding your man there. I believe he's quite comfortable, doing a bit of work about the place with the earl's own men."

"Forced labor?"

"I believe he was distracted, having little or nothing to do. No, Sir Montgomery, we did not drag out whips and chains! So what we need is time. A few days of time!"

"A few days," he said, wary.

She rose. "I'll send a bath and a maid to shave you. I've surely some kind of clean clothing around here for you.

You're a tall man, lean, somewhat like Lord Stirling's father. And you must be starving."

"Indeed, if you say I must, then I must."

She smiled loftily again, and left him.

Tristan laced his fingers behind his head and leaned back. He had been nothing more than a common thief, dragged before the lord's temper. And now he was being entreated to stay. He couldn't help but smile.

"Mrs. Prior?"

She had been about to leave the room, but she hesitated, looking back.

"Do I have any meal options?"

"Roast beef or fish?"

"Um…a taste of both?"

She inclined her head. "As you wish."

The door closed behind her as she left with a rustle of silk. His smile nearly split his features, but he grew somber after a moment. There was a fairy tale by the Brothers Grimm about a witch who was gracious and kind, doting upon the children Hansel and Gretel, because… Because she was fattening them up for the kill.

LORD WIMBLY INSISTED that he and Brian dine at his gentleman's club. Brian's parents had frequented the establishment, and he maintained their membership. But because he could still see them, far too easily, as they had once sat in the fine leather sofas and chairs, he had kept far from the place after their deaths.

Too much time had passed. And since Evelyn had prodded—and Camille Montgomery had either fallen into his lap or was somehow slipping into it with a far more sinister scheme—he knew it was time to take his own game back into the public.

He was greeted by old friends, acquaintances, waiters

and management, those who had known his parents. Some stared at his mask. Others tried to pretend they did not see it. Some old soldiers, bearing scars, a few minus limbs, were quick to sympathize, and a few of the old codgers, like Wimbly himself, suggested that he opt for more subtle attire, hedging before warning him that he was becoming known as "The Beast."

He was gracious and assured them all that he would take their suggestions to heart, but that he had to admit he found his solitude quite rewarding.

"Bah!" Viscount Ledger, an old cavalryman, told him. "It's the modern-day world we must seize by the horns! Never has England ruled over a more glorious empire! You, good fellow, are spending your days seeking the past. Now I know you do the good Queen's bidding at her command. And she speaks so well of you, waving a hand in the air when some would worry that you have become such a recluse. But that dear lady has made a lifetime of mourning. I mean, good God, she's made mourning a new way of life in society itself! Brian Stirling, you are a young fellow, and if you hide your face away, what of it? Look at you! Fine, tall, robust!"

"And quite wealthy," added Sir Bartholomew Greer, at his side.

"Yes, wealthy. That does stand for everything, doesn't it?" murmured Lord Wimbly, somewhat amused.

"I have a daughter of the proper age for marriage myself," Sir Bartholomew said.

"Ugly as sin, she is!" Viscount Ledger whispered to him in an aside.

Sir Bartholomew must have heard him because he straightened like a fire poker. "Sadly, I'm afraid that our dear Lord Stirling wears the mask for a reason."

"Thankfully," Lord Wimbly said, rushing to the defense, "Brian is the *Earl of Carlyle*."

"Yes…there's your title," Sir Bartholomew said. He remained stiff—and titleless. "Forgive me, Brian, but you *are* wearing a mask."

"But you are an earl, a wealthy earl," Viscount Ledger said, twirling his moustache. He let out a sigh. "Frankly, Brian, were you as old as the hills, hideous beyond belief, decaying with each move you made, you would still find a proper wife, you know."

He laughed easily, accepting a brandy from the waiter who quietly served them, nodding his head in thanks. "No matter who or what I am as a man, I am an earl. A wealthy one," he murmured dryly. "I've not ventured out to find a proper wife, I'm afraid. I don't believe I'm quite ready for that, though, I must say, were I looking for a bride, I'd far prefer she love the man and not the manor."

"Good lord, there is society to think of!" Viscount Ledger said.

"There is society and there is life. Am I not right?" Brian murmured. "But the point, at the moment, is moot. I've just decided to step outside my boundaries again, learn more about London and England. And as has been suggested, since I was blessed with such riches, I must decide for myself how best to become a more useful member of society."

Brian was glad that, at that very moment, they were interrupted by the club's host and discreetly informed that their table was ready. He and Lord Wimbly excused themselves.

When they were seated, Lord Wimbly again remarked on his pleasure that Brian was determined to become involved with the museum again.

"No reason, even if a fellow has a so-called curse upon him, that a man of your means and responsibility should be shut away in a medieval castle day after day!" Lord

Wimbly chastised. "Brian, the Empire stands upon her finest hour! And though we have the French to deal with, our importance in Egypt is monumental."

Brian took a sip of an excellent claret. "Lord Wimbly," he reminded the man, "without the French, we'd not have the Rosetta Stone today, nor would we begin to have the knowledge and resources that we have available."

"Yes, yes, well…Empire, my boy. Empire!" He raised his glass.

He went on to talk about the incredible work that Brian's parents had done in Egypt, seeking knowledge and learning to live among the people.

"And finding treasures," Brian murmured.

"Indeed! Tragically, though, no treasure so great as life. They were so beautiful, so brilliant, such brightly shining stars! It is for you to take up where they left off, in their memory."

Brian smiled. He had hoped to gain something more from the lunch than a reminder of what had been, and what he should be doing. When the bill arrived, Lord Wimbly did not protest when Brian said that the meal must be on him.

At the cloakroom, they parted ways. Brian, a bit behind Lord Wimbly, overheard a fellow speaking to the lord, asking softly about a debt.

Lord Wimbly replied almost as softly, but his voice carried more easily. "Indeed, my good man. How remiss! I've quite forgotten my exchequer. But I've not forgotten our game." He looked around quickly.

Brian pretended to be staring out one of the beautiful etched windows before the mudroom.

"There's to be another game. We can try for double or nothing, eh?" he said, and laughed heartily.

As the man left, slipping by Lord Wimbly, Brian tried to get a good look at him. He was sallow-faced and had a limp. Brian determined that he must be a soldier, and had perhaps been doing duty in the Middle Eastern section of the Empire, since his face showed signs of exposure to the sun and his limp suggested an injury. Brian did not know the man.

Yet, as he left the club, he had a curious feeling that he had discovered more than met the eye. And that the luncheon hadn't been a complete waste of time after all.

CAMILLE SAT BACK, aware that she had to move. Her shoulders were taut, and she was certain that she was way too young to have a crick in the back of her neck. She stood, stretching, looking about her tiny workspace. So far, the ancients had not revealed any more to her than she already knew.

"And I don't believe in curses!" she said aloud.

She exited her little room. Sir John was not at his desk, so she removed her apron, determined just to take a short walk around the facility and then get back to work. At the moment, she thought wryly, she was something of a golden child, and while the Earl of Carlyle was professing his interest in her, she would remain so. But she was nothing more than a pawn in his chess game, and she was well aware of it.

She walked back out to the Egyptian galleries. As usual, a number of people stared with fascination at the mummies, which always drew a crowd. The museum had done an excellent job of explaining the beliefs of the people during the different dynasties. Some of the dead were displayed unwrapped, some halfway wrapped, some in their complete wrappings and still others in their sarcophagi.

The Rosetta Stone, one of her favorite pieces, was another draw. But people looked at it, and then left. It was, after all, a stone, an inanimate object. It had never lived, walked the earth, laughed, cried and loved. Mummies drew the people.

Along with their current exhibit, this one was a special display, tracing the life of Cleopatra. With her passions, her determination to rule and her reputed beauty, she, too, drew a great deal of attention, although they didn't have her actual mummy on display. Still, they had an excellent waxwork of the legendary Queen of the Nile, much about her life and times, and, to finish the allure of the exhibition, an Egyptian cobra, just like the asp that historically did in the dramatic queen.

Camille found herself drawn to the cobra in its glass tank, despite the fact that it was already surrounded by a group of bragging schoolboys.

"He's just a snake! He's all skinny!" said one.

"I could pick him up and wring his neck in a second," boasted another.

"Does he have a neck?" wondered a third.

One tapped on the glass. The snake, which had not been in attack mode, suddenly reared up, head winged. It darted toward the boys—and struck the glass. The boys fell back in a flash.

"Let's get out of here!" cried the one who had wanted to know about the neck.

"If you don't tease the creature, it's quite safe to look at it," Camille said, walking by them. The cobra was actually beautiful. She turned to the boys. "You know, according to legend, Cleopatra asked that a basket of figs, with a cobra in it, be delivered to her. She didn't just want to commit suicide, you see. The cobra was a symbol of divine royalty, and she believed that if she was bitten by an asp and died, she would become immortal."

"Was that true?" asked one of the wide-eyed boys.

"Well, she's legendary, so in a way she's immortal. But

as far as the asp bite is concerned, I'm pretty sure she was just dead." She smiled. "Museums are places to see things and to learn, not to tease or to damage artifacts," she said. She turned away from the boys, then paused and added, "And yes, snakes do have necks."

"How do you know where the neck is?" the boy asked.

"Behind the head," Camille said, smiling.

"The whole rest of the body is behind the head!" one of the other boys noted, scowling.

"*Right* behind the head," Camille amended.

"Are there more snakes in the museum?" the fascinated boy asked.

"Just this one," she assured him. "And when the exhibit on Cleopatra moves, so will the snake."

"Wow! He's the best thing in the place!" another of the boys said.

"There's a lot more. Just read and use your imaginations!" Camille advised.

They frowned.

"Why don't you take us around?" asked the inquisitive one. "Please," he added quickly.

"I can't. I have to get back to work," she explained.

"What do you do?" the boy asked.

"Translate."

"You can read the signs on the tombs?" Even the boy who had ridiculed the place seemed fascinated.

She smiled and nodded. "Really, go on and read the little placards everywhere. It will be fun, if you use your imaginations. I promise!"

"Let's see the Rosetta Stone," one of the older boys said.

They left, the one boy thanking her and looking at her with awe. Camille grinned at him and waved.

She turned to the snake again. Cobras, she knew, killed

many people. But she'd also learned that they seldom attacked unprovoked. Camille watched it, suddenly sorry for
the creature. It had surely hurt to hit the glass. And
yet…she wondered what she would be feeling if the glass
were not there, protecting her from the creature.

She wondered how Lord and Lady Stirling had felt.
Had they seen the snakes that would bring about their ag-
onized ends? And had it all been a sad accident…or murder, indeed? Murder most foul.

CHAPTER SIX

CAMILLE FOUND IT QUITE AMAZING that she had been able
to slip so easily from work just the day before. This
evening, she was accompanied. Hunter, who rarely stayed
long in the halls of the museum, was at her one side, Alex
at the other. Sir John strode just a few feet behind.

And when they reached the street, the great carriage belonging to the Earl of Carlyle was there, awaiting her.

"Don't go!" Alex whispered to her, sounding a little desperate.

"Camille…" Hunter whispered awkwardly. Then, and
for her ears alone, he said, "I'll marry you. Honestly."

"She shouldn't be doing this!" Alex said aloud to Sir
John. "A young woman alone, in the company of such
a…beast!" he finished lamely.

"Ach!" Sir John said, shaking his head at the two of
them. "We're speaking of the Earl of Carlyle! Respected,
a war hero, a onetime friend to us all!" he reminded them
indignantly.

"A man who is injured, scarred and embittered," Hunter
reminded them. "She can't go."

"She must," Sir John said.

"*She* will make up her own mind," Camille said firmly.
Shelby was alighting from the coachman's chair, smiling
like a gentle giant. He bowed, then opened the door for her
to take her seat.

She felt a moment's panic, and more. Hunter MacDonald had just said that he would marry her! Take him up on the offer, call the fellow's bluff! she thought on the one hand. He was attractive, renowned and definitely a man with the kind of charisma that could seduce. And she had felt herself drawn to him so very often....

But the Earl of Carlyle, wretched though he might be, held Tristan. And strangely, she realized that, although the man was boldly bribing and using her, there was something about him and his passion that was equally alluring. He offered no false deference to her sex, age or appearance. Even in his anger, and despite his ruse, there was an honesty about him that seemed as great a pull upon her now as any other. She was intrigued, and she wanted answers for the man, whether they proved innocence and accident, or...something far more sinister.

She turned to the men surrounding her. "I thank you all. The Earl of Carlyle has offered hospitality to my guardian, and I must go."

As the carriage pulled away, she couldn't help but wonder at the true thoughts their words might have masked.

EVELYN FOUND BRIAN hard at work in his library, once again poring over the journal his mother had kept on that last, fateful trip to Egypt.

"Brian, you are going to make yourself quite insane," she told him gently.

He looked up at her, as if unaware that he had bid her to enter or even that she had come into his private realm. Ajax, of course, had given her a woof and wagged his tail. As usual, he dozed at his master's feet, taking on the task of watching out for the world, since his beloved human seemed quite incapable of noticing all else when he was involved.

Brian stared at her, as if weighing her words. He had taken to wearing the mask at all times, even in his own castle, since they were offering hospitality to certain "guests."

He shook his head. "I'm close, Evelyn. I know it. I'm very close."

"Yes," she said gently, "but you've read that journal a thousand times over."

He arched a brow. "I thought you'd be pleased. I went out, I had lunch at the club with Lord Wimbly. And, you'll be pleased to know, I've made arrangements for the fund-raiser this weekend."

"Have you?"

"Yes, yes," he said impatiently. "I'm taking Miss Montgomery. Though I must say, the woman is something of an enigma. Her guardian may have been knighted for service to our Queen, but he is a petty thief nonetheless. So where did she come across her excellent knowledge of Egyptology?"

"I've an idea how you might find out," Evelyn murmured.

"Yes, I intend to get one of the men delving into her past immediately," Brian said.

"My idea was easier," Evelyn said.

"Really? Pray, do share your thoughts with me."

"Ask her," Evelyn said.

He smiled ruefully. "Ah, but will she tell me the truth?"

"It is a place to start," Evelyn said. "Shelby should be returning with her at any moment. I've set you up to dine here together, alone, at eight."

"I can't actually force her to stay," he reminded her.

She smiled. "Ah, but her guardian is doing poorly."

"I thought he was but bruised."

"I've seen to it that the bruises still cause pain."

"Good Lord, Evelyn, you did not do injury to the man?"

She laughed. "No, Brian! We've simply had a discussion, that is all."

He gazed at her, shaking his head. "You're quite a marvel, you know."

"I simply do my best to serve," she said, smiling sweetly. Then she looked solemnly. "Seriously, Brian. Ask her what you want to know. Perhaps she will tell you the truth about herself. And if it's not the truth, you'll discover that easily enough, I'm certain."

"Perhaps. But…"

"But?"

"Well, when we first spoke, she was masking the truth with a far greater fervor than I usually cloak it in myself."

"You can't seriously believe that Miss Montgomery is part of a conspiracy against you!" Evelyn said.

"All I know, Evelyn, is that it seems everyone is playing at some kind of masquerade or another. And that Miss Montgomery definitely has her secrets."

AS SHE OPENED THE DOOR, Camille heard the soft moan. Fear swept into her heart.

"Tristan?"

"Camie, love, is that you?"

His voice sounded faint, weak. Camille rushed to the bed and sat at Tristan's side, looking down at him anxiously. "Are you all right?" she demanded.

"Righter than rain, child, with you before my face!" he said. Still, he winced as he spoke.

"What's hurting you, Tristan? Perhaps you have broken bones. I've really got to get you out of here and into a hospital!" Camille said worriedly.

"No, Camie. No!" He grasped her hand then. He might appear weak, and it seemed that he was suffering, but his grip was surprisingly strong.

"No, lass, my bones are not broken. That I can tell, for

I can move the old things without going into crushing agony. No, child, it's just that I'm aching, you know?"

She sat back, staring down at him, not at all sure whether to be worried or furious. She set her free hand on his forehead. "You're suffering no fever," she told him.

"There you are, see? I'm just…weak. And sore. I'll be better, given a wee bit of time to heal." He gave her a tremulous smile. "It's not life-threatening, child, I'm certain."

"Oh, it may be!" she warned. "I just might throttle you when we get out of here!"

"Ah, now—"

"Tristan, you might have jeopardized my employment."

"A lass should not be working," he said, and his misery sounded real enough.

She sighed. "I'll not throttle you on one condition."

"And what is that, love?"

"You never, ever do something so incredibly stupid again! This man is a monster, Tristan. I'm not certain he could have gotten you hanged, but he could have seen to it that you rotted in prison for a very long time," Camille reprimanded.

"Ah, now…the man has so much!"

"And intends to keep it. I'm not at all sure he's sane."

Tristan suddenly seemed to get a fresh surge of strength. He sat up halfway in the bed, frowning fiercely. "Why, lass, if he's so much as lain a finger upon you—"

"Tristan! Nothing like that. It's just that…oh, never mind. He's associated with the museum, you know, through his parents and their deep interest in Egyptology. And he's convinced that they were murdered."

Tristan frowned then. "They were killed by asps, or so I believe."

"Yes, I guess he can't accept that truth. If it is the truth."

"What are you saying?" Tristan demanded.

She set her hands upon his shoulders, suddenly concerned that she had said too much. "Never mind, Tristan. It's just that I'm anxious that you get well, and I'm so angry with you! How could you do this!"

"Camille, I'm so sorry. But I should be providing for you. 'Tis sad, lass, that you have to…go out and work for a living!"

"Tristan, I like what I do. I *love* what I do. And it's not sad in the least. You looked after me when I was too young to do so. Now, you must allow me to look after you. And don't help me! You mustn't help me anymore, do you understand? What you're doing is no good."

"Actually," Tristan murmured, "I'm usually a pretty good thief."

"Tristan! You must swear to me right now and before God that you will never, ever go out to steal anything ever again!"

"Ah, now, lass…"

"Tristan!"

He settled back like a sulking child. "I *am* good."

"Tristan!"

"Well, now, we made our way on my charms, as they say, for a good many years."

"We don't need to do so any longer! At least if you behave yourself, we will never have to live on your 'charms,' as you say, again. Swear to me that you'll never pull another foolish caper such as this!"

He mumbled something.

"Swear!" she demanded.

He looked up at her. "I swear, lass. There, are you happy? I'll never pull a foolish caper such as this one again."

She cocked her head. "Not good enough."

"What?"

"You'll do some other foolish deed and say that it wasn't a foolish caper such as this one. You know what I want you to say—and mean. That you'll never seek to steal, commit fraud or do anything illegal—whatsoever!—again."

"Camille!" he protested indignantly.

"Now!" she said firmly.

And so he repeated her words, leaning back on his pillow, crossing his arms over his chest. He looked worn indeed, and rather like a petulant child. "You shouldn't have to work," he said again with a sigh. "You should be married, lass, to a fine man who'll give you all the fine things in life."

"I don't want the fine things in life," she insisted softly. "Tristan, I love you and Ralph. I'm happy to take care of you—"

She winced, aware that she had said the wrong thing. Tristan had his pride. That was why he saw his working as a thief to support her preferable to the honest employment with which she could support him.

"Camille!" he said firmly, indignantly. "It's not right for a lass to support a man."

"Tristan, do you believe that we are living in the Dark Ages?" she countered. "You fostered my love of learning as much as—"

She broke off as they heard a tap at the door. Without being bidden, Evelyn Prior cracked the door open. "Miss Montgomery, you have returned," she said pleasantly.

Camille stiffened. "Yes. Shelby left me at the door. *Naturally,* I came to see Tristan immediately."

"Naturally," Mrs. Prior agreed. "However, the earl awaits you now, in the master's sitting room, where dinner will be served."

Camille smiled sweetly. "I had thought that I should

dine quietly with Tristan, and not take such undue advantage of the earl's…hospitality."

"Ah, but the earl awaits you."

"I've supped already," Tristan told her.

Camille glanced at him, frowning. "We are most *accidentally* guests here, sir!" she reminded him.

"Miss Montgomery, if you would be so kind…" Mrs. Prior persisted.

Camille inhaled, staring at Tristan.

He grinned. "You must go, lass. The Earl of Carlyle insists."

Forcing a smile, Camille rose. "You are certain that you are growing stronger here? That there is nothing so serious that we shouldn't get you to a hospital?"

She thought that Tristan glanced a little uneasily across the room at Mrs. Prior. "Camille, I am certain that I don't need a hospital. Only time to repair and gather my strength."

Camille turned sharply to stare at the woman. She gave no hint of having offered Tristan any dire warnings; she appeared to politely await Camille and nothing more.

"As you wish," Camille murmured. She kissed Tristan on the forehead and followed Mrs. Prior out the door.

"He seems to be doing very well," Mrs. Prior said, smiling as if she really felt a sense of keen relief.

"Yes," Camille murmured. The day now seemed tediously long and traumatic. She was exhausted and not sure she wanted to spend the evening with the man who was so blatantly using her to his purposes.

Apparently Mrs. Prior realized that she was not in the mood for small talk, and kept silent as they traversed the long hall leading to the master's quarters.

Once again, Brian Stirling awaited her, hands clasped behind his back as he stared out the windows into the darkness of the grounds.

Ajax sat before the hearth. Tonight, however, the dog offered her something of a welcoming whine as he thumped his tail on the floor. He did not rise. He wouldn't come to her, she knew, unless given the go-ahead by his master.

"Miss Montgomery. My Lord," Evelyn murmured.

She started to turn and leave, but the earl swung around, calling her back.

"Evelyn!"

Mrs. Prior walked in, waiting as bidden.

He turned to give Camille a long and careful assessment, his eyes teal that night as they took in her length, head to toe.

"We must find Miss Montgomery some suitable clothing," he said at last.

"There are certainly some garments we have here that will suffice," Mrs. Prior said. "I will look into the matter immediately."

He waved a hand in the air. "For her work, yes. Certainly we'll find enough that's…serviceable. But if she's to attend the fund-raiser with me, she must be properly attired."

"She's quite slim," Mrs. Prior mused.

Camille felt her cheeks flaming. This was simply rude, whether the man was an earl or the Prince of Wales himself.

"Excuse me, but *she* is standing right here," she informed them both. "And if you will allow me time to go home, I have my own, very *serviceable* clothing there."

"I'm quite aware that you're there, Miss Montgomery. We humbly beg your pardon," he murmured. He didn't *humbly* beg a thing, she was quite certain. "There hasn't been a convenient time for you to go home, I'm afraid. I believe that, even on such short notice, the sisters could make up something wonderful for Miss Montgomery," he said. "Evelyn, please tell Shelby that he must bring Miss Montgomery to the cottage in the woods before coming here tomorrow evening."

"Shelby could just bring me by my own home," Camille protested. "Please, Mrs. Prior, ask him if he will be so kind as to make such a stop."

"I'm afraid that this will be a very grand gala, Miss Montgomery. It will be my deepest pleasure to see that you are fittingly attired."

"Lord Stirling—"

"How is your guardian doing this evening? You did stop to see him, I believe?" the earl said pleasantly.

Camille gritted her teeth. "He's doing well," she said icily.

"I shall find Shelby," Mrs. Prior said, leaving them. The door closed.

Camille remained very still, seething as she stared at Lord Stirling.

"Hungry?" he asked pleasantly.

"You really are a monster, and it hasn't a thing to do with the mask," she told him.

"Be that as it may, dinner is served," he told her, indicating the table with its snowy white cloth and silver-domed plates. "I may be a monster, but that doesn't change the fact that one must eat. Pray, tell me, why is it that I'm such a monster because I'd be pleased to see you well dressed?"

"I don't take charity."

"No, but your guardian does take…well, other people's belongings."

"Did you actually catch him stealing anything?" she inquired. "Were the goods in his hands?"

"Actually, no."

"Then how do you know he didn't just fall over the wall. Perhaps he was simply curious, looking in upon your property."

"Please, let's not insult the both of us, Miss Montgomery."

"Why not? You have no difficulty insulting me."

"How on earth is that? I've invited you to an affair. The gown is not for you, but for me. Therefore, it isn't charity."

She let out a cry of exasperation, then decided that, if nothing else, she was going to have dinner. She headed for the table.

He was capable of swift and agile movement and was there to draw back the chair for her before she could industriously do so herself. She kept silent, her jaw locked, as he pushed her in and walked around to the other side.

He poured her a glass of red wine, then lifted the silver heating dome from her plate. That night, the fare appeared to be lamb, tenderly broiled, served with peas and new potatoes. At the aroma she felt an instant stab of hunger.

He disposed of the heating domes and lifted his glass to her. "Please. To the museum, Miss Montgomery."

"So, your sudden revitalized interest in the museum is real?" she inquired pleasantly, lifting her glass, taking a sip of wine.

"I have never lost interest in the museum, my dear. Never."

"Well, I do believe you have quite fooled those others who find it to be their passion."

"Yes, the others," he mused, watching his wine as he swirled it in his glass. Then his eyes fell directly upon her. "How were the others today? I could almost hear their whispers and protests all the way down the street."

"What were you expecting?" she asked.

"Ah!" His eyes widened. "That they would be in horror, of course. You are their ingénue, admired and coveted by many, protected by a few, and sheltered in that domain where they would tease and flirt and hope you remain one of them. Then in walks the wolf, the beast with a title and money! Let's see, I can tell you how it went. Sir John, good fellow, would simply want it all to go about easily and with no confrontation. He's looking at you through new eyes, wondering just how you've drawn my attention to such a degree. Of course, he knows he's harboring a beautiful young woman, but…well, in the young, beauty is a common enough commodity. Still, if it's what would please me, he's delighted. On the one hand, he's trying to discover just what is so amazing about you. On the other hand, he doesn't want to look this gift horse too deeply in the mouth."

"Your flattery will go to my head," she said.

"There is no offense intended. I am simply telling you what I'm sure went on after I left. Lord Wimbly is actually not going to comment, given that I mentioned to him the fact that I'm bringing you. A number of my colleagues are quite convinced that I should be looking for a wife, you see, but from the right class. And they believe that my wealth and title will enable me to find such a pillar of virtue—despite the mask. Then there is Alex, ever aware of his humble birth, yet a man who has thought himself right for you. Not a persistent or eloquent fellow, he is surely deeply dismayed. And last but never least, there is Hunter. I'd almost wager he was so stunned and appalled that you're my guest that he was willing to offer his own services—dare I suggest so far as *marriage?*—just to get you from my side!"

She hoped that no flicker of her expression betrayed just how correctly he had assessed the reactions of the others to his appearance and announcements.

"I would never marry Hunter," she told him, not allowing her lashes to slip over her eyes.

"Aha! So he did make such a suggestion."

"I didn't say that. I said that I would never marry Hunter."

"Oh? And why not? The fellow has looks and charm. And, I dare say, he has that certain dash that makes him appear to be a man's man, an adventurer, the sort to make many a fair maid of good breeding swoon."

"Are you mocking him?"

"Not in the least. I'm just curious as to why the fellow would have no appeal for you. But then, you didn't say that he didn't have his appeal. You merely said that you wouldn't marry him."

"Just what are you implying?"

"I'm implying nothing. I'm trying not to put words in your mouth, since you are so quick to correct me."

"Oh, Lord Stirling, you are making implications. Of the worst kind."

"Well, would you consider a liaison with the man?" he asked bluntly.

She was tempted to toss the very excellent wine right into his face, but she somehow managed to refrain.

"Quite frankly," she said, her tone pure ice, "it's none of your affair."

"I do apologize, Camille. But I consider every aspect of your life my affair at this time."

"I do not."

She saw his slow smile beneath his mask, and found that a strange tremor swept through her. He was rude, a total boor. A beast. Yet...even as he angered her, he made something within her quicken. His eyes, that slow smile. She wondered what the man had been like before life—and death—had so embittered him.

"I am the Earl of Carlyle," he reminded her. "And I am escorting you to a fund-raiser. Tongues will wag. It's rather important that I not appear the fool in such matters."

"Well, Lord Stirling, you should have thought of that before announcing that you intended to go to the gala with me on your arm."

"But we have an agreement."

"We have no agreement. You are bribing me, or threatening me. Or both."

"Both, I believe. I am doing a service for you. You are doing one for me."

"It's a *service* that you not prosecute a man? Think, Lord Stirling. A court might well deem him not guilty."

"Oh, I doubt that. And so do you," he told her easily.

She sat back, folded her arms over her chest and tried for a look of dignity and disdain. "You created this charade."

"Yet I am still assessing my actress."

"It seems that you assess everyone in your path—as you did the gentlemen at the museum today."

She was startled when he suddenly launched a new assault. "Tell me, Camille, and tell me the truth. Where did you gain your knowledge of history and Egyptology, and how on earth did you learn to read hieroglyphs?"

She was startled by the question, barely breathing for a minute. Then she said simply, "From my mother."

He frowned, sitting back. "Your mother?"

"When I was a child, we went to the museum on a daily basis."

"Is that how you came to work there? Did she know Sir John?"

Her lashes fell at that. "I'm weary of this third degree, Lord Stirling."

"Then talk to me. And end it."

"You're worried about what relationship I have with Hunter MacDonald? Well, there is none."

"I already gathered that," he said.

She jumped up. He was toying with her, and she was suddenly so angry that she was determined he would know the truth he was seeking—all of it. "Hunter, My Lord, is the least of your worries where I am concerned. You want the truth about me? Well, here it is. My mother was an East End prostitute. Oh, she didn't start out that way! But few women, sir, are born whores. She was the seventh child of an Anglican minister up in York, and therefore well educated. I was led to believe that my father was a man of some prominence or title, but even in this great age of enlightenment, that cannot change the fact that I am a bastard. My mother, knowing that she would be cast out, hurried to London, hoping to obtain a respectable job with her education. But her effort to gain such while carrying a child proved futile. Yet, despite her own sad circumstances, my mother wanted a better life for me."

Camille paused a moment, wondering at the desperation her mother must have felt to enter into such a profession. And she wondered to what lengths *she* would go for her family.

"She did her best to hide the ugliness of her life from me. By day, she taught me. She read, she sang, she took me to museums. We spent hours and hours in the Victoria and Albert, learning about history and language and…ancient Egypt. She read, so I read voraciously. And I taught myself much of what I know. You don't want to be made a fool? Well, My Lord, press this far enough and trust me, someone will discover the truth! If you've any brains behind that mask of yours, you will stop this ridiculousness right now. And if you've a shred of mercy left behind those claws, you'll somehow let it all slip back into enough normalcy that I can maintain my employment!"

By the end of her tirade she had planted her palms on the table and leaned toward him. She was shaking and all but yelling. Fury raced through her in an avalanche, and it was only when all the words were out that she began to rue the fact that he had goaded her into speaking them.

But he didn't recoil in horror. He merely watched her. Once again, she was startled to see the hint of a smile beneath the mask, a light of brightness and not just amusement, and maybe even admiration in his eyes.

She pushed away from the table, stepping back. "Say something," she murmured.

"You taught *yourself* hieroglyphs?" he demanded.

"Did you hear what I said?" she cried out, exasperated.

"Perfectly. And I am amazed. You were able to teach yourself hieroglyphs?"

She threw up her hands, totally at a loss. "You've missed the point, you fool!" she cried. "My mother was a prostitute! If anyone starts delving around, that fact will come out."

"She must have been quite an amazing woman," he murmured.

Her jaw nearly dropped. "Have I not said enough for you to stop this idiocy?" she demanded.

He rose then, as well, and she was reminded again of his height and muscled physique. She refused to acknowledge that he towered over her, yet she found her fingers knotting into her palms, and she took another step backward.

"I will thank you not to call me a fool in the future," he said flatly. "Ever!" He swept out an arm, indicating the table. "I will leave you, Miss Montgomery, since I'm quite certain you need the sustenance, and my presence, beastly as it is, keeps you from your repast."

He turned and strode across the room, ready to exit.

"Stop!" she found herself all but shrieking.

He turned, and she felt the piercing blue anger in his eyes as they fell upon her.

"What now, Miss Montgomery?"

"Let me give you the rest, Lord Stirling, since you've insisted this far! There is little in the world I will not do for Tristan Montgomery. He saved me, expecting nothing in return. He has given me the best of whatever he has had these many years. So I will play out your charade. I will do my best to humor you in any way. I will be what you want me to be, and go where you want me to go. But I will not abide a meal in this house with you again if you insist on believing that I would find any man hideous just because of his looks. Besides, it is not your appearance that makes you a beast!"

"A lovely speech," he said, but she could not tell his emotion.

"It is your constant suspicion and your cruelty in manner that make you a horrid monster. So if you would have my cooperation in any way, you will stop with your insinuations and suspicions where I am concerned."

He took a long stride toward her, and for a moment, she was tempted to back away again. She had pushed him too far. She was about to find out about the violence that seemed to lurk beneath his well-dressed facade, always leashed, always there, like a current of electricity.

He walked around her, arms crossed over his chest. And when he had circled her he said, "Sit, Camille. Please."

She did so. Not really because he had invited her, but because she was afraid that her knees were going to give.

He leaned over, an arm on either side of her. She breathed in the aroma of his soap and cologne, a faint scent of leather and good pipe tobacco. She felt the sharp, stinging blue of his eyes, and the combustible heat that lurked ever beneath the surface.

"What?" she managed to say, breathlessly.

"I have a name."

"Lord Stirling, the Earl of Carlyle."

"Brian. You will use it, please."

She swallowed. "I will gladly do so, if…"

"If? More conditions? Who is bribing and threatening whom here?"

"You must quit being such a monster!"

For a moment he was very close. And to her horror, she was warm, flushed and fascinated. Then he moved away.

"Your meal will grow cold," he said.

"As will yours."

"I mean to leave you in peace."

"You invited me to dinner. Therefore, it would be exceedingly rude of you to leave."

He laughed out loud, walked around the table and took his seat. He didn't immediately pick up his fork, but continued to stare at her. "Your lamb," he said.

"I will eat when you do so," she said.

"There is no shame in your birth, you know. The sins of the parents do not fall upon the offspring."

Camille bit into her lower lip. "I don't believe that she sinned," she whispered. "I think that she just…she loved too deeply, too rashly."

"Well, I'm afraid then that your father was an ass."

"Ah!" she said. "Something upon which we might agree."

His hand moved over hers, oddly warm and assuring. "As I have said, there is no shame."

She was surprisingly touched by his words, and the warmth and power of his hand upon hers. "That, Lord

Stirling, is not how most of the world would view the situation. But you are warned. And I beg you, remember this—you could well cost me my livelihood."

"If there is ever such a ridiculous repercussion, I could well afford a pension."

"My livelihood is also my passion."

"I have tremendous influence upon the museum," he reminded her.

Her eyes fell. His hand was still closed over hers. She was ridiculously tempted to draw it to her face, to feel the palm against her cheek. In fact, her heart was beating far too quickly and erratically. The flush that had come over her stirred sensation into heart and limbs and torso.

She drew her hand back, frightened, not so much by the man as by her reaction to him.

"You'll forgive me. I'm exhausted," she told him. "Please…I've got to retire."

"I'll escort you to your room."

"I'm sure I can find it."

The gentle man she had glimpsed so briefly made an abrupt change. "I will escort you," he snapped firmly. He strode to the door, opened it for her.

She passed by him, acutely aware of everything about him. She was even convinced that she heard him breathe, felt his heart beat…. Felt again the leashed tension, the violence that could erupt.

When she was out the door, he followed, then took the lead. Ajax had risen and followed. Curiously, he remained by her side, rather than hurrying to catch up with his master's tread.

They traversed the long hallway, and at last came to her door. He opened it for her.

"Thank you," she told him stiffly.

"Indeed."

"I could have found my own way."

"No," he said harshly. "No. And don't ever—ever—wander these halls at night, do you understand? Ever!"

"Good night, Lord Stirling."

"Good night. Ajax!" As he said the dog's name, the animal dutifully loped ahead into Camille's room. With a glance of blue fire, Lord Stirling pulled the door shut.

She heard his footsteps echo down the hallway. And it occurred to her that, though it seemed they had come a long distance, the master's chambers might well abut the very room in which she slept.

CHAPTER SEVEN

CAMILLE MONTGOMERY was dressed in deep blue when Brian saw her in the solarium. Evidently Evelyn had found some garments that would provide the proper wear for her workday.

"Quite lovely," he informed her.

Her eyes, with their beautiful marbled hazel color, flashed at the compliment. "It pleases me to no end that you approve, since it seems that I am unable to return to my abode for my own clothing."

She wasn't pleased in the least, of course. But he didn't intend to argue at that moment. As he poured himself coffee, he wondered if she was aware just how enticing she could appear. That her features were perfectly hewn was one thing; that she had a rich head of hair in a glorious color was another. She was slender, yet delightfully shaped, with a tiny waist, slim hips and perfect breasts. But it wasn't just in her appearance that she exuded such an allure; it was in her every expression, her determination not to be cowed, even by a man such as himself. The flash of her eyes held a keen intelligence and pride.

He walked some distance from her. Yes, he had asked his questions. And she had replied with such anger and passion that he had not doubted her words. He had dragged her in on this. Evidence seemed to show that he could trust her. As yet, though, he could not put his faith in her, and neither did he want to feel the growing attraction for her that was beginning to tease his senses mercilessly.

He set his coffee cup down, locking his jaw, hardening his resolve. "Shelby will be there to pick you up at four this afternoon."

"I cannot possibly leave at four!"

"Yes, you can. Sir John will give you permission. The sisters are quite talented, Camille, but they must have a few days if they are to create a ball gown."

She looked as if she was struggling to maintain her temper. "Lord Stirling, this whole thing is quite ridiculous. You're on a hunt—whether justified or not, I do not know! But this charade will end, and I must keep my employment!"

"Trust me. I have written a letter that Shelby will deliver to Sir John. You will be given the time."

"Lord Stirling—"

He turned to leave the hall, having a great deal of business to attend to that day. She was disturbing in many ways, like a rose—with thorns.

"Good morning, Camille. I will see you this evening, in my quarters, for dinner as usual. And I will appreciate a report on the events at the museum."

She rose, irritated, calling after him. "Events at the museum! I will put on an apron and work over ages of dust! There. I have given you the events of the museum that concern me."

He stopped, turned. "Oh, Miss Montgomery. You are ever so much more observant and clever than that!"

He didn't allow her to reply, but headed quickly for the exit.

THAT MORNING, CAMILLE found it difficult to concentrate. As she stared at her work, the symbols continued to meld before her eyes. She hadn't managed an exact translation of the continuation of the text, but it seemed that the warning involved something about the curse falling upon not only those who invaded and defiled the tomb, but upon their offspring, as well. However, that didn't seem so startling, since the "Beast" of Carlyle Castle was already reputed to be cursed.

Anxious that she needed a break, she emerged from her little workroom and looked to Sir John's desk, determined to ask him if she might step out for a cup of tea, anything to settle her nerves. But Sir John wasn't there.

Restlessly she wandered the office, then sat at his desk. His top drawer was ajar, and when she went to close it, she discovered that it was stuck. Wrangling with it, she managed to draw it wide-open. When she would have closed it properly, she stopped, her eyes caught by the newspaper clipping that had been left on top of the assorted pens, pencils and paperwork utensils.

It was the front page of the *Times* from a little over a year ago. And the headline was definitely provocative.

Curse From The Grave Takes The Lives Of London's Finest

There was a photograph below the line. Though poor and grainy due to the newsprint, Camille recognized the woman in the picture as being Lady Abigail Stirling. The fellow at her side, the late Lord Stirling, was quite tall and imposing with a handsome, well-chiseled face. They were standing at the site of a dig. Both smiled radiantly. The lord's arm was around the shoulders of his lady. She was dressed simply in a light blouse and long skirt, while he was in a tweed jacket. There were others around them, Egyptian workers and fellow Europeans.

Camille floundered in Sir John's top drawer, seeking his magnifying glass. She continued to study the picture. Seated on a slab of Egyptian marble was Mrs. Prior. At her side, mopping his brow, was Lord Wimbly. Two men were close to the entry of the tomb, involved in carrying out artifacts that were carefully wrapped for transportation. They were Hunter and Alex. In the doorway of the tomb itself stood Sir John. And she had to stare to see that it was Aubrey Sizemore directing the Egyptian workers in the background as they transported a coffin up a hill.

Below the picture and caption, another line read,

Exultation to tragedy; noble lord and lady fall prey to Egyptian cobras. Even the Queen mourns, as revenge from the grave seems to reach out with skeletal fingers and bring about a terrible demise.

Someone was coming! Camille wanted to read the entire article, but she couldn't risk being caught delving into Sir John's desk. She quickly returned the article and shut the drawer, then set the magnifying glass back in its place. She leaped to her feet.

Her heart was thundering and she didn't know why. What she had done wasn't so terrible. She had righted a drawer. She had seen an article and started to read it. Certainly she had seen it when it came out, but that was a year ago, before she had become part of the museum. She read the paper constantly. The news would have faded behind that which had occurred more recently.

Sir John entered, seeming preoccupied at first, but then frowning when he noticed her standing there.

"Is there something wrong, Camille?" he asked. The silent question behind that, of course, was, why aren't you working?

"I'm sorry, Sir John. I have been doing well, but I'm feeling a bit tired. I was hoping to slip out for a cup of tea. I won't take any lunch at all later. You've been so kind to agree with Lord Stirling that I must leave early to meet with the dressmaker."

To her surprise, Sir John waved a hand in the air, returning to his somewhat distracted state. "If you were not to come in at all during the week, my dear, it would be quite all right. You've done us great service in a day's time. Go, enjoy some tea. Your work will wait."

"Thank you. I do not mean, however, to neglect my responsibility in any way!"

"Even I need a cup of tea upon occasion. Or a whiskey! Something to clear the head." As if thinking in that direction and seeking another cure, he shook his own. "Tea, yes. And take what time you need."

With that blessing, Camille eschewed her apron and picked up the little blue reticule that matched so well with the sedate but beautiful gown Mrs. Prior had afforded her. Then she fled the offices.

Heading out through the exhibits, she found herself pausing. The cobra was lying relaxed and dormant. There were no children about to tease it. She walked close to the glass, wondering if they really were wise to keep the creature on display. Glass could break after all.

She frowned. It was Aubrey's responsibility to care for the cobra. He knew something about the creatures from his time on expeditions. An unease filled her. She had seen Aubrey in the picture of the last expedition the Stirlings had sponsored. Just as she had seen the others.

She turned to leave, then stopped, an uneasy feeling trickling down her spine.

She turned, glanced around, then gave herself a shake. Had she really been afraid that the snake had leaped from its terrarium to come slithering after her? No... She hadn't been afraid that the snake had been following her. But she had felt someone...watching. Yet there was no one around. At least, no one she could see.

Still not able to shake the odd sensation that she was being followed, Camille hurried on out of the building and headed for the tea garden directly across the street.

GREGORY ALTHORP WAS SEATED on a stool, deeply focused on the object beneath his microscope.

Brian had to clear his throat to get his attention.

Gregory looked up. "Brian!" he said with surprise. "Uh, sorry, Lord Stirling."

"Brian suffices just fine, thank you," Brian said, walking forward and shaking hands with the man. They had served together in the Queen's Service. To Brian, that put the two of them on a first-name basis.

Gregory was so tall and thin, calling him lanky was a kindness. He had taken his medical expertise onto the fields of war, but then shrapnel in his calf had sent him home. He didn't need to be in the teaching college, yet there he was, as usual, because the field of medicine fascinated him endlessly. He had once told Brian that if he worked every minute of his life, there would not be enough time to begin to explore all the areas that called to him, all the areas that *needed* to be explored.

A skeleton hung on a frame nearby. As Gregory's passion was discovering the true source of death, he usually worked in one of the dissecting labs. A body lay covered on a table, awaiting the cold scalpels of teachers or students.

Though the soul of the departed was surely long gone, Brian couldn't help but feel an inkling of sympathy for the corpse. There had been, in the past, hideous ado over the procurement of bodies for medical schools. There had been terrible incidents of ghastly murders since many a man and woman had been worth more dead than alive. The trial of Burke and Hare, the "body snatchers," in Edinburgh had brought attention to the dangers of making corpses so valuable.

They were still valuable, though the government had worked hard to make them more available. Therefore, Gregory would use every inch of the dead man, just as a poor hunter might make use of every bit of a slain animal. Gregory's determination, however, would be to advance his own passion—an understanding of the human body and how it worked. And what forces brought about death.

"How are you?" Gregory studied Brian's eyes. "Surely, the wounds have healed and cannot be quite so fearsome as that mask!"

Brian shrugged. "Maybe the mask is what I've become," he said lightly.

Gregory continued his study. "It's been a while since you visited. I'm sorry I've not pursued some of your questions further. I'm afraid that the police have requested my help many times in the past several months. I wish that there was more I could tell you, Brian. Actually, since it seems I've been able to give you questions rather than answers, I'm rather sorry I ever called upon you when… when your parents died."

Brian shook his head. "You did the right thing."

"I sent you on a horrible quest, and it seems that there is no answer. If there had been, you'd not be here now."

"Observant, of course," Brian told him, grinning ruefully. "But I'd like to go over your notes again, if I might."

"I've created an obsession," Gregory said sorrowfully.

"Is justice an obsession?"

"Is revenge justice?"

Brian shook his head. "I believe someone so coveted riches and fame that they were willing to kill. It isn't revenge to see that such a crime never occurs again."

"Ah, Brian!" Gregory murmured.

"It's true, I'm angry. And perhaps I do seek vengeance, of a kind. But time has passed and my anger is now cold and calculating. And though the scar I bear on my heart is far deeper than any of my flesh, it is truly justice I'm seeking."

"After all this time…? We're talking about asps! How will you ever prove it?"

"Perhaps I can't."

"Then…"

"Perhaps, with the proper knowledge, I can force the killer to show his true colors."

"I cannot dissuade you?"

"You did start me on the quest."

Gregory sighed. He rose, a slim man in a white coat among Bunsen lamps, test tubes, chemicals, a skeleton and a corpse. "I'll get my notes."

THE REST OF THE DAY passed quickly enough. Camille was happier with her work after having taken her break, and the symbols seemed to fall into place nicely, verifying what she had already suspected. She understood quite well how Brian Stirling had acquired his reputation as "the beast," since the curse was to be visited upon the heirs of those "who dared defile" into perpetuity. It was natural that anyone in the least superstitious would find themselves embracing a certain fear of the earl. Therefore, he became a beast. Not that his behavior at times didn't warrant such a reaction!

Alex stopped by as she worked into the early afternoon, not having much to say but staring at her morosely. "He may be quite mad, you know," he said from the doorway.

"Pardon?"

"The Earl of Carlyle. Camille, I am so afraid for you!"

She sighed. "I don't think he's insane."

"Do you call it rational that he should choose such a mask, let his grounds become a jungle and live within those walls of his as if he were a cornered animal?" Alex demanded.

Behind him, she could see the old fellow Aubrey had been seeking the day before. Stooped and bent, with long gray whiskers and a beard to match, Jim Arboc was busy sweeping the outer office.

"A man has a right to be eccentric," Camille told Alex.

Alex shook his head. "He has everything in the world. A man born with a title can get away with anything. Why, if I were an earl, with that kind of money, with his resources…"

"Alex, he's not doing anything terrible. He prefers to live a quiet life within his own walls."

"You don't get a reputation for being a beast without a reason."

She arched her brows. "Alex, you've seen him in here. He can be entirely courteous."

"Ah, Camille. Even you!"

"Even I…what?" she demanded, feeling a surge of raw anger.

"It's his title. You're enraptured by that title."

"Alex, you're my friend," she said softly. "I suggest you get out before your words to me indicate that you are something other."

"Oh, Camille!" he said miserably. "I'm so sorry."

"Apology accepted."

He came into the room then, obviously still distressed. "What if I were rich?" he asked her.

"Pardon?"

"If I were…well, if I were a man of greater means. Would you care about me then?"

"Alex! I do care about you."

"That's not what I mean, Camille, and you know it."

She shook her head. "Alex, I repeat, you're my friend and I care about you. But at this stage of my life, I am concerned with my work. You know that it was difficult for me to actually obtain my position here. I am dedicated to doing the best work that I can and keeping this job!"

"Then why are you living with the man?"

"I am not living with the man!" she said with indignant horror.

"Why stay there? Get Tristan away. Surely, unless he were seriously injured, he could be moved by now."

"I don't know what you're implying, Alex, but I am taking great offense at your words."

"I care about you far too much to see…well, to see this happening to you."

"Just what is happening to me, Alex?" she demanded.

"There will be a terrible scandal," he told her.

"Oh, and why?"

"You're a commoner, Camille. That is not meant as offense, but simple fact. And you are staying with the Earl of Carlyle. He is going to escort you to a gala. Surely, you know, tongues will wag."

"Then they will just have to do so," she said sharply. She stood then, furious. "Alex, I am going to have to ask you to leave. The world has called Lord Stirling a monster. I can tell you that he is not. He has asked me to attend a museum function with him. I will do so. And I am not afraid of being with the man. Indeed, you and Hunter have behaved with far less decorum and courtesy. So let the tongues wag. I will defend the man. He has been hurt, scarred, wounded. That is all. I do not find him repulsive, nor do I find him a monster in any way. Once again, if you would have our friendship continue, I suggest you leave without further words to drive us apart."

"Camille!"

"Alex, go!"

He turned, obviously still distressed. She heard him muttering as he left. "Titles…and riches!"

With a sigh, she went back to her work.

I cannot describe in words the joy felt upon our discovery! Nor, I suppose, can I begin to explain the absolute fascination dear George and I have found delving into the past and the present of this exquisite, yet suffering, country. The ancients left such treasures, while the people now suffer in such poverty. It is my dearest hope that in finding the riches of the past, we may give back to those who now so desperately need our help. If we are to be a great empire, then we must take care that we do not rob these people of their heritage. We must see that they are given all that they need to enter into the quickly coming twentieth century. That said, let me try to put down everything about that glorious first day and all the wonders of excavation since!

It was early when Abdul found the first steps. Eagerly, we dug, myself included! And there, slowly, we at last found the sealed doorway! There was, of course, a warning upon it. One of the poor diggers was in horror, certain that we had unearthed something unholy. I felt such sorrow for the poor man that I discreetly paid him his day's wage and sent him on his way. Lord Wimbly was a bit put out that I paid the fellow, saying that they were nothing but superstitious fools and shouldn't be rewarded for such behavior. Hunter, of course, shrugged and said that I must do what I must. He is ever such a flirt and intrigued only with what he shall do next! I

think Alex, too, was upset, but the poor dear has been
out so often, truly ill a few times. I tried to cheer him
as I understand that he is often frustrated, not being
able to finance many a project that he would find
rewarding himself.

Other workers were brought in to break the seal. And
then, behold! The tomb came to light. We were amazed,
for though we had not found the grand tomb of a pharaoh, we had discovered the next best thing—the resting place of a great vizier, prophet or holy man. And, as
we delicately moved into the entry, we realized that we
had made a tremendous find. Sir John shared our ecstasy,
and it was difficult to keep Aubrey from plowing like an
elephant into the tomb, he was so anxious and eager.

We knew that every find would need to be carefully
removed. And there would be so many decisions to
make. Finds must go into the museum at Cairo, for truly,
in my heart, I see that these treasures belong to the
Egyptian people. And finds must go to our own great
center of culture and learning, for I fervently believe
that it is from the past that we discover the future. If
there is anything I can do to repay God above who has
blessed me with such a life, it is to give the gift of learning and education to our people…to *all* people.

And though we have explored and dusted and
cleaned and catalogued and packed, we have just begun
to see the treasures. I am exhausted, but so excited. Poor
George! Even here, he troubles himself with mysteries
from back home. While I grow so terribly involved here,
he is talking about Carlyle and how anxious he is to get
back and discover if his theory regarding our lovely castle is correct!

BRIAN SET DOWN his mother's journal. He had read it time and again, desperately seeking between the lines to discover if she'd had serious difficulty with any of the erstwhile *scholars* who had been with them on the last expedition. But in her journal, as in her speech, Lady Abigail was ever kind.

He picked up the autopsy notes he had received that afternoon, and tried not to think about the state of his parents' bodies by the time they had reached England. Just where, exactly, had the asps been when his parents had come upon them?

He closed his eyes. A drawer? Had his mother reached in and been bitten immediately? She had been bitten on her lower arms, twice. Had her cries alerted his father? He would have run to her immediately, taken her desperately into his arms.

She must have fallen. That would explain the fracture at the back of her head. So she had cried out, fallen, then his father had come.

But how then had his father been bitten on the arms, too? If the snakes had been in a drawer, and his mother had fallen, and his father had gone to her assistance, the snakes should have…either remained in the drawer or been on the ground, in which case his father would have been bitten about the legs or ankles.

He studied the autopsy notes again. There had been a cut on his father's throat. A shaving mishap? And then there had been the curious bruise on his mother's shoulder.

He set the notes down and rubbed his face, glad, in his private chambers, to be free from the mask, idly tracing the scar that ran down his cheek.

He had been certain from the start that his parents had been murdered. He had always assumed that the murder had been perpetuated by someone seeing to it that the asps

were in a place where they would instinctively strike before being seen. But now he began to wonder if the murderer hadn't actually been there in the room. Had his
parents seen the face of their killer and known just exactly
what they were facing?

He shuddered, torn apart once again to think of what
had been done. Anger seared into him, and with the anger
came the repeated question that tortured his mind. *Why?*

The answer was somewhere. And by God, he was going
to find it.

"Oh, my, how delightful!" the woman cried, admitting
Camille into the cottage. "Shelby dear, you are coming in,
of course?"

Camille turned to her great hulk of an escort, a little surprised that anyone could call such a giant "Shelby dear!"

"Ah, Merry, of course, if you don't be minding. I'd
never leave without a spot of your fine tea and one of those
scones I can smell on the air!" He cleared his throat.
"Merry, this is Miss Camille Montgomery, a scholar at the
museum. Camille, may I present Merry and the other
lasses, Edith and Violet."

Again, she had to smile at the choice of words. The
"lasses" were all well into their sixties, Camille thought.
Yet, maybe Shelby was right to label them as such, for the
women were all lovely, with beautiful, pert, young smiles.

And she herself was hardly considered a scholar. She
didn't have the credentials that made one so.

Violet was very tall and thin, whereas Merry was short
and a bit squat with an ample bosom. Edith was somewhere between the two.

"Camille…what a lovely name. I dare say someone
loved opera!" Edith said.

"Come, come, perhaps her mother just liked the name,"

Merry said, pleasantly grinning away. "Edith was a teacher for years, my dear, and we still listen to opera day after day on the wonderful machine there. A bit scratchy, but…oh!" She turned to her sisters. "She's so lovely, isn't she?" Then back to Camille. "This will be such a pleasure!"

Camille flushed. "Thank you."

"Merry, dear, you fix the tea," Edith said. "Violet and I will do the measuring! Come along, dear."

Violet caught her arm and she was drawn through the little cottage to a room in the rear with a sewing machine, a dressmaker's dummy, shelves full of material bolts, spools of thread and all kinds of paraphernalia. The women were charming, carrying on a conversation with one another, asking her questions, not really waiting for answers. Before she knew it, and before she could feel the least awkward, she was standing in nothing but a shift, with a tape measure going about her here and there. Somewhere along the line, she managed to get in a question.

"Edith, you were a teacher?"

"Oh, yes, dear. And I did love teaching!"

"But now…you are all dressmakers?"

"Oh, no!" Violet told her. "Well, we do have a love of it, as you see. But we're sisters, of course—all widows, I'm afraid."

"How nice that you have one another," Camille murmured.

"Delightful!" Violet said.

"Oh, we've much more, as well," Edith told her. "Merry has a wonderful son, with Her Majesty's troops in India."

"And he has three sons!" Violet supplied.

"I see. Is that how you know Lord Stirling?" Camille asked.

Edith laughed charmingly. "Oh, no, dear. We've had this cottage now for…twenty years, is it, Violet?"

"Indeed."

Camille must have looked a little baffled because Violet continued. "My dear, we're on property belonging to the Earl of Carlyle. Of course, we moved here when George and his dear lady were still living…we made all of Lady Stirling's clothing. Now we only make shirts for Brian. How I miss his dear mother! Not that he isn't the most generous of men to us. A great sense of responsibility, he has. Now, please turn for me, dear."

Camille did so, and was startled to see a child standing in the doorway, a beautiful little girl of four or five. She had glorious dark ringlets, huge eyes and dimples. She didn't seem at all shy as she stared at Camille.

"Um…hello," Camille said.

Violet swung around. "Ally! Child, what on earth are you doing out of bed?"

Ally gave Camille a secretive smile. "Thirsty!" she said sweetly. "And hungry, Auntie Vi!"

"Ah, she smells the scones, she does!" Edith said, chiding with no real thought of discipline. "Oh, where are my manners? Ally, you must meet Miss Montgomery. Miss Montgomery, Ally."

They offered no last name.

"Hello, miss!" Ally said, bobbing a curtsy.

"Hello, a pleasure to meet you, Miss Ally," Camille told her.

She looked at Violet. "One of Merry's grandchildren?" she asked.

"Oh, no! The grandchildren all live with their mothers," Violet said.

"Ally is our dear little ward," Edith told her, folding the measuring tape. "Well, there, that's done and set. Oh, dear! You must see the fabric." She drew a bolt from one of the shelves. "Well, it's for the overskirt, you see. I do hope you'll be pleased. We're so excited about this gown!"

She admired the fabric. It looked like spun gold, and yet…there was an underlying hint of green to it.

Ally came in, tentatively touching the fabric. She smiled her beautiful little dimpled, impish smile at Camille.

"Like your eyes."

"Exactly!" Violet said. "Well, it is what Lord Stirling told us, isn't it, Edith?"

"Oh, yes, and it does match."

"Here, dear, let's get your clothing back on you, and then, tea!"

"Oh, yes! Tea!" Ally said with a clap of her hands.

Violet had the borrowed blue work dress quickly over Camille's head. Edith was there to help with the lacing and petticoats in seconds flat. Between them, they were incredibly deft and efficient.

And yet, while the dress went over her, Camille couldn't help but wonder, whose child was it? And why did she live here with her "aunties"? Was the lovely little girl Brian Stirling's…child? His illegitimate child?

"Come, come, tea!" Violet said, turning down the lamp. Edith was leading the way out.

Ally came to Camille and slipped her little hand into hers. "Miss, tea. Oh, do come, please! The scones are so very, very good!"

As the child had promised, they were. It was a lovely setting, having tea at the kitchen table in the little cottage. It was warm, and the aroma of the fresh-baked scones enwrapped them. Shelby, the great hulk, was obviously a favorite with the aunties, and with Ally, as well. She squealed with delight as he hiked her onto his back and gave her a horsy ride around the room. Camille found herself forgetting all else for a time as she enjoyed the child's laughter, the comfort of the tea and the delicious scones.

At last, it was time to leave. "You'll have to come again tomorrow, dear, for a fitting," Violet told her.

"Well, everything should be perfect. We do know what we're doing!" Edith said, then grinned. "But we want it to be perfect, so you really should have a fitting."

"This is needed in such a rush, dear," Merry murmured, shaking her head.

"But you will be so beautiful, miss," Ally told her.

For some reason, the child's wide-eyed compliment suddenly seemed to bring a rush of tears to Camille's eyes, and she didn't know why. Maybe because she could remember being so young, and then a little older…

She'd never had such ladies as these to raise her. No, she'd had Tristan. He hadn't been like an auntie, and he certainly had never baked scones, but he had given her all of his heart—he'd given her a life.

"Thank you," she told the little girl. Yet she was suddenly angry, as well. Torn. So Lord Stirling was seeing to it that his child was properly raised! He was no better than the other rich and titled men who ran about using young women who had not been blessed at birth with wealth and inheritance, then left them to brave the world with no name, no dignity.

She dared hug the child tightly to her. "Thank you!" she repeated.

Ally pushed away from her to study her eyes. "Are you scared to go to the ball?"

"Uh, no…no," Camille said. "And it's not exactly a ball. It's a fund-raiser for the museum."

"Scared? Silly little moppet," Violet said, affectionately tousling the girl's hair. "And it *is* a ball, a grand gala for the museum. It will be elegant and beautiful, and Miss Montgomery will dance the hours away. It will be lovely!"

"You'll be the most beautiful one there," Ally told her,

taking Camille's cheeks between her chubby little hands. "Like a princess."

"You are very, very sweet, but I'm hardly a princess. I work for the museum, you see."

"And that should keep you from spending a night dancing just like a princess?" Merry demanded. "Oh, no, dear! You will put on that golden dress, and for the night you will be magical. I cannot wait to see you dressed and on your way."

"On our way is what we must be right now," Shelby interrupted. "Lord Stirling will be waiting."

"Oh, right! Absolutely. Shoo, shoo!" Merry said cheerfully. "And don't forget, a final fitting tomorrow!"

Camille paused, looking from them to Shelby. "I'm not sure that can be arranged. I am employed by the museum."

"Lord Stirling can arrange anything," Violet said. "Get along now!"

They were ushered out. Before she knew it, Camille was back in the carriage with the huge crest of the house of Stirling emblazoned upon it. As they drove, she wondered just how far the Stirling wealth and holdings went. And again, she found herself wondering about the child, and the way that Lord Stirling could "arrange anything." By the time they returned to the castle, she found that she was really simmering in a state of anger. And she wasn't even sure exactly why.

BRIAN DISCOVERED that he was looking forward to the evening. Shelby informed him immediately when Camille returned, and Brian allowed time for her to visit with Tristan and freshen up from the day before sending Evelyn to her room to escort her to his quarters.

The day hadn't brought forth much new in his quest for truth, but it had allowed for a few pleasing and refreshing surprises.

He realized that Camille entertained him. That she was quick with her wit and her responses, and that she stood her ground. No, she more than entertained him, he thought.

When he heard the door open, he quickly turned. "Good evening, Miss Montgomery."

"Is it?" she replied.

"It's not?" he inquired, frowning. She always stood straight, and when she walked she seemed to glide. Tonight, she moved with purely regal disdain.

"It is evening, that much is certain," she agreed.

"Did something happen?" he inquired.

"Indeed. My guardian is here, and therefore, so am I," she informed him. She swept out a hand, indicating the table. "I am afraid that nothing happened at the museum today that I can report, so your meal is a waste."

"I believe you're mistaken, actually," he told her. "A great deal might have happened at the museum, of which you might not be aware."

"My day was boring," she informed him.

"Tell me about it. I'll see if I agree."

He drew out her chair. She swept by him. He frowned, still puzzled by her hostility. As she sat, he was brushed by the fabric of her gown, teased by a touch of her hair against his fingers. He was startled by the quickening that seized him, and he moved back behind her, glad that she faced forward, not certain if even the mask he wore could hide the sensation that had ripped into him. Simple. Basic. Instinctive. Purely carnal.

She was a beautiful young woman. Such thoughts would not be far from the mind of any man. But such thoughts most often existed without such a fierce response from within.

He gritted his teeth, angry with himself. Composed, he walked around the table and drew out his own chair. "Were the sisters difficult? I cannot believe that they were."

"They were charming. I remain displeased, however, that you're forcing me to have a gown made."

"Why?"

"I am not a charity case."

"It is not being offered as if you were."

"If I didn't have to attend the fund-raiser, I would not need a gown."

"But you are attending. Therefore, you need a gown. You are attending because I have asked you to do so. Therefore, the gown is my responsibility. Not charity in the least."

He poured wine. She picked up her glass a bit too quickly, he thought. Sipped it immediately. More than sipped. Was she seeking courage? Or had something seriously disturbed her?

"Tell me about your day."

"I went to work. Shelby came at four. I went for the fitting."

He gauged his response, inhaling slowly for patience. "What happened at work?"

"I worked."

"Miss Montgomery—"

"I continued my translation. I'm afraid that the symbols promised a curse upon those who defiled the tomb and their heirs into perpetuity."

He smiled coldly. "I'm well aware that a curse is supposed to be eternal. Did you think that such news would be upsetting to me? I don't believe in curses, Miss Montgomery. I do believe in evil, but it comes from men. I thought I'd rather established that fact. You worked, you translated. And what more?"

She hesitated, taking another swallow of wine. "I saw…a newspaper clipping. Of your parents and the others at the dig."

"Ah," he murmured. "And where did you see it?"

She said slowly, "In Sir John's drawer."

"There, you see? Your day does offer light on the subject most passionate to my heart."

"Sir John is not a murderer," she insisted.

"Ah! Does that mean you actually believe that someone may be?"

Her lashes fell over her eyes. She leaned forward suddenly. "Suppose someone did see to it that the asps were where your parents would be. There is no way to know! No way to prove foul play. So you are torturing yourself and nothing more."

For a moment, the glass encasing she seemed to be wearing that evening had slipped away. She straightened almost immediately, though, as if irritated that she had shown him any real emotion.

"What of my illustrious colleagues in the quest of ancient Egypt?" he asked.

"What do you mean?"

"Sir John was there. And...the others?"

She sighed. "Alex was working. I saw Aubrey moving about. Neither Hunter nor Lord Wimbly were in today, at least, not that I saw."

"And what about Alex?"

She stared across the table at him. "What about him?"

"Did he say or do anything unusual. Did you share a conversation?"

She frowned. "We do work in the same department. Since we are both fairly polite and courteous people, we tend to have conversations daily."

"Did he say anything special? And did you have a reply?"

She finished the last of her wine. He kept his eyes locked with hers as he waited for her reply and refilled her glass.

"He said nothing new. He is afraid for me."

"Because he believes me to be a monster?"

She lifted her hands, refusing to tell him that Alex might have used those words.

He lowered his head, smiling, then asked, "And what did you tell him?"

"What does it matter? In truth, I begin to believe that all men are monsters!"

"And that would definitely include me," he murmured.

"Well, you've worked hard to make yourself one, haven't you?" she demanded, staring at him and reaching for her wineglass once again. "But then, it doesn't always take work, does it? Sometimes behavior just comes naturally. A man is born into a world of privilege, so he feels free to toy with those beneath him!"

"Oh, yes, I should be opening the grounds to orphans, I remember," he murmured.

She stood, and to his astonishment let out an infuriated "Oh!" before slamming her napkin down on the table and heading for the door.

He let her go so far, then called out her name sharply. "Miss Montgomery!"

She went as rigid as steel and turned back to him slowly. "Forgive me, but I am not hungry this evening. And I'm very afraid that I've told you everything I can about events at the museum today."

He stood, walking toward her.

"You cannot force me to eat dinner!" she cried.

He stopped in front of her. To his frustration, he found it a difficult place to be. Every muscle in his body seemed to blaze and stretch and groan. It took every fiber of self-control not to seize her by the shoulders, pull her to him…

"You will not wander the castle alone," he said, the words somehow sharply enunciated despite the tight clench of his teeth.

He threw open the door, eyes burning and narrowed, and waited for her to exit. She did so with a slight lift of her chin. When they reached her door, he reminded her, "Don't ever, ever, wander the castle alone at night, do you understand?"

"Oh, yes! I understand."

"Do you?"

"Far too much!" she replied.

And to his absolute astonishment, she had the nerve to slam the door in his face.

CHAPTER EIGHT

THE DOG WASN'T WITH HER that night. Either the earl didn't think she needed to be guarded anymore, or else he didn't believe that the castle needed to be guarded against *her* anymore.

It had been a very long day, and a long bath had been in order. And when she was done, she should have been very tired, but thoughts continued to race through her head and she couldn't sleep. *He wasn't always a monster.* He had tried to be courteous at dinner.

Surely he knew she had seen the child. Was he just so callous that he didn't care she knew the truth? Really! After the confession she had raged out to him the other night, he might have realized that men having children but refusing to be responsible for them was a real issue for her.

Yet he was responsible. The child was being raised by loving sisters—without a father.

She hadn't known her biological father, but at least she'd been blessed with Tristan… Well, *blessed* might not be the right word. After all, she wouldn't be here now if he could just learn to behave.

She frowned suddenly, aware again of a noise. She heard it…and then she didn't. She wondered if she was imagining it, and then she was certain that she wasn't. It almost seemed to have come from within her room.

She sat up, turning on the oil lamp at her bedside. From

across the room, the deadlike eyes of an Egyptian clay cat stared back at her. She ignored it; she had studied all things Egyptian in the museum since she'd been a small child. The past did not frighten her. But the sound…

She got out of bed and walked around the room, trying to find the source. Finally, she thought that it wasn't coming from the room, but from below it. She hesitated. Then, carefully walking with bare feet, she went to the door. She hesitated, wondering if she would find it locked from without. But it wasn't locked.

She opened it carefully and looked into the hallway. She saw nothing, no one. The hall lights were very dim, but she sensed there was no one near her.

Then…the sound came from somewhere below.

She moved out into the hall, not really intending to go down the stairs. But the noise propelled her. Instinctively she moved against the wall, following the stairway down to the entry of the castle. In the dim light afforded by a few low-burning lamps, the arms upon the walls took on a faint but sinister glow. She moved through the great hall, realizing that she knew nothing of the layout of the castle. She had come up and down the stairway before, and traveled the hall above, but she didn't know what lay to the left or the right of the great entry.

At the foot of the stairs, she turned to her right, since she was certain the strange scraping noise had come from beneath her. Thankfully massive double doors beneath a Norman arch were ajar; it was easy enough to slip into the next room. There, the light was even dimmer. Only one lamp burned against the night. She held still for a minute, allowing her eyes to adjust.

She had come to another long hall, which in better times, might have been used as a ballroom. There were love seats and settees against the wall. A large piano

loomed at one end, and near it a harp and several string instruments rested on stands.

She traveled the hallway, aware that an uneasy feeling
was creeping over her as she did so. She tried not to shake.
The empty ballroom, however, seemed to whisper of ghosts
of the past as no object, artifact or even mummy could do.

In the center of the great room, she paused, swirling
around, feeling as if she were followed. But there was no
one behind her; she was alone in the cavernous space.

She continued onward until she came to two doors, the
wood beautifully carved, beneath ancient archways. She
hesitated, then chose the left. As quietly as she could, she
pressed against the door. Someone used it frequently, for
it opened without a sound on well-oiled hinges.

The room she entered was a chapel, small but distinct.
Unchanged, she thought, in hundreds of years. The altar
was of stone. A metal crucifix rose above it. There were
flowers placed upon it; their aroma struck her immediately.

She hesitated again, some part of her longing to return
the way she had come, to race back up the stairs and bolt
herself into her room. But something stronger drew her onward, toward another door at the end of the chapel. Though
she called herself an idiot with every step, she knew that
she must discover where it led.

Slowly, carefully, she opened the door. From somewhere down below, a light burned. It occurred to her that
since she was in the chapel, the stairs probably led to a family crypt. But why would a light be burning in the crypt?

Don't go down! a sane and fervent voice begged in her
mind. But her feet were already moving. The stone stairs
were old, hundreds of years old, worn, slick and smooth.
And cold, like ice against her feet.

Still, the flickering light drew her as if she were the pro-
verbial moth.

The steps curved, and she told her thundering heart that all she needed to do was get low enough to peer around and discover the source of the light. Then she would obey all reason and sanity and race straight back up to her bedroom. Just a few more steps and she'd be able to turn.

She reached the bottom, but an old stone support blocked her view. Her hands were against the dampness of the wall. Suddenly, the light went out and the world was cast into absolute pitch. There was a whisk of sound from….behind her on the stairs? Or had it come from the darkness that lay before her?

She froze, straining with every sense, trying to fathom the source of danger. Then hands reached out, touching her.

IT WAS LATE AT NIGHT, very late. But time made little difference to Sir John Matthews.

The rest of the museum lay in shadow. Just recently, in 1890, the galleries had been fully lit with electricity. But it was an expensive undertaking, and when the museum closed down, so did most of the light. He worked in his office, the soft glow from the lamp on his desk casting eerie shadows on his face.

Notebooks and news clippings were strewn before him. He muttered to himself, carefully reading a clipping, casting it down, frowning and picking it up again. From beneath the pile of clippings he drew out a small journal. His own. From that time. The expedition to Egypt.

It had been extraordinary. All of them there. Arguing, of course! They were scholars. They were opinionated. They were well-read. And they all had their ideas.

He read a page in his journal, then closed his eyes, shaking his head sorrowfully. He could still see Abigail Stirling so clearly! Her simple skirt, so perfect for the desert sands! Her light-colored shirt, utilitarian, as well, yet with the embroidery that gave it a feminine touch. He could hear the sound of her laughter. She would always smile and say that the next day would be better. She never gave way to exhaustion; she never lost her enthusiasm. Gentle and kind, she was a woman the workers would move mountains for, and in the end, that's what they had nearly done.

Then there was Lord Stirling—George. Not to be fooled. Not to be taken. He loved the quest as much as any of them, but never forgot that he was Lord Stirling. He was a man with responsibilities to country and Queen, and his own home, as well. He was concerned with his property, with his tenants and with his obligations to Parliament.

Wherever he went, he had a movable office. The telegraph wires clicked constantly. Yet that didn't stop him from seeing everything, from knowing everything. The man had been endowed with keen powers of observation. He kept a mental catalogue in his head, and knew if anything—the smallest object—had been moved.

Lady Abigail had been sweetness itself. And Lord George was a man of steel. But they had died.

No one could best death. They all knew that, had all seen the pathetic remains of the ancient Egyptians who thought they could cheat death and take their treasures with them into the afterworld.

Lord George had been the first one into the tomb, with Lady Abigail at his side. And there had been a curse.

Suddenly, a little desperately, Sir John began to dig through the news clippings once again, seeking a certain paper, an Egyptian paper. A noise startled him. He looked around in the darkness but saw nothing.

"Good God, old man!" he chided himself. "You'll be thinking that the mummies awaken and walk!"

It was his exhaustion. He had been a fool to come here

tonight, but his workload had been so heavy lately. It was time to leave.

He shoved the papers and the notebooks into his desk drawer and slammed it shut. He rose, amazed to realize that he was suddenly frightened. Truly frightened.

"I'm leaving now!" he announced aloud.

He hurried out, not stopping to lock the office door, not stopping at all until he was out on the street. There, as required by his position, he assured himself that the great doors to Britain's national treasure were secured. He nodded to the policeman on night duty.

He turned and rushed from the great edifice. Only later, when he had reached his cozy little flat, when he was sipping tea and whiskey, did he realize that he had fled the museum when he thought someone might have been up to no good, when it was his duty to make sure that no one invaded the hallowed halls.

But even as the thought struck, he remembered his journal, and his hands began to shake, his teacup clattering against the saucer.

TO HER AMAZEMENT, Camille didn't scream. At least, not out loud. But then, her terror at that moment was so great, no sound would issue from her lips. Surely the whole of the castle had to hear the pounding of her heart; it thundered in her own ears.

Despite the sheer loss of sight in the stygian darkness, other senses rose to the fore. The touch fell upon her shoulders. Knuckles brushed over her breasts, barely covered by the thin material of the nightgown. In seconds, she knew the figure that had come upon her, knew him innately before his fierce and ragged whisper touched her ears.

"Camille!"

He was furious. And maskless.

Amazingly, she was no longer afraid, but as the sense of relief and security filled her, a voice awakened within her. Instinct cried that she should trust him, but logic condemned her.

She reached out blindly, touching his face in turn, and felt the texture of his skin. Her fingers swept over high cheekbones, a strong nose, full lips. She was about to speak when he caught her hand, and she heard his whisper.

"No!"

She swallowed hard. He indicated that she should remain where she was. Then he disappeared.

She waited for a flood of light to break through the world of ebony, but no light came. She remained totally motionless against the stone-cold walls of the castle. He must be seeking a source of light, she thought. He would know, certainly, where any source would be; he was master of the castle.

And when the light flared, she would see his face. See what must be so horrible and monstrous beneath the mask.

But still no light came. She nearly cried out when he returned to her, for she had heard nothing. Indeed, seconds before he touched her something within warned her that he was near. Scent, body heat, a whisper in the air, but not so much as a whisper of sound. Perhaps the total darkness played havoc with her mind, for when he touched her again, foolish as it might be, she clung to him, trembling. Beneath the cotton fabric of whatever covered his arms and torso, she felt the tension and power that constricted his muscles. He leaned against her. She felt his breath against her ear, and the word he whispered had bare substance.

"Up."

She nodded. Still clinging to his arm, she turned. The stone wall was cold as ice to her left, while to her right was the warmth and vitality of his length and form and the reassuring pressure of his fingers upon her wrist. They reached the top of the stairs that led to the chapel. They entered and he firmly closed the door behind them.

She realized then that he hadn't left her to find light; he had gone into the black netherworld to procure a mask. He must have several, for this one was different, a simple, thin tanned leather without the least resemblance to any beast, real or mythical.

The light here in the chapel was still dim. With the door to the stairs and the crypts closed behind him, Camille felt a certainty that they were alone.

"Why did you do that?" she asked.

"You were told not to wander the castle alone at night!" he returned.

"I—"

"You were told not to wander the castle alone at night!"

She wrenched free from his hold and started quickly out of the chapel. He came up behind her, his strides long. She knew when he was almost upon her, and spun around. To her astonishment, he swept her up and threw her over his shoulder. The impetus robbed her of breath, and she couldn't protest for several seconds. In that time, determined strides brought them to the stairway. As he took the first steps, she tried to rise against him, but the force of his angry movements sent her flopping back on his shoulder, breathless once again.

They passed the door to her room and came to the carved entry of his chambers. He pushed open the door with his foot, slammed it behind him in like manner and deposited her crudely in one of the great upholstered chairs before the hearth.

By then she was trembling in earnest, absolutely indignant. Her teeth were chattering and she gripped the sides of the chair, staring at him with eyes that all but spit fury as she said, "How dare you! I don't care if you are the earl and I the child of a prostitute! How dare you!"

He was hunkered down before her, the flash of his blue gaze like a smoldering flame as he returned her anger. "How dare *you!* You were told not to wander. How can a guest abuse her position so blatantly?"

"Guest! I'm a prisoner."

"You were told not to wander. What in God's name would allow any sane person to seek out family crypts in the middle of the night—even if they *hadn't* been told not to wander!"

"I heard…a noise."

"Ah! So something might be wrong—that would make you rush right to it?"

She didn't know why she had done what she had done, didn't know how to explain to him that she had been compelled to go forward when all sanity suggested she retreat.

His next words stunned her.

"What are you really doing here?"

"What?"

"Which one of those bastards are you working for?"

"What?"

"There is an entry, right?"

"I don't know what in God's name you're talking about!" she cried, suddenly alarmed. He was on fire, his jaw clenched, eyes brilliant, muscles constricting with such tension that she could feel the ripple even beneath the simple cotton shirt he wore. She recoiled on the chair.

"Good God! After all this, don't act the innocent with me," he warned.

She exhaled, understanding then exactly what he meant. "You are not just a beast or a monster, but a lunatic!" she said icily. "You are obsessed, and you've come to see so much evil in life that you think it exists everywhere. I am not working for anyone—I work for the museum."

"Why else wander naked in the night?" he demanded.

"I am not naked!"

"You might as well be," he informed her.

She hadn't realized that the nightgown was so sheer, or that words could have such a profound and instant effect upon one. She suddenly felt as if she burned, as if her flesh, blood and even bones were on fire. The sensation stole breath from her.

Then she wondered if it was the words that caused such a reaction, or the fact they were spoken by him. What was it about him?

For the first time in her life she felt a rush of hunger, of longing. She wanted to be held by him, to feel the molten-steel strength of his arms around her, the whisper of his voice in assurance rather than anger. She yearned to know the man beneath the mask, the man with fire and fury and raw determination.

"I—"

"You what?" he demanded.

She shook her head helplessly, hugging her arms around her chest. "I don't know what to say to you. I don't know how to prove that I have no evil intentions. Damn you! I'd help you if I could, if there were a way…don't you see? But there is no way! We can't put asps on trial. They cannot bear witness. Nor am I part of the hierarchy of the museum. I wasn't employed there when the expedition took place. I wish that I could help you but I cannot!"

He was still for a long time, and when he did move, she froze at first, afraid that he intended some kind of violence. But to her amazement, he reached out for her, pulling her up and into his arms.

Just as she might have wished, desired…

He took the chair himself, cradling her there, his arms around her to give her warmth. "You're shaking like a leaf blown in winter, you little fool," he said gruffly. "Dammit, lass, I'm not going to tear you to shreds. I'm merely trying to give you warmth!"

She nodded, unable to speak, and afraid of any sound that might issue from her lips. Again, her pulse was racing. She didn't need to feel any warmer; her flesh might have felt cool to his touch, but rampant fires had ignited inside her. She closed her eyes, praying that he remain certain her shaking was from the cold.

She couldn't bear for him to guess the truth, that he had stripped away the certainties and logic of a lifetime, making her believe that the world could be forgotten, that there could be no tomorrow, that everything important in existence lay in the way that he held her. It was like being intoxicated. She couldn't begin to understand it, for logic struggled fiercely with sensation in her mind. She should have been horrified, repelled, but she was not.

His fingers found her chin and lifted it. She stared into the deep and endless cobalt of his eyes. And it all became worse when his thumb stroked over her cheek and he whispered softly, "You are either the most magnificently honest and courageous woman I've ever met, or the most beguiling liar."

She stiffened, fighting the urge to remain where she was, held so tenderly. She had never allowed herself such vulnerability before.

"Don't bristle, Camille. I tend to believe the first. As you say, I am bitter and angry and baffled. Time has not changed that."

"Could you be wrong?" she whispered. "Perhaps…"

He shook his head, smiling ruefully. "No. One stray asp, one bite, maybe. But both my parents? And there's more.

Too many artifacts have disappeared. Then there are the noises."

She stared at him, newly mystified. "There is a huge wall around the place. It's an overgrown forest. And you have the dog. If there are noises—"

"You know that there are," he reminded her.

She shook her head. "But they have to be the natural settling of the building. This place is medieval. Besides, it's impossible for anyone to get in here, isn't it?"

"Your guardian managed."

"Yes, but you caught him immediately."

He shifted slightly, the better to meet her eyes, and the absurdity of her position struck her again. There was something more intimate about the way they sat together, speaking softly, feeling the warmth of the flames, than if…

She didn't dare think about the "if." Her cheeks would flame too brightly.

"What made you wander in the night?" he asked.

She exhaled, still meeting his eyes. "A…sound. Of course, you don't believe me. You don't have it in you to believe in anyone anymore—"

"I believe there's a passage from beyond the grounds to the house," he said, looking toward the fire.

"A passage?"

"An underground tunnel."

"But wouldn't you have known about it?"

He shrugged. "There are all kinds of stories associated with Carlyle Castle. The first walls were built not long after the Conquest. Different sides found a haven during the Wars of the Roses. Royalists were supposedly hidden here in Cromwell's time. It's said that Prince Charles once escaped to Scotland after taking refuge in the castle. It's very likely that there is a secret entrance."

"But you're the earl. Wouldn't you know about it?"

"We haven't had any great civil conflicts in a very long time now," he said softly. "My father was keen on the idea that such a passage existed. He was an explorer, loved mysteries. And God knows he might have found out something. I was away, in the military, for a long time before they died. He was always writing me with tremendous excitement, thinking he was on to something that would prove to be a wondrous surprise. At one time, I shared his and my mother's enthusiasm for the past, for history, for lost civilizations. But my father was an English earl, you must remember. That meant we had responsibilities. A man in my position served the Empire, and that was that. Luckily I did have a knack for horse-soldiering. So I spent years away from home, returning on holiday, meeting them in Egypt a few times. But I lost that edge I'd known when I was younger, living here at Carlyle. So if my father ever found his secret tunnel, I know nothing about it. But if he had found one, I'm sure he would have written to me about it."

His eyes narrowed, as he studied the fire. Camille thought for a moment that he had forgotten all about her, he seemed so deep in thought. She was afraid to move, afraid to distract him, afraid to create a greater contact herself. She was amazed by the overwhelming desire not to escape, but to draw even closer. The words he had said earlier haunted her, for she suddenly felt nearly naked, as if they were flesh against flesh. Again, she tried desperately to remind herself that this man might not be sane, that his temper could flare as hotly as the flames before them. But the logic of such facts failed her as she breathed his scent, felt his powerful length beneath her.

"He would have written to me," he murmured. Then he stared at Camille again. "And that's just it. There should have been…well, there should have been a half-written letter somewhere. My mother kept her journals. My father wrote letters. He would send one and then begin another. But when he died, there was nothing."

She swallowed, trying to dredge her mind from sensation, and reply with reason and intelligence. "They had just made the discovery, right? Opened the tomb? It had been just a matter of days. Perhaps your father simply hadn't had time to write," she suggested.

"Perhaps. But he was obsessive."

"Imagine," she murmured softly.

"Miss Montgomery!"

She looked at him and saw that he was smiling beneath the mask.

"I rather believe that, were you in my position, you'd be no less determined. After all, you are here, burdened by hospitality in order to save a wretched thief from his just rewards."

She started to stiffen again, furious, but then realized that he had said the words to rile her, but with no malice.

"Thief—"

"Yes, thief! But the point is, you could do no less. You would not be able to live with yourself. So surely you understand my position?"

He was inclined toward her now, intense, yet ever so slightly teasing. She was aware again of the tripping of her heart, the windswept stagger of her breath, the vitality of the man. She longed to reach up and touch the cheeks beneath the mask, to feel his flesh. He was so close…and his lips were surely going to form over hers any second. She was aware of his touch. It was like a form of enchantment or intoxication. She wanted, yearned…

He drew back, hard again, distant, and rose in a single

strong, swift movement, setting her upon her feet. Yet he steadied her; she would have stumbled had he not.

"I've now kept you up half the night. I'll get you back to your room."

He walked to his own door, seeming stiffer, more severe than ever, restrained to total dignity, yet molten beneath the exterior of civility.

He brought her back to her door. "Camille, I do mean every word. Don't, under any circumstance, go wandering in the halls again. I pray God, I've made it clear that it could be quite dangerous."

She nodded. "I...enjoyed having Ajax."

"Yes, well, he's on duty. Out on the grounds."

"Ah."

"Camille..."

Her name had never sounded so like a warm whisper on the seductive air of night. There might even have been a touch of tenderness. And beneath that, something she had felt herself, deep and searing in her soul.

Again, he was so close, his head bowed down to hers. And she, who had sworn that such things could not exist, longed for more....

"Sleep well," he murmured, and stepped back. "Tomorrow will be another long day for you."

He turned and started out.

"Wait!" she heard herself cry, finding life, moving forward.

He paused at her door.

"What if I hear something in the night?" she asked.

He smiled. "Scream like bloody hell."

"And you'll hear me?"

His smile deepened. "Indeed, I will."

"You are so close, then?"

"The portrait there, of Nefertiti..."

"Yes?"

"It's a door. To my room. You need only pull the painting by the left side of the frame. Good night, Miss Montgomery," he said. And he was gone.

CHAPTER NINE

CAMILLE HAD BARELY LEFT the house when Brian was startled from his morning coffee by a visitor.

Tristan, shaved, neat and clean, and admittedly, appearing quite the gentleman, strode in upon him. He came in with strong, sure steps, his head high, fingers knotting and unknotting into fists at his side. Then he stopped. His chin went a shade higher. "Good morning, Lord Stirling."

"Good morning," he returned, not rising, just waiting. The fellow certainly looked to be in the best of health.

"I'll not make either of us out to be fools," Tristan said after a moment.

Brian lowered his head slightly, aware of the courage this was taking the man. "Aye, that's a good thing," he said.

Tristan squared his shoulders and continued. "I came here, thinking you'd not notice a little piece gone that might have paid the rent a good many day."

"Aye."

"But me lass is worth ten of me," Tristan said, and a tender humility came into his voice. "I'd not have her paying any price for me. So…"

"You know the underworld a bit, eh?" Brian queried.

"Well, it's not as if I frequent the truly degraded alehouses and brothels of the city!" he said indignantly. Then he frowned. "But, aye," he admitted with a weary sigh. "I do know a place or two where those of unsavory character are known to be found."

Brian leaned back, surveying the man. He was lean and spry, and he well imagined that at one time, he'd been a fine soldier, and had thus acquired his knighthood.

"Sit, Mr. Montgomery. There is coffee and food, if you've not breakfasted as yet."

Tristan's brow knitted into a wary frown. "Ye'd have me at your table?"

"Please."

Now more wary than ever, Tristan poured coffee with hands that suddenly shook so badly, Brian took over the task for him.

"Thank you," Tristan murmured, taking the cup, and then the seat Brian indicated. Once seated, he tried to state his case again. "She's everything to me, you see," he said softly.

Brian smiled, again lowering his head. "I intend her no harm."

"What may be no harm to one is like a lifetime of shame to another," he said.

"Ah, I see."

"She's not…she's not to be taken lightly, My Lord."

Brian leaned forward, his eyes straight and level with the older man's. "Sir Tristan, I assure you, no man would take your ward lightly."

"Well, frankly, sir, I'm disturbed. And there's no help for it!"

"She works for the museum—in Egyptology."

Tristan nodded, still frowning. "And mostly self-taught, she is."

"I'm escorting her to a ball, a fund-raiser."

"Aye, so I've heard."

"She indeed has her talents."

"Sir!"

"In Egyptology, Sir Tristan. Just as I believe you have yours."

Again, wariness and fear seeped into Tristan's eyes. He met Brian's gaze. "Apparently, me talents aren't quite what they once were. You caught me, you did."

Brian laughed softly.

"What do you intend to do, Lord Stirling? Scared as I am, I'll not hide behind me ward's skirts any longer."

"I intend to offer a business proposition."

"Sir!"

"Having nothing to do with your ward," Brian assured him.

"Then…"

"I intend to give you a piece to sell."

"What?"

"I need you to get out into the streets for me."

Tristan sipped his coffee, at a loss. "I came to steal a piece of ancient art, but now you intend to give me one to sell?"

"Precisely."

"Ah, Lord Stirling! If ye're meaning to teach me a lesson—have the coppers after me once I'm gone—ye needn't bother. I've admitted my guilt."

Brian shook his head. "Tristan, you're not listening to me. I'm offering you a position. I need you out on the streets. I need you to get into many a place I don't know, and find out if there are a number of pieces being sold off on the black market."

The man straightened. A light came into his eyes. "Are you serious?"

"Dead serious."

"I'd be working for you?"

"I'm assuming you and your man, Ralph, are known at a few of these places?"

"I know my way around the city, aye. And I know something about Egyptian artifacts, of course. I raised the lass, you know!"

"And taught her everything you know?"

Tristan frowned, not liking any suggestion that Camille was not a total paragon of virtue.

Brian was startled to feel a sudden tension himself. Could she really be all that she seemed, not just innocent of any conspiracy with her co-workers, but as impervious to such a hideous mask and reputation as she appeared? She knew his position and title—was that enough to make her blind? Yet she'd been eager that he know her own beginnings, so he would understand what a Pandora's box he could be opening, subjecting her to a social scrutiny. He hadn't given a damn where she had come from. But then, he had been doing nothing but using her. And now...

He rose, suddenly afraid that even his mask would not be enough to cloak the sudden agitation that had seized him. Last night he had felt alive again, *human* again, in a way he hadn't since it all began. Since he had heard the terrible news, gone into battle, wielded his own fury and felt the steel rip into his flesh. Nothing had disturbed the steadfast cold that had fallen over his heart, no matter what his charade, where he had been, what he had done. Until last night.

He hadn't realized what she could make him feel. It had happened slowly, and yet so suddenly. He hadn't lived as a monk, but he hadn't *felt* anything inwardly, either.

Last night there had been seconds of pure, unadulterated lust. And the temptation to touch and hold, to forget the world in a sea of carnal fire and energy had been almost overwhelming.

He let out a sound of irritation, suddenly angry with himself for letting his thoughts get away from him. He turned and stared at Tristan. "Spend the day with your valet, Ralph. Think, talk and make plans of where you might go on a selling mission. Return to your bed by night, though. I'd have the world believe you were in sorry shape until tomorrow at least. After the fund-raiser, you can rise, at long last feeling somewhat healed. Word will be out that you're looking forward to raising a few pints to your renewed good health."

Tristan stood, reminding Brian of a fierce little terrier. "I'll find out what you want to know, Lord Stirling," he swore. "That I will."

THE TRAFFIC GOING IN to the museum that morning was wretched. A pony cart had overturned on Russell Square, its load of vegetables spewing here and there. Despite the efforts of the police, people were everywhere, some trying to help the injured driver and collect his belongings, others trying to take what they could. Great carriages, bicycles, hansoms and other cabs were twisted about and caught in a jam. Onlookers stopped in their tracks, while those anxious to reach their places of business on foot tried to veer around them.

At length, Camille tapped on the roof and stuck her head out the window, telling Shelby that she would walk the remaining distance. Before he could stop her, she slipped out of the carriage and into the crowd.

Arriving at the museum late, she saw that they had already opened for business. She hurried through the exhibits and saw that a great crowd was arrayed around the terrarium. Aubrey had fed the snake.

With a shiver, she hurried on up to her office. Sir John was at his desk, but offered her no rebuke for tardiness. He merely gave her a weak smile.

"It's a mess out there, eh?" And he shook his head. "It's

worse and worse all the time! Ah, traffic in the city!" Then he turned his attention back to the graphs and records on his desk.

Symbols swam before her and she found her mind wandering. Just a little more than a year ago, each of the men in the department had been on the expedition. At first it had appeared that it would end brilliantly with an incredible discovery. Then triumph had turned to tragedy.

She left her work, running out of the room. Sir John remained at his desk. He looked up at her.

"Yes?"

"Um...Sir John. What happened when the Stirlings died?" she asked.

"What do you mean, what happened?"

"You were all there, right?"

A clouded look crossed Sir John's eyes. "Yes."

"They were brought back to England for burial, but the discoveries had just been made. Certainly there was a lot to be done after their deaths."

He looked at her, then shook his head. He stared back at his papers. "It wasn't so immediate. We'd been in the tomb, cataloguing finds. Most important objects had been removed, and many were already prepared for shipping. A telegram was sent to Brian, who apparently learned about the deaths right before a skirmish. He was wounded, but still managed to arrive quickly to Cairo. The bodies had been preserved in ice. He saw that they were returned to England, anxious for autopsies to be done, though God knows why. The cause of death was very evident."

"Did anyone ever find the snakes?"

"Pardon?"

"The asps. The creatures that killed them," Camille said.

"I don't believe so. I'm sure that a nest somehow got

into their rooms. Once they had killed, the snakes probably made their way out. Camille, many people die due to
cobra bites. It is an inherent danger when living and working in the desert."

"Of course," she murmured.

He looked back at his work, dismissing her, but she
walked over to his desk. "Was there an investigation?"

He looked up again. "Of course! Egyptian authorities
and English authorities were all called in. Good God, child,
George was the Earl of Carlyle!"

"Yes, yes, of course."

"I have work, Camille. And so do you."

She nodded and returned to her little workroom. What
usually fascinated her seemed dry today; her mind kept on
spinning. For several lines, she translated more of the
threat. Then she came to a stretch of symbols that excited
her. She spoke aloud, slowly.

"'Know that the Great Cobra, with its eyes of flame and
light, formed by Hethre's will and power, and by the creation of her own hands, will bring down the retribution of
the greatest nobility.'"

She stared at the text, carefully looked over her every
translation. Then she jumped up and ran back out to Sir
John's desk.

He was gone.

The newspaper clipping about the death of the Stirlings
lay on top of his other papers. Something pinned it down.
Camille walked around the table. A small pocketknife attached the paper to the wood, the point pierced through a
face in the picture. That of Sir John.

DESPITE THE OUTCRY that had arisen during the time of the
so-called Jack the Ripper murders, the East End had
changed very little.

Dirty, scrawny, wide-eyed children, already acquiring the look of street rats, sat on doorsteps and played in the streets. None came near Brian. They looked his way and scattered. Though in his Jim Arboc attire, he was still a man, bulkier with the workman's coat he wore, and still a man with eyes that seemed to warn of danger.

The idea of becoming Jim Arboc had been born a good three months hence, when the position in the museum became available. He had been willing to sweep up the offices of the curators dealing with Asian works, certain he could bide his time and thus arrange a transfer without appearing suspicious. Had this occurred just a bit earlier, he might have known Camille Montgomery when he had seen her at the castle. But the closest he had come before meeting her at his estate had been those times he managed to slip into the storage rooms and begin a slow and methodical search. Blatant accusations would not work, especially when he wasn't certain whom he should be accusing. Therefore, he had needed patience.

And as Arboc, he had learned to be a patient man.

Poor but honest seamstresses hurried down the roads, along with butchers, their aprons bloodied, and factory workers, hats pulled low over their eyes. Hawkers sold gin and meat pastries, most lacking meat but tempting hungry buyers with the smear of gravy. Legitimate businesses hired on immigrants for a few pence and long, tired faces were the norm. Prostitutes with rheumy eyes and broken teeth lolled by many a pub, and the stench in the area was enough to make one ill.

Shuffling along at his awkward but steady "Arboc" pace, Brian hurried after the figures ahead of him, keeping a distance. The two he followed came to an establishment with a sign that read McNally's Public House—All Are Welcome. He let the two enter and then followed behind.

There was a large group at the bar, and gin was flowing freely. Aye, as well it must, for the working women plying their trade there were long past their days of glory or seduction. "Gin blossoms" rode many a cheek, and a few of the noses had most obviously been broken more than once. But there were dark alleys in abundance, places to close one's eyes and seek only the gratification of the moment. That a few of the whores could entice the work-worn and world-weary fellows at the bar to pay for their gin made them attractive to the pub owner.

A few hardwood tables, broken at strange and odd levels, lined the area opposite the bar. He elbowed his way through the crowd, bought a gin and retreated to one of the tables. And watched.

Tristan Montgomery was obviously not a fool. He had changed his clothing before starting out on his trip, and now wore the jacket and cap of a dockworker. Ralph was likewise attired. And though he hadn't Tristan's jovial manner, he was a likely enough companion.

Tristan ordered his gin, complaining of the price, and flirted with the one prostitute who seemed to have all her teeth. Compared to the rest, she might have been considered in her prime. She was small, somewhat lithe and apparently glad of the gin he bought her, and ready to remain close.

"'Ave we business to discuss, gov'nur?" she asked him, playing with the collar of his jacket.

Tristan looked at the woman, a little brunette with dark eyes and a winsome smile. She had ferreted out the fact that Tristan, despite his attire and manner, was a cut above the majority of the clientele in the smoky gloom.

"Business, indeed!" Tristan said softly, producing a shining coin.

Those around the pair seemed oblivious to the transaction. Such business was done constantly.

"Shall we slip out? Or would you 'ave another gin, luv?"

Tristan caught the woman by the arm, moving her from the bar area and closer to the table where Brian sat, his hat lowered over his eyes. "I've real business, money business," Tristan told the woman. "And there's more of these for the likes of you if you can give me a lead on it."

"Oh?" The prostitute eagerly cocked her head.

"I've something to sell."

"Ah!" She frowned. "If it be jewels you've snuffed off a rich one—"

"Better than that. But I need a special buyer. I've something from—" He paused, whispering into her ear.

The whore backed away a bit, shaking her head with disgust. "Don't be tellin' me ye've got a mummy or the like! They're fire-fodder and little more! A chap sold one a while back, and all the amulets and little pieces that shoulda been in the wrappings were stole out already!"

Tristan motioned with a finger to his lip. "What I have is gold," he said. "The best you'll find on the market."

"And what do you know of the market?"

Her accent, Brian noted, was slipping away. He had the feeling that this particular lady of the night came to the bar with more than one agenda.

"So…others are selling such antiquities?"

"Oh, aye. And they be the best."

"Who is selling them?"

Tristan had a fierce grip on her wrist.

She struggled, aware that she hadn't taken on a drunken sot. "He ain't here now!" the woman cried softly.

"I'll be back tomorrow," Tristan said. He slid the coin into her hand, closed her fingers around it. "It's a business I'm coming in on," he said. "Now, you can give me a hand, get me the buyers, show me my competition and make good money. Or…"

"Or?"

"Well, it's a hard life, isn't it?" Tristan demanded.

"This coin isn't enough," she said flatly.

He grinned slowly. "Then we are understood." Tristan produced another coin. He stared at the woman, then nodded to Ralph, and the two went out.

The whore returned to the bar and whispered something to the burly man drying glasses behind it. The fellow whispered back. With a pout, the woman produced one of her coins. The fellow looked to the exit, where Tristan and Ralph had just departed. Then he walked to the far end of the bar and whispered to another man. He was lean, with a sharp, hawkish nose.

The man rose and exited. Brian did the same.

As Camille stood by Sir John's desk, he returned. Camille looked up.

"What are you doing?" Sir John demanded.

"I…I came out to talk to you."

"What is that paper doing on my desk? With my knife!"

She shook her head. "I just came out. The paper was here. And the knife."

Sir John frowned and walked to the desk. Angrily he ripped the knife from the desk, folded it and returned it to his pocket. He opened his middle drawer and swept the paper into it. Then he stared at Camille.

"Who was here?"

"I don't know."

Now Sir John was looking suspicious. "How can you not know?" he demanded. He sounded angry; his voice was rough. But, she thought, there was more than anger in it. There was fear.

"I was in my room working. I'm sorry, truly sorry. I just stepped out to talk to you, and this is what I found," she told him.

He shook his head, not really addressing her but wondering aloud. "I had a lecture…in the reading room. I spoke about the wonders of the Nile and the last expedition. I wasn't gone more than an hour." He sagged suddenly, nearly falling into his chair, then pressed his hands to his temples. "I've a headache, a terrible headache. I'm going home for the afternoon."

He rose, suddenly stronger again. He barely glanced at her as he hurried out.

She watched him go, worried. He hadn't even asked her why she had come out to talk to him. *Because he was afraid?*

She started to walk back to her room but her toe nudged something. Looking down, she saw that he had dropped his keys in his haste. Picking them up, she started after him. "Sir John!"

But he was gone. In fact, their entire work area seemed eerily silent. She hadn't seen Hunter that day—which wasn't unusual. But neither had she seen Aubrey Sizemore or Alex Mittleman. Not even the old fellow who cleaned was around anywhere.

She stood in the deep quiet for a long moment. She would never catch Sir John. It seemed she was alone.

She tightened her fingers around the keys. It was time to see the storeroom again.

BRIAN QUICKLY REALIZED that the hawk-nosed man from the bar was keeping pace with Tristan and Ralph. They wove through alleys and busy streets, then back into a section of alleyways again, coming near the river and the old Roman wall. Brian could see the rise of the White Tower across the river. Then that view disappeared.

They made a turn into a crowded street. That was when he saw the hawk-nosed fellow run up behind Tristan and shove him into a narrow, dark alley.

Brian followed in haste. Hawk-nose had a gun. By the time Brian made it into the little square at the end of the alley, he had it out and aimed at Tristan and Ralph.

"What have you got and where are you getting it from?" the fellow demanded.

Brian moved up behind him. He saw Tristan's eyes widen but he shook his head, and before the fellow could turn to see the danger behind him, Brian had lashed out. He struck the fellow's right arm with a crushing blow. The gun went flying into the dirt of the overgrown, trash-strewn alley. The fellow made a move for the knife at his calf, but Brian hooked him with a right jab, sending him flying back.

That was when the sound of gunfire ripped through the air.

CLUTCHING THE KEYS, Camille hurried back down to the exhibit area. It wasn't terribly busy, but still, she saw a few couples, students and scholars taking notes, art students with their workbooks out as they sat or stood before various statues and reliefs. The cobra, satisfied with its recent meal, was coiled and sleeping. Aubrey was nowhere to be seen.

With a deep breath, she retraced the steps she had taken with Sir John just a few days earlier, heading down into the bowels of the museum to the storage rooms.

The lighting was very dim, and it took her several seconds to adjust to it. But once her eyes were accustomed to the shadows, she was fine. She strode through aisles and stacks of cartons and treasures until she came to the Egyptian antiquities—specifically those boxes that had been brought back from the Stirlings' last expedition.

There were a number of mummies that were not in their sarcophagi, either having already been opened, or because they were from a mass burial in which they hadn't been allotted separate coffins. She glanced over the forms, noting that the wrappings had been done carefully and were of the best quality. In the latter dynasties, many of the embalmers began to shirk their religious fervor for that of earthly gain, doing poor work upon their clients.

She wasn't really interested in mummies at the moment, though. She went from box to box, reading the contents, searching for a mention of a golden cobra. If the piece had been put into the tomb as a special talisman— handmade by a revered priestess or witch—it had to be an exquisite work of art. Solid gold? Possibly. And the eyes…rubies? Diamonds? Gem stones at the very least.

But going crate by crate, she could find no mention of such a piece. And though she tried carefully to rummage through the open boxes, she couldn't find anything that resembled the description, either.

She returned to the boxes that held mummies, wondering if it had perhaps been something smaller, maybe buried with the mummy Hethre herself.

But she didn't think one of the casually opened mummies could be Hethre. No Egyptologist worth his salt would have opened the sarcophagus of such a renowned individual without all proper care and precaution. Just as the tombs might have sand traps, falling stones and other grave-robbing deterrents, so might such a coffin.

Frustrated, she stood staring at one of the mummies, somewhat saddened to realize that none of man's efforts could really stop the onslaught of death and decay.

Then, what dim lights burned in the storeroom suddenly went out. And as she stood amidst the mummies, the world went black.

"GET DOWN!" Brian roared, falling to the ground himself and rolling for the comparative shelter of a watering trough. He felt a burning sensation against his arm, and knew that he had been winged by one of the bullets.

Then, abruptly, the firing ceased.

He crept around the trough.

"Hey! Hey, there, old chap!"

It was Tristan's voice. Brian breathed a sigh of relief. Carefully, he looked around the trough. Both Tristan and Ralph were coming from behind the wheels of a broken-down carriage.

The man who had followed them was on the ground. Brian walked over and hunched down by him. A bullet had torn straight into the fellow's forehead. There was no question that he was dead.

Brian quickly rifled his pockets. He glanced up at Tristan and Ralph, who were standing by him, gaping like children who had wound up in a schoolyard fight gone bad.

"Get out of here, quickly, both of you," he said.

"What?" Tristan said thickly.

Brian realized that neither of them had the least idea of who he was. "Get out of here before the police come, before they want to know what you're doing here, and what your relationship was with this fellow."

"Right...right..." Tristan murmured.

"But who shot him?" Ralph demanded.

"A relationship with this fellow..." Tristan murmured. "I don't know the bloke!"

"He was in the pub," Ralph said, eyes widening. "Sitting at the far end of the bar, down from us."

"But if the police question us, we really don't know a damn thing," Tristan said.

"No," Ralph agreed.

"So, do you want to be questioned?" Brian demanded.

"No!" Ralph said.

Brian continued to dig into the man's pockets, but the fellow carried no identification of any kind. There was nothing on him but a few coins and a wad of tobacco.

He looked up. The pair remained, just staring down at him. "Go!" he urged them. "Go, quickly."

He stood himself and surveyed the small square. It was surrounded by houses, the kind that had once housed Flemish weavers but which were now the typical, wretched housing for the poor, where single rooms were often home to over ten family members. Each house would have at least seven or eight rooms. Two of them were three-storied. Each had a back balcony or spit of flat roofing.

The two still stood there, waiting.

"Get!" Brian warned.

They started for the alley, but Brian could hear police whistles. There was a path between the two houses straight back and to the right.

"That way."

Brian rose and pushed the pair forward. He needed more time to linger, but he didn't want to be questioned by the police, either.

With him propelling Ralph and Tristan forward, they reached another small yard in what would be the front of the first house. He shoved them toward the crowd and hurried in the other direction.

CAMILLE STOOD, gripping the crate that held the mummy she had so recently pitied, and listened. At first, there was nothing. Then she heard a rustling. The sound was coming from within the box.

It couldn't be! Though her heart hammered, she refused to believe that a mummy had come to life. But if it hadn't, then someone was there. Someone was in the darkness with her, standing on the other side of the crate, making the noise, searching as she had been searching, trying to scare her….

An image of the knife thrust into the newspaper clipping, right through Sir John's face, came to her mind's eye. This person was interested in more than simply scaring her.

She fought to remain silent, to back away from the crate. Then she heard the voice. The whisper. The rasping sound.

"Camille…"

She had nothing whatsoever that could be used as a weapon. She loathed being terrified, and she didn't believe a word about curses, but…that voice. It seemed to rake right along her spine. To tear into her very flesh. There was something about it that was…evil.

She had to run, but it was impossible in the clutter and the boxes, in the darkness. And if she was stopped, what then?

"Camille…"

It came again, like sandpaper against the air… taunting, amused. Warning. Deadly.

She gritted her teeth and turned, totally blinded. She instantly walked into a box. She heard movement from behind her. Someone was coming around the side of the crate, seeking to find her, blinded in the darkness, as well.

She groped at the box and reached inside, hoping desperately to find some kind of weapon. Her arms gripped something covered in dust, but long and hard. A scepter, perhaps. She curled her fingers around it, felt for the box and circled around.

She remembered something of the pattern of the storage cartons and boxes and began weaving her way through. She heard footsteps, bold now, following in her wake. And again, the voice.

"Camille…!"

The door out! She could see it ahead, for it was surrounded by tiny slits of light. She raced for it.

She heard the footsteps, felt someone reach out with bony fingers…catching her hair.

She screamed, turned with her weapon and lashed out, then tore for the door and the light that lay beyond.

CHAPTER TEN

"TRISTAN, WHAT ARE YOU DOING, man?" Ralph demanded.

Tristan had stopped. They were a good three blocks from the square, surrounded by folk, some who were rushing toward the sound of the police whistles, others who just kept walking or going, accustomed to the sound. Murder was not a rarity in this area.

"Come on, let's get far away. You heard the old bearded fellow."

Tristan shook his head. "Ralph! Good God! You must know who that was by now."

Ralph stared at him, arching a brow. He looked around, anxious to be on his way. It was quite one thing to be a petty thief. He wasn't accustomed to the way the world had gone since Tristan came up with the brilliant idea to help himself to a bit of Lord Stirling's property. Until today, the debacle had stood rather well with him—lounging in the fine apartments granted him among the servants' quarters at the castle, eating well, living the life of a gentleman, completely at ease. But now! Well, he wasn't accustomed to being shot at.

Tristan sighed, looking at him. "It was Lord Stirling."

"No!"

"Aye."

"No!"

"Aye!"

"Lord Stirling!" Ralph breathed. "But if he was there, in such a disguise, why did he send us in?"

"Because we do know our way around such places, and we have been known to pawn off an illegal trinket or two," Tristan said.

"Fine. That's all well and good. So let's move on now, shall we. He told us to go."

Tristan shook his head, eyes sparkling. "I'm going back."

"Back! To the place we were nearly shot down along with that fellow!" Ralph said with amazement. He tried hard to draw forth some serious authority and dignity. "If it was Lord Stirling, as you say, he very sternly ordered us to move on!"

"Of course, he didn't want us involved in the questioning." Tristan shrugged. "It's not likely the murder of such a bloke will draw much attention, but in case it makes the newspapers at all, he wouldn't have us involved."

"Right. So let's not be involved."

"We're not involved any longer. We're just part of the curious public, drawn to the excitement. A man shot dead in a square! They'll be people amassing around the scene now, so we'll not be noticed in the least."

"I don't want to go back to see a dead man bleeding on cobblestones!"

"Ah, but people do! Just as they used to line up for a public hanging. Come on, my man. We'll not be noticed. And we may hear a thing or two."

"Oh, Tristan!" Ralph moaned.

"We need to find out what we can for Lord Stirling," Tristan said firmly. He turned and started back the way they had come.

Groaning again, Ralph followed in his wake.

THE DOOR CLOSED behind Camille, and the world was suddenly flooded with light. The chamber to the storeroom door, however, was empty, so she tore for the stairs, racing up them.

She burst out into one of the galleries, where a few people milled around exhibits. Everyone turned and stared at her. One woman gasped; all looked at her in shock.

For a moment she was simply frozen in place, not understanding. Then she looked down at the weapon she had grabbed from the mummy crate. She was holding an arm.

Wrapped, its linen darkened by years of entombment and decay, it indeed appeared to be some kind of strange and grisly trophy.

She dropped it in horror. Then, realizing she was about to create a scene in the gallery, she smiled ruefully, smoothed back her hair and retrieved the ancient body part. "I'm so sorry. A new exhibit," she explained.

She tore for the stairs to the offices, her mind racing. The logical thing to do was go for one of the policemen charged with museum security. But then she would have to explain what she had been doing in the storeroom. Still, whoever had been taunting her might still be lingering in the storeroom. It was time to catch the culprit!

As she ran into the office, determined to go for help and damn the consequences, she was startled from immediate action when she saw that Sir John's desk was occupied.

Evelyn Prior was waiting in the chair.

"There you are, dear!" she exclaimed. "I was getting worried…a workday and no one about. No one at all. Why, Camille, what's wrong? You look as if you've seen a ghost." She raised a brow. "And you're carrying its earthly remains around with you."

"I…I'm fine," she murmured. Her heart was thundering. She wasn't in the least sure why—she had liked Evelyn very much—but she was suddenly wary. Was it possible that Evelyn had been down in the storage vaults, that she had been the one whispering Camille's name and was now sitting at the desk, just to allay suspicion?

"Oh, this!" She forced herself to smile. "Yes…terrible of me. I must get it back. I'm embarrassed to say that I saw a rat and panicked. One would think I'd be accustomed to dealing with such things, but… Excuse me, I have to—" She broke off. "Evelyn, what are you doing here?"

"It's after four, my dear. I've come with Shelby to take a ride out to the sisters' cottage with you. We must make sure your gown for tomorrow night is complete, that it fits perfectly and that you'll be ready for the ball."

"After four?" Camille murmured. "Of course, I need just a minute…if you don't mind waiting? Excuse me, Evelyn, I'll be right back."

She exited the offices, closing the door behind her. It was absurd to think that Evelyn might have been stalking her in the storeroom! The woman was Brian Stirling's right hand, so it seemed. And she had been calm and serene, simply baffled by the fact that no one had been in the office. And surely more baffled than ever to see Camille with a death grip on a mummy's arm.

She turned quickly, realizing that there was definitely a reason for her to find one of the officers and hurry back. The mummy's arm was still in her hands. She needed to return it. She tried to hide it in the folds of her skirt, not wanting to shock any more of the museum's visitors, then realized there was an even more serious matter. She had dropped Sir John's keys somewhere. And she had left the door open.

She found the guard resting in a chair in the hall with the Rosetta Stone. She was grateful to discover the man on duty was a fellow they all called Gramps, though his real name was James Smithfield. He had drawn museum duty, she thought, because of his age. He was a tall, lean man, left with just a few wisps of gray hair beneath his hat. His powder-blue eyes were faded but kind, and he had wonderful stories to tell about his early days in the police force.

"Jim!" Camille said, shaking him by the shoulder.

He had apparently dozed off. He looked up with a start. He saw her face, knew he shouldn't have been napping on the job and jumped up. "Camille!" He looked around, certain there must be some trouble.

She had to smile, despite her situation. "I need some help, please."

"Yes, yes, of course, what is it lass?"

"I had to check on something in the storeroom. I think someone was down there with me. I'd like to make sure it's empty and lock it back up."

He frowned. She wondered if he knew that she didn't really have the authority to be prowling around the storeroom.

"Someone prowling about?" he demanded.

"I'm sure it's nothing. Maybe even my imagination. But if you wouldn't mind coming with me?"

"Of course not, lass! It's my job!"

Feeling a great deal more secure—even if James Smithfield was nearly as old as some of the museum's exhibits—Camille led the way.

The door to the storeroom was still closed, but unlocked. And when Camille pushed it open, the dim lights were back on, just as if they had burned as they were supposed to, all throughout the day.

She retraced her steps, Jim behind her, poking around containers here and there, determined that he'd not be caught napping on the job again.

Camille found the carton with the armless mummy and did her best to return the limb. The keys were on the floor by the massive container. She picked them up. Jim was looking at her, a slight smile teasing his lips. "Now, lass, there's no one here, nothing looks amiss! Have you been listening to much lore about mummies and curses? Whatever they thought, Camille, these fellows don't rise again and come after the living! Ah, but then you're young. Easy to let the mind find fear in such things, eh?"

She forced a smile. "No, I think someone was down here. But I do agree, whoever it was is gone now."

"Probably just someone from another department," Jim said, still smiling pleasantly, amused, yet affectionately so. He was a good man, confused as to why certain things were so important to the scholarly types in the museum when the sums they cost could feed dozens of families for weeks on end, but still tolerant. A most fatherly figure.

She caught his arm. "Thank you, James."

"Any time you need me, Camille."

"Thank you."

When they left the storeroom, Camille saw to it that the door was securely locked, though she wondered just what good she was doing. It had been locked when she first arrived!

There were other keys out to department heads. Other people had access. But another department head wasn't likely to make all the lights go out! And she was certain that it wasn't a curator from another area who had been in the darkness with her.

They walked back. As they neared the Rosetta Stone, he paused. "I won't be saying a thing about this, you know." And he winked at her.

She started to tell him that it was all right, but then decided that she would be glad of his silence.

"Thank you, Jim," she said, and started back for the offices.

Brian had barely finished treating the wound where the bullet had grazed his arm when there was a tap on his door. Ajax, sitting sentinel before the hearth, lifted his head and thumped his tail.

"Yes?"

"It's Corwin, My Lord."

"Come in, please."

He tied the mask at the back of his head as the fellow entered.

"What is it?" Brian asked.

"The fellow, Sir Tristan Montgomery, is here to see you."

"Send him in."

Corwin nodded and Tristan entered. "Good evening, Lord Stirling."

"Good evening. So…you have a report to make? You found a place where antiquities are being sold on the black market?"

"You know that I did," Tristan said quietly and with a great deal of dignity.

Brian stared at him for a minute and then shrugged. "I will assume then that you and your cohort made it safely away before the police arrived?"

"We made it away, but we went back," Tristan told him.

"Oh?" Brian was definitely surprised. A man with Tristan's past didn't usually seek out the police.

"I thought you'd want the bloke's name," Tristan said.

Definitely surprised, a smile on his lips, Brian walked to a small side table with a brandy decanter and glasses and poured out two portions.

"Indeed," he said, handing a glass to Tristan.

"He was a shady character, well-known to the coppers. Joseph Buttonwood. As of late, he's not been the type to be in the clink. Apparently, that's what got the coppers most suspicious of him. Seems they suspected he was doing some dirty work for someone maybe of a higher class, since he'd given up his street robberies in Mayfair."

"I see," Brian murmured.

"City of London bobbies have the case—we were within the mile," Tristan continued. "But there's not much interest. The detective who arrived at the scene after the street boys is a jaded old fellow, Sergeant Garth Vickford. He thinks it's well enough that the criminal element take out the criminal element, for it avoids a trial and saves the Crown and the taxpayers money. I don't think that there will be much of an investigation."

"You found all this out?" Brian asked.

Tristan shrugged. "I know how to get close and listen."

Brian took a seat in the great upholstered chair before the hearth. For a moment, he didn't reply. Despite the amazing fact that he was closer than he had ever been before to an answer, he was momentarily distracted.

It was here that he had sat the other night, holding Camille. It was too easy to remember her scent, the softness of her skin and the way her eyes had looked into his, marbled and brilliant, golden flames and emeralds, not seeming to notice the mask and, apparently, oblivious to the fact that he was known as the beast, a man cursed and scarred beyond all hope....

"I dare say," Tristan continued, "that the dead man was no more than a runner, and his attack on Ralph and me probably foolish. That's why someone, maybe whoever he was working for or just someone with a higher place in the thieves den, decided that he had to be silenced."

"Yes, yes," Brian said. He stood. "Thank you. You did me a service today. You owe me nothing more. I hadn't really thought that I'd be putting your lives in danger."

"But you were there. And you took a bullet in your arm."

"A scratch, nothing more. And since I can't guarantee that I will always be there if there is trouble, I repeat, you have done me a great service. And you owe me nothing more."

Tristan stretched to his full height. "Lord Stirling, it's well known that you led men and fought not from behind the ranks, but at the head of them. But I, too, was a soldier for Her Majesty. I'm not a coward, nor do I love life over honor. I'm pleased to be of greater service."

"If I were to cause injury to you," Brian said quietly, "Camille would loathe me and never forgive me."

"If I were to refuse the just and righteous work offered to me by a man such as yourself and eschew the life I had been living, Camille would despair of me," Tristan countered. "Perhaps I didn't make a fine showing today, Lord Stirling. Perhaps, as well, I hadn't quite believed the truth in what you're seeking to discover. But I can take care of myself. And I will. Don't ask me to step back now. I'm in this, and I feel as I haven't felt in many a year."

Brian leaned down and stroked Ajax's great head, then rose and faced Tristan again. "All right. But I'll ask that you not take things upon your own shoulders. Nothing is to be done without my knowledge, and you will keep your own life and limb in mind."

Tristan grinned. "I'm back to bed then—worn and bruised and ailing! Just in case my Camie gets in early!" He saluted and departed the room.

Brian sat and stroked Ajax's head again. "What have I done?" he murmured.

THE SISTERS, Camille was convinced, were not just wonderful, they were fairy godmothers.

Despite the events of the day and Evelyn Prior's current company, Camille couldn't help finding excitement in the garment. She'd never worn anything like it in her life. Surely there had to be something magical about it, simply because it existed. In one day's time they'd created a gown so lovely that it was breathtaking, and it fit with absolute precision.

Of course, they had seen to it that she had the right undergarments. A lace-edged corset, matching petticoats, a perfectly sized bustle. Camille was amazed herself at just how alive, how glowing she looked in the dress. Against the color, her hair was dark and her eyes were pools of brilliance. And when she turned in it, she indeed felt like a princess. The bodice was low, but not too low. The little sleeves capped off the bodice, with the line an arc at her shoulders. The fabric shimmered over an ever so slight underskirt, and the beaded bodice fit tight to her natural curves.

"Oh, miss! You're too beautiful!" little Ally told her.

She smiled at the child, losing just a bit of her enthusiasm as she couldn't help but wonder about her parentage.

"Thank you," she told the girl.

"I helped, you know," Ally said proudly.

"You did?"

"Well, only a little. But they let me do a few stitches on the hem."

"Wonderful. And really, thank you so very much!"

The sisters were grouped together, proudly surveying their accomplishment with impish little smiles.

Evelyn Prior walked around her, nodding approval, yet Camille felt as if she were part of new furnishings that had been ordered for a room. She was meant to convey a certain appearance, and, as per agreement, she did so.

"Lovely, lovely," Evelyn said, then looked at the sisters with a smile. "So…let's get her back out of it. We've got to pack it quite carefully for the castle, and his lordship will be waiting."

"You can't stay for tea?" Edith asked, deeply disappointed.

"I'm afraid not. Lord Stirling awaits Miss Montgomery before having his own supper."

"Oh, that's too bad," Ally said.

Evelyn smiled at the child with great and honest affection. "Ally, dear, we can come back, you know."

Ally nodded with a bit too much wisdom for a child her age.

As they headed out, Shelby waited by the carriage door to help Camille. He offered her a smile and gruff words of encouragement. "There can be no woman, no lady, great or common, more beautiful than you at the ball tomorrow night."

"My deepest thanks. For all your kindness," she told him.

Evelyn was coming quickly behind them. Still uncertain as to why she was so suddenly suspicious of the woman, Camille slid into the carriage.

"I'M NOT SO SURE about this," Evelyn murmured. "I'm not sure at all." She had come to his quarters immediately following her return from the cottage. Camille had stopped by to spend time with Tristan, who had taken back to his bed.

Brian arched a brow beneath his mask. "You're not sure? You're the one who insisted I slide back into society, find a woman to appear on my arm. You thought it was all just perfect when Miss Montgomery walked into our lives."

"Yes, but…"

"But?"

"The girl is strange! And I do mean strange," Evelyn told him.

"How so?"

"She wasn't in her workroom when I arrived. I waited at Sir John's desk. And then she came back with…"

"Yes?"

"With a mummy's arm in her hands!"

"Evelyn, it is the department of Egyptology."

"Yes, yes, but what normal young woman runs around with body parts?"

"She must have had it for a reason."

"Maybe, but her behavior was beyond strange. She was totally disheveled, covered in all that tomb dust, hair escaping, somewhat ashen. And walking around with a petrified arm."

"Evelyn, you've been there when large grave sites were discovered. Locals and foreigners alike have used petrified mummies like firewood."

"Yes, but even I really don't like handling them!" she said with a shiver.

"How did the fitting go?" he asked, changing the subject.

Evelyn was silent a minute.

"Was anything wrong?"

"No. Everything was right. Unbelievably right," Evelyn murmured.

"Well, then…?"

"I don't know. I'm worried, I suppose. Well, let me go fetch our little mummy-loving belle for you." She rose and left him, pausing at the door one last time to look back, "I'm sorry, Brian. Yes, it was my idea, but the girl is weird."

Puzzled, he watched Evelyn go. Since he'd taken his old character of Arboc to the museum, he'd followed people, assessed their work. Nothing out of the ordinary had taken place, nothing at all. But something must have happened today!

Another tap on the door signaled Camille's arrival. He

bid her enter and told her gravely, "Good evening, Miss Montgomery."

"Good evening."

Her hair was damp, he noted. She had apparently bathed upon her return to the castle, taking precious moments from her time with her guardian before their nightly meal. Had the mummy dust been too much?

He pulled out her chair, poured the wine, then took his seat across the table from her.

"Long day?"

"Yes, it seemed so," she murmured.

"Did anything happen out of the ordinary?"

"Everything was out of the ordinary."

"Oh?"

"No one seemed to be working today."

"Sir John didn't come in?"

"No, he was in, but he left. Under peculiar circumstances," she informed him, eyes on his. "He had to give a lecture in the reading room. I went out to find him to discuss a piece referred to in the hieroglyphs. He wasn't there, but a clipping about your parents' last expedition was on his desk. His little jackknife was on the desk, as well—with the blade through his face in the picture."

"Interesting. Go on."

"Well, Sir John returned and was very distraught. Then he left."

"Do you think he's being blackmailed?" Brian asked.

"Blackmailed!"

"Yes, it happens. As you know."

"Um," she murmured dryly. "You think he knows something and he's being threatened?"

"Possibly."

"Do you know anything about a golden cobra with jeweled eyes?" she asked him.

"A golden cobra? No. I never saw such a piece listed, not on the crates that came here or those that went to the museum. The cobra was the symbol for royalty, of course, but I haven't heard of many such pieces. Was it supposed to be part of a funerary mask?"

"I don't think so. I don't know. But it's mentioned in the text I translated."

She leaned forward suddenly, looking at him intently. "I've been thinking, trying desperately to sort this all out. You truly believe that your parents were murdered, and that may well be what happened. But there must be a reason, a…"

"Motive?"

"Yes, exactly. If someone working at the museum really wanted to steal something for a great deal of money, well…there are many pieces worth a fortune. Yet to sell something here, in England, even illegally, well…someone would surely find out. Why have such a treasure without being able to show it off?"

"One might well find such a piece and get it to France, the United States, or some other country," he told her.

She nodded. "But still, if we're talking about someone at the museum, they would have the opportunity to steal many an object."

"But those objects on display are all recorded, accounted for," he said simply. "My turn. What else happened today?"

She eased back and shrugged. He thought that she was watching him carefully, weighing her words.

"Sir John dropped his keys. I used them to get into the storage room."

"And is that where you decided to inspect a mummy's arm?"

She looked at him with stark surprise.

"A little bird with a big beak told me," he said.

"You see, there was someone in there with me, and the lights went out."

He frowned fiercely, tension constricting his muscles. "You know that someone else was in there, and the place went black? Are you certain?"

She was staring back at him evenly. "Yes. Actually, I think it was Mrs. Prior in there with me. I'm going to assume Mrs. Prior is the little bird with the big beak."

"What!" He was so startled that he stood, not realizing he towered over her, or that his voice was harsh and rasping.

Her features went rigid. She didn't cower or back away. "I told you, none of the usual workers were in the museum. But Mrs. Prior was there."

"Yes, at the museum, and you found her in the offices. As to lurking around with the mummies, may I remind you that Evelyn was not just mother's lady's maid, she was her best friend."

She stood, as well, leaning toward him, her teeth clenched, her eyes flashing. "Fine! You started this, bringing me here every night to question me. I've tried to give you answers as honestly as I can. You ask, I answer. I'm sorry if you don't like the answers I give!"

"Are you supposed to be in that storeroom?" he demanded.

Her eyes faltered.

"Don't go in it again. Don't go anywhere in the museum where there aren't other people and lights, do you understand?"

"You are constantly asking me if I understand!" she cried. "Yes, I understand! You lost people you loved dearly. You owe it to them to know the truth. Yes, I understand! That someone might be dangerous, yes, I understand. You're using me in your own pursuits, yes, I understand that, as well. You're the fierce, rich, titled Earl of Carlyle, I even understand that. But I am heartily tired of you shouting at me, roaring like a beast. Do *you* understand?"

Her passionate outburst startled him into utter silence. With her words out, though, she, too, appeared at a loss, an impasse, not sure whether to fight further or retreat. She chose retreat, a dignified retreat. Tossing her napkin down on the table, she said, "Forgive me, Lord Stirling. It has been an excruciatingly long day."

She turned, heading for the door.

"Lock yourself in," he told her harshly.

At the door she paused, turning back. "Yes, *I understand*. And don't come out at night, because God alone knows what really goes on here!"

"That's what I'm trying to find out, Miss Montgomery."

"At the cost of all else!" she informed him.

With that she exited, not slamming the door but closing it firmly in her wake.

He was stunned at the sudden coldness, the loss of life and vitality that seemed to pervade the room. He was tempted to race after her, to stop her in the hallway and drag her back, by force if necessary. She didn't understand… And he didn't understand himself.

He swore vociferously. Ajax whined. He looked over to the hearth. "Sorry, old boy!" he said, gaining control. Good God, she was the ward of a thief who had just happened in here, and he was the damn Earl of Carlyle! A beast. An image he had created himself and seemed to be maintaining quite well.

CHAPTER ELEVEN

HE WAS CERTAINLY the most infuriating creature on earth, Camille decided. She hadn't slammed his door, exiting with all the dignity she could muster, but she slammed her own, simply because it felt good. Really good. She hoped she broke it, ripped the hinges right off!

But, of course, she didn't. The hinges and the door were solid. Ancient. They'd been working for hundreds of years and they would continue to do so.

She prowled the room restlessly, furious, and not completely sure why. He asked her to be his eyes and ears and then he didn't trust her! So he had known his precious Evelyn for years. She had been his mother's best friend. She was... What? Was she more to him? Another mistress? And the child, Ally...

"Why do I care?" she whispered miserably to herself.

But she did care. Even when she was furious with him, he was everything. A towering figure, seeming so indomitable, keyed with constant energy and fire. She knew the sound of his voice so well, the length of his fingers. She had watched his hands time and time again, and his eyes...

"He *is* a monster," she said aloud, but she knew the real problem was that she *did* understand him. And she was drawn to him for his passion and fury just as much as she was drawn to him for that gentle, tender side she had glimpsed so briefly.

She paced the room, admitting to herself that perhaps she shouldn't have suggested that someone he apparently loved and trusted might be working against him. It had just been a suspicion on her part, nothing solid.

Her fire was dying. She prodded the logs and ashes, took a deep breath and reminded herself that tomorrow would be a longer day. The fund-raiser would last long into the night. And she had her gown, her beautiful gown. For a few minutes, she would be able to shine, to dance in his arms.

Biting her lower lip, she changed into the nightgown Evelyn had supplied for her and crawled into bed. But she was loath to douse the lights completely, so she allowed the little lamp at her bedside to burn. She beat her pillow, determined that she was going to sleep.

She lay awake.

She wasn't afraid of mummies or curses. But that day, with the dead and all that they had taken with them to their graves, she had felt a terrible chill. And when she had heard that voice… She tossed, hit the pillow again and then went dead still.

There it was again…that sound. Like a scrape against rock from deep below. It was almost as if the castle were a living entity itself, groaning from the depths of its being.

She shot out of bed, listening. Nothing. Then…again.

She hesitated, frightened, yet so weary of being afraid that she wanted to race out into the hall, turn on all the lights, cry out her presence and demand to know why everyone wasn't awake and searching.

No! She couldn't race into the hall. Right or wrong, something warned her not to do so. Then her eyes fell upon the portrait of Nefertiti and she remembered his words.

If you need me, just pull on the left side of the portrait.

She hesitated, recalling how they had parted. But she couldn't stand it any longer, so she walked resolutely to the portrait, set her hand upon the left side and pulled.

The wall opened toward her. It was dark within his chambers, but there was a soft glow from his hearth.

"Brian?" She whispered his name.

Then she longed to close the panel, pretend that she had never opened it. She was suddenly aware of exactly why she hadn't gone into the hall screaming. She wanted to go to him alone. She still wasn't certain that he wasn't a little mad, that he hadn't taken his quest so far that he was creating the drama around him. Yet…

"Camille?"

His voice came to her, rich and reassuring through the shadows. And all anger was gone.

She stepped in, still half blinded by the dimness. He had risen and was wrapping a robe around himself, coming toward her.

"Did you hear it?" she whispered.

"Come in," he said, and she found herself doing so, shivering once she was on the other side of the panel. The fire burned low. She could make out the massive, draped and canopied bed, the wardrobe before it. A record player sat on a table to the right, and books and newspapers were scattered on various dressers and tables.

"Did you hear it?" she asked him.

"Yes," he said. And then he added, "Stay here."

"No!"

"Camille, I'm begging you, listen to me, please."

She realized then that the dog was by his side, whining softly. She saw Brian, felt him, sensed him, as he stepped by her, securing the hidden door. She couldn't make out the painting that had caused it to open from his side.

His hands fell on her shoulders. She knew then, too, that

before he had slipped on his robe, he had gone for his mask. She found herself wondering just how hideous his face might be. And not caring.

"Stay, please."

"But—"

"Camille, someone is playing for keeps."

"I don't want to stay alone!" she told him.

"I'll leave the dog."

"No! You need to take Ajax with you."

"I doubt that I'll discover more tonight than before. The noise always stops before I find the source. Please, Camille, wait here. Lock yourself in."

He must have decided to trust her, because he left without her agreeing, going out through the sitting room. She followed him, locking the door as he had commanded.

She turned around. There was more light here. Perhaps his grounds were a wild tangle, but the room had been cleared of their dinner and appeared spotless. She saw the small occasional table with its decanter of brandy and rushed to it, deciding to help herself. As she sipped it, she wondered if he didn't have at least a small suspicion that danger might come from within his own house. Why else insist that she lock herself in all the time?

She started, hearing a noise, closer this time. She turned around. And then she wasn't sure... Was someone trying the knob to the door? Had it turned or had she just imagined it? Was it twisting again?

BRIAN HURRIED DOWN the stairs, Ajax at his heels. It had taken Brian months, but he knew that the source of the noise came from the crypts.

He crossed through the great hall, the ballroom, into the chapel and then, as silently as possible, followed the stairs down.

On the crypt level, he came first to the large, cold, outer chamber. At one time it had housed instruments of torture, but that was long ago. It had been a workroom and storage area for his parents. There were two desks, his father's and his mother's, file cabinets, boxes and a number of the artifacts they had kept themselves for study. Cartons from the last expedition were piled high, some that he had gone through, some which he had not. All were neatly catalogued.

Beyond the main chamber were the family crypts. His parents were not there. They rested in Carlyle Church, centered in the farmland that surrounded the castle. No one had been interred in the family crypts in over a hundred years. The massive iron gates that separated the burials from the workroom hadn't even been oiled in aeons.

Ajax sniffed and barked and ran around the workroom. At last he stopped, sat, looked at Brian. The noise hadn't come again.

"Good thing I don't believe my own ancestors are rising, boy, eh?" he asked. He had gone over every inch of the stone that made up the work area. Now, he stared at the rusting iron gates.

"Tomorrow we get an iron worker in here," he said softly. "Come on, boy. There's nothing to find tonight."

Ajax followed him as he made his way back up the stairs. The castle seemed empty and yet mocking as he walked back through the great rooms. At his own door, he tapped lightly. It swung open immediately.

She was there, eyes brilliant, hair free and flowing down her shoulders. And that gown…sheer, soft, floating about her form like a wisp of cloud. He could actually see the beat of her heart as it thundered against her chest.

He pulled her to him before even closing the door. "What's wrong?" he murmured.

She didn't pull away. She lay against his chest. At length, he felt her shake her head.

"Night, darkness, the human imagination," she whispered in return. Then she pulled back, searching out his eyes again. "There was nothing…no one, right?"

"Oh, there is someone. I didn't find anything tonight, but I will." He smoothed back her hair. An ungodly agony suddenly burned through him. He needed to step away, but he didn't.

"You're cold again," he said. She shivered with a tremendous energy and every measure of movement against him was a stroke of the sweetest touch, bringing about a rise of heat that should have surely consumed them both.

"Cold," he murmured again, but the word that echoed in his mind was anything but. Her hair, so subtly scented, teased his chin and nose. Simply breathing was intoxicating. She lifted her head, and the eyes that met his were bright. He felt again that he could drown in the color, the marbling of emerald and gold, dark and light in one, the mere crystal of the tone allowing for a sheen that mesmerized. He touched her cheek with his knuckles, wanting to assure, and finding that his throat was thick, his jaw all but locked.

She whispered, "Not with you."

A groan ripped from his lips. He cupped her chin, his thumb padding over her lips before his mouth moved down upon hers. All the tension leashed within him became a vibrant explosion of want and need and desire. She tasted sweetly of brandy and mint. Her lips held for a moment, then gave. Again, he felt that he would drown in the wild sweep of staggering liquid and warmth the depths of her mouth seemed to promise. He was a man of reason and logic, but both fled. His fingers tangled into her hair, and just the silk of it was another unbearable sensation against his flesh. His hand swept down the perfect line of her back, cradled her hips, curved over her buttocks and drew her ever closer. Her fingers crept around his neck, and he realized that she, too, had discovered any bit of space between them to be too much. She craved the erotic contact of flesh against flesh, figure against form. Warning voices arose at the back of his mind and were promptly dispelled in another wave of stark desire.

He lifted her, swiftly striding into the next room where the massive bed awaited in the gloom lit only by dying embers. At her side, he hungered. As if some long-dormant energy had exploded from the deep, he felt the electricity of life and longing rip violently through him. His fingers played upon her face. Again he found her lips. His hands strayed over the gossamer fabric of her gown and found the fire beneath, the heat of her body and the feminine perfection of it. His fingers teased her collarbone and the fullness of her breast. She moved against him, volatile, smooth…a little gasp escaping her lips beneath the frenzied onslaught of his kisses.

He drew back, bones locking, muscles clenching, as a measure of sanity entered his mind. "You've got to go back," he told her, and the words sounded as harsh as they felt. But she didn't move, and he felt the rampant beating of her heart, the ragged draw of her breath.

She touched his face. "The mask," she whispered. "Please…you are not a beast to me."

He was lost, and he knew it. Chivalry was gone, and consequence meant nothing. He ripped the mask from his face, tossing it heedlessly to the floor. He kissed her again, and the true drowning began.

Her fingers moved tenderly over his face, seeking what she couldn't see. They were a caress over the length of the scar, a whisper of movement, and then they were tangled in his hair, drawing him to her.

He kissed her lips, her throat, the valley of her breasts. Tenderness fell to a growing passion as his hands caressed, his mouth and tongue teased. Urgency was like an explosive in his head, yet he forced the anguish, alive in the seeking, his kisses still reigning above the fabric, following the length of her, liquid fires touching against her abdomen, trailing to her hips, down to her thighs. She began to writhe, her touch light upon his hair, his shoulders. Then she began to move. Arching, sounds slipped from her lips, urging him on as the pounding of his heart pulsed through him like a wicked drumbeat.

His fingers moved to the hem of her gown, slipped beneath it and found naked flesh. He teased and sought and plundered. She tore at his shoulders, and her hands slipped beneath the open robe he'd worn until it was tangled around them like the gossamer sheet of her gown. He needed to touch her with all of his length, to press his lips, teeth and tongue to the softness of her bare skin and beyond. A cacophony clamored in his blood, as he brushed thighs and hips and abdomen anew, teasing in circles around the very crux of her sex, then delving a breath into the heart of her need and desire and giving free reign. She arched in a fierce motion, whispers tumbling from her lips. The hunger in him had grown to a deafening chorus, and when he heard the soft cry that tore from her lips, he rose above her at last, desperately leashing the fierceness of his hunger, parting her thighs, sinking into her....

He knew, in that distant corner of his mind, that there were seconds when he might have withdrawn, ordered her away. But then she touched him in the darkness, played her fingers over his face again, threaded them into his hair and drew him back to her, hungrily reaching for his kiss. They had both lost all reason. He drew her limbs about him.

As she began to move, the thunder of his blood beat to

a frenzy and filled his limbs, drove his muscles, rippled through his flesh. Her fingers dug into his back with a startling strength and her lips found his again and again. Then the explosion of his climax tore through him with a vengeance, ripping through blood, flesh and muscle, tearing through the heart and mind. He gripped her to him, falling to her side, arms cradling her against him as tremors shook them both, as the fires fell to ash and the rasp of breath slowly eased.

She was silent, head against his chest, and though sanity made a brutal return, she didn't pull away from him. He marveled anew at the scent and feel of her, and the way she remained against him.

"Sweet Jesu, Camille," he said then, smoothing the wild tangle of her hair. "God, I am sorry. Not sorry, exactly, what man could be? But—"

"Don't talk!" she begged.

"I've worked hard to gain a reputation as a beast, but it's not my desire to—"

She came against him violently, pressing a finger to his lips. "Don't talk!" she repeated.

"Camille, I'm the Earl of Carlyle, and I don't make a habit of—"

"I have always made my own choices!" she said fiercely.

"I shouldn't have—"

"Please, stop."

"If you were afraid—"

"Good God, it had nothing to do with fear. I made this choice! I am neither inebriated nor a fool," she told him.

He thought that she was close to tears now…when it was over. And it wasn't what he had done, it was what he was saying.

Baffled, yet unable to really rue his actions, he said

softly, "Shh!" He reached out, cradling her to him again. "You are truly unique," he whispered, and knew that his words were true. She had done far more than invade his senses. Then he added, "I will always see that you are cared for."

Ah, he was wrong again. She bolted up against him, chin high. And in the dim light, she was more exotically beautiful than ever, for the shadows accented the length of her throat, the slim line of her torso and the fullness of her breasts, splayed with the wild tangle of the curls and waves of her long rich hair.

"I will never need be taken care of!" she assured him. "I can take care of myself!"

"Camille…!" He was tempted to laugh—she was such a bristling little beauty—but he knew that would drive her away from him completely. He managed no more than a smile in the darkness and reached out for her once again, drawing her down to him despite the fierce protest she began. "We all need to be taken care of, now and then," he told her tenderly, and when she would have protested, he kissed her again. She strained against him for only a moment, and then all the wonders of discovery seemed to burst upon them again.

Yet she drew away, murmuring, "I should return to my own room."

"No," he told her. "Lass, the damage is done."

Again, he had uttered the wrong words. "Damage! I am not damaged!"

He pulled her back. "No. You are perfection," he whispered, and he knew that her protests and anger had not been for him but for herself. And he knew that she had truly chosen to be with him, despite logic, reason—and her own birth.

And he was humbled.

"You are sheer perfection," he told her again, and began

slowly, with the utmost tenderness, to make love to her, striving to seduce and cherish. Sensual, exquisite, she gave as sweetly as she received. Perhaps she had been right all along. They shouldn't talk. For when they came together, the natural beauty of being a man and a woman in one another's arms seemed to demand no explanation.

Later, as she lay against him, nestled, he whispered again, "You are truly perfection, Camille."

She whispered back, "And you, My Lord, are no beast."

In the morning, as faint whispers of light began to ease the darkness of the room, he rose carefully and found his mask.

The night was gone, and day could be far too brutal.

CAMILLE MADE HER OWN CHOICES, but that didn't mean she didn't make mistakes. Yet, when she awoke, the memory of the night still vibrantly clear, she knew that she had done what she wanted. And she understood her mother as she never had before.

The first emotion she had ever felt for Brian Stirling had been anger. But in seconds, she had been awakened and aroused. He was like no man she had ever met. And ever since, he had created more turmoil within her, whether he evoked tenderness or fury. The brush of his fingers had elicited a fire in her flesh, while the sound of his voice had entered into her mind. And finally, the tempest he created had made its way into her heart. All the sound logic and wisdom she had embraced for a lifetime had deserted her, and she had begun to fall in love with the man.

Even as she lay in the light, she tried to deny the possibility of such an emotion. Yet she was certain that nothing less would have allowed her to throw such caution to the wind. She had brought about what had happened. She had wanted it more than she had ever wanted anything in her life. She had wanted him. And now… Dear God, she was her mother's child.

Tears suddenly sprang to her eyes for the woman who had loved her so dearly and with such devotion until the harsh realities of life had swept away dreams, health and, finally, her last grip upon life itself.

Tristan had then been there for Camille. But if she were to have one, who would be there for her child?

She rose swiftly, finding her nightgown and fleeing back behind the picture. In this room, the great portrait was of Rameses II, and she had to grip it by the right side to force the hidden door to give.

She was shaking when she bathed, at war with herself, trying to convince herself that one night's abandonment to the heart and senses did not necessarily create a new life.

In the mirror above the sink, her face was ashen and grave. Yet, she had made her choice. She would not take that night back, whatever the future might hold. It would be a long day, and a very long evening. She would have to face him again, the man with whom she had fallen in love, whom she knew too well and didn't know at all.

Just then she remembered one thing. He had taken off his mask…for her. Though the light had been dim, she knew that he had been living a lie. He wasn't a beast at all.

"HERE IT IS!" Evelyn said. "There's a small mention of the shooting of a criminal, page seven of the *Daily Telegraph.* The staff journalist seems to be taking a few liberties with his reporting!" She looked across the table at Brian. Only then did her words register in his mind, he was feeling so distracted that morning. "Brian!" she said firmly, demanding his attention. "I found mention of the dead man in the paper!"

"Sorry. Let me see it, please." He took the paper from

her, found the small column and read aloud. "Violent death in Whitechapel. Thief is shot down in square. No witnesses found."

The notation went on to say that the detective in charge was certain the man had been shot by a fellow miscreant. The reporter's words implied that those who lived by such means died by such means. At least the writer had changed the old quote a bit.

He should return to the pub, he thought, but he was loath to do so. If he ever needed to be at the museum, it was today. Had there really been someone in the storage area, following Camille? Were they trying to frighten her? Or worse?

Good God, Camille had thought that it was Evelyn. And Evelyn, it seemed, thought that Camille was losing her mind, or up to something that she shouldn't be. He had been the suspicious one at first. But now he knew that Camille was as honorable and honest as it was possible to be.

A niggling thought gave him pause. Did he know it? Or was he now so entranced by the woman that he was falling into place, exactly as planned? He forced the thought from his mind.

He had lived in suspicion for so long that he didn't know how to trust in anyone. But he was suddenly frightened as he had never been before, afraid of what he had done. Afraid for her.

He didn't dare risk following up on the events at the pub, or searching out more information on the dead man. He would have to tell Tristan and Ralph that they weren't to go snooping that afternoon; he didn't dare risk their lives, either. He had to be at the museum.

He rose abruptly. "Evelyn, ask Shelby to see to it that Miss Montgomery leaves the museum by four at the absolute latest. We have to be dressed and back by eight-thirty."

"Brian, what are you—" Evelyn began, but he was already treading quickly, wanting to be at the museum before Camille arrived.

A new sense of urgency had seized him. Before, his efforts hadn't taken him anywhere. But then *she* had come into his life.

THAT DAY, THANKFULLY, was so busy that Camille had little time to think. Exhibits were being moved, caterers arrived to set up in the Egyptian hall and guards prowled everywhere. Whereas no one had been around yesterday, today, everyone was in attendance. Even Lord Wimbly was working, eager that the seating for the evening be arranged perfectly, which meant that those who would supply the best donations to future expeditions and the upkeep of the museum itself had to be in prime positions.

Aubrey was directing most of the painstaking menial labor, barking at the poor old fellow who seemed big enough to manage what was needed, but who was so stooped and gray, it seemed a crime to work him so hard. Aubrey's temperament was not the best, and he only showed signs of tolerance when Lord Wimbly was about.

At one point, there was a major argument over the cobra.

"It's got to be out of sight for the evening," Sir John insisted.

"Don't be ridiculous, John!" Lord Wimbly protested. "We're leaving up the display on Cleopatra. Her legend is part of what so intrigues people regarding Egypt. The terrarium is perfectly safe!"

"The snake needs to go," Sir John insisted.

"I believe that I am the man to make that decision," Lord Wimbly said.

"Lord Stirling will be in attendance this evening."

Everyone, it seemed, stopped and stared at Camille, who, at that point, had been rescuing an ancient canopic jar.

Sir John turned back to Lord Wimbly. "Does he need such a reminder of the past?" he inquired quietly.

Lord Wimbly looked at Aubrey. "All right. The cobra should be moved into the offices," he said brusquely, determined not to let it appear to anyone that he was not the man directing all their efforts.

"The cobra must be moved!" Aubrey muttered, then gritted his teeth, as if remembering that Lord Wimbly could end his employment at will. "There's been a lot left to the last minute, but I'll get to it."

"I can move the terrarium," Alex said. "Old Arboc can give me a hand."

Outside help had been brought in for the day, but those in the department were determined to deal with their precious artifacts themselves. At one point, Camille was sent to the office to find a roster on Sir John's desk; she was startled to find him there, his hands folded prayer fashion below his chin, his eyes appearing distant.

"Sir John?" she asked quietly. "Are you all right?"

He started. "Ah, Camille."

She was surprised by the assessing look he gave. He saw her on a daily basis, but it was as if he expected to see something new in her.

"Dear Camille. Yes, yes, of course. I'm fine."

"You seem very worried."

"Do I? I guess that I keep reliving the past, now that Lord Stirling has entered our lives again."

"Are you starting to think that…"

"That someone might have murdered his parents?" He shook his head. "No…no. It's just too heinous a thought. Why in God's name would anyone have wanted to harm the Stirlings? They did nothing but give to the museum."

"Right. They gave *to* the museum," Camille murmured.

"What do you mean?" Sir John asked sharply.

"Some of the artifacts found are priceless. Priceless objects are tempting to thieves. Some thieves would murder for gain."

"Artifacts are catalogued, Camille. No one can just make them disappear."

"They haven't been catalogued if they haven't actually been found within the boxes shipped here from Egypt."

"My dear, why kill someone for something that hasn't even been discovered?"

"Because it's known to be somewhere." She hesitated. "Sir John, I found a reference to a piece I haven't seen listed anywhere. A golden cobra. And I think that it was studded with precious jewels. Sir, just a piece, even taken apart, would be worth…well, it would be priceless."

He shook his head. "There is no golden cobra."

"I believe there was."

They were interrupted when Hunter came striding into the room. "Camille, what's taking you so long? Lord Wimbly is becoming a bear out there, and you don't want to get on the old fellow's bad side, do you? Or…do you not care anymore?" he asked.

He sounded bitter and hurt as he looked at her, but she was still tempted to slap him. He and Alex were both behaving as if their friendship allowed them such affronts.

"Hunter!" Sir John said, appalled for her.

"Sorry, Camille," Hunter said, but he didn't mean it. "She is abiding at the beast's castle!" he reminded Sir John.

"Take the list. Bring it in to Lord Wimbly." He rose, shoving the list at Hunter, who could only scowl as he left them.

"I believe he was really quite enraptured with you, my dear," Sir John murmured. "Come!"

"Come?" she said. "Where? Sir John, we need to be in the hall—"

"To the storeroom."

"Sir John, I took your keys and looked in the storeroom, reading the contents of all the cartons yesterday."

He frowned. "You took my keys?"

"I'm sorry. You had left them, and I had found the reference…."

He started out, his keys in his hand. She followed, certain that they would be stopped when they went through the hall. But they didn't go through the hall. She found out then that there was indeed another way down to the storerooms as Sir John led her past a few doors and through a maintenance room. She was lost for a moment as they traveled the back halls, but then they descended a staircase and arrived at the door.

"Sir John," she said quickly, breathlessly. "Someone followed me down here yesterday. The lights went out while I was in here. Whether you want to believe it or not, something is definitely going on that isn't right at all."

He glared at her, pushing the door open. She followed him in. He was like a man obsessed suddenly, going from carton to carton. He thrashed carelessly through packing, shaking his head all the while. "I would know!" he said.

Once again, Camille was startled by a noise. The old fellow, Arboc, came around one of the great shipping cartons, clearing his throat as if he had just arrived. "They be wantin' ye up the stairs, Sir John," he said.

Sir John seemed to regain some sense of sanity. "Yes, of course! Let's go, Camille. Tomorrow…we're open tomorrow. Yes, I'll come in then."

As if barely aware that Camille had followed him there, he headed for the door. The old man shuffled before them. They returned upstairs, where things now seemed to be coming to a place of order. Lord Wimbly had left, needing to take time with his personal barber and valet before the event began.

"Sir John, if you would just give the seating arrangements a final inspection?" Hunter said.

Sir John took the list. He wasn't really seeing it, Camille knew.

"Yes, fine," he said.

"I'm leaving," Hunter told him. "I have to prepare." He looked over Sir John's shoulder at Camille, then walked around to her. "You'll forgive me, Camille. And may I beg a dance from you this evening?" He offered her a rueful, truly apologetic smile.

"At your own risk," she assured him, smiling back.

"I swear, my dear, you will be able to follow me," he said lightly, then turned, striding out.

Hearing someone behind her, Camille turned. Alex was there, looking tense and white.

"What about me, Camille? I haven't even a 'sir' before my name."

"Alex! Of course I'll dance with you," she said with a sigh.

"I may never have any kind of title," he said quietly, "but we are living in a great age, and I could become a very rich and powerful man one day. Stranger things have happened." His smile seemed a little wistful.

"Alex, I swear to you, my position here is so very important to me because I don't ever want to care about someone just because they have wealth or a title. You are my friend, and your finances will never matter to me. I'll be happy to dance with you at the ball."

He nodded. "But—"

"But what?"

"You are coming with *Lord* Stirling."

"He asked me."

"But his title means nothing to you? You are enduring the dictates of a beast?" he said.

She sighed, trying to keep her temper. "His title means nothing to me, Alex, nor does his wealth. Nor does his face or the destruction thereof! There is a very decent man beneath the facade."

"I don't believe it," Alex murmured.

"I'm telling you—"

"No! Camille, please, I beg of you! Let me tell you— no! Warn you. You're falling under some kind of spell with this man. And you really don't know him. He is vengeful! He is coming here to destroy us all, not to renew his interest in the museum."

She looked around. Only the caterers and musicians were moving about, and they were at a distance. But entering the great hall was Shelby.

"I have to go, Alex. Please believe me, Brian Stirling does not want to destroy us all."

"Ah, *Brian* Stirling. So you are becoming more and more…intimate."

Despite herself, her cheeks burned. "I have to go," she told Alex.

"Camille, wait, please!" he said.

"What, Alex?"

He stood humbly, words forming on his lips but not finding voice. He reached out, touched her hair. "I just care for you so much. I dreamed that one day…that one day I might be the right man for you. We truly find the same things fascinating. We're of the same social strata. It wasn't the right time, but I always knew we were perfect for one another. I've…oh, dear God, this is so difficult. I've been in…in love with you since I first saw you. And I believed that one day I would have what I needed to…to ask for your hand. In marriage. And I thought that you cared about me. But now…" He finished miserably.

She caught his hand, held it tightly. "Alex, I care about you very much. You are my dear, dear friend!"

"But you'll never love me, will you," he said. "And you might have, if it weren't for him."

"I'm a guest at the castle, Alex."

He looked up at her intently. "Not a guest in his bed?"

"Alex, I will not forgive the rudeness with which you have been speaking to me much longer," she told him.

"I apologize for my rudeness, sincerely," he said. "I can't help it. I'm so afraid for you. It would be better if you had engaged in a liaison with Hunter! But, Camille, I am the one who will be there. For you. Always. And I swear, I will be a rich man one day. Those I have bowed to will know my name!"

"Alex—"

He turned away from her, speaking over his shoulder. "Watch out for your precious 'beast,' Camille. The man is cursed. And the curse that haunts him will fall upon you if you stay too close beside him." He swung back. "He is obsessed. Maimed, bitter, destroyed, ready to sacrifice anyone for his goals. Camille, you are a sacrifice for him, whether you see it or not! Believe me, he's dangerous! And dear God, Camille, I am so afraid that you will discover the truth of my words!"

CHAPTER TWELVE

CAMILLE WAITED restlessly in the entry, feeling at war with herself. Edith and Merry had come to help her dress, which had actually been a tremendous amount of fun. The sisters were so sweet, so encouraging and so…normal!

She wished heartily that they had stayed on, that they had promised to be there when she returned from the gala. But though they were giving and focused on their task, willing to have a spot of spiked tea after they had trussed her into their elaborate creation, they were equally anxious to get back to their own little cottage in the woods. Still, they had been there for her. And the gown, she was certain, was magical.

When she was finally dressed, the sisters had gone for Tristan. And he had made her feel as if she really were a princess for the night. Edith and Merry had looked on like proud mother hens. But then they had gone, leaving her to her own devices. Tristan, after complimenting with all his love and pride, had seemed to weaken, and she had insisted he return to his bed.

She'd never worn anything so exquisite in her life. And seeing her reflection in the mirror, she actually felt beautiful.

The only thing that gave her pause was the topaz earrings left on her nightstand for use that evening. They had come with a note: *Please wear these tonight.*

Her heart was hammering. She hadn't seen Brian

since…she had fallen asleep at his side. As she had said, she had made her own choices. But now she felt acutely uncomfortable. She had almost decided not to wear the earrings. Their appearance had seemed almost like…a payment. But the note hadn't indicated that they were a present, only a loan.

She stood by the great hearth with the fire blazing. She shouldn't have been cold, but she was. The evening yawned before her like an abyss. Everything in her life was suddenly a charade, a lie, because every movement Brian Stirling made was an effort to draw out a killer.

And now, another mystery. Why was Alex so certain he was going to be a rich man? She felt ill. Alex had been on the expedition. Alex had free rein of the museum. He wasn't the keeper of the keys, but, as she had discovered, it was easy enough to get hold of Sir John's set. And what about Sir John and his oh-so-strange behavior? And the newspaper clipping on his desk? If he hadn't had it out, then someone had gone into his desk, taken the clipping and stabbed the point of the blade right through his face. And that someone wouldn't have been noticed in the office. *Alex?*

She turned away from the fire, seething over these dilemmas—very real and totally emotional. Then she saw him.

Despite the mask, he was the epitome of masculine attraction. He wore the swallow-tailed coat, starched white shirt, black vest and tie with both elegance and grandeur, carrying the proper white kid gloves in his hand. His buttons and studs were simple gold, as was the watch fob that seemed to arc at the perfect angle from his pocket. He walked down the stairs as a man who might not usually choose such attire, yet was able to wear it with the nonchalance of one who knew it well.

On the fourth step he stopped, staring at her.

"My God!" he breathed.

She felt a flush come over her, reminding her of everything she had felt the night before. On the one hand she longed to rush forward, but on the other, she wished she could run away.

"Good evening," she murmured.

He continued down the steps after a moment, then came to her, took both her hands, stepped away and surveyed her again. She was sure that she was as red as a lobster, it seemed her flesh was burning so hotly.

"And the earrings," he murmured. "They're perfect."

"I shall see that they're given back to you the moment we've returned," she said, and winced, for there was a brittleness to her tone that she had not intended.

He frowned. "I don't wish to have them back."

"As I've said before, I've no interest in charity."

"Their value is not so great."

"Nevertheless, I want no such gift."

His eyes, which had glittered so brightly with appreciation, took on a hard sheen. "I understand. You see them as something other than a simple gesture for the evening?"

"I don't accept gifts," she said stiffly.

He pulled her close. "My dear, if I were to give you a gift of appreciation, trust me, it would be of a far higher value."

She started to wrench away, but his grip was firm. His voice was soft, as if he was determined they would not be overheard, should anyone be near. "What on earth has gotten into you?"

"Nothing. I simply know the world for what it is."

"And what is that?"

"It's a place where…we all have our place!" she said a little desperately.

"Our place, at times, can be where we choose to be, Miss Montgomery," he said. "I have not meant to offend you. I knew the fabric of the gown, of course, and the earrings have been in the family for decades. Forgive me, but I assumed we'd come to a point where it was possible, at the very least, to be friends."

She exhaled slowly, wondering if what Alex had said hadn't gotten to her after all. She had wanted him, yes...so badly. And she had allowed everything that had happened, caused everything that had happened. Alex had been wrong, though. It had nothing to do with title or wealth. And perhaps the earrings had hinted of just such a possibility.

"I can accept no gifts," she said again, but gently, wishing that she didn't like the strength of his hands on hers, or that she didn't savor just being near him. Or crave the tenderness and flattery his eyes had offered.

"Did something happen at the museum?" he asked.

"Today? Nothing worth mentioning," she said.

He drew back, as if he were suddenly the one mistrusting her. "Nothing?"

"They prepared for tonight," she said. Had anything been worth mentioning? Sir John was acting strangely to her, but what did that mean, and how did she explain it? Lord Wimbly and Sir John had argued about the cobra, but there was no way for her to bring that up without mentioning why the argument had raged.

"Oh, my!"

They pulled apart as they heard Evelyn's voice from the stairway. She, too, was the height of elegance, with her hair piled high atop her head, a tiny diamond at her throat and a gown of cobalt blue over a sea of aqua petticoats. She had stopped halfway down the stairway, much as Brian had done. She clapped her hands together, her smile radiant. "My God! I do hope they've arranged for a photographer.

You should see yourselves together. You are quite beyond description, really."

"Thank you, Evelyn," Brian said. "I'm afraid that evening wear for men is quite regulated in our society, but you ladies…" He inclined his head toward Camille. "I have never seen a more stunning vision, Miss Montgomery, and Evelyn…"

"I know. You've never seen a more stunning version of a woman my age—is that it, Brian?"

Evelyn turned to Camille as she came the rest of the way down the stairs. "I'm sorry, you looked a bit shocked. I didn't mean to intrude upon the evening, to be a third wheel, but Brian insisted."

"Evelyn, I believe I'm actually the third wheel this evening."

"Oh, my dear! Don't be silly," Evelyn protested. "Just forgive my presence. I do know the fellows at the museum quite well, and since I've been in the roasting sun and the wretched sand with them all, it seemed only fair that I should attend the ball."

"Of course," Camille said.

The door opened. Even Shelby had changed for the evening; his livery was perfectly tailored and his top hat seemed to gleam. "Lord Stirling? The carriage is ready at your leisure."

"Excellent. Well, ladies, shall we?"

THE MUSEUM WAS ABLAZE with light, and the most elegant of carriages were aligned before the steps. One by one, they were emptied of their glittering occupants. Women dazzling with jewels alighted, and men, tall and short, lean and squat, all in their black, helped them as they made their grand entrances up the steps.

Brian Stirling was recognized the minute he stepped out

of the carriage, and a number of shocked whispers reached their ears.

"Good God! It is the Earl of Carlyle!"

"So the old boy has really come out of it."

"Must have been one hell of a saber wound. He's still wearing the mask."

"Ah, but he does wear it exceedingly well!" That came from one of the female guests.

"Well, he'll be giving you a run for the money with the rich old darlings' daughters, eh, Rupert?" That was said in an amused and taunting drawl.

As Brian acknowledged those who openly called out to him, Camille became an object of wonder for the not-so-discreet whisperers herself.

"Who on earth is she? Why, she's glorious!"

"Evelyn Prior, his mum's old friend."

"Not Evelyn, you dunce! The stunning creature in gold!"

"Must be foreign nobility, I dare say."

"Maybe they're related, and thus I'd have a chance."

"No! I've heard tell he was coming with some little commoner. An *employee* of the museum, can you imagine that?"

Near the entrance, they came upon the group that had been doing the speaking, Camille quickly became certain.

"Brian! Lord God, Brian, I'd heard you were coming! Couldn't quite believe it was true!" said a fellow stepping forward. Dressed in like fashion, the speaker was a handsome blond fellow.

"Robert, good to see you," Brian said, shaking his hand. "Rupert, Lavinia, what a pleasure." He turned to Camille. "My dear, good old chums. We were all at Oxford together, and Rupert and I saw some service in the Sudan. Count Robert Offenbach, Prince Rupert and his sister,

Lady Lavinia Estes. May I present to you Miss Camille Montgomery. And I believe you all know Mrs. Prior."

As the greetings went around, Camille forced a smile. The men were staring at her with poorly concealed curiosity, and Lady Lavinia was openly making an assessment, her nose rather high in the air. She was, Camille had to admit, an extraordinary woman, petite, blond, with immense blue eyes and a lovely face. She dazzled in a white gown resplendent with crystals and beads, and a diamond chain about her throat.

"So, Brian! You're taking up an interest in the place again," Robert said, sounding pleased. "That's wonderful. I really can't even envision the department without a Stirling having a hand in it."

"Right, quite seriously," Rupert agreed. "I was rather afraid you'd be putting a uniform back on, heading down to India, the Sudan or perhaps South Africa. It's just wonderful to see you back."

"Yes, well, being a great Empire is not easy, is it?" Brian said. "But no, unless I'm specifically asked, I intend to remain in England for some time."

"Poor dear!" exclaimed Lavinia. "You were so dreadfully wounded."

"What I received is nothing, it's simply not pretty, Lavinia," Brian said gravely. "I walked away with all my limbs, and for that I am grateful. Though I dare say, despite our wondrous medical advances, most of my fellow chaps fell prey to typhoid and dysentery. Anyway, it's really not the subject for this evening. Shall we go in?"

And so they did. The halls were brilliantly lit. The orchestra was situated between giant Armenian statues. Tables were arrayed by the walls, allowing for a dance floor toward the center of the large west hall, where the exhibits had been moved to allow for the evening's entertainment. As they walked in, the strains of a Strauss waltz were being played.

Before they had even crossed into the gathering, Brian turned to Camille. "Shall we? Evelyn, do you mind?"

"Of course not, children. Dance away!" Evelyn encouraged.

"Wait!" Camille cried, but it was too late. She was in his arms and being swept in a rapid tempo across the floor.

She thanked God for her skirts, and for the fact that she didn't really need to worry too much about where she put her feet. The way he held her, she was all but carried. And…she couldn't be happier, couldn't feel a greater sense of well-being than the second his arms had come around her, holding her so tightly, when she had felt a hint of the fever that had seized her the night before, a sense of closeness, intimacy, electricity and fire.

"Do relax, my dear Miss Montgomery."

"Easy for you to say!" she said, lifting her chin. "I was taught Egyptology. I grew up in a museum. And I am sorry to say that they did not teach dance here!"

"You've never danced?"

"Well, of course I have, but not on a dance floor," she murmured, flushing.

"Where did you dance?"

"Around our pathetic little rooms, with Tristan and Ralph," she admitted.

"But you're dancing just fine. Those fellows were excellent teachers."

"I know only a few steps!"

"You follow delightfully."

"You're being polite."

He laughed softly. "Why would I suddenly start being polite? I'm speaking nothing but the truth."

"Ah, the truth. Are we out here now just because you

enjoy your friends being so flabbergasted to see you with an *employee* of the museum?"

He shrugged, amusement in his eyes. "Partially."

"Partially? Then why else?"

"Because you are the most stunning beauty, and I quite honestly swear to you, Miss Montgomery, that I would far rather dance with you than any woman here."

"Now you are being polite."

"I wouldn't ruin a relationship of such honesty by putting courtesy before truth, Miss Montgomery!" he told her.

"Such flattery will truly go to my head."

"Oh, no, my dear Miss Montgomery. Never. You are far too levelheaded to ever be swayed by a man's comments."

"Not his comments, perhaps," she murmured.

Brian suddenly stopped dancing, and she realized that he'd been tapped on the shoulder. By Hunter.

"Forgive me, Lord Stirling, but may I be so bold? I'm afraid that the sight of Miss Montgomery, sweeping ever so gracefully across the dance floor, will soon draw attention from every man here. She will be whisked away at every possible moment as the night wears on. And as she is my dear friend and associate, I would beg your forgiveness, your patience—and this dance?"

Brian politely stepped aside, bowing his head. "Naturally, Hunter."

And so, she who wasn't at all sure about her ability to sweep gracefully about a dance floor was swept off anew.

"You are so far beyond beautiful tonight," Hunter told her. "The prim little scholar has been reborn."

"It's just a ball gown, Hunter. It doesn't change who or what I am," she told him.

"Mmm. Maybe it does," he said. "Well, what do you think?"

"I think that I don't actually dance very well, and that I need to concentrate not to step on your feet."

He laughed. "Ever pragmatic! Don't worry about my feet. How does the hall look, with the lights and the elite?"

"Lovely. I hope we are able to raise the funds Sir John desires."

"And what of you?" he asked intently.

"What about me?"

"Are you anxious for funds, anxious for a new expedition down the Nile?"

"I hardly think I'll be asked."

"Really? But then, you didn't expect to be here."

"No. But it seems that we are all present. I see Alex speaking with Lord Wimbly over there, and I don't believe that he had originally been included on the guest list, either."

"You were never excluded."

"I was never invited."

"Perhaps Lord Wimbly believed that buying such a gown would be beyond your means." He said the words with a pleasant enough smile. Then the smile faded. "Get away from him, Camille. I swear, I don't believe the man is sane. I told you I will marry you."

"Hunter, that's extreme, don't you think?" she asked him, trying not to smile.

"It would save you."

"Hunter, I will never marry to be 'saved,'" she assured him.

"Camille!" he exclaimed. "You know that I've always found you enchanting. And tonight, in that gown…"

"Hunter—" she began.

But then Hunter stopped dancing; he had been tapped on the shoulder. Alex was behind him, looking a little uncertain, but determined.

"May I?" he asked.

"Of course," Hunter said ruefully.

And so she moved across the floor with Alex. Together, they did stumble.

"I'm sorry," Alex said.

"It was probably me." And it probably was. She could see Brian dancing with the oh-so-aristocratic Lavinia.

"We don't really belong here, do we."

"Of course we do," she said, smiling, distracted.

Brian was no longer dancing with Lavinia, and they had drawn to the side. An older woman with a lovely young girl of perhaps nineteen or twenty had cornered him, and both were speaking animatedly.

"No, we don't."

"We don't what?"

"Belong here!"

"We work here," she said.

He sighed. "Well, I haven't much of your attention, have I? Oh, come, Camille, you must have expected this! Beast or no, he was one of the most sought-after men in England before he went off to fight for our great Empire in Her Majesty's services! The great, strong, handsome son of the Earl of Carlyle, now the earl himself. A man who can wear a mask like a demon and have it make him all the more attractive and elusive! What were you expecting when you came on his arm? You remain a commoner, a mere employee of the museum. There are dozens of mamas out there who would sell their daughters to the devil himself if it meant they could have an earl for an in-law. As I said, Camille. *We don't belong here!*"

"Alex, if you were going to be that uncomfortable, you shouldn't have come."

"Oh, at the last minute old Wimbly decided we all had to be here. It wasn't an invitation I accepted, it was an order I obeyed."

"So, please, enjoy the night!"

"I can try," he told her.

"So smile."

"You know how I feel."

"Then smile anyway!" she said with exasperation.

"Do you know who else doesn't belong here?"

"No, and I assume you're going to tell me."

"Evelyn. His precious Mrs. Prior."

"She was on that last expedition, for the discovery of the tomb," Camille said.

"Oh, yes, she was there. Did she tell you?"

"Not exactly. I saw her in one of the newspaper photographs."

He nodded, then cocked his head slightly. "Did anyone tell you that she was the last one to see the Stirlings alive?"

Camille shook her head. "I…no, I didn't know."

Alex sniffed. "She had a little cottage, like a caretaker's place, just off the apartments the Stirlings had taken. She was usually with the Stirlings, but had gone to a nearby hotel for tea. Just think, if she hadn't gone out, she might have heard them screaming, might have gone to their rescue."

"If the Stirlings chanced upon a nest of cobras, she might well have died, too," Camille said. "From what I've read, Egyptian cobras will strike over and over again, once they feel threatened. And their poison brings about paralysis. In most cases, respiration is stopped and death comes in fifteen minutes, unless the poison can be sucked out quickly enough. Even then, the possibility of a full recovery is—"

"People have survived cobra bites. When they had help. Look," Alex murmured, drawing to a halt on the floor. "Lord Wimbly is about to speak. I'll get you some champagne. We can listen. We've a table near the podium. Apparently Lord Stirling insisted that the staff be at a table with him."

As Alex escorted her across the floor, her cheeks burned. She knew that she was the subject of a great deal of gossip.

Alex led her to a seat at a table covered in snow-white linen and adorned with silver place settings and crystal. Brian, Evelyn, Sir John, Hunter and Aubrey were already seated.

When Alex would have gone to procure champagne, Brian indicated that there was a bottle in an ice bucket by the table. Delicate flutes had already been filled for them.

Lord Wimbly took center stage, speaking of the importance of the museum and its work, and of the more serious importance of funds to support such work. He did have a way with words. And by the time he was done, everyone there felt that they were contributing to the one true temple of knowledge, learning and civilization in the world.

Sir John was called up to say a few words next. Lord Wimbly, however, cut him short, because he began to speak about expeditions and the inherent dangers. Then Lord Wimbly introduced Brian Stirling, the Earl of Carlyle.

She wondered if Brian had known that he would be called, for he hesitated before rising. There was a sudden burst of applause.

At the podium, he smiled, raised his hands and thanked his friends. He was gracious and charming, speaking of his appreciation that so many had been patient with him during his period of mourning. He joked about being the "Beast" of Carlyle, and admitted that he had let a fine landmark, a treasure that belonged to Britain as well as himself, slide into decay. But, of course, he'd been cursed.

"If a curse comes upon one by an ancient form of magic—a dire Egyptian warning, as so many believed—

it's only natural that the forces of a far more powerful magic should lift it. Therefore, I'd like to take this opportunity to make an announcement." Despite the mask, and its very beastlike form, his smile was apparent. "I'm afraid that a very real form of curse created the darkness that came upon me, and a very real form of magic has lifted it. My friends, I would like to introduce my fiancée, the light that has come into my world. Miss Camille Montgomery."

She couldn't have been more surprised if he'd walked straight up to her and slapped her in the face. She was quite certain he hadn't intended to say such words before being asked to the podium. Fury filled her. It was just another ploy in his quest; the words were said to shock someone. She was nothing but a sacrificial lamb. She would definitely lose her job, and the press would investigate her background.

And the words hurt! They were like a knife in her heart!

"My dear, please, your jaw is gaping. You really must shut it," Evelyn whispered to her dryly.

She managed to close her mouth. Her fists clenched at her sides. She was tempted to jump up and denounce him.

"Well, I can see why my proposal meant nothing," Hunter muttered at her other side.

Alex was gaping. Sir John was staring at her. Lord Wimbly's neck whipped around as if he were a puppet with strings.

There was an audible, collective gasp. Then the room went silent.

It was Lord Wimbly who stepped into the fray. "By Jove! Congratulations, old chap!" he said, clapping a hand upon Brian's back. Then he strode toward Camille, catching her hands, causing her to rise. He kissed her on both cheeks. "I do say, congratulations to you both!"

Some kind soul began to clap, and though there were

surely those who thought it the least applaudable situation ever, the sound began to fill the room. Brian strode toward her in Lord Wimbly's wake. And there, before the company, he pulled her into his arms and planted a quick kiss upon her lips.

"A waltz!" Evelyn cried, rising.

There was a slight clatter of instruments and then the music began again.

As they moved around the floor, Camille had her chance to protest. "What are you *doing?*" she demanded fiercely.

"Letting everyone know how happy and enamored I am," he replied.

"You are a charlatan and a liar!" she accused. "And I have become your sacrificial lamb!"

His eyes narrowed. "If anything, Camille, I have just offered you the protection and power of my name."

"But how dare you! You had no right to say such a thing. You never discussed your newest ruse with me. You had no right!"

"Ruse?"

"Obviously!"

"Maybe I meant what I said. Maybe it wasn't a lie at all, just completely right."

She felt her cheeks burn. "No! There is no right thing, no…obligation!" she sputtered. "I told you—"

"Oh, yes, you make your own choices."

"And I wouldn't have chosen for you to make such a ridiculous announcement!"

"I make my own choices, too, Camille."

"It's not your choice when it involves me!" she cried. "You're going to cost me everything. I love my work. My life was finally respectable. Don't you realize? All your wonderful so-called friends here will be determined to find out all they can about the wretched little commoner who has apparently so ensnared you! Everything will turn into a travesty. Don't you see? They'll drag Tristan and me through the dirt. I'll become the scheming social climber willing to seduce a 'beast' to get ahead. I'll—"

"Not really ready to stand up next to a beast, eh?"

"What?"

She was unable to continue. He went dead still.

Rupert suddenly stood behind him. "Congratulations, Brian! I am green with envy. May I?"

"Thank you, Rupert. And of course."

Rupert slipped into dance position with her. "My dear Miss Montgomery. My deepest and most sincere congratulations to you! It's amazing. You are the girl to snare old Brian at last! They had all said it would be quite impossible for anyone to get past the barriers he had erected, but you have done so, and I can quite see why! I must confess, you have captivated the audience this evening! Well, you had done so even before the announcement, but now—"

"Snake!" came a scream.

"Oh, my God!" came another.

"It's Cleopatra's *asp!*"

Dancers piled onto one another. The waltz screeched to a halt. In the jostle, Camille was instantly parted from Rupert. She was quite certain the man had run.

"It's a cobra!" someone else shouted.

Then came the rush. Musicians dropping their instruments. Beautiful, bejeweled women, running. Tall, stalwart, elegant men following in their wake. Even the police guards hired as extra security for the evening were escaping!

"Dear God! I'll get it…I'll get it!"

She recognized the voice. Alex.

Suddenly another sound ripped through the air. A cry, loud and anguished.

As others tripped over themselves to get away, Camille rushed forward to find her friend. And there, in the midst of overturned chairs and shattered glass, lay Alex. Beside him, the asp was in a defensive position, raised high off the ground, collar flared. He lashed out, but missed a strike as everyone had scampered so far back. The creature was surely terrified and overwhelmed.

"Kill it!" someone shouted as it began to slither wildly, not knowing in which direction it should be going.

"Sweet Jesu!" It was Brian. He stepped forward swiftly, capturing the asp just behind the head with the stomp of his boot. He reached down, catching the creature. It hissed and struggled madly, but his grip was firm.

"Here!" came a cry. It was Aubrey, rushing forward with a canvas bag. The snake was slipped into it, and Aubrey took it away to the cries of "Kill it! Kill it!"

"Good God, why did they have such a creature here!"

Camille knew that the snake had done nothing but be a snake. Whoever had failed to secure its habitat properly was to blame. *Alex!*

Camille rushed forward, falling to her knees by his side, seeking the spot on his body where the snake's fangs had punctured his flesh. She found the marks on his left hand. A dinner knife lay on the floor. She quickly slashed the flesh, set her lips on the marks and began to suck and spit venom. A hand fell on her shoulder, pulling her up. She protested, looking into Brian's intense blue eyes ringed by the leather of his mask.

"Leave me be, I know what I'm doing."

"Camille!" he said sharply. "You're risking your own life."

"I know what I'm doing, I swear—"

"From?"

She lifted her chin. "Books! Of course!"

And still, he forced her aside.

"I can better take what venom might be ingested," he said flatly, and then he was down on his knees, repeating her procedure.

"A doctor! There must be a doctor among us!" Lord Wimbly shouted as he strode through the hall, furious. "I ordered that creature put well out of the way for the night. Aubrey, how did it get out? This is a disaster. The fund-raiser is a disaster!"

Camille stared at the man, feeling as if ice water lashed through her veins. Alex might well die and Lord Wimbly was worried about his fund-raiser!

"Aubrey! Damn you, man!"

"Lord Wimbly, Alex was the one who saw to it that the asp was removed from the hall!" Aubrey said, rushing forward to defend himself.

Throughout the argument, Brian continued to draw in venom and spit, over and over again. He stood at last, shouting, "Has anyone found a doctor?"

Someone had. The fellow, looking a little nervous himself, came forward. He made a face when he kneeled down in the venom before he saw it.

"The man is dying!" Camille cried, choking in fury.

"I'll do what I can, I'll do what I can…" the man muttered. He pulled a stethoscope from his black bag and listened to Alex's chest. He then looked up at the small group that had stayed, gathered around Alex's side. He shook his head sadly.

"No!" Camille cried. "No!" She fell back by Alex's side again, leaning against his chest herself, listening. Nothing.

CHAPTER THIRTEEN

EVELYN STOOD OUTSIDE the museum with Rupert.

"It's been caught. It's away," Lady Lavinia said, hurrying to reach the two.

"Doesn't matter much now, does it? The party is over, I'd say," Rupert said with a shrug.

"Rupert! That studious fellow who rushed forward to save us all is dead!" Lavinia chastised.

"Poor bloke. I hope it went easy. They say it's a horrible death."

"Yes, horrible," Evelyn murmured.

Rupert studied her. "Oh, Evy! Sorry. You were the first to come upon Brian's parents, weren't you? It must have been devastating." Noticing her shocked expression, he said, "Sorry, don't mean to bring back the past. Hard not to tonight, though. Pity, it was a good party, too. Delicious gossip. Evelyn, old girl! You didn't give us a word of warning."

"I didn't know myself," she said.

"You're joking!" Lavinia said.

"I've sent for the carriage. I believe that's your driver coming now, Rupert."

"Pity," Rupert said. "I'd hoped to simply ply Evy here with questions! Find out all about Brian's little unknown beauty. The girl is dazzling, isn't she, Lavinia?"

"Mmm."

"So, Evy, where did she come from?"

Evelyn hesitated. "She rather just stumbled into our lives, actually."

"How so?"

"There was an accident. Her guardian was hurt."

Rupert's eyes narrowed. "Her guardian? Who is the fellow?"

"A man named Sir Tristan Montgomery."

"Montgomery!" Rupert said with shock.

"You know him?" Evelyn asked.

"Of him!"

She waited on pins and needles for what he would say next. "The old fellow was a legend in the cavalry. He earned that knighthood in India."

Evelyn exhaled. His words had not been what she had expected.

"Well, at any rate, there was an accident. Sir Tristan was recuperating—is recuperating—at the castle. Naturally his ward has been loath to leave him."

"Amazing, still, even with her obvious assets!" Rupert said, eyes flashing.

The object of their conversation suddenly came bursting out upon them, distressed, her hair tumbling down and still more beautiful than ever. "Evelyn! Please! You must find Shelby quickly. We need another conveyance, an ambulance."

"An ambulance?"

"He's alive!" Camille cried. "Barely, just barely, but he is breathing."

"He needs a hospital!" Evelyn said.

Camille shook her head, flushing. "We're taking him to the castle."

"Brian has said this?" Evelyn demanded, shocked.

"Yes, yes! His condition is so dire, Evelyn. At a hospital he might pick up any number of illnesses that could destroy his chances. Please, Evelyn, get Shelby on this quickly!"

"I'll find your man," Rupert volunteered, as Camille spun around, returning to the hall.

"Thank you," Evelyn told him. "Excuse me, Lady Lavinia…"

She followed Camille back into the hall, but she skirted around the area where the rich and elite had danced, heading quickly up the stairs. She pushed open the door to the office, fumbling for the electric light switch. The terrarium was behind Sir John's desk. The cobra was now sleeping.

She walked over and read the placard on the front of the glass. *Naja haje, Egyptian cobra, asp. Symbol of the Sun, dominance, strength and power and, most importantly, royalty. Part of the Uraeus, a solar disk supported by two asps. This marks the right of the power to rule, the eye of Ra, the sun god. Signifies the destruction of enemies as well as light, life and death.*

Life and death. Alex Mittleman was still alive.

Hinges now secured the lid of the terrarium. Evelyn reached for them. Then she turned and left the office, careful to douse the lights.

CAMILLE HAD CHOSEN to ride in the ambulance, thus Brian had done the same. It was on loan from the Metropolitan Asylums Board, and Brian had been relieved to see that it had been thoroughly cleaned. And the fellow with them— despite the fact that he hadn't seemed much like a medical man at first—was proving to be competent. He had tended the bite with carbolic acid, the same substance that had kept Brian from dying of his own injuries in India. Equally, though it might have been a bit late, he had ordered both Brian and Camille to rinse their mouths with whiskey and drink a fair amount, as well, though it was most likely that whatever toxin they had taken in during their attempts to save Alex were already imbibed or on their way into the bloodstream.

There was little room in the ambulance. Such carriages had not been intended as passenger vehicles, but rather provided a mattress that stretched where one would customarily find seats. There was room for a passenger by the driver's side in this particular conveyance. Brian had taken that position while Camille and the doctor, a gentleman in private practice named Ethan Morton, rode in the cramped quarters by the patient.

As they rode, he wondered why he hadn't killed the cobra. Such creatures had, whether put to the task or not, killed his parents. He realized that, amazingly, he had pitied the snake. And he knew that someone there had purposely let the creature free. Alex might well have been declared dead, sent for autopsy, if not for Camille's insistence that the fellow was still breathing. And God knows he wasn't conscious, wasn't out of the woods yet.

"Long way for you in a poor seat," the driver apologized. "Usually we just make the run from hospital to hospital, institution to institution, in these carriages. I'm sorry, My Lord."

"I've ridden in worse," Brian assured him.

"You know, your lass is fearing the worst. There was a time when I'd agree that the best care was in the home. But we've come a long way in this age! Sterilization, antiseptics! This fellow might have done as well in the hospital. Why, once rich folks feared the very sight of such a place, but I tell you, folks are actually coming to be cured these days, and not because they're so poor they haven't another choice."

"I'm sure he would have been fine. Actually, I'm not at all sure he'll be fine. His state is still dire. But as long as he is breathing, my home is large enough to provide for him and his care."

"A castle! Lord Stirling, I agree, you've got the room!" the driver told him.

When they reached the outer wall, the man pulled the horse to a stop. Corwin was waiting, and Shelby had apparently gone ahead with Evelyn. The gates were open.

The driver urged the horse forward again. Brian realized that he was afraid of the grounds, but steadfast he went on.

"Pardon me, My Lord, but if you need help with your grounds…well, I would suggest a new gardener!"

"Thank you. I'll keep that in mind."

They crossed the moat, into the courtyard. There, Brian leaped down. The doctor had opened the wide doors and Brian reached in, lifting Alex Mittleman and carrying him straight for the castle. Evelyn was waiting just within the door.

"The west chamber is ready for him," she said, straightening her hair.

Brian nodded, hurrying up the stairs with his burden. Shelby waited in the room, but Brian shook his head when the man would have helped him. The bed had been covered with clean sheets, a fire burned in the hearth and clean clothes and cold water waited on a little occasional table drawn up by the bed. Brian carefully eased the unconscious man down.

"I've a nightshirt for him on the back of the chair," Evelyn murmured.

Shelby said, "I'll help the doctor see to him."

Brian nodded and turned to exit. Camille was in the doorway, wide-eyed, silent and distraught.

"There's nothing you can do now," he said.

"I'll sit with him through the night."

"I can tend to him," Evelyn said.

"Thank you, but I want to sit with him," Camille said firmly.

She didn't look at him as she spoke. The woman who had come to him the night before did not exist. This one was distant, suddenly a stranger.

He closed the door, forcing her back. "You have to give the doctor time to get him settled," he said.

She blamed him, he realized. For some ungodly reason, she blamed him for what had happened. Suddenly angry, he told her, "Do what you please," and he strode down the hall to his own quarters.

He should have killed the damn snake! Because while it existed, this could happen again.

DISTRAUGHT, CAMILLE KNEW that she had to wait. And she believed that Alex would be safe enough while Shelby and the doctor attended him.

Nervously she hurried down the hall to Tristan's room. She started to knock, then hesitated, thinking he might be asleep. She opened the door and looked in.

He was there, in bed, his head upon the pillow. But he wasn't sleeping.

"Camille?" he asked, sounding a bit groggy.

"Tristan, I'm sorry, I didn't mean to wake you."

"Come in, come in! What's happened?"

He stepped out of bed in his long nightgown and bed cap, and hurried to the door to urge her inside. "Come, come. You left here so aglow, what is it?"

"The cobra got out somehow. Tristan, Alex was bitten. He's here now, a few doors down."

"He's alive?"

She nodded, deciding not to tell him that she had worked to suck the venom out of the wound. As had Brian

Stirling, she reminded herself, and she felt a small twinge of guilt. But even if she trusted him, she wasn't at all certain she trusted his household anymore.

She had been so suspicious of Alex! And now, he lay near death's door.

"But he's alive?" Tristan demanded.

"Just barely," she murmured.

"They killed the wretched snake?" Tristan demanded.

"No. Actually, it's back in its terrarium."

She walked with agitation before the hearth. "Someone let the snake out, Tristan. They had to have done so."

"Oh, Camie, I don't know." Tristan scratched his chin thoughtfully. "A snake in a crowded room… It's not as if anyone would know just who the creature would attack, right?"

She exhaled slowly, studying him. "I supposed you're right. Oh, Tristan! It will be so terrible if Alex dies. It will be as if—"

"As if there were a curse, eh, lass?" Tristan demanded.

She shook her head. "Maybe."

"Camille!"

"Nothing terrible had happened at the museum, not until Brian Stirling came back to it."

Tristan shook his head, looking away from her. "You can't go back there."

"What?"

"You can't go back to the museum."

"That's ridiculous! There's my job. I'll never find anything like it again—"

"I can take care of you, Camie!"

"Tristan! We'll have no more illegal doings," she told him.

He shook his head. "I know! I've learned me lesson, girl. But I don't think you should go back."

"Maybe we shouldn't be here," she murmured. "You're better, Tristan, so much better. We can just go home—"

She broke off, choking suddenly, aware that the idea brought tears to her eyes. She didn't *want* to leave. She didn't even want to be angry. She just didn't want to be a mockery. A pawn. Because that's what she was, no matter what yearning and temptation had taken her into the arms of a man who now…made ridiculous announcements about marriage!

"Home!" Tristan said.

"Home, our little apartments, where we live!" she said, but then she shook her head. Tristan certainly appeared well enough tonight. But now Alex was here. She couldn't desert Alex. Especially since she had decided that she didn't trust Evelyn Prior.

He was silent. "You can't go back there."

"Where? Home?"

"The museum!" Tristan said, shaking his head.

"Tristan, my work is like a miracle gift." She was suddenly sorry that she had come in. Naturally, he would have to know what had happened. All of London would know by morning. But she should have let him have the night. After all, he was still healing. And she had spoken so hastily. She couldn't leave, not while Alex hovered between life and death!

"Camille, now I'm telling you, lass—"

"Tristan, I'm sorry so sorry I disturbed you tonight. I want to sit by Alex, make sure he makes it through the night. We'll talk in the morning, all right?"

Tristan had the most serious and somber look she could ever remember seeing on his face. She walked to him, hugging him fiercely. "Hopefully Alex will be out of the woods by morning."

"Camille, I'll come and sit with you," he said.

"Good heavens, no! You need to be in your bed, getting some rest."

He stared at her for a moment. She thought that he looked guilty, but guilty of what? It was probably just her imagination. She was tired and distraught. Now she was even believing that Tristan was part of a conspiracy!

"I can stay with you—"

"I'll be fine, right down the hall," she told him. "Tristan, please, get back into bed before you wind up hurt again or ill. Please!"

"Camie—"

"I'm begging you!"

He sighed, then wagged a finger at her. "I sleep light, lass. If you need me, if you need anything at all, just scream! Call my name."

She smiled. He wasn't a light sleeper, and he'd been on sedatives several nights. That's why the scraping sounds that came at night never aroused him.

"I'll call out for you if I need you, I swear." She kissed his forehead, prodded him toward his bed, then tucked the covers in around him.

"Actually, you're looking exceptionally well, you know," she murmured.

He nodded. "Don't you even think about going into that museum tomorrow, though!"

She smiled without answering. It hadn't been all that long ago that the museum didn't open on Saturdays.

"Good night," she said.

When she walked back down the hall, she saw that Shelby was standing guard by the door, arms crossed over his chest.

"He's—" she whispered.

"Still breathing, Miss Camille. Still breathing," he assured her. He smiled. "You go on in. The doctor is staying for the night, as well. And I'll be right here."

"Thank you."

She went on into the room. Alex looked very young and fragile, dressed in a long white nightgown, his face pale, hair unruly. She walked toward the bed. Dr. Ethan Morton had made himself comfortable in a plushly upholstered chair and appeared to be sleeping already. When Camille walked gingerly toward the bed, though, he spoke.

"Keep the cloths on him, if you'd be of any help. We don't want him getting a fever. So far he's breathing, and his pulse has gotten steadier. Keep him comfortable, and keep his forehead cool."

She nodded. "Thank you."

"And what about you?"

"Me?"

"You sucked in that venom."

"I'm fine. I spit it all out immediately."

"And are you often called upon to rescue snake-bite victims?"

"I've never done such a thing before."

He arched a brow.

"I read a great deal," she told him.

He nodded, eyeing her through half-closed lids. "It was a dangerous thing to do, young lady. If you'd had a cut in your mouth…well, you'd have the venom in you now."

"I feel fine, honestly. And thank you."

She cooled Alex's head as instructed, longing to believe that it made a difference. And she thought it did, because every few minutes, there was a shiny glow of sweat arising, and her administrations kept it at bay.

At some point she began to doze, leaning upon her arm, which rested on his chest. She woke with a jerk when she heard a rumbling. At first, panic seized her. His lungs were giving out. But that wasn't the case. He was restless, and his lips were moving. She glanced at Dr. Morton, but the man appeared to be sleeping. She touched Alex's cheek. It wasn't hot.

"Alex, it's all right. You're going to be all right," she murmured.

"He keeps them," Alex said, his head tossing. "Keeps them...keeps them in the crypt. The crypt...dangerous...."

"What, Alex? What is dangerous?"

"Asps...in the crypt." His eyes suddenly opened fully upon hers. "Cobras...in the crypt. And when he's ready...he'll kill. He'll kill us all."

His eyes closed again. Camille sat in icy silence, shaken into deep fear by his wild comments. She glanced at Dr. Morton. His eyes remained closed. She leaned closer to Alex.

"What are you saying, Alex?" she asked softly.

He tossed and twisted again. She bit into her lower lip, praying that she wasn't making him worse. But she was, of course.

His eyes opened again, wide. She didn't think that he was actually seeing her face. Then he stared into her eyes. His fingers flailed on the sheets.

"The beast!" he exploded in a whisper. "The Beast of Carlyle. Beware the beast! He has a bitter plan. He wants vengeance. He wants to kill us all!"

Then his eyes closed, his fingers went still and it was as if he had never spoken.

From somewhere, a clock chimed the hour of three. Dr. Morton let out a snore and twisted in his chair. Then all was silent.

BRIAN LAY AWAKE, listening. But that night there were no strange noises to awaken him and draw him down the stairs to the crypts. Ajax slept peacefully by the hearth. He swore to himself in the darkness, remembering that he was having someone in to clean and oil the hinges.

The evening had certainly ended in disaster. Again he wondered why he hadn't killed the asp in a fury. Maybe he had realized that the animal was just that, and though its defenses were lethal to human beings, it had been cornered and was probably far more terrified than the elite who had fled at the very mention of its existence. But how had the creature come to be among the company?

Alex Mittleman's lack of riches had made him a likely suspect, but now he was stricken. He had nearly died that night, the same way Lord and Lady Stirling had met their demise.

Brian halfway rose and sent a fist into his pillow. Then there was Lord Wimbly, who apparently had gambling debts. But would such a man risk so much? And Aubrey? Aubrey was the main man to handle the asp at the museum, but there wasn't a soul among those who worked there who hadn't been to Egypt, except for Camille. Those who had been in the desert, and in the cities and towns along the Nile, had experience with the Egyptian cobra.

He gritted his teeth, concentrating. Maybe Sir Hunter, the great adventurer? But even Brian had to admit that his main issue with Hunter was the man's apparent interest in Camille.

He still had no real indication of who the guilty party might be, but he believed now that whoever it was had information that he did not—knowledge his father had apparently discovered just before his death. There was a piece of tremendous value that had not been catalogued, that existed somewhere. And if it wasn't at the museum, then it was among the relics and artifacts below.

He had kept the grounds a jungle, and they were known to be inhabited by wolves. He had allowed doctors onto the property, but only because it had been necessary. Other than that, Evelyn had brought in a few local women from time to time to help with the cleaning. Only those he truly trusted with his life had real access to the estate, despite its rambling size—Shelby, Corwin and Evelyn. And among them, only Evelyn had been in Egypt.

None of this was a conspiracy he was solely creating out of loss, bitterness and anger. That had become evident when the fellow they had followed at the bar was killed. Oddly enough, that rascal Tristan had proved to be an asset. Except now, what should have been simple, cut-and-dried, was complicated. He had allowed Camille and her guardian in because he had intended to make use of both of them, not counting on his own feelings in the matter.

But now….

He rose, causing Ajax to leap to his feet, as well. The great wolfhound looked at him, wagging his tail, waiting.

"It's suddenly cold and lonely in here, isn't it, boy?" he asked. "So let's explore."

First things first. He silently moved down the hall. Shelby had fallen asleep at his position before the door. Ever the faithful friend, however, he opened his eyes and nearly jumped up with alarm at Brian's arrival.

"It's me," Brian assured him. Shelby nodded, leaning against the wall again.

Brian slipped open the door where Alex Mittleman lay, fighting for his life. The doctor dozed in the chair. Camille had fallen asleep, slumped over Alex, still in her elegant gold. Neither stirred when he entered.

He set a finger against a vein in Alex's throat. The pulse was strong.

Tenderly he shifted a lock of hair from Camille's face. He felt a wave of warmth and then a tautness constrict his limbs as he surveyed her, captured again by all that he had come to admire and covet, and feeling as well a steely sense of self-doubt. She cared about this man. Because he was her co-worker? Or was there something more sinister between them?

He drew a throw from the one chair remaining by the fire and carefully set it around her shoulders. Still she didn't move. He returned to the hall, left Shelby dozing at his post and headed down the stairs.

ALEX SHIFTED.

The movement woke Camille. For a moment, she lay confused, eyes on the fire, unable to remember where she was. Then the horror of the night rushed in on her and she jerked up, quickly looking at the man on the bed. His color seemed good. His face was not shining with sweat. She set a finger against his throat and felt the steady beat of his pulse.

She sat back, relieved. Dr. Morton was snoring. After a moment, she rose and stretched, rubbing her neck where it was tight.

Suddenly she had the strange feeling that the castle was alive. Pinpricks of unease filled her as she remembered Alex's delirious words. The crypts here, he had said, were filled with asps. It was ridiculous. How could he know such a thing? And whatever might make him suspect it?

She glanced at the door, aware that Shelby kept guard, though why, she wasn't certain. Unless Brian had his own doubts about Evelyn Prior? Or his doubts about her, the half-dead Alex and Dr. Morton.

She walked to the door, silently opened it. Shelby was instantly alert.

"It's just me," she whispered.

"How's the patient?"

"His pulse is strong."

"Thank God."

She feigned a yawn. "I believe he is well enough that I

will seek out my own bed for a while. Shelby, are you quite
all right there? Should I bring you a pillow, a blanket?"

"Oh, no, Miss Camille. I've slept in many a worse situation, in India…in the Sudan. I'm quite comfortable,
thank you."

"Good night, then."

She left him, hurrying down the hall to her own room.
She entered it, but didn't close the door all the way. She
waited several seconds, her heart pounding, wondering
just what she was so determined to do. Assure herself that
there were no cobras in the crypts, she realized.

She waited. Time seemed to stretch, but she wanted to
make sure that Shelby had gone back to sleep so that she
could slip out her door and down the stairs without being
noticed. It occurred to her to take a lamp, so she ran quickly
into the room to procure that, along with a box of matches.

She went back to the door and peeked out. Shelby appeared to have returned to sleep, his head resting atop his
arms, which were folded over his knees in his position
against the wall by Alex's door.

She walked on out, silent as a wraith, tiptoed to the stairway, started down it, then looked back. Shelby hadn't
moved. She hurried downward. At the stairs, she moved
into the side hall and continued on, coming to the tiny
chapel.

She opened the door to the dark curving stairs that
seemed to go downward into emptiness. But as her eyes
adjusted, she realized that from somewhere, the faintest
light glowed. She hesitated, set down her own lamp and
started downward.

Inch by inch, aware of the sound of her own breathing,
she entered ever farther into the pit of bare illumination.
At last, her feet fell upon the final step and she started
around the corner.

The first room of the crypts was not what she had expected. Though it was so dismal down here that the one lamp burning on the floor did little more than provide for shapes and shadows, Camille could make out something of the room.

No vaults of the ancient dead were neatly aligned, nor were there musty tombs surrounded by spiderwebs. It was an office. The floor was stone and appeared to have been swept clean.

She strained to see against the darkness. Far across from her, and leading into a true stygian darkness, were massive iron gates. Those, she was certain, would lead to the long dead, yet not of an ancient Egyptian world.

Here in the office there were ordinary things—desks, files and cartons. Parts of the vast area were very much like the storeroom of the museum. Relics that might be of tremendous value were always carefully packed, and just as carefully unpacked. She had come upon the cache of items sent straight to Castle Carlyle, rather than the museum! She blinked as she realized that one of the cartons lay open. She inched toward it, wishing that she had brought her oil lamp. Drawn, yet unable to force her limbs to move quickly, she slowly came to the wooden carton. It was immense. The nails had been pried from the wooden lid, which lay at an angle to the side of the now gaping box.

Slowly, barely daring to breathe, she came closer. She stared down at the treasure in the straw packing.

Within the huge shipping carton was a sarcophagus. The beautifully painted and adorned receptacle for the dead had been opened, as well; its lid lay against that of the shipping carton. Moving ever closer, she saw that the mummy remained within its resting place. Darkened by time and the resin used to assure immortality, the mummy lay in typical fashion, its wrappings in place, arms folded over its chest.

Then something scurried near her. She nearly cried out, but saw the rat heading for a tiny hole in the wall. Her heart was thundering. Why? There had been no noises tonight. And she didn't begin to believe that a nest of cobras lived beneath the long-dead being in the box.

So what was she doing? What had she hoped to prove? That there was no dark, dank, evil laboratory here. That Brian Stirling had not gone mad and begun breeding cobras in his crypts. Fine. She had discovered all that she needed to know. She could retreat.

Suddenly the lid of the carton burst outward. A dark figure leaped toward her. Before she could scream, a hand clamped over her mouth, and a low, furious, rasping whisper touched her ears.

"Now, you'll pay the price!"

CHAPTER FOURTEEN

SOFTNESS. Pleasant, clean sheets. A bed. A fire burning near.

Alex Mittleman opened his eyes. He tried to speak, but nothing came out except a croaking noise.

"Here, here, son. Water, take a sip."

Alex looked into the eyes of a total stranger. He blinked and accepted sips of water. He was parched, desperately parched.

"Slowly, boy. Slowly. Take it easy now."

Alex nodded, and though he longed to inhale the water, he sipped. His jaw hurt. Everything hurt. His vision seemed clouded.

"You're lucky to be alive," the stranger said.

He nodded, then frowned, confused.

"I'm Dr. Morton," the stranger said. "Do you remember? You were bitten by an asp, an Egyptian cobra, at the museum."

Alex nodded slowly. He swallowed, signaling an entreaty for another sip of water. Then, he asked, "Where am I?"

"Carlyle Castle."

His body gave an involuntary spasm. His frown deepened. "Camille… I thought…I spoke, I saw her, saw her face."

"She was here, son. Earlier. She stayed awake with you

for hours, cooling your brow, keeping your fever down. Poor girl. She must have awakened and gone to get some sleep herself." The doctor cleared his throat. "She saved your life. Well, she and the Earl of Carlyle. They both seemed to know something about snake venom."

"Camille...she saved my life?"

"Yes, son. And the earl."

The Earl of Carlyle had helped save his life!

"You've got to rest now. I'd say that your survival, even with the quick thinking of that pair, is something of a miracle."

"Camille..."

"No, no, you've got to let the lass rest now, and get some sleep yourself. I'll stay until midday, son. Then you'll be on your way to mending, and the lass can attend to you again."

Alex nodded, settling in. He'd been bitten by a cobra. But he was at Castle Carlyle. And *Camille* was going to tend to him.

Life was a miracle.

EVELYN PRIOR couldn't sleep. She rose, found her robe, turned on the lamp at her bedside and hesitated. Then she silently opened her door and walked down the hall.

The door to Alex's room was closed. Shelby slept by it, leaning against the wall. She had known the man a very long time. She took a few steps closer and hesitated. She nearly jumped a mile when a voice sounded behind her.

"Why, Mrs. Prior!"

She whirled around. Tristan, standing in the long white cotton nightgown she had provided him, was right behind her. The man had moved without a sound. But then again, he was a sneak thief. She should have expected that he could do so.

"Are you all right?" he asked politely.

Naturally, Shelby woke up.

"What? What is it? What's going on?" he demanded with a voice like a growl.

"I came out to see to the welfare of our patient," Evelyn said, her chin high as she stared at Tristan. "What our guest is doing, I do not know!"

"I heard noises in the hall," Tristan said with a shrug. He frowned fiercely, staring at both of them. "And my ward is residing here. There's not a chance that I will not look after her welfare!"

"Go back to bed, the both of you!" Shelby admonished, apparently disgusted that his sleep had been interrupted. "The patient's doing well enough—looks like he'll live. And under the circumstances, that's damn well. And Miss Camille is sound asleep—neither of you will disturb her!" he said firmly.

"Perhaps I should just check on Alex Mittleman," Evelyn said.

"Be my guest," Shelby told her. "But the doctor's still in with him. Get some sleep and save your strength. The doctor will be leaving by noon tomorrow, and the lot of nursing will fall to you all again." He glowered, obviously very grumpy.

"Get back in your room!" Evelyn said firmly to Tristan, not to be outdone by Shelby.

"Let me escort you to your own first," Tristan suggested, very politely.

"As you wish," she said. But she looked back at Shelby. "See that Sir Tristan makes his own way back to sleep, will you?"

"Everyone is to go to sleep!" he said, and shaking his head, he sat back down again, leaning his massive shoulders against the wall. But his eyes didn't close. He was watching.

CAMILLE WAS FIERCELY SPUN around in stark terror. A light was suddenly shone in her eyes and she backed away, blinking.

"Camille!"

Breath rushed from her in a terrible expulsion. It was Brian.

"Oh, my God!" She was so relieved that she sank down to the floor, catching herself on her knees, her hand flying to her throat.

But then again, what was he doing down here in the darkness, hiding by a mummy?

"Get up!" He set his lamp down on the ground, caught her hands and dragged her to a standing position. She swallowed, staring at him, catching sight of his face. His real face. And that scared her more than she might have imagined.

"What the hell are you doing down here?" he demanded angrily. "Sweet Jesu, what in God's name do I need to do with you? Tie you down at night?"

There was nothing wrong with his face, nothing at all. Except for the scar that slashed from his forehead across his cheek on the left side, but it was barely a white line. It certainly didn't detract from the line of his skeletal structure, high cheekbones, firm jaw, almost aquiline nose, and high, well-set brow. He was exceptionally striking, handsome in a rugged and classic sense, and there was nothing of a beast or monster about his appearance at all. It was all a lie. A charade.

"What are you doing down here?" she cried.

His hands fell to his hips. He was dressed in nothing but a pair of white knickers, and his chest gleamed in the candlelight, muscled shoulders and abdomen a taut ripple of shadow and pulse. "I am the Earl of Carlyle," he reminded her coldly. "I have title to the castle. I live here, Camille. And beyond that, you are more than aware that I am always searching for the cause of the noise at night!"

She swallowed hard, aware that she was far less than

presentable herself. If she were clad with a bit more dignity it would be an easier task to explain her presence. As it was, her hair was half up, half trailing in pins, and her elegant gown was askew.

He crossed his arms over his chest and his eyes glittered upon her. "It was my understanding that you were desperate to watch over your friend during the night. I will assume that he's doing well. Did he send you down here?"

"No!" she gasped with horror, although, in a way he had. She had come looking for cobras. Which was not the wisest thing to do, not when a man had just been bitten by such an asp. But, she was certain, had the Earl of Carlyle been raising the creatures for some perverted reason, they would surely not have been allowed to roam free.

"There...there is something going on here," she said.

"Obviously. We've established that."

She shook her head. "I heard noises again."

"And you didn't come for me? How odd. This was the one night I didn't hear any noise."

"Then I must have heard you," she said. Her words had a lovely ring of possible truth to them, but she went on the offensive again. "And you, My Lord? Suddenly, in the middle of the night, you found it expedient to start opening up sarcophagi?"

He didn't so much as blink. "I repeat, my dear, I own the castle. And all that lies within it. If I choose to open boxes in the middle of the night, it's entirely my right to do so."

"But one would have to admit, as well, that it's quite odd!" she said. Then she backed away. "And you! Your very existence is a lie! Why the mask, why the pretense? There is nothing wrong with you!"

He walked forward, reaching for her arm. She backed away. "No!"

He caught her anyway. "Hush up, will you! You'll wake the entire house."

She fell silent, staring at him. And as she did so, she felt anew the incredible magnetism that he could exert. She wanted every evil possibility about him to be a lie. She wanted to reach out in the light and touch his face, to marvel at it.

And she wanted it to be true, that she had come into his life and changed it. And that he had been as blind to her poor status and sad start in life as she had been to the scarring of his face. She wanted to believe...

"Let's get out of here," he said. He doused the lamp he had carried, leaving it on one of the desks. Then he caught hold of her hand and led her up the stairs. In the chapel, he closed the door firmly behind him. He frowned. "You got past Shelby?"

"Don't you dare be angry with him."

"I'm not. I'm sure you were cautious—and amazingly cunning—when you decided to make your way down."

She turned away, starting up the steps. He came behind her fleetly. As she rose up the stairway to the second landing, he was just inches away. At the top of the stairs, she hesitated. Shelby appeared to be sleeping again. She started to tiptoe by him, heading for her own room. But Brian came behind her. The hold he planted at the base of her spine was firm as he ushered her swiftly down the hall to his room. When he'd opened the door, he propelled her in firmly.

She spun around. "You've no right to just assume—"

"I'm not assuming anything. I don't intend to leave you alone again at night. Ever. And I don't care which of your so-called friends is ailing next, or from what cause!"

"Oh, my God! You would imply that that poor man was not stricken, when he rushed in to save others, when your grand and rich peers ran like rabbits!" she exclaimed.

"I imply nothing of the kind. I merely state that I will not leave you alone at night anymore!"

She suddenly started to tremble, aware that he meant it, aware that she couldn't bear being this near him without...

"It's all a game, isn't it?" she asked softly.

"A very deadly game."

She backed away. "I can't play it with you anymore!" she said.

He blocked the door. There was no exit in that direction. She turned, yet got nowhere, for in seconds he was at her back, his hands upon her. With gentle force he turned her around. His eyes were cobalt with tension, his muscles locked. He looked as if he longed to speak, yet shook his head. Then he crushed her to him, caught her chin, and his lips found hers.

She felt as if she exploded against him. Before, she hadn't even really known what she sought. Now she knew.

Right or wrong, she trembled anew, falling against him, feeling the plunge of his tongue in her mouth, the passion behind it, and the overwhelming desire. Her hands, rising to his chest, marveled in the bare flesh, the play of muscle beneath. Her fingers crept to his shoulders, and she clung there as they kissed. Her fingers fell down the length of his back, tracing the spine, again glorying in the simple feel of naked flesh and all that burned beneath.

His lips broke from hers at last, and he spun her easily in his arms, then began working at the cord that laced her bodice. An oath escaped him after a moment. She heard the slight snap of the cord in his fingers, and it didn't matter in the least. She could scarcely breathe now and his haste mattered more dearly. In seconds she had wrangled from the tightness of bodice, and his hands were there when the length of it was pulled over her head.

He swore again, spinning her once more, starting at the
laces of the corset, tearing into them, as well. It took forever, and when she was freed from it she could wait no
longer. Turning back into his arms, she melted against his
chest, feeling the chafe of it against her breasts, knowing
that she willing to live and die there. Again his mouth
found hers while his hands busied themselves with the
petticoat tie. When that fell to her feet, he went to his
knees. She clutched hard upon his shoulders as he removed the elegant little slippers and then the garters.

Suddenly his touch was slow as his fingers brushed
against her thighs and behind her knees, rolling down the
length of silk. She shivered, standing, longing to come
down to him. His lips found her kneecaps, her inner thighs,
her calves…the top of her foot. One stocking was gone.
He began to remove the other. Again hands, fingertips, lips,
tongue lingered upon her flesh as the silk slipped from it.
And he halfway rose, burying his face against her belly,
teasing her thighs, falling to her hips…bathing her.

At last she fell to meet him. His arms crushed around
her again, his mouth falling upon and consuming hers.
Firelight played upon them, intoxicating them with the
headiness of sight and touch and taste and scent. She knew
then, as they burned as one along with the flames, that
come what may, she was lost. He was all that she craved
in life, all that she needed, all that she…loved.

His whisper touched her ear. "How is it that you can do
this to me?" It was a breath, barely discernible, yet it continued. "I forget the world, and reason, and even sanity…."

They were the words she should have been saying to
him, but she refused to let them come to her lips, refused
to let them enter her heart. Her fingers threaded into his
hair, down his nape, down the length of his back. She
came closer, her hands riding over the leanness of his hips

to the muscled walls of his buttocks as she inched herself ever closer. She felt herself lifted and slowly eased down upon him. The focus of her entire being became the sensation of him within her, part of her. She could not come closer, could not feel anything so penetrating and wildly exciting ever again.

Before, she had followed. Now she could lead. And she did.

Digging into his shoulders, she was aware of each painstaking sensation—fingertips upon his flesh, breasts scraping against the matt of his chest, arms tightening around him. His hands upon her, catching her hips, adding to the momentum, touching, guiding.

As she exploded in ecstasy, he swept her around and beneath him. The world blazed with the blue flames from the hearth, and the winds that had seized her tore through the forests surrounding them.

And then, as the wind shifted to the slow catch of her breath, she reached out and touched his face.

"Why?" she asked softly.

She thought he would move away, but he did not. His arms lifted his weight from her, but his flesh still hovered over hers, his limbs parting her own.

"At first? Because I was monstrous."

"But there…there is nothing but a scar."

"Is that so terrible?" he asked softly.

She shook her head. "But it's a lie."

"Not a lie. It's because I'm not ready to know the world."

"The mask is not what you've become!" she insisted.

He laughed then, found her lips and kissed her again. "So fierce! Ever so fierce. We all have secrets."

She shook her head. "Sadly, Lord Stirling, I am an open book."

"With pages that run very deep."

"You're playing games again."

"It remains a game. A deadly game," he said, rising.

Then, naked in the pile of her cast-off clothing, she felt the force of all that she had once believed so ardently come falling down upon her again. What was she doing?

She moved to rise. He didn't let her do so on her own, but came down again, drawing her into his arms as he pulled her to her feet. His fingers cradled her head as he pulled her against him, his lips against hers.

"I have to go."

He shook his head.

"But I can't…stay in here."

"Why not?"

She pulled away. "You are the Earl of Carlyle," she said.

"Ah, but you are the enchantress who can't seem to stay in a room in the lord's castle," he murmured.

He picked her up then and passed through to the next room, then fell with her upon the cool, clean expanse of his majestic bed. He held her there. "You really can't go running around the castle at night," he said.

"I won't."

"So you've said upon nights gone by."

"Have I made such a vow before?"

"You seem averse to making vows."

"They can only be made when they are meant."

"There, you see, you would return to your room—or to hover over your dear friend Alex—and some temptation would arise and you would be headed down to the crypts again. Ah! And you think that *I* am strange!"

She reached out, touching his face, running her finger down the length of the scar. "It is scarcely visible," she murmured.

"I'm sorry. Apparently I'm not living up to your expectations."

She studied him. "I have no expectations," she told him. "Yet neither do I like to be deceived."

"I did not set out to deceive you."

"No, I came upon a charade long in progress," she said, and then added, "But tonight you saved Alex, and I'm grateful."

"*You* saved him."

She shook her head. "You were far more adept than I."

"I have had occasion before to deal with snake bites," he told her. "In India…the Sudan." He shrugged, turning away from her suddenly. "Even in Cairo," he added bitterly.

His words sent a sudden unease into her. "But you never have bred or raised snakes, have you?"

He looked at her surprised. "Why on earth would I? They're very dangerous—as you saw tonight." He turned away, lacing his fingers behind his head, his focus on the ceiling. "Alex was lucky, terribly lucky. That venom is brutally toxic. It seems that he has pulled through, though I daresay he'll be in pain and fog tomorrow. But if he continues to do so well…" He shrugged. "I have business in the morning. I assume you'll be tending to your good friend tomorrow."

Camille didn't answer. She decided to let him have his assumptions. She did, however, have a few plans of her own for the day.

Apparently, he misunderstood her silence. "Camille, I believe that Alex is going to survive. He's come this far, and I have seen men survive such bites."

"Yes," she murmured. "I believe he will survive."

"He is your very good friend, right?"

She stared back at him, feeling a small flutter of anger

in her heart. Brian Stirling certainly knew that they had never been more.

"Yes, Alex is my friend." Now was the time to tell him again that he'd had no right to make the absurd announcement about their engagement. But he was the Earl of Carlyle, as he was so fond of reminding her. His words were all part of the game he played, the charade. He was a peer, had been a soldier, had traveled the world.

It would be so easy to speak. So many things could be solved with conversation. Yet, she wasn't sure she wanted to hear what he would have to say. She was, after all, the one who had assured him that she made her own choices.

"Thank you for agreeing to bring Alex here," she said, a little stiffly. Her voice sounded prim, especially considering her position, lying naked next to him. But they were honest words. Naturally she would tend to Alex. But Sir John would be at the museum; he had said so when he had been called away from his search of the storeroom. And she meant to be there, too. It would prove far easier than she had hoped, since Brian would be gone.

"Camille, seriously—"

"Seriously, I'm exhausted," she murmured. "Let your game rest, I beg of you."

He fell silent. For the moment, she desperately wanted to avoid further conversation, questions, accusations and mentions of the future, so she reached out and touched him.

He took her into his arms. "I thought you were exhausted."

"Far too tired to argue," she told him. "It's far too easy for us to argue."

He rolled in the bed, meeting her eyes, stroking her face. "Ah, my dear Miss Montgomery, I'm afraid I find it far too easy *not* to argue."

He was right. Because when he touched her, there was no future. No child living in the woods. No reproach for the charade he played. No suspicion cast against her.

There was nothing but the moment.

CHAPTER FIFTEEN

NATURALLY, THE INCIDENT at the museum made headlines of all the newspapers. And naturally, all the talk regarding the curse was brought back to the fore. Every reporter diligently noted that the snake bite occurred just after Lord Stirling returned to a place of prominence at the institution after a year of mourning and announced his engagement. To a commoner. An employee of the museum.

So far, the pieces Brian quickly scanned said nothing about Camille's background. The reporters were far too busy questioning the possibility of a real curse since he had stepped back into the picture and another man had been bitten. It was mentioned that both he and his fiancée attended to the victim. The papers also heralded Alex Mittleman for his courage in attempting to secure the reptile, and went on to say that the young man was now desperately fighting for his life.

He had just finished reading the articles when Shelby came to the solarium, telling him that Sir Tristan had asked to have a moment to speak with him. He was somewhat surprised, wondering why the man hadn't just come on his own.

In Tristan's room, he was impressed and somewhat amused by the man's rationale. "I didn't want to come walking out looking too healthy!" he told Brian. "Camille is here this morning, eh?"

"I believe she'll be spending the day tending to Alex, yes."

Tristan nodded. "Well, I was thinking that Ralph and I

should slip out. Go back to the pub in the East End and have another chat with that prostitute."

Brian smiled. "I appreciate your willingness to serve, Sir Tristan. I truly do. But not today. I have business myself, and I'd prefer you stay here. Camille will be here, as you have said."

"But, as you have said, she'll be tending to Alex. Not that she doesn't care about her dear old guardian, but I'm on the mend."

"So is Alex, I believe," Brian said. "Tristan, I'd not have you out today, though again, I do appreciate your willingness to help. We'll get back to it next week, eh?"

Tristan frowned and nodded. "I know me way about, you know, Lord Stirling. I was taken a bit off guard the other day, but I'm an old soldier. I can hold me own."

"I don't doubt that," Brian assured him. "But you'd be serving me best to keep an eye on events about the castle today."

"You don't trust her, either, eh?"

"Who? Camille?"

Tristan waved a hand impatiently in the air. "Not Camille! That woman Mrs. Prior! Prowling around at night."

"What?"

"Mrs. Prior," Tristan said sagely. "Last night she was prowling the halls, and that's a fact."

Brian sighed. "Tristan, she's the housekeeper here. She has a right to be prowling the halls."

"In the dead of night?"

"What were you doing prowling the halls?"

"Heard noises," Tristan told him. "And it was her. Sneaking on down the hall to the room where you've got the young fellow, Alex."

"She probably wanted to see how he was doing," Brian said.

"So she claimed. But was she really trying to see to his welfare? Or was she trying to finish off what the asp started?"

"Tristan, Evelyn was my mother's best friend. She has stood by me through a great deal. I believe in her."

Tristan sniffed. "She's got you hornswoggled, eh?" he muttered. "An attractive woman she is, and I can see how in loneliness…well, a woman can twist a man around, can't she."

Brian wasn't sure whether to be angry or amused. "There is nothing between Mrs. Prior and me, Tristan. Nothing, except friendship."

"She may be a witch," Tristan said knowingly.

"I don't believe in witchcraft."

"Maybe you should, young fellow. Maybe you should."

"And that from an old soldier?"

Tristan flushed uneasily. "Begging your pardon, you are the Earl of Carlyle, My Lord. But I'd not be of any good to anyone if I didn't speak me mind!"

"Warning taken. So there you have it, Sir Tristan. I need you here today."

"Maybe you do, maybe you do," Tristan muttered. "Have ye seen me Camille yet this morning?"

Brian hesitated. Had he seen her? Yes, sweetly sleeping, the elegance of her length and flesh, the rich luxury of her hair, splayed upon sheets and pillow. She was breathtaking in sleep.

"I've not spoken with her. And I'm leaving on business immediately. So, Tristan, it's up to you to tend to the household. Shelby will be driving me, but Corwin will be here, should you need help of any kind."

Sir Tristan took that gravely. "And I've me own man, Ralph, as well." That seemed to mean that he could handle about anything.

"WE ARE LISTENING, Lord Wimbly."

Lord Wimbly cleared his throat. The Queen said that she was listening, and she was. Yet she wasn't looking at him, but rather giving attention to the correspondence on her desk.

Once Victoria had been lovely and young. And when Albert lived, she had been avid and passionate in so many ways. Now, though Albert had been gone decades, she still chose dark colors, and she had taken to living his ethics as if chastity and pure living assured an entrance to heaven. Albert, in life, had been her dearly beloved husband. In death, he was put on a pedestal that could never be toppled. Admittedly those who had come immediately before Victoria had led lives of debauchery, but Victoria had created a stifling world of do-good-or-die around herself. As she still seldom let the world in around her, she wasn't really aware that the common man needed to laugh upon occasion, have a pint or two… Live a life with just a touch of debauchery!

"The section does not need to be closed down for any length of time. Naturally I returned to the museum first thing this morning. And again, quite naturally, Your Majesty, the section is closed today. But the young man has survived the attack, and…dear God, Victoria!" he said, remembering the years gone past. He had resorted to the way he had spoken when they were both young, years and years gone, before she had become the Queen of England. She looked up at that instantly, one brow lifted so imperiously that he knew he had made a major mistake.

"We will not have it said that our museums are cursed," she told him.

"Forgive me!" he pleaded, but added, "Perhaps you should suggest to the Earl of Carlyle that he take a step away from the museum again. I was pleased to see him, of course, when he showed his renewed interest in our precious national treasure, but…maybe the man is cursed!" He nearly said *damn it all*. Thankfully, he managed to refrain. Surely, his swearing might well have sent her into apoplexy.

"The Earl of Carlyle has suffered grievously, and he and his late parents have served me well." She clenched her teeth for a moment. "Not a single one of my prime ministers has even had a negative word for the Stirlings and their contributions, either military or financial." She glanced at him sharply, but then her eyes returned to the papers before her. She seemed to lose focus for a moment. He had heard that her physician had prescribed cannabis for her monthlies years ago. With gritted teeth, he wondered if she had stayed on the substance.

"Your Majesty, I've already seen to it that the exhibit will be changed, and the creature that somehow managed to get loose has been given to the zoological park."

"A cobra never should have been part of an exhibit!" she snapped angrily.

No, the old girl was sharp as nails, and angry. It wasn't a good day to be having a discussion with the Queen, but he hadn't chosen to do so—he had been summoned. Of course, he had been expecting this since the debacle of the night before.

"Your Majesty, I repeat, the snake is gone." He hesitated. He desperately needed the Egyptology department of the museum to thrive. Desperately! With his gambling debts…

He tried an old ploy, striding to her desk, falling down on one knee. Victoria, despite her great age, could still be flattered. "Most noble Majesty, I beg of you! Don't let the great display of so much that creates our great Empire be hidden! I do believe that…well, forgive me, but it was your dear Prince Albert who gave us the Great Exhibition, so much of learning and industry and invention—and history, as well! Please, trust in me. Let me pave the way for even greater displays, and take away nothing from what we have!"

Her lips were still pursed, but the flattery—and the mention of her dear, departed Albert and his thirst for knowledge—seemed to have helped his appeal.

"We will give you leave to open your section on Monday," she told him. "We will trust you to take personal charge."

He lowered his head. "Thank you, Your Majesty!" he said.

"We are quite tired now," she told him.

"Yes, of course, forgive me! I have taken your time on a Saturday morning."

She turned back to her papers, dismissing him. He got out quickly. Good God, yes, the Egyptology section had to remain open! And now, not only would it do so, but he had actually been give a royal command to spend his time within it!

AT MCNALLY'S PUBLIC HOUSE, Brian put in an order for the rotgut gin the place served, and chose one of the dirty tables that looked out onto the street. He watched for a while and saw the small prostitute with whom Tristan had been talking the day before. She teased and played with the men at the bar, allowing herself to be fondled and pulled this way and that. But from what Brian could see, she wasn't making any arrangements for quick trysts in any secluded alleyways.

After a while the woman spotted him at the table and noted the fact that he was watching her. She approached and took the chair opposite him, leaning low against the table. It was a practiced move, allowing for her breasts to be pushed up to a more than abundant size and to nearly spill on the man being graced with her attentions.

"So, old timer! What y' be doin' here? Looking is free, as long as you keep the gin coming. Think there'd be more ye could manage?" Her foot slid along the length of his leg.

He ran his fingers up and down his glass, looking down at it. "I don't be needing entertainment, dearie," he said.

With shrewd, narrowed eyes, she leaned back. "Didn't appear that ye're the type to be getting it up to par, old man. But then again, I've been known to raise a few with sheer ability, if ye get me drift o' things."

She was waiting for his reaction, watching him.

"I need money myself," he told her.

"And you've a way of making it?" Once again, the woman's accent disappeared.

"I have things to sell."

"There is enough garbage around here."

"I have good things."

She eyed him up and down. His clothing was tattered; he'd rubbed dirt in the glued-on beard.

"I've no time for you, old man," she told him. "Sorry. That's the way it is." She started to rise.

"I work at the museum," he told her.

She sat back down. Her eyes narrowed again. "And you've stolen from the museum?"

He shrugged. "Who suspects an old man who can barely wield his broom?"

"I could get you arrested, you know."

Again, he shrugged. "You'd rather make money. And I don't believe that the buyers you know are from this area."

"What do you have?"

He leaned forward, whispering. She drew back, her eyes growing wider.

"Maybe…maybe I can make some arrangements."

"I don't want any 'maybes.' I saw that fellow's body the other day, the bloke at the bar there when I'd been in."

"Murder happens all the time here," she said.

He snaked his hand out suddenly, encircling her wrist. "There were other men in here trying to sell trinkets. Your man—and he *was* your man—meant to rob them, but someone killed him. Before he could get too close to the pair? You don't need to speak, I know you're not going to answer me. But when you set up a sale for me, there won't be any petty thieves following me around. I'll want a name and a place. I'll pay your price. But if I'm followed, I promise you, there will only be more dead men. As you said, murder happens all the time. You should be taking care yourself."

With that warning, he released her wrist. She sat rubbing it, staring at him.

"Do we have a deal?"

She nodded. He saw the hatred in her eyes, and dug into his pocket, producing a gold coin, which he slid straight into her hand. If they were noticed, it would appear that they were making arrangements for a dark alley.

He smiled. "I'll be watching…and waiting," he told her, and exited the pub.

Outside, he hesitated. He wanted to give her plenty of time to send a goon out after him. He believed that she did have buyers. But she didn't believe that he had anything to sell that wasn't already on his person.

Now all he had to do was move slowly.

GETTING OUT OF THE HOUSE was going to prove more difficult than Camille had realized. Shelby was gone, off somewhere with the Earl of Carlyle. The doctor was preparing to leave. And though it appeared that Alex was

fighting the remaining toxins in his system with a steady
tenacity, she was very afraid to leave him alone.

Corwin, she noticed, had taken up Shelby's position by
the door. He had greeted her with courtesy when she entered. And when she was ready to leave the room, she
spoke with him.

"Corwin, the earl is out?"

"Aye, miss."

"I need you to bring me into London."

He frowned. "Miss, I can't leave my post. And I don't
believe the earl intended for you to go into the city."

"Corwin, I'm not a prisoner, am I?"

"No, indeed not."

"I…have an appointment. Today. For confession."

"Confession?"

"I'm Catholic, Corwin." She waited, wondering if God
would strike her down for the lie. But she was certain that
a power far greater than any of them would know that her
intentions were honest.

"Ah, a Catholic," he murmured. Then, perplexed, he
said, "It's Saturday!"

"Yes, Corwin, I know the day. You confess Saturday so
that you're ready for God's grace on Sunday. Can you
please get me into London? And, of course," she added,
determined to convince him of the outright lie, "wait for
me and bring me back."

"I don't like leaving Mr. Mittleman."

"You won't be leaving him. Ralph and Tristan will look
after him."

Corwin mulled it over.

"I must get to confession!" she said, sounding desperate.

He nodded. "As you wish. And I'll be waiting for you,
you needn't worry."

She went to Tristan and found him in his room, playing chess with Ralph. He was up and dressed and looking very well.

She greeted him with a kiss on the cheek and whispered a possible move to him. Tristan's eyes widened with delight. He made the move. Ralph scratched his head.

"Ah, Camie, that's not at all fair! I'd have had his sorry hide, I would have!"

"Oh, Ralph! You're right, I shouldn't have helped. It's just that he is a recuperating man, and we wouldn't want him to feel as if he hadn't all his senses going for him, would we?"

"Your friend, Alex, is doing well?" Tristan asked.

She nodded. "Tristan, that's what I wanted to talk to you about. I'd…I'd dearly like to get to church."

"Church? It's Saturday," Tristan said.

Again, she sighed. "I know, but…." She was lying, and lying about church. That couldn't be good. Still, it was important. "I've an appointment to talk, you know."

"You can talk to me."

"She wants to speak with someone a bit more holy than the likes of us!" Ralph said.

"I feel it's important for the welfare of my soul."

"I'd imagine, Camie, that your soul is in wondrous shape!" Ralph told her.

She smiled. "It's troubled, I'm afraid. And you two have definitely put some of the trouble into my soul!" she told him, but without reprimand. "I've asked Corwin to get me into London, but I'm afraid to leave Alex alone. I mean—" She hesitated. "I mean that I don't want him left alone for a minute, not a minute."

Tristan looked at her gravely.

"I'll see to him," he swore gravely.

"Ralph, if Tristan leaves, you must see to him," she said.

Ralph nodded to her solemnly, as well.

She thanked them both.

Now, all she had to do was get out of the house without Evelyn Prior being aware that she was leaving!

HE KNEW, as soon as he started down the street, despite the bustle around him as many hurried on to the Saturday market, that he was being followed.

He made a point of joining in the market rush, pausing to inspect vegetables. Fishmongers hawked their fresh catches, and farmers crowed about the taste of their crops. He inspected fruits that were advertised to have arrived just that morning from the south, and each time he paused, he noted the man behind him.

He bought a bag of oranges, fresh in from the Mediterranean if the fellow selling them was to be believed. The bag was heavy. Perfect.

He continued his way along the streets, then set forth through a string of alleys, stepping over a drunk here and there, tossing a few coins to children begging.

At last he found what he was seeking—an overgrown square, littered with gin bottles and debris, surrounded by houses with boarded-up windows.

And when he entered, the fellow followed.

"I HAVE A GREAT DEAL on my conscience," Camille told Corwin. "If you wish to have a spot of tea or a pint of ale, I'll be a good hour or so."

"Whatever you wish, Miss Camille. I will be here," he swore, leaving her at the entrance to St. Mary's.

She quickly walked up the path to the great front doors. Once inside, she felt the guilt of her lie upon her. She wasn't Catholic, but she crossed herself before the high altar, then hurried out through the cloister.

On a back street, she found a hansom. When she arrived

at the museum, crowds were all about in the street. The fiasco of the night before had not kept them away. Indeed, it appeared they were more fascinated than ever to view the remnants of ancient Egypt. The thrill of believing that there was a curse was like an aphrodisiac.

Camille caught bits and pieces of conversation as she hurried through the Saturday crowds, then through the area where the elegantly adorned tables had been placed just the night before. Everything was as it had been, as if the gala had never taken place. Except that the terrarium was gone.

She ran up the steps and came into the offices. Sir John was not there, but his coat rested on the back of his chair. Knowing where he was, Camille sped back down the stairs to the storage rooms.

To her surprise, the door was open. She stepped in. "Sir John?" There was no answer.

She walked on in, certain that he had to be in there somewhere. "Sir John!" Still, there was no answer. She began to move through the vast aisles of cartons, coming to the rear where the massive crates had held the sarcophagi of the dead found at the last expedition. Most crates now lay open.

There was a *ping!* The light, poor at best, faded as one of the few overhead bulbs exploded.

"Sir John?"

"Camille…!" That voice again, calling out to her. Then, from within one of the crates, something slowly began to rise.

"Camille…!"

Dust from thousands of years formed a sudden haze. The mummy began to rise from the sarcophagus, then staggered to its feet and came jolting after her….

It was so dark. Her heart began to thunder as she backed away, her mind denying the possibility that such a thing could occur. And then, the cracked and terrible whisper again.

"Camille…"

AS SOON AS HE SENSED the man directly behind him, Brian spun around, planting his fingers around the fellow's throat.

"Wait! Stop, for the love of God!"

Brian held tight, feeling the man's fingers tearing at his hand in desperation. He quickly ascertained that the man wasn't filthy, and though his clothing was poor it was not shabby. He didn't seem the type to inhabit the pub.

"Start talking!" he commanded.

"I didn't come to hurt you," the man choked out.

"Why were you following me."

The fellow hesitated.

"Let's go to the police, shall we?" Brian said.

"What?"

"Let's go to the police. Now!"

The man let out a long exhaust of air. "I am the police."

It was Brian's turn to be confused. *"What?"*

"I'm Detective Clancy, Scotland Yard!" the man said quickly.

Not at all certain, Brian warily eased his hold. The fellow stepped back, rubbing his throat.

"You were at the pub," Brian said.

"You were at the pub," he said, and added nervously, "And you're under arrest."

"For...?"

"Robbery—and murder!"

CAMILLE STARED at the apparition, panic rising in her breast. She backed away, ready to turn and flee. And then, suddenly, sense and fury overrode terror. Mummies were nothing but the pathetic remains of people who had believed that their bodies would serve them in an afterlife. They did *not* come back to life. But someone willing to go to the lengths of playing a mummy might well be a murderer, though wrapped as they were, they could not do much harm. It was her chance.

She played the game, turning to run in terror. But as the creature stumbled after her, she looked for a weapon along the way.

She passed the crate she had delved into the other day. And, of course, she knew that the mummy's arm was already broken off. She reached into the crate, came to a standstill and swung with all her might, catching the lumbering being hard in the ribs.

"Damnation!" a voice cried out in agony. The figure doubled over.

Camille gave it another hard smack on the head for good measure. The creature fell to the ground, clasping its head now with wrapped hands. The ancient arm had taken too much abuse, as well. It crumpled into pieces.

"Lord God!" the thing on the floor swore.

"Who the hell are you?" Camille raged in fury, no longer afraid in the least, though she might have used more common sense.

"It's me, Camille. I was just trying to scare you."

"Me who?"

The creature was already maneuvering around to sit up. Camille reached forward, grabbing hold of a loose piece of tattered linen and pulling.

"Ouch! Go slow, please!"

The man grabbed hold of her hand, then the wrapping.

"Hunter!" she gasped.

"Yes, it's me."

"You idiot! I could have killed you."

In the darkness he looked at her dryly. "Not with a mummy's arm, though I admit, you took me by surprise and you pack a strength that hurts abominably!"

"Hunter, what in God's name are you doing?" she demanded.

"I told you! Trying to scare you."

"Why?"

"So that you get away from Brian Stirling and the wretched curse he's brought down on all of us again! Help me up, will you? And please, I beg of you, don't let it get out that I was beat to the floor by a…a woman."

"Beat to the floor! Hunter, this is far more serious than that!"

"Yes, it is. You're living with the man. And you're engaged to him."

"Hunter, stand up. Let's get the rest of these wrappings off you."

"Yes, I guess we should hurry, before Sir John makes an appearance."

"Where is he? His coat is in the office."

As they finished taking off the wrappings—half real, from some poor naked mummy, and half, apparently, concocted from museum canvas—Camille was astounded that he had been able to fool her, even for a second.

"I saw him earlier, not since," Hunter said.

"Well, you're an idiot," she told him flatly. "Sir John is somewhere. And how did you even know that I'd be in today?"

"I knew you'd be in. After last night."

"That's a ridiculous assumption. After last night, I shouldn't be anywhere near the place today!"

He grew somber suddenly. "How is old Alex doing?"

"He was sound asleep when I left, but the doctor said that he was doing very well. Steady pulse, good respiratory. It's a miracle."

"Hmm." Hunter wound all the wrappings together and set them in one of the cases. "How is my hair? Too much dust or dirt?"

"You look all right, for a grown man who played at

being a mummy," she said. "Hunter, that was truly cruel! And what did you think you'd achieve?"

He sighed. "Camille, I cannot tell you just how concerned I am. Perhaps I can't convince you that there is such a thing as a curse. But there is something very wrong at Carlyle Castle, and with Brian Stirling. He has stayed away from the museum and things have gone well. He appears, and Alex is bitten by an asp, Lord Wimbly is called before the Queen—"

"Oh, no!"

"Oh, yes!"

"And it seems that Sir John has gone slightly mad. He doesn't really hear anyone, he's never at his desk… Camille, please. I swear, I am terrified for you."

He was so sincere, it was touching. But she retained her anger and indignation. "You might have given me a heart attack, you know."

"Hardly!" he protested. "You weren't even out of here before you'd convinced yourself that a mummy couldn't rise."

"Perhaps we'd best leave now," Camille said. Then she looked at him, puzzled. "How on earth did you manage to make the lightbulb break?" she demanded.

"I didn't," he admitted with a rueful grin. "It was simply rather convenient timing."

She sighed, shaking her head. "Hunter, if you ever—"

"Camille, please, tell me that you'll at least think about what I'm saying?" he begged.

"Hunter, you're right. I don't believe in curses. We shouldn't have kept a cobra at the museum. Naturally Lord Wimbly has to face the music regarding what happened. However, I believe it will all work out."

"There's something evil afoot, whether it's a curse or a madman," he said.

She sighed, looking downward.

He stepped forward, catching her chin. "Why, you're in love with the bastard, aren't you?"

"Hunter—" she began to say, then froze.

They were both dead still as they heard the eerie sound of a groan in the near darkness.

CHAPTER SIXTEEN

BRIAN SAT in one of the few private offices at the Metropolitan police station with Detective Clancy and Sergeant Garth Vickford, the first one at the scene of the shooting yesterday.

Though he hadn't shed his costume hair or beard, Brian had identified himself in the square. At first, Clancy had a bit of difficulty believing him or grasping the situation. But since Brian had been the one with the upper hand there, he'd been forced to listen.

Brian had been averse to continuing their discussion in the square, not certain if there had been others following him from the pub, as well. He did not care to have Clancy or himself shot down by a sniper on a distant roof or by bold ruffians simply running in from the alley, so he had insisted that they head for the station to further their conversation.

"We know that the fellow killed in the square was the man actually arranging the sales of black market items," Detective Clancy explained to Brian. "His name, we know now, was William Green, or at least that's as close as we'll get to his true identity. That woman at McNally's apparently changed her line of work during the days of Jack the Ripper, though I imagine she takes on a fellow now and then. But mainly she pretends to be a whore, and acts as a go-between for all manner of criminals. We knew there was such a place, we just didn't know where many of the illegal Egyptian transactions were taking place until Green was killed the other day and some bystanders mentioned that he'd come from McNally's."

"There have been those dealing in the black market forever," Brian said. "What drew this sudden interest and determination from your department?"

Clancy flushed, looking at Vickford. "Well, it's come down the line, you see." He cleared his throat. "We all know that our good Queen Victoria once believed in mesmerism and the like. And as eager as she is for her Empire, for Britain's stake in Egypt and the Commonwealth, it seems she might also believe in tombs being cursed and all that rot. But then she recently discovered that a number of treasures bound for Britain were winding up in France. There's nothing to annoy her like the French taking a lead in anything, you know. She's had warnings out with our superiors, Lord Stirling, since you returned from Egypt with…with your parents' remains. We've gotten our hands on a few of the petty dealers, but there's a Frenchman who has diplomatic immunity. The fellow's name is Lacroisse, Henri Lacroisse. He's frequently at court, and just as frequently taking trips home. We believe he's looking to buy a very specific object that someone has promised him. When we found Green shot, we managed to bring in a few witnesses. Twice, when we showed them sketches, they recognized Henri Lacroisse as a man who had been seen on the streets with Green."

"If you suspect him of murder, why don't you bring him in?" Brian demanded.

"He is a French diplomat," Vickford supplied, shaking his head. "It's not an easy matter." He frowned. "And we don't believe he shot Green. He was at a tea at the time, or so a number of witnesses will swear. We did go so far as to discreetly ascertain his whereabouts."

Brian looked at the two policemen. "The buyer is not going to kill his messenger," he said.

"Of course," Detective Clancy said with dignity. "But we still had to make sure. Naturally our assumption is that the person with the treasure either killed Mr. Green or had him killed. God knows why. Maybe he had threatened to talk to save his own skin. Anyway, he's paid the ultimate price for his crimes, and like as not, with a fellow like him, the hangman has been saved some work."

"Does the Queen or the Marquis of Salisbury know that you are suspicious of this man, Lacroisse?"

Clancy looked uncomfortable. "So far, all that I've been is suspicious. And you know Her Majesty. As fine and good as she is a ruler for a Constitutional Monarchy, she remains…well, she remains the Queen. The prime minister is far more pragmatic. Still, without proof, his hands are tied. And this moment Her Majesty is still deeply disturbed that there were whispers about the Royal House during the Ripper terror, and she is not going to allow us to accuse Lacroisse without evidence. But Lacroisse couldn't be buying treasures if someone wasn't selling them. I'm afraid, Lord Stirling, that I was delighted to think I had my man, or at least an involved culprit, when I followed you from the pub. Now I fear we are all but back to square one."

"Maybe not," Brian mused.

"How so?" Clancy asked.

Brian rose. "Perhaps, Detective Clancy, diplomatic protocol prevents you from questioning this Monsieur Lacroisse. But it does not prevent me from asking him to dine with curators and staff of the museum."

CAMILLE TURNED, following the sound of the groan.

"Camille! Wait, you could be…hurt!" Hunter called after her. He followed quickly behind.

She didn't fear being hurt. Whoever was groaning was in pain.

She went down one wrong row of cartons and boxes and sarcophagi, then turned and backtracked along the right row. She saw the body on the floor next to the boxes before recognizing the man. *Sir John.*

"Oh!" she cried, falling to her knees at his side. He was struggling to sit up. She caught his shoulders. "Sir John…"

It would be inane to ask him if he was all right; he definitely wasn't. But he was blinking, steadying himself. "What happened? Are you seriously hurt?" she said, looking at him anxiously.

He shook his head, swallowing, closing his eyes and frowning. "Help me up!" he said.

By then, Hunter was at her side. "Sir John, here, take my arm."

"Maybe you shouldn't be getting up so fast! Take it easy. What happened?" she asked at last, seeing that he didn't intend to heed her words of warning, and that he was rising.

"How long have I been…unconscious?" he asked in return.

Camille shook her head. Hunter's eyes widened and he lifted his shoulders, assuring her he was as baffled as she.

"It, um, had to be a while," he said, not admitting that he had been in the storeroom for some time.

"Sir John!" Camille said firmly. "What happened to you?"

"Let's get him upstairs, get him some water," Hunter suggested.

Camille glared at him. "Did someone attack you?" she demanded, taking his other arm, helping Hunter lead him toward the door.

"I—" He stopped walking. "I don't know! I was down here, looking. It has to exist, you know."

"What has to exist?" Hunter said.

"Why, the cobra, of course," Sir John said, as if puzzled that Hunter shouldn't understand.

"Sir John, I think we need to go to the police," she said.

"What cobra?" Hunter asked.

"The police!" Sir John protested, alarmed. "No…no!" He shook his head, an emphatic no and another attempt to clear his mind. He pulled free from her hold and Hunter's, backing away. "No. It was the lid of the packing carton. No one came after me. I was foolish, careless. And annoyed. The cleaning fellow had been around the place, and I wanted to be annoyed. I'm afraid I was rather sharp with the old man. And then I was impatient. It's one of those lids that has hinges. I put it up but I didn't secure it. It fell on my head!"

Camille didn't believe him. And she was suddenly suspicious of the cleaning man. It was true that since the fellow had been hired, he did a lot more hovering than cleaning and sweeping!

"Arboc was here?" she said.

"Yes. Everything was in quite a state after last night, as you can imagine."

"Sir John, maybe the fellow hit you," Camille said.

"Camille, I have told you what happened."

"What cobra?" Hunter said again.

Camille sighed, shaking her head. "There was mention of a golden, jeweled cobra in the work I'm transcribing, that's all. And it isn't in any of the catalogues or lists."

"But I believe it exists!" Sir John said. "And it must be found. I must find it before…before it cannot be found."

"Sir John, perhaps next week we should take a day where we bring in the police and the entire staff, and just go through everything here."

He glanced at her, but he wasn't really giving her his

attention. "It needs to be found." He touched his forehead and closed his eyes. He looked as if he was about to faint again.

Camille reached out, touching the back of his head. She cried out. "Sir John! You've an enormous knot on your crown. You need a doctor—"

"No! It's a bump, it will go down. I do not want a doctor. There will be no more attention drawn to this museum at the moment. There will be no more doctors brought in, and there will be no more talk about curses!" he said.

"Then you must get home," she told him firmly.

"Yes, you must go home!" Hunter agreed.

He looked from one to the other and then sighed, seeming to lose strength. "All right, all right. I'll go home immediately." He managed to get the strength together to walk ahead of the two of them. "I'll get one of the officers down here, have him watching. There are too many keys out. Too many keys."

He stopped at the door and turned to them, his eyes suddenly suspicious. "Are you coming?"

"Yes, yes, of course," Camille murmured, looking worriedly at Hunter. Then she glanced at the watch locket she wore around her chest and winced. Good Lord, she must have been admitting to scores of sins!

"Hunter, I must…go," she said. "Will you see to it, please, that Sir John actually gets into a hansom or a carriage. He must go home!"

"I'll see to it," Hunter swore.

She bid Sir John a safe and restful Sunday, left him with Hunter and hurried out of the building, eagerly seeking a cab at the entrance.

SIR JOHN WAS IN AGONY, and so rattled that he couldn't think straight. Hunter was there, with him. They stood in one of the exhibition halls, yet he couldn't quite grasp where he was. He needed to stay, to finish what he had started. No, no...he needed to get home. To get rid of the pounding in his head.

"Come on, Sir John, I've got to see you out of here," Hunter said. "I've promised Camille."

"Yes...and she'll be a countess now, soon, right?" Sir John murmured.

"Do you believe that? I don't," Hunter said harshly. "He's using her. All he wants is revenge. Against us."

"No...no..." Sir John said.

"She'll see it soon enough. And I won't let him continue to use her—against us."

"What do you intend to do?" Sir John asked worriedly.

"Expose him."

"You'll ruin us all."

"Oh, come, come, Sir John. He isn't the only rich man in England! And he's not sane, no matter what the pretense, the show. Come on, I've got to get you out of here."

Despite the pain, Sir John shook his head. "I need a little time."

"Sir John, I promised Camille that I'd see you home!"

"Then wait for me here. I have something to do first."

"I'll come with you."

"No!" Sir John said firmly. He looked at Hunter suspiciously. "You wait right here!"

"Right here, in the Old Kingdom exhibit, eh?" Hunter said.

"Just wait!" Sir John said, and he forced himself not to stagger as he hurried for the stairs.

CAMILLE RETURNED TO THE CHURCH, hurried through the cloisters, nearly knocked over a priest and stopped for a second to offer an abject apology.

Out on the street again, she felt her heart skip a few
beats. She didn't see Corwin in the crowds.

"Miss Camille!" he called her, and she turned, grate-
fully heading for the carriage. He helped her in, saying
nothing about the amount of time she'd been gone.

The drive back to the castle seemed long and, indeed,
with the traffic in the streets, it was. She wondered what
business Brian had been about that day; she prayed she
reached Carlyle Castle before he returned.

It was nearly dark when they came to the outer gates.
As the carriage ventured in, she heard the wolves crying
in the forest, foretelling the coming of night. The horses'
hooves clip-clopped over the drawbridge.

At the doorway to the castle proper, she thanked Corwin and hurried in. She went immediately to Alex's room
and was relieved to find him there with both Tristan and
Ralph. They had brought their chess set in.

"How is he?" she asked anxiously.

"He wakes now and then. He has had a spot of tea, a bit
of broth. I believe he's doing well," Tristan said.

"*She* brought the broth," Ralph said.

"But we sniffed it good, then tasted it," Tristan told her.
"And we've not dropped dead yet!"

Camille frowned. They were taking their guard duties
very much to heart. Evelyn Prior might be suspicious, but
she'd hardly dare poison anyone in the earl's house!

"I'll stay with him now, if you two have…well, anything to do," she said. There was little they could do. Now
that Tristan was well, they could leave the castle. Except
that, at her own insistence, Alex was here now.

As the men stared at her, she found herself wondering
what she would do if it weren't for Alex. Tristan was obviously well enough for them to return home. But…did she
want to return home?

It was one thing to be used by a nobleman who was passionately bitter, determined on the truth. It was another when he began announcing that they were engaged when they were not. And when...she was in love with him.

"We could take a bit of a walk," Tristan told Ralph.

"A walk is good," Ralph agreed. "Except for the wolves."

"Well, the wolves aren't this side of the bridge. We'll stroll the courtyard. And then we'll come back here. And I'll trounce you again, Ralph!"

"Humph!" Ralph said indignantly. He looked at Camille. "When I was winning, Sir Tristan had the strangest tic in his leg. Toppled the board over, he did."

"Tristan, I hope you conceded that game to Ralph," she said.

Tristan smiled ruefully. "Aye, it was Ralph's game! Well, shall we? Let's see if the old Iron Maiden tries to stop us!"

"Let her try!" Ralph said.

The two men left, but Camille had the feeling that if they were to so much as see Evelyn Prior in the hall, they'd be running back.

She sat on the bed next to Alex, noting that his color was good indeed, and that his pulse was strong. As she held his wrist, he opened his eyes. He tried a weak smile.

"Camille."

"I'm here. How do you feel?"

"Stronger," he said. He hesitated and tried to sit.

She caught his shoulders, easing him back. "You were bitten by a cobra, Alex. You must take is slowly."

"Camille," he said again, and it was as if the effort to speak cost him a great deal.

"I'm here."

He shook his head. "We...we have to leave. All of us. You, me, Tristan, his man, Ralph. I...can't stay. Can't be here."

"Alex, you must get better."

He shook his head. "He'll try to kill me again."

"Who?"

"The Earl of Carlyle."

His voice was so hoarse and rasping that it sent a chill through her limbs.

"Alex, Brian didn't try to kill you. You were bitten by a cobra."

"He...he let it loose."

"Alex, I came to the museum with Brian. He wasn't there before me."

"He was there. I know that he's been there." His voice was weak, then he suddenly gripped her hand tightly. "Camille, that's it, don't you see? He blames us all. His parents died and he blames us. All of us who were there. And he intends to have us all die, as well, one by one, in ways that can't be traced, can't be proven—like his parents."

"Alex, that's madness!"

"Yes, it's madness."

"Alex, listen. Brian hasn't been at the museum!"

"He's been there. I know he's been there. And he means to find ways for all of us to die. Because they died, and we didn't."

"Alex—"

"We've got to leave here, Camille."

She sighed. "Alex, we can't leave. You're still too weak, and I was the one who insisted on bringing you here."

"He'll never really marry you, you know," Alex said distractedly.

I know! she cried inwardly.

"He has a way about him, he always did. He is the Earl of Carlyle now, of course. But people always believed him, believed in him. He is seducing you to madness, Camille. You've got to see this, realize it."

"Alex! Please—" She broke off, hearing a tapping at the door. She rose and opened it.

Evelyn Prior stood there. "So, dear, you have returned."

"Yes."

"And are tending to Alex."

"Yes, and I will do so myself through the night, Mrs. Prior."

"Certainly. I can tend to him while you go to Mass tomorrow."

"Mass?"

"Dear child, I know that you will naturally be eager to go to Mass. All those hours of confession today…I had not realized you were quite so religious. The earl, of course, is Anglican. Our beliefs are a bit different from yours."

"With all the hours I spent in church today, Mrs. Prior, I believe God will forgive me when I don't attend tomorrow. Alex is my friend. I will look after him."

"Or have Tristan do so," she said.

"It's my responsibility," Camille told her.

"I see. Shall I have supper sent for you here, then?"

"That would be very kind," Camille said, and hesitated. "Has Lord Stirling returned to the castle yet?"

"I have not seen him."

"Well, thank you."

"Your supper will arrive shortly," Mrs. Prior said, and giving Camille a long assessing look, she turned and left at last.

Camille went back to sit by the bed. Alex, however, had slipped into a fitful doze. She drew up one of the heavy armchairs, leaned against it. Despite the insanity of the thoughts rushing through her mind, it was only minutes before she fell asleep herself.

Sɪʀ Jᴏʜɴ ᴡᴀs ᴇxᴘᴇᴄᴛɪɴɢ the knock at his door. He rubbed the knot on the back of his head, hesitated and fingered the little pistol in front of him on his drawing room desk.

The knock sounded again. Hard.

He slipped the pistol into his drawer, on top of his papers—where he could reach it easily.

"Come in," he said, "the door is not locked."

His visitor entered. The door closed. Minutes later, the muted sound of gunfire could have been heard on the street—had anyone been about to hear it.

Sʜᴇʟʙʏ sʜᴏᴏᴋ ʜɪs ʜᴇᴀᴅ at Brian Stirling. He had served with the man in India, seen him under the harshest conditions, watched him cast his own life into danger before ever asking that sacrifice of another man. He had followed him to Cairo, and sat with him through the anguish, the rages and the loss. He had served him not because he had needed the work so much as because Brian Stirling had never asked a man to think less of himself as a human being based on the class he had been born into.

But at the moment, Shelby was wondering at Brian's sanity.

"It's an impossible task."

"Impossible? Nothing is impossible," Brian said.

"It's been quite a day. I didn't know whether to show myself or not when the culprit in the square turned out to be a police officer," Shelby said. "Now, Lord Stirling! You've a real lead, a chance to discover what is going on. Can't you rest for the night? Must we start this now?"

"Shelby, every night, someone is coming closer. The castle is riddled with doors and stairways. My father was convinced there was a tunnel, I feel the same. Yes, the expanse around the wall is monstrous. But there will be some sign that the area is disturbed." He grinned, rubbing his bearded chin, which was starting to give him quite a fit. "Haven't you ever heard the story about the little squirrel in winter, Shelby?"

"Didn't hear many stories growing up in a family of ten, Lord Stirling. My folks were working in one way or another most of the time," Shelby said. He sighed. "You are going to tell me the story, though, eh?"

"Indeed, Shelby. When winter is coming, does a little squirrel try to take twenty acorns into his hole? No, he takes the acorns one by one. Tonight, we'll take it from both ends. You'll start by the gate and go each night, bit by bit, until the entire property has been circled. I'll get rid of this wretched beard, we'll get Corwin, and the two of you will start as soon as the moon is up. I'll be taking it from the other end. First, however, to your apartments. If I remain as Arboc for another minute, I will be a monster indeed, clawing my own skin from my face!"

Shelby stared at Brian for a minute, then shook his head.

"What is it?" Brian asked.

"You've spent months looking in the crypts," he said at last.

"Actually," Brian said, "I've spent months in the office area, the old torture chamber. I've not been into the crypts at all yet."

Shelby groaned softly. "You must do it at night?"

"If we're to catch a thief and a killer, that's when he works, Shelby."

Shelby nodded. "Aye, then. We'll start as you wish."

CAMILLE WOKE WITH A START, and looked at Alex. He continued to sleep. She wondered what had awakened her. And then she knew.

The stonework of the ancient castle always made the

noise sound distant and muted, but still it came, a grating—
sometimes sharp, sometimes like a groaning sound.

She glanced at Alex again, but he seemed to be sleeping like a lamb. She touched his forehead and found that
it wasn't hot. His pulse was strong.

She realized that the door had cracked open, and someone was looking in. Before she could move, the door
closed. A feeling of ice trickling within her veins seized
her, then she rose. She walked to the door, cracked it open
again and looked into the hallway.

Evelyn Prior was in the hall, now retreating from Alex's
door, heading for the stairway. She was in her nightdress
and robe, which were both white, and it almost seemed that
she was floating along the floor. She carried no lamp. But,
of course, Evelyn wouldn't need one. She knew her way
in the dark.

Camille longed to follow her. She looked back at Alex;
he was still sleeping, yet she was afraid to leave him. And
why? Because he was so afraid. And his fear was…conta-
gious.

None of his fears could possibly be true. Still, Camille
couldn't shake the dread that if Alex was left alone, in his
weakened state, someone would slip in and finish what the
cobra had started.

She went to the chair by Alex and sat back down. And
as she did so, she found herself longing for the night before, longing for a touch of the man, for a night in which
she could forget everything except being held, tempted,
teased and taken…in the darkness—where reality had no
hold over desires.

Brian Stirling was probably below. In the crypts.
Searching madly, as he always was, seeking answers in
what had become his obsessed quest. If Evelyn came upon
him… That was insane. Evelyn had been here with him,

forever. If she offered any danger to Brian Stirling, it would have come long ago. And Ajax was surely with his master.

Something inside her cried out suddenly, *Where had Brian been all day?* And more importantly, why hadn't he come to see her, find her, coerce her back across the hall with him…?

OPENING THE RUSTED GATES produced a sound like a banshee's wail. He might have tried to draw them open bit by bit, but decided instead that one rough and shrieking tug would be best. He damned himself for again putting off the idea of bringing workmen in.

The crypts, untouched for so many years, were surprisingly clear of dust. But then again, nothing had moved, nothing had been disturbed here. There were tombs set in a line down the length of the main aisle, and crypts within the wall. They'd been designed in a cross fashion, so a secondary hall sliced across the first about three-quarters of the way down. The oldest grave dated from 1310, and was that of one of his ancestors, born Count Morwyth Stirling, later to become the first Earl of Carlyle. In the late 1700s, one of his industrious great-great-great-aunts had set about a renovation of the crypts, so the stones were clearly etched where brass and copper had not been used for memorials, and there were no open crypts with ancestors aligned merely upon shelves, as did remain in some old family vaults. Here and there, there were spiderwebs, and crumbled stone. And as he walked along, he heard the squeal of a rat.

He turned back at a moaning sound, then nearly laughed aloud at himself. Ajax was on the other side of the gate, moaning softly, as if warning Brian that he shouldn't go in.

"They're all just family, boy," he told the dog softly. Frowning, Brian left the crypts and returned to the office area, quietly walking to the foot of the stairs. He held very still, waiting.

"Someone is there, eh, boy?" he asked softly, and Ajax began to bark. Brian headed quickly up the stairs, but whoever had been there was gone. Was it Camille, making another trek into the night?

He hurried up to the second floor. All was silent; he hadn't been quick enough. Yet once there, he felt his heart thudding. He walked to the door behind which Alex Mittleman lay recovering.

Camille was in the chair by his bed, eyes closed, her head resting on her hands on the chair arm. He longed to go to her. Was she only pretending? Had she tiptoed down the stairs to see what he was doing?

"Watch over them, Ajax," he told the dog.

Then he turned and went back down to his task.

CAMILLE WAS STARTLED to hear many voices in the breakfast room when she approached it at last, late and feeling the aches and pains of sleeping in a chair that not even a long, hot bath had been able to ease. She was apparently the last in the household to arrive.

Brian Stirling was seated with his newspapers, as always. Evelyn Prior was across from him. Tristan and Ralph were in attendance, courteously complimenting Evelyn on her scones. Ralph, though he had been considered a family member in all the years he had lived with Tristan and Camille, looked a little awed to have been invited into such a grand place as the breakfast solarium. Even Alex, looking ashen and weak, had managed to bring himself into the room. And they also had another visitor—Lord Wimbly.

His plate was piled high with thick bacon and fluffy eggs, and though it appeared he had been talking all the while, he was also enjoying his breakfast.

"Good timing, I do say," he said to Brian as Camille came in. "Mrs. Prior, you are an excellent cook!"

"Thank you, Lord Wimbly," she said demurely, rising as she noted Camille coming in. "Coffee, dear? Or tea?"

"Coffee, please," she said.

Brian looked up sharply from his paper. He didn't look pleased as he assessed her. He rose, though, and pulled out a chair for her.

"Good morning, Camille."

"My dear, dear child!" Lord Wimbly said.

"Camille!" Tristan looked at her with tremendous reproach. "You're to be married!"

"I—" She glanced at Brian.

"Now, quite rightly, Lord Stirling has asked for my blessing. But you didn't say a word to me about the announcement at the gala!" Tristan reproached her.

"Ah…well, Alex was near death!" she said.

Alex smiled weakly.

"But such a thing is still…monumental!" Tristan said proudly.

And it's all a lie! she wanted to shout.

"When will the wedding take place?" Lord Wimbly asked. "A grand affair, I imagine. Takes time, planning," he said pragmatically.

Evelyn handed Camille a cup of coffee. "Indeed, it will take planning and discussion, since Lord Stirling is an Anglican and the bride-to-be is Roman Catholic."

"We're not Catholic," Tristan said, frowning. "We belong to the Anglican Church."

"Oh?" Evelyn said, looking pointedly at Camille.

She was definitely on the spot. "We have always attended the Anglican Church officially," she said, "but I'm afraid that I've always been fond of the Roman Catholic ritual, so…I follow many of their practices." God, she decided, was really going to have to forgive her.

"Well, we are living in a world where tolerance is demanded. Still, you will be marrying the Earl of Carlyle," Evelyn said.

"Kings have married Catholics," Ralph put in.

"And a few of them have lost their heads," Evelyn said sweetly.

"Only Charles I lost his head!" Tristan protested.

"Ah, but a great deal of royalty has gone to the scaffold!" Evelyn argued.

"This is nonsense! We are living in a great age, beneath one of the finest constitutional monarchies ever to exist," Lord Wimbly said. "Honestly, at this meeting tonight, however grave, Brian, we must really celebrate your engagement to our dear Camille!"

"Meeting tonight?" she asked.

"Yes." Brian's eyes remained hard. She realized that he had heard the reports of her activities yesterday and was both angry and suspicious. But where had *he* been all day?

"Actually, we're having a dinner," Brian said. "Thankfully, Alex will be well enough to attend. Sir John will be there, Lord Wimbly, a French envoy, a Monsieur Lacroisse, a few of the gentlemen on the board of trustees. Naturally Aubrey will be invited, as well as Sir Hunter. After the events of the gala, it seems that we needed to regroup, as it were."

She stared back at him. Regroup, indeed!

"Eggs, dear?" Evelyn asked.

"No, thank you, I'm afraid I'm not very hungry this morning."

"Well, it will be a very busy place today, lots to do, caterers coming in!" Evelyn said. She looked flushed and pleased, and added hesitantly, "Like the old days."

"Yes, well, I'd best be off!" Lord Wimbly said. He, too, sounded pleased. "Much to do before I return. Brian, I must say I'm delighted. I was deeply disturbed when I had my man drive me out this morning. Your solution for a quiet dinner to establish some sound conversation regarding the future is brilliant, simply brilliant."

"I'm glad you approve, Lord Wimbly," Brian said, rising.

"Until this evening," Lord Wimbly told them all, and took his exit.

"I believe I'd best retire for more rest, if I'm to appear my brightest and best this evening," Alex said.

"I'll sit with you, of course," Camille said.

"No," Brian said sharply. "Tristan and Ralph are into a chess tournament of a kind. They intend to keep Alex company and see to anything he might want or need. I'd like to have a word with you myself, my dear."

She nodded pleasantly, though her heart was pounding.

"So much to do!" Evelyn murmured. "Oh, dear, there are so many eggs left. Ah, well, they are supposedly quite good for Ajax's coat! Ajax, you come along with me."

Ajax, who had been sleeping at Brian's feet, arose. *Don't go with her!* Camille longed to cry out. But she held silent. The great wolfhound was up, wagging his tail, apparently understanding completely that he was being offered a breakfast treat.

"Camille, if you will be so kind, my dear?" Brian said.

She forced a smile and preceded him out of the solarium, and down the hall. At the entrance to his suite, he opened the door, once again allowing her to move ahead of him. But the second she was in the room, he closed the door and leaned against it. His eyes were ice beneath the mask.

"Where in God's name were you yesterday?" he demanded.

"Where were *you?*"

"I had business. Where were you?"

"I had business."

"Confession?"

"I do have a great deal to confess," she murmured.

"Think of me as your confessor, then. Where were you?"

"I went into the museum," she told him.

"What?"

She took a deep breath and repeated, "I went into the museum."

"Are you mad?"

"It's where I work!"

"It's where a cobra was loose the night before. Whatever made you go in? You knew, obviously, that it was a dangerous thing to do because you lied to Corwin. And he, being the trusting fellow he is, sat outside a church for hours waiting for you."

"I did go into the church," she murmured.

"Why did you go to the museum?"

"To find the cobra—the golden cobra. The object that seems to be of the greatest interest to everyone!"

"You will not go into the museum anymore," he said angrily.

"I will go where I choose!" she told him. "I am not your prisoner. You can't hold Tristan here any longer, either!" she claimed, but her voice was faltering. He was the Earl of Carlyle. He could make many things happen.

"Are you so eager to go, then? You despise it here so much?" he demanded.

"I make my own choices!" she reminded him. "And you cannot order me around. Where were you? Why do you disappear all the time? What insanity are you playing at?"

"No insanity. Camille, as I told you, this is a dangerous game. I never should have brought you in on it. God knows

I had not even suspected the turns it would take. I had not expected...damn you, Camille!" He took one step toward her, gripping her by the shoulders, looking as if he longed to shake her, fingers remaining tense on her instead.

"Damn you, Camille. Damn you!"

"Damn you!" she cried back.

His fingers tensed anew. He shook his head, gritting his teeth. Then an oath left his lips. Suddenly his mouth was upon hers, filled with the passion and fury of his anger, yet eliciting an instant arousal within her that soared at that mere touch. The fever was greater than ever before, perhaps because she had become so familiar with his touch, taste, perhaps because anticipation was knowledge now. Or perhaps because she could not bear the fact that she had not lain beside him the night before.

Instinct, raw, earthy and sweet, had come to live within her heart. She met his touch, both tender and savage, with a volatile hunger and fury of her own, returning his kiss, falling against him, melting into him, fingers tangling into his hair and trailing with electric energy down his shoulders, tearing at his shirt.... Only one thing caused her to draw away.

"The mask!" she whispered.

For a second, he hesitated. Then it was gone.

In a tangle of fused lips and arms, they shed clothing in a whirl of frantic need, desire overriding anger, breathlessness stealing words, a fire in the blood driving all else. Just a short time ago, she would have mocked such a desperate abandon. But now she needed only to be in his arms, to feel his naked flesh against hers, to know the heat and warmth and power that engulfed him when he touched her. His hands were everywhere, so quickly. Shed clothing was tossed where it lay as he continued to kiss, caress and stroke while inching ever closer to the door separating the rooms of his suite. Finally they were before the great canopied bed and she was falling against it, feeling the weight of him atop her. There, she discovered her own prowess, lips finding his throat, the expanse of his chest, hands savoring the feel of the man beneath her. She inched against him, body flush with body, breasts pressing against him, skin and muscle and searing heat, lips playing over his flesh in a need both desperate and instinctive. The ragged sound of his breath, the fire of his fingers upon her, all drove her. She touched and licked and teased, and felt the explosion of him beneath. Then his hands turned her to his own will as he coerced and seduced anew, creating the steady rise of magic and lava that she had come to know, yet coveted more each time. Like magic, he brought her higher, and ever more beneath the urgent spell of hunger and fulfillment.

When he touched her, when he was within her, when his arms were around her…there was no world beyond.

There was only the soaring, the ever rampant, thundering rise, and the volatile climax that rocked her, shattering all else.

In the shadow of his arms, she lay for long, sweet moments, with only the feel of him, the music of their hearts, their breathing coming together. It was a moment to cherish, a sweet moment for dreams.

His gentle fingers smoothed her hair. His lips just brushed her forehead. And then, his words.

"You cannot go back to the museum anymore."

"I *must*."

"You will not."

"You will not tell me what to do."

"I am the Earl of Carlyle."

"This is not feudal England! I am not your subject! I make my own—"

"You will not make your own choice, not in this!"

"Damn you!"

"Damn *you!*"

And then she was in his arms again, with his fierce kisses and her own angry response to them.

Much later, he sighed softly. "Regrettably, we cannot do this all day."

"The argument has not ended!"

"I pray that's true," he said, and rose. "There's much to do. Much," he murmured. He left her upon the expanse of the bed and began collecting the clothing he had shed. And she knew, though she could not see him, that he re-donned the mask before anything else.

"You must meet at the entry in an hour," he said.

"But you just said that there's so much to do!"

"Indeed, there is. But I announced an engagement last night. It's now Sunday. And since you felt that desperate need for confession and were let off before a Catholic church, I believe that we must make an appearance at the parish church. We wouldn't want anyone questioning our intentions. And surely you wouldn't want to waste the pureness of soul you acquired yesterday! An appearance will be expected!"

"But—"

Too late. She heard the outer door open and close, then Evelyn's voice in the hallway. Camille leaped up in a fury, hastily scrambling around for the clothing she had shed. To repair her hair took some effort. But at last, groomed to respectability, she walked back out into the hall, her heart hammering. But no one was in sight.

She hurried down the hall to Alex's room and peeked in. Alex himself was back in bed. Tristan and Ralph were at their chess game before the fire, whispering to one an-

other, glancing over their shoulders now and then to see
that Alex slept.

She was about to announce herself when Tristan said,
"It's not insanity. Not with a man dead in the streets, and
the Earl of Carlyle right there—well, there disguised as
Arboc as it were, following us."

Camille froze in the doorway, stunned.

"It's time to get ourselves and the lass out of here, Tristan. I'm telling you."

"He's engaged to her!"

Ralph looked sadly at Tristan. "Is he? He risks his life.
Now, he is risking hers."

"He's looked out for her at the museum, playing at
being the old fellow," Tristan said.

Arboc! Her blood chilled to ice. He was Arboc, and he
had never told her. He had been at the museum yesterday
morning, when Sir John had received the wound to his
head.

Brian Stirling was Jim Arboc. And according to Tristan's words, people *died* when he was near.

She closed the door and ran to her room. Inside, she
walked fretfully to the mantel and leaned against it, shivering. Alex, with the toxin from the cobra racing through
his system, had said, *He wants vengeance. He wants to kill
us all.*

And though her heart denied it, she was forced to acknowledge that the Earl of Carlyle was always a man in
disguise, whether he wore a mask or not.

CHAPTER SEVENTEEN

THANKFULLY THEIR TRIP to church was quick and public. Back at the castle, Camille spent the remainder of the afternoon trying desperately to organize her thoughts and feelings about what she knew. Point one: Brian Stirling was Jim Arboc. And as she kept coming back to it, she became more and more disturbed. Arboc was cobra spelled backward. The name had been an anagram.

Point two: Tristan had become involved in what was going on, and had told her nothing about it. That meant that tonight or first thing tomorrow, she was going to have a good row with Tristan!

Point three: She had found mention of a golden, jeweled cobra while transcribing. There were cases from the expedition in two places, the museum and the castle.

Point four: They had all been there when the late Lord and Lady Stirling died.

But what was her part in this? She knew that she was being used! He had intended to use her, of course, and had openly stated that from the beginning. He could not be accused of taking his actions in more than one direction. And she had made her own choices.

Still, how did she trust him? He questioned her mercilessly, but gave nothing of himself. He wore a mask he did not need. And more than one person thought that he really was insane. God knows, he was bitter enough.

She prowled her room, more anxious than ever to get back to her work. Hethre had been the concubine, the mistress with the power. Hers had been the name used to strike terror into the hearts of would-be tomb robbers. She stopped pacing, suddenly certain that she knew where to find the gold and bejeweled cobra.

She was anxious, desperately anxious, to prove her theory be fact. But there would be no question of her leaving the castle this evening. So she would have to wait. So she went back to her notes.

If the Stirlings had indeed been murdered, it had surely had been for the golden cobra. What better, more sadistic way to kill than with cobras.

That thought was with her when she came down the stairs at last.

CHAMPAGNE WAS BEING PASSED about in the entry. Evelyn, who was serving as hostess, handed her a flute. She was instantly hailed by Brian, elegant in attire once again, and summoned to meet a stranger by the doorway.

Brian set an arm around her shoulder. It was a natural move, as if she were cherished, truly the woman with whom he intended to spend the rest of his life. It felt wonderful. And she felt…a little ill. She was in love with him, and she was afraid of him in oh so many ways!

"My dear, I'd like you to meet Monsieur Lacroisse. He is an envoy from France, and a man as dedicated as any at our own fine museum in the pursuit of all things from ancient Egypt. Monsieur, Miss Camille Montgomery, my fiancée."

The Frenchman was trim, tall and elegant, as well, with lean, aesthetic features, a mustache and a trim little goatee. He bowed elaborately over Camille's hand. "I am enchanted, mademoiselle."

Lord Wimbly strode up. "Henri! Congratulations! They have said that you managed to acquire one of the finest pieces in recent history, a mammoth bust of Nefertiti. Was there no difficulty with the department of antiquities in Cairo?"

"I have worked with the department often," the Frenchman told Lord Wimbly. "The bust has been purchased legally—there were actually many in the cache." He shrugged. "At least, when the Egyptian scholars deal with us, we English and French, they are paid. Too often, the difficulties lie with their own poor, desperate to sell anything. There is an entire city of grave robbers, you know—families who have survived through the centuries by slipping into ancient tombs and selling what they find to foreigners. But, Lord Wimbly, you and your group of curators, trustees and explorers are far more to be congratulated. There has been no find to rival that made by Lord and Lady Stirling in years and years!"

"Quite right," Lord Wimbly said. "Ah, and here is our true adventurer, Sir Hunter MacDonald. Hunter, have you met Henri?"

Hunter moved into the group. "No, I haven't as yet had the pleasure," he said, shaking the Frenchman's hand.

Aubrey Sizemore stepped forward. "I believe we've met, in the Cairo museum, Monsieur Lacroisse. I'm Aubrey Sizemore."

Lacroisse looked perplexed for a minute. "Yes, yes…of course. I remember you." The look on the man's face implied that he did not, really, but that he was being polite.

"Where on earth is Sir John?" Evelyn demanded. "Lord Wimbly, you did go to his flat and request his presence?"

"Well, of course I did, Evelyn. Sir John wasn't there, or at least, he wasn't answering his door," Lord Wimbly said. "I did, however, slip a note beneath it."

"Perhaps he didn't receive the invitation," Evelyn mused. "But that wouldn't be like him! When he's not at the museum, he's working at home."

"We'll hold dinner a few minutes longer," Brian said.

"He's brilliant. Just a brilliant man!" Lord Wimbly said of Sir John.

"An incredible speaker," Hunter agreed.

"Excuse me, please," Camille murmured. She hadn't seen Tristan and Ralph as yet, nor Alex Mittleman. And it seemed that the forced enthusiasm of the others for the missing Sir John was a bit on the cutting side, no matter what the words. "I'll just see if I can find Tristan."

"Camille," Brian murmured with a frown.

But she ignored him, and hurried up the stairs.

Alex was not in his room. Neither could she find Tristan or Ralph. However, when she returned downstairs, the diners were gathering in the ballroom. She had no choice but to join them.

The ballroom had been completely transformed. A long table, set more elegantly than even those at the fund-raiser just nights before, had been set out, resplendent with a fine cloth, delicate china and place settings in etched silver. Servers had been hired for the night, and everyone within the household, including Shelby, Corwin, Ralph and Evelyn Prior, had a place set.

Brian was seated at one end of the long table, she was seated at the other. And a number of others had arrived, trustees from the museum she had never met, several with wives and daughters. Two place settings were removed. One, of course, had been Sir John's.

She searched the company and discovered Shelby, too, was gone.

Talk about the subject filled the room. Arguments about the death of Hatshepsut—had she, or had she not been hastened to her death by her stepson, Tuthmosis III, who believed that she had usurped the throne at the rightful time for him to become pharaoh? And what of his rule in Egypt? He had been a great warrior, vastly expanding his empire.

Of course there was excitement in the talk because the find the Stirlings had made involved the reign of Tuthmosis III, and the powerful man who had stood behind the pharaoh, followed him into battle and, according to an ancient legend, lent him more than a touch of sorcery.

"No one has identified Hatshepsut's mummy as yet," Henri Lacroisse mused. "Now that would be a find!"

"So many were identified from the cache of mummies discovered in the 1880s near Deir el-Bahari, around Thebes," Lord Wimbly provided for Camille's benefit, since most of the others—those, at least, who knew what he was talking about—had been to Egypt. "So many pharaohs from the New Kingdom, hidden away by priests two thousand years ago! Still, a mummy is a mummy, and therefore fascinating. And any great tomb that is found intact…well, that is magnificent. Ah, my dear! You can't imagine the heat, the frustration, the terrible conditions, and then the delight of discovery! Perhaps, once you're married, your husband will set out on a new expedition, in honor and memory of his parents!"

Camille stared at Lord Wimbly, who apparently had decided that there was nothing odd in the least about Brian Stirling's startling and sudden announcement of the previous evening.

Brian was watching her down the length of the table. She saw his fingers locked around the stem of his wineglass so tightly that she thought it would shatter.

"Such an expedition would be entirely up to Camille, Lord Wimbly," he said.

Excited chatter rose about the possibility of a new expedition being mounted. Hunter seemed bemused, Alex looked ashen. Aubrey seemed fascinated with his food, and Sir John had yet to make an appearance.

Camille wanted to scream. She didn't believe that the evening would ever come to an end. Brian was being an exceptionally gracious host, drawing their French guest into very polite and animated conversation about different finds and purchases, and French and English relations with one another and with the Egyptians. At last, it was suggested that the gentlemen retire for cigars and brandy, and that the ladies should enjoy their coffee and tea in the pleasantry of the upstairs solarium.

Her mind raced. She smiled and rose, and with Evelyn, tried to be the most pleasant hostess, guiding their guests up the stairs. But it was all a charade, perpetuated by a man with a mask.

At last, people began to leave. Camille was with the others in the entry, but Evelyn Prior had taken over her natural duty, seeking wraps and overcoats, and bidding their guests farewell. With the confusion at the door, Camille thought she might have found her chance.

She walked through the great ballroom where caterers were cleaning, and slipped into the chapel room off the side. The door to the winding stairway to the crypts was closed. She eased it open, and started down. But then she halted. Someone was down there already. No, two people. And they were whispering fervently.

"She knows too much! Something must be done."

"Good God, you can't mean…"

"I do!"

"Don't be ridiculous. There are too many dead!"

"But there's a curse, isn't there? And it's easy to cause an accidental death."

How had these two gotten down there? Taken the winding stairway, as she had done? Or was there another entrance?

Her heart slammed against her chest. There was a chance they had slipped down here, and all she would have to do is wait at the doorway to the chapel, where caterers were moving about, where a scream would bring someone, and the killer...*killers* would be unmasked.

As she stood there, she heard a sudden uproar of horror coming from the front of the house. Shouts ripped through the old stone of the castle, tearing through the very night. Cries rose high in denial. The whisperers stopped speaking. Any minute, they would come up the steps; they would catch her standing there.

She turned, frantic, and headed up. The sound of her own footfalls and the thunder of her heart drowned out the sound of someone coming behind her. She reached the chapel and flew for the door out to the ballroom.

And it was then that she was attacked. Blinded. Something came flying over her head. A sheet. A shroud, she realized, stolen from down below.

She shrieked as loud as she could. She was shoved hard to the ground. Fighting the length of the ancient, stifling fabric around her, she tried to rise. She slammed into something. The altar?

She was dimly aware of footsteps, someone running. In panic she continued to battle the cloth over her head, spinning madly to avoid the next blow that would come at her. Arms came around her, she was lifted. She struggled fiercely as she was carried several steps. And then she was falling.

"SIR JOHN IS DEAD!"

Tristan had enjoyed the evening incredibly, having found himself seated next to a lovely widow who had been invited as her son was on the board of trustees. And he had been seeing the widow to her carriage when the announcement was made.

Shelby, who had apparently been sent to discern the whereabouts of Sir John, had returned with his dramatic and horrifying declaration as if on cue, right when everyone was hovering at the door, awaiting their carriages.

Being such a huge fellow, Shelby was able to make the crowd fall back as he walked through it, looking around, seeking Lord Stirling but not seeing him. And he made his announcement because he could not keep the news quiet any longer.

"Dead!" cried the lovely widow.

Someone else demanded, "How?"

"The police have not ascertained that as yet," Shelby said. Then, for several minutes, he could say nothing else because everyone was shouting out questions and voicing horror and dismay.

"My God! It can't be true?"

"Was it natural?"

"The police haven't said."

"Surely, he was murdered."

"Maybe another cobra bite."

"He was cursed!"

"Oh, my God!" cried Tristan's widow. "Perhaps they're all cursed in truth, all involved with that dreadful expedition! Oh! Maybe it will fall on all of us to be cursed, all of us associated in any way with the museum."

"Nothing happened until Stirling became involved again!" someone shouted.

Tristan looked around. Brian Stirling was not there to defend himself. But then he burst out into the entryway, tall and oddly forbidding in his beastly mask and elegant dinner attire.

"There are no such things as curses!" he announced loudly and angrily. "Only men with evil intent." His eyes shot out like blue fire around the crowd. "My parents were not cursed. They were murdered."

"My God, he believes it!" someone close to Tristan whispered. "Do you think Lord Stirling could have come out of his mourning and seclusion to kill the rest of them, one by one?"

It was a man speaking, but people were milling tighter and tighter, and Tristan couldn't see who had let out the explosive suggestion.

"People, there are no such things as curses!" Brian Stirling repeated. He looked around the group. "But there are such things as murderers, and the police will find the truth behind Sir John's death. When it is discovered, a murderer will face justice and swing from the hangman's noose!"

CAMILLE LAY AT THE FOOT of the winding stairs, stunned and bruised. Then, to her amazement, she realized that everything around her was silent. In panic, she fought her way out of the linen shroud. One small lamp burned on a desk, but for the most part, the room was in shadows and darkness.

She was here alone, trapped if someone were to come down the stairs. She'd be dead now if it hadn't been for the rise of voices so excited that they had filled the entire castle. Perhaps someone was hoping right now that she'd broken her neck after she'd been thrown down the treacherous stairway.

With that thought, she leaped to her feet. Her plan to search the cartons here for the mummy of Hethre now seemed insanely dangerous; she had to get out. Down here, in the dark, in the very bowels of the castle, she was trapped and in tremendous peril.

She threw the ancient linen shroud far from her, forcing herself to run up the stairs with a modicum of control, lest she lose her footing and come flying back down.

Someone had tried to kill her, someone who knew about Brian Stirling's crypts, the office, the cartons. And whatever else went on down here!

She had to get out, and quickly. Then the truth could be discovered. Yet at the top of the stairs, she found that the door was locked, bolted from the outside.

Again, panic filled her. Did she dare bang on it? With all the other excitement going on at the castle entry, would she be heard? And by anyone other than whoever had cast her down here?

She backed away from the door and returned to the office and storage area, looking desperately around for an escape—and a weapon. She flew to the desk where the single lamp burned and quickly rifled through the drawers. Nothing! Unless she could protect herself from a cunning killer with a pen!

She turned around to look at the room, praying for calm and an objective eye. The iron doors to the crypts were ajar, she noticed. Walking toward them, she saw that there was plenty of room for a body to slip through. It was dark beyond.

She went for the lamp on the desk, then moved into the vault area, listening warily for the arrival of anyone at the chapel door. She walked down the length of the tombs. It was cold here, very cold. Despite her firm hold on logic, the dank darkness seemed to slip beneath her skin. These weren't the ancient mummies of a different society, or a world so long gone that it was difficult to really feel the touch of the bygone lives.

Here the dead were Brian Stirling's family, knights, lords and ladies of old.

"Lady Eleanora, wife of James, Fifth Earl of Carlyle," she murmured aloud, raising the lamp.

A squealing sound nearly caused her to drop it. She spun around, her flesh crawling. To her horror, she saw a bat slamming against stone, trying to find a perch. A bat!

But if a bat was in here, then…there was another way out.

She held the lamp high, looking at the tombs that lined the wall. Then, setting the lamp down, she began to press against the stone slabs that closed each burial in. Time was ticking, she knew. Was she missed? *Were the whisperers waiting for just the right moment to return, to finish what they had started?*

She worked in a fever, pressing, pushing, shoving, tapping. Then she saw the fissure, small, barely ajar. But it wasn't right, wasn't flush with the others. There was a name on the stone, but it gave no date of birth. It said nothing except Sarah.

She pressed against the stone. And there it was, that noise she had heard time and time again. A scraping sound, stone against stone.

Swallowing hard, she pushed with greater force. The stone pushed backward and she stared into a gaping hole of darkness. Hesitantly, she grabbed the lamp. She set it into the hole, then hoisted herself up. It was difficult going, crawling along, moving the lamp, trying to see what lay ahead. And the space was suffocating. She had to steady herself against the walls, and try to maintain some sense of distance.

She hesitated, inhaling deeply, panic setting in as she felt the cramped darkness and the poor air all around her. She realized then that she really was trapped if someone came in from…from where? She didn't know where the passage led. The lamp would not offer a good enough view.

She forced herself to keep crawling, then realized that she was moving at an angle. Not downward, upward. She paused, fighting the dizziness caused by the cramped quarters and the lack of air. She moved the lamp, then steadied herself with a hand against the wall to her left. It gave way, crumbling. And she could see light at the end of the shaft now uncovered.

She blew out the lamp and began to crawl in that direction. Something covered the light, but still it was there. She kept moving, seeing an end in sight now, eager for air, for freedom from the tight wall of stone that had done no more than allow her to creep and crawl.

The light became brighter. She came to the end of the corridor. There was light, yes, but something barred an exit here. She pushed against it hard. Bit by bit, it gave. Desperate then, she managed to turn around in the shaft, to position herself and shove with all her might with her feet. She heard a groaning sound, a scraping.

The thing budged, barely. She pushed harder and harder. There was an inch, then another inch. Finally, there was room for her to slither out. She squeezed through the small opening she had created.

Then she looked around, with horror, realizing where she was.

BRIAN WASN'T SURPRISED that Shelby's announcement had created such an uproar. But as the news was absorbed and he vowed that the police would find out the truth about old crimes and new, the uproar died down. Now people were anxious to leave.

It was then that he realized he had not seen Camille. Tristan was standing at the entry, blankly watching the carriages as they left.

"Where is Camille?" he asked.

"What? I don't know. Dear God! I have to find her. This is going to be terribly upsetting to her. She worked with

Sir John day in, day out. This is terrible!" He lowered his voice. "The man in the square. Now Sir John. I have to find Camille!"

"Try her room, and I'll search this level," Brian said.

Tristan headed for the stairs. Brian strode swiftly back through the ballroom, but when he didn't see her, he started to turn. He hesitated, then headed for the chapel and opened the door to the curving stairway that led down to the dark crypts.

Striding back through to the ballroom, he snatched up one of the elegant candles from the dining table and hurried back, slowly descending the stairs, aware that a trap might await him. When he reached the office area, there was no one, but cartons had been moved about. Just slightly. By lowering his candle, he could see that dust marks on the floor were slightly off from the cartons. And there was a tattered, dust-covered linen shroud thrown on the floor.

He straightened, looking toward the great iron doors to the crypt itself. They were opened enough for a body to slip through. He entered the crypts. What he had looked for during a solid year was now boldly visible. One of the great stone slabs that covered every sarcophagus was open. It had been cleverly attached on hinges, the hardware apparently several hundred years old, yet as basic and sound as any that might have been made in their great age of industry.

There was no grave behind the stone, only a passage. He crawled into it. The going was rough, tight, and carrying the candle was difficult. Ventilation was almost non-existent. The candle, with no oxygen to feed upon, soon went out. Pitch darkness seemed to swim before his eyes. Then…a pale and distant light.

He followed it, dread beginning to fill him as he did so. At the end of the passage, he was blocked. There was a small opening, but it was not large enough for him to escape. Straining, he shoved at the object that blocked him, knowing exactly what it was and damning himself a thousand times over.

How had he not known?

CAMILLE TOOK A DEEP BREATH. She looked around. Then she fled.

Flying down the stairs, she heard voices. They were coming from the ballroom. She inched that way, but stopped, looking in, a fever in her heart. She no longer knew who to trust. Tristan? But Tristan wasn't in the ballroom. Nor was Ralph. She peeked in, and saw that Hunter and Evelyn Prior were there alone. Whispering.

"And now the announcement that Sir John is dead! Without the police even giving out the how and why," Hunter was saying.

Sir John...dead!

The horror of it struck her. No! She nearly cried out in anguish, but clapped a hand against her mouth. Sir John dead...

Hunter had been with him at the museum, when he'd supposedly struck his head on the carton lid. And old Arboc had been there, as well. Oh, God!

"Yes, well, you know what it all means?" Evelyn said. Their heads were bowed; they were close to one another. She said something else, something that Camille couldn't hear. Then she looked up suddenly, as if sensing that they were being watched.

Camille backed away from the door. She couldn't race back up the stairs, and she couldn't trust either of the pair in the ballroom at the moment. There seemed only one thing to do.

She ran out the front door. She could see a carriage just crossing the drawbridge to the forested property that comprised so much of the estate. Picking up her skirts, she ran. Her breathing was labored; she was in pain in a million places. Her heart thundered but she ran as fast as she could. Still, the carriage was moving far more quickly. She slowed, desperately gasping for breath.

Then she heard the snap of a twig behind her. She jerked around. No one was to be seen. But there, back by the courtyard entrance to the castle, there was someone. Someone who had seen her. Someone who was coming after her.

In sheer terror, she bolted into the woods.

BRIAN STEPPED OUT of the passage into his own room. His massive wardrobe, in place since the 1600s, had been the heavy object to block the small, square opening to the tunnel.

His heart thundered. Only one person could have slipped through so small a space from the tunnel. Camille! So what in God's name would she be thinking now? And had she heard the announcement about Sir John? Where the hell was she?

He tore out of his room and down the stairs. The entry was empty, no sign of anyone. A few carriages remained across the courtyard, their drivers most probably sleeping. Then, looking across the locked drawbridge, he saw a figure, dark in the night, running.

His heart sank. Camille! She was fleeing, terrified. *And terrified of him!*

She'd be ready to throw herself into the arms of anyone she knew and trusted. She was running into the woods. And into danger. Someone was a killer, and that killer could be anywhere.

As Brian started after her, he saw another figure emerge from the woods. Someone who was now chasing Camille….

As SHE RAN, CAMILLE realized that Tristan and Ralph were back at the castle—in danger. But she didn't dare go back! She had to elude whoever was following her! She couldn't help those she loved if she was dead herself!

Terror threatened to close her throat, to choke her. Brian was Arboc, and Arboc had been at the museum that day when Sir John had been injured. He had not returned…. He could well have discovered that Sir John was not dead and gone to his flat. But why?

Because they all had to pay the price. No! Brian was not a murderer. He was just determined to solve the riddle. She so desperately wanted to believe in him! But he had lied and worn that mask over and over again, in so many ways! The passage from the crypts led to his bedroom!

A cry sounded in the woods. Her heart thundered to a stop. He was calling out to her, trying to find her. She should stop, go to him. He wouldn't dare dispose of her then and there, in his own woods!

But she knew she couldn't talk to him. If he were to do no more than touch her, she was afraid that she would forget all logic.

She heard her name shouted again. It was Hunter's voice, she thought. She stopped for a moment, holding on to a tree trunk. Hunter! But Hunter had been whispering with Evelyn in the ballroom. And there had been someone whispering below in the crypts, whispering that she knew too much!

The wolves howled. She ran again, spurred on by plaintive cries to the moon.

BRIAN KNEW the forest trails. Camille did not.

He burst into the area where he had seen her head, and even in the moonlight, her flight had been so desperate and thrashing that he could easily follow her trail. But as he rushed at her, he was nearly flung back, the tie at the back of his mask catching on a dangling branch. Swearing, he ripped the thing from his head and went on.

He heard the cry of the wolves, and knew that they were near. He had encouraged the creatures to live in these woods; they had been part of his life as a bitter, monstrous recluse. The wolves were actually afraid of people. They wouldn't hurt Camille; they wouldn't come near her. They would run from the sounds of footsteps in the forest.

"Camille!"

There she was, at last, before him. She spun and faced him, and the way that she looked at him made his heart sink. He stopped, not coming closer.

"Camille! Camille, please, for the love of God, come with me. Come with me now." He spoke softly, reaching out to her.

They were both aware of the snap of branches just a few feet away, in the opposite direction. Hunter stepped into the clearing.

"Camille, thank God!" He strode for her instantly, and Brian, his voice rich with fury, snapped out a fierce warning.

"Touch her and you're a dead man."

Hunter narrowed his eyes at him, all pretense of friendship, courtesy and civility gone. He turned to Camille. "He's going to kill you, Camille."

Brian shook his head, his tone and posture pure steel. "Never!"

Hunter cast him a scathing and wary gaze. "You know that one of us is a murderer," he said to Camille. "For the love of God! Camille, the man is a monster and it's been proven. Carefully, quickly, come to me."

And Camille, her hair a tangle around her shoulders, her beautiful gown torn and dirtied, her face smudged, her eyes brilliant in the moonlight, looked from one to the other, torn.

He thought that she was about to go to Hunter! His muscles constricted painfully. She didn't know who to trust.

"Think carefully, my love," he told her. "Think of all that you have seen, learned and felt. Think back, Camille, and ask yourself, which man here is the monster?"

CHAPTER EIGHTEEN

"I DON'T TRUST EITHER OF YOU!" she cried.

Hunter took a step toward her, taking her by the arm, too roughly. "Camille, look at him! There's nothing wrong with his face. He's been wearing a mask just to play at lies and charades. He's obviously a madman!"

Brian strode toward him and wrenched him away from Camille, flinging him around. Hunter took a swing at him. There was no mocking the man's ability. He was muscled and strong, had fought with the Queen's troops and traveled far and wide, learning to defend himself. But he swung too quickly and too wildly. Brian avoided the blow, ducking below it. When he straightened, Hunter was already preparing to swing again. Brian caught him with an upper jab to the lower jaw just before Hunter's blow flailed against his shoulder. But he staggered back, and as he did, Brian tackled him.

"You're trying to kill us all!" Hunter roared.

"You bastard! All I want is the truth."

"Sir John is dead!" Hunter roared.

"I didn't kill him," Brian returned. "Good God, you might well have—"

"You wretch! I didn't kill him!" Hunter tried an upswing, but Brian had him down, his fingers around his throat then.

"Stop it!"

He heard the cry as Camille's fingers tore into his hair. "Stop it, you're going to kill him!"

He fought to regain his temper, and eased his hold on Hunter. He came to his feet just as a light came bursting into the forest. Shelby had arrived on horseback.

"Lord Stirling!" he cried.

Hunter rose on his own, attempting to dust himself off. Another horse arrived right behind Shelby. Tristan and Ralph were with him.

"Camille!" Tristan was off his horse in a flash, hurrying to Camille's side, taking her into his arms.

For a moment, Shelby remained upon his mount, as did Ralph. Hunter and Brian glared at one another, and Tristan looked at them both as if they were tigers in a zoo.

Tristan frowned at Brian. "There's nothing wrong with your face!"

"Precisely!" Hunter declared. "But there's everything wrong with his blackened soul!"

Camille gently disentangled herself from her guardian's hold, smoothing back her hair as if that could change the fact that she was covered in white chalky dust, twigs and dirt. "How did Sir John die?" she demanded icily.

They were all silent for a minute. Shelby answered her at last.

"A bite."

"By an asp?" she inquired incredulously.

"Yes."

"How?"

"No one knows," Brian said. "At least, as yet they don't know. The asp was in his flat. Apparently, he knew the creature was in there with him. He shot and killed it, but not before it got him."

She walked up to Brian, furiously slamming a hand against his chest, eyes blazing. "You were in there! You were in the museum with him on Saturday. As *Arboc!* And what a group of fools we were! None of us realized it!"

"I was in early. I never saw Sir John," Brian told her.

"Why?" she demanded.

"To take a look at the terrarium and find out if anyone had tampered with it." He hesitated. "Besides, Arboc was hired as manual labor. I had to put in a few hours cleaning and sweeping the debris from the night before."

"You've been lying to me!" she told him.

"He lies every step of the way," Hunter agreed.

But Brian kept his eyes locked on Camille's. "No, I never lied to you. I didn't tell you certain things because I had to be sure that I could trust you, that you really weren't working with any of these men."

"Working with us!" Hunter repeated. "At what?"

Brian turned to him at last. "At finding whatever it was that my parents were killed for. You see, there is a medieval entrance to the castle and tunnels that run from the crypts to that secret entrance beyond. I believe my father finally figured out the how and where of the entrance and the layout of the tunnels before he died. Someone else knows and has been breaking in."

He couldn't help it; he was moving toward Hunter again. "I can imagine what happened in Egypt, and when I do, I feel ill all over again. The killer threatened my mother first, until my father told him everything that he could. Crates had already been shipped. There were probably things he couldn't answer. But he must have told the killer—or killers—just where he believed the outer, secret entrance to the tunnels, and thus the crypts, to be. If the crates were here, at the estate, and someone was armed with that information, they could conceivably slip in without anyone being aware. My father would have said or done anything to save my mother. So he talked, and he was good. He probably talked a very long time while praying for time, desperate to save her life. He must have known that no matter what he said, the killers didn't intend for either of them to live. But he played for time, praying help would come before—"

Brian had to pause, the pain was overwhelming. Then he continued, "They didn't die easily. They were tortured first. The autopsy done here clearly shows the bruises on my mother's arms. No chances were taken. They were bitten time and time again. Do I want vengeance? Dear God, yes! Do I have any desire to kill randomly? No, you fool! I want the truth. I want a trial, and I want the killers to know every day before their executions that they are going to die, just as my father surely knew that the help he so desperately needed wasn't coming."

Silence followed. Then Hunter shook his head. "Brian, what you're saying…it can't be true."

"Come study the autopsy notes, Hunter," he said. "I have a strange feeling that Sir John knew. I don't know exactly what he suspected, but there was something. And that's why he's dead now, too."

The forlorn cry of a wolf rose to the heavens just then.

"We should go back to the castle," Tristan said, suddenly the man of reason. "There's nothing to be done out here, in the woods."

Brian was suddenly afraid that Camille would refuse to go. That she would insist it was time that she, Tristan and Ralph returned to their own humble little home—far away from all of this. But she didn't.

"Yes," she said. "It's time to return." And she walked straight to Ralph, who still sat on his horse. "A hand, Ralph? I am really weary, with no desire to walk back."

Ralph leaned down, catching her arm, helping her to a

sidesaddle position before him. Tristan went back for his own mount.

Brian realized ruefully that he might well be the Earl of Carlyle, but, apparently, everyone had decided that he and Hunter could just walk themselves back. And if they decided to tear into one another again in the process, well then, they could beat one another to pieces, if they so chose.

Brian turned and started back for the castle. Hunter fell into step with him.

"Secret entrance, did you say?"

"My father believed, from family diaries, that a tunnel had been dug—an ancestor was a staunch supporter of Charles I. I believe that messages, and people, came and went through the tunnel at that time. In the years that followed, there was no need. There was no more mention of it after the days of Anne Stuart, and the 1750 Act of Union with the Scots. The story fascinated him. He talked about it now and then. His passion was ancient Egypt, but he was also a huge believer that there was much for us to discover here at home." He was quiet for a moment. "Had he only stayed here."

They were both long legged and walked quickly. They crossed the drawbridge and approached the castle through the courtyard.

Hunter indicated the carriage, sitting at the far side. "I'll take my leave. I—really thought that you intended harm to Camille," he said. It wasn't exactly an apology. "I was a fool, I guess. The minute I met her…well, she wasn't just beautiful, but so incredibly intelligent and sure of herself. She would even flirt a bit and tease, but she had no intention of falling into any kind of an affair. I thought that I must marry above myself, being a lowly sir! But then you made your announcement, and I realized that I was a true

horse's ass! Oh, she knew I was enchanted. But I thought
that I was too good to offer more, since her background…
Ah, well, I am the loser. But I will remain her most ardent
defender! And, Lord Stirling, if you are not serious in your
intentions, if you…well, if you do harm to her in any way,
I swear, you will know how fervent an enemy I can be!"

Brian was startled by Hunter's sudden and truly
passionate declaration.

"You see, I have sense now," Hunter added. "I would
marry her. And cherish her the rest of my life."

Was it all an act? Brian wondered. So much of Hunter
was an act. Maybe they all put on acts. But was this a true
declaration? Or a scene calculatingly played out now, so
that suspicion would be averted from him in all ways?

"You may rest assured, Hunter, that I would not allow
Camille to be hurt in any way. And if I discovered that
someone did intend her harm, I'd kill him on the spot and
risk an assignation with the hangman."

Their eyes held as a breeze picked up in the courtyard.

"Well, then, where do we go from here? It appears that
the gloves are off, that we all suspect one another of all
manner of things. What do we do? There must be some answers, some reckoning. Sir John is dead," Hunter said.
"And God help us all, the museum is an incredibly fine institution. We'll be bringing it down along with ourselves
if we don't find a way out of the insanity!"

"Insanity? Yes and no. Someone is selling treasures out of
the country. Insane? Not when there's a fortune to be made."

"Lacroisse! You suspect Lacroisse of buying from…
who?"

"If I knew, we'd know who was guilty," Brian said,
watching him intently.

"In a thousand years, I'd have done no harm to your
mother!" Hunter told him. He shook his head.

"And I would not blindly go about murdering people!" Brian countered. "I believe that the police will begin questioning all of us."

"And if we're lucky, they'll find the answers," Hunter said.

"No. If the killers are lucky, the police will find the answers. Because if I discover the truth first...well, I'm afraid that I will remember exactly how my parents died. Good night, then, Hunter," Brian said, and he walked wearily into the castle.

TRISTAN WAS MARKEDLY UPSET, suggesting that they leave the castle as they rode.

"We can't do that," Camille told him.

"Why?"

"The answers are here."

"But we're in danger! People are dying," Ralph said.

She slid down the horse as they reached the courtyard and the great entry to the castle. "Ralph, if you're worried, you must go on home."

"What?" Ralph demanded.

"Camille, Ralph is making sense," Tristan said. "Alex bitten, and now Sir John dead! I'm not worried for Ralph and meself, we've lived good lives. But Camille, lass... dear God! I know you're engaged to an *earl,* but child, your life is worth more than any title!"

"Tristan, this has nothing to do with a title! Tonight there have been answers. And we are nearly to the end of it. We're not leaving," she said firmly. "Well, I'm not leaving. Perhaps the two of you should go—"

"And leave you!" he said with horror.

"I wouldn't want either of you hurt," she said softly.

"Camille—"

"Excuse me. I'm taking a bath," she informed him. And

she left them there. She walked back into the house, ignoring Evelyn, who was worriedly pacing the entry.

"Camille!" Evelyn said, horrified at her appearance. "What's happened? Where is Lord Stirling…Hunter? He said he saw you run out of the house. Into the woods!"

"Yes, I ran into the woods. Brian and Tristan should be back any minute. Good night, now. I'm going to my room."

"Camille!" the woman called after her, her voice sounding frantic.

"Good night!" Camille repeated.

Upstairs, she locked the door and began peeling off her filthy clothing. She ran water in the bath, grateful for the great iron tub and the fire heater beneath it. It didn't do to sit too long—one could scorch one's self in certain places—but the hot water was such a luxury!

Unfortunately, she needed more time for it to really heat, and she couldn't bear the dirt and dust upon her another minute. She sank into the water, knowing that he would come. And, of course, he did.

She didn't hear him enter the room, until he was standing in the entry to the bath, leaning against the frame, watching her.

"I had thought you'd be gone. That you'd have run far away," he said softly. "I thought that you'd still be angry."

She studiously scrubbed an elbow. "I am furious. I am beyond furious. And my heart is bleeding for Sir John. My little corner of the world is a disaster. And you are a monster!"

"But you're still here."

She looked over at him. His features were tense, his eyes dark.

"I am a part of the department," she said. "Sir John is dead, and that is quite personal, Lord Stirling. In truth, though I lack the men's college degrees and experience in the field, I am a scholar, though I've not thought so all these years."

"Ah."

She dropped the soap and cloth and stood, dripping, reaching for her towel. She approached him, eyes narrowed. "You…cad!" she told him, slamming against his chest as she had earlier. "You had to know that your wardrobe hid a tunnel!"

"I didn't," he swore, catching her wrists. "I swear to you, I knew nothing about it until tonight!"

She realized it was unlikely that he had. She had broken through a decaying wall to take the path she had. She looked up at him, knowing her eyes showed fear. "That wasn't the only tunnel. There was another passageway. Actually I broke into that route by accident. Brian, someone could get in—and now get up here!"

He shook his head reassuringly. "No. No more."

"But—"

"Shelby and Corwin are in the crypts now, sealing the tunnel with bricks and mortar."

She searched his eyes and sighed. "So…when you've heard that noise, someone has been in the crypts."

"I believe so. Definitely tonight." He said sternly, "What were you doing down there tonight? You little fool! With a household like that, you went down those stairs?"

She lifted her chin. "I was thrown down those stairs."

"What?"

She was sure that he hadn't intentionally locked her wrists in such a vise.

"I heard whispering."

"In the crypts? And where did you hear this whispering from?"

"All right, I did intend to go down. But I paused on the stairs." She stopped speaking, studying his face. She did believe him. She had seen truth in his eyes during his passionate speech in the forest.

And yet, she could have sworn that Hunter, too, had been passionate in his quest to save her.

She started to tell him that she was nearly certain she knew where to find the golden cobra, that piece which seemed to be drawing the murderer to acts of greater and greater recklessness. And she meant to tell him that the whispers she had heard had been threats against her life. But she didn't have a chance.

"Camille, I'm taking you out of this castle."

"What?"

"Tomorrow. No one will know. I'll bring you to stay with the sisters in the cottage."

She jerked free from his hold. "With...your child?" she demanded.

He looked at her, frowning fiercely. "My child?"

"They're raising your child for you, aren't they? Well, they are lovely ladies but, no, I will not go and live out there with them, another responsibility that you ask of them!"

He glared at her for a moment, then turned away, toward his own room. She hesitated, then followed him.

"You have done nothing but play games and lie to me since I met you!" she cried.

"No, Camille, I have never lied to you."

"You have just avoided telling me the truth."

"You can't stay here any longer," he said. "It's too dangerous for you."

"Well, I won't leave!"

He spun around, coming back to her. He groaned aloud, reaching out for her, pulling her against him.

"One more night!" he murmured.

And she lifted her chin to demand to know exactly what

that meant, but she found herself crushed against him, held…her mouth seized in a passion and fury that left no room for protest or denial. The tempest alive within her rose to meet the trembling fever in him. She dropped the towel and came into his arms, held him fiercely. His fingers slid into the sleek wetness of her hair and down the length of her back, cradling the naked curve of her rear, pressing her ever closer to him until he broke from her, studying her eyes, seeking words, shaking his head, kissing her again.

She drew away from him, eyes serious as she worked his jacket from his shoulders, pulled the perfect knot of his white tie, and worked industriously at the mother-of-pearl buttons on his vest and shirt. He let go of her, still studying her face intently as he eased his shoulders from the shirt and pulled her close again. She lowered her head for a moment, wondering if he knew that she was willing to risk her life to be with him, just to feel the muscled heat and vitality of him as she lay against him, just to feel him breathe. The rough-hewn touch of his palm found her chin, lifted it again, and his lips formed over hers with temperance guiding all that was leashed and desperate, with a tenderness joining fire and flame. And though she hungered against him, he was slow, kissing her lips, teasing her earlobes, pressing his mouth to her shoulders, her throat, and even those light provocative brushes of touch seemed to steal away what strength she had left. She ran her fingers down his back, teased along the spine, and slid her hands beneath the waist of the elegant black silk-lined trousers he wore, and at last found the buttons in front, sliding her hands beneath them, her touch insistent.

She could only tease so long, and his tenderness gave way to ardor and action. He caught her to him hard, his body angling, as he held a kiss while tossing aside a shoe, and then the other. His trousers were shed, and she was pressed against the pulse of his erection, distantly thinking that it was she who was insane, and not caring in the least as he lifted her, as they fell upon the bed where she had so seldom slept, heedless of covers, pillows and all else. Their mouths traced wet paths upon one another's bodies, met and melded again, tore away, until they were fused as their bodies were fused, and the madness of need and desire had locked them together as one. And as he moved, she knew how much she loved him, just what a fool she was, but that, yes, indeed, she would gladly risk her life for him, because he had managed to become her life, and it didn't matter at that moment what was a lie and what was true, being there could be no truth such as this that they shared.

Yet that night, he didn't stay.

When it seemed that the ceiling had become the sky and had burst into stars and that nothing in all the universe could be so passionate, so heated, he barely stayed within her, or beside her, but rose abruptly.

"Tomorrow, you go," he said harshly.

And to her amazement, he walked away from her, returning to his own room, closing the hidden door between the rooms that he had opened.

Stunned, she stared upward, at what had become nothing more than a ceiling once again. Her flesh still burning, her heartbeat rampant....

At last, she sat up. She found the nightgown that Evelyn Prior had given her the first night and slipped into it, then stared at the picture of Nefertiti. Brian had once told her that if she had needed him, all she had to do was pull at the left side.

She hesitated, then went closer. And she set her hand upon it, opening the hidden doorway once again.

He wasn't in his room, but in the second part of the master's suite beyond, in a robe with his family insignia embroidered upon it. He sat at his desk, studying some notes, and he looked up at her as if she were an unwelcome stranger.

"I will not leave here," she said. "Not when I have the answers."

"No one has the answers," he said harshly. "The police are now aware of what is going on. They are on to the sale of antiquities from England to buyers in other countries. They know that men have been murdered. It's in their hands now."

"But, I know—"

"Stop it! If you know anything, know this—you are in danger! You little fool, no matter what, you have to go where you shouldn't. You could have been killed tonight. But you had to go into the darkness anyway, you had to delve into the dead!"

"I found what you couldn't in a year's time!" she told him angrily.

"Did you? Come to think of it, just how did you find the passage, the right grave marker?"

"I found it because I was locked in the crypts and had to get out. And whoever is plaguing your castle hadn't quite gotten it lined up properly again!"

"That's the point. You were locked in the crypts."

"Didn't you bring me into this for information, to use me as a catalyst?" she demanded.

He stared. "Yes. Precisely. And your use and function are no longer required."

A rapping at the door startled them both.

Brian lifted a brow. She folded her arms over her chest, said, "We are engaged."

"No. The engagement is broken. Good God, Camille, what did you think? You're a commoner!"

The words were the cruelest blow she had ever received, though she had always been the one to deny the fact that he really intended marriage. Yet the concept of living with him, waking up beside him, sleeping with him nightly, had become part of the dream.

"Good Lord! Don't look at me like that. The engagement is off. You'll be well compensated," he said curtly. "But you will no longer live in this castle!"

"Brian?" His name was called as the rapping on the door sounded again. Evelyn Prior.

"Brian, I'm sorry, but Ajax has been in my room. He's going insane, though, scratching the door."

Afraid of betraying any more emotion, Camille turned to flee. She didn't do so fast enough. Or perhaps Brian was truly a callous beast and just didn't care. He rose abruptly and threw open the door.

Ajax bounded in, raced to his master.

"Down, Ajax, down!" Brian said, gentling his words by scratching the great hound's ears.

Evelyn was staring at Camille. Camille stared back. Then Ajax bounded at her. She wasn't ready, and he nearly knocked her over.

"Oh, Brian, I'm so sorry," Evelyn murmured.

"It's all right, he's here now. Let's try to get some sleep tonight, for the love of God!" Brian said impatiently.

"Ah, yes. Sleep," Evelyn murmured and departed.

"Why did you do that?" Camille cried, furious and near to tears. "Tristan is likely to call you out, you know!"

"You wouldn't leave," he said. "What was I to do? And don't worry about Tristan. We're not living in the Dark Ages. He can slap me in the face with a dozen white gloves, but you needn't worry. I'll do no ill to your guardian."

She stood stock-still, staring at him shocked. In a second, she would have turned and hurried away. But he groaned, coming to her, picking her up gently and taking her in his lap to sit before the hearth, as he had done before. He stroked her hair, shaking his head.

"I have to hide you away. I cannot risk your life."

"It's my choice—"

"No! This time, it is not your choice!"

"I believe," she said, "that I know where the golden cobra is. Or, at least, I know where to look to find it."

He drew back from her, studying her face. "Where?"

"They often bury mummies with amulets, actually in the wrappings," she said.

"Yes, of course," he said. "But for this golden cobra to be worth killing for, it can't be such a small thing as an amulet."

She shook her head. "I don't really know what it is. And I'm not sure how anyone else would know, since it was certainly never catalogued. And if it had been taken out of the tomb with the other treasures, arranged in a design or with a purpose, someone would have seen it, and it would surely have been catalogued."

"I'm lost. You're saying that it's probably not an amulet. Then…?"

"It's a larger piece, but I do believe it's in with the mummy."

He shook his head. "The priest's body has been unwrapped."

"What about Hethre's mummy? Is it here or at the museum?" she asked.

"Neither," he said. "Not that we know about, anyway. Hethre's mummy was never found—or never identified, at any rate."

"Maybe it hasn't been identified because those who buried her tried very hard to see that she wasn't identified. The golden cobra might have been a powerful piece, not just to keep away tomb robbers, but also, possibly, to protect the people."

"From what?"

"From Hethre. The ancient Egyptians themselves might have been afraid of her power. And so she was interred without identification, yet with a talisman that would assure she did not come back to work her power against them."

CHAPTER NINETEEN

SHE MUST HAVE SLEPT VERY HARD when she finally did so, because it was a long time before the rapping sound woke her. For several seconds she lay in comfort, listening until the sound became annoying. Then she realized that it was coming from the door to her actual bedroom, and that she was sleeping in Brian's room. And Brian was no longer beside her.

She leaped up, closed the hidden door, found a robe and called out that she'd be right there.

It was Corwin.

"I'm to take you to the woods, Miss Camille," he told her.

"What?"

"I'm to pack you up and take you to the woods. To the sisters' cottage," he explained, growing a little impatient.

She tried to remain expressionless, as her heart sank. Everything in her denied what Corwin was saying. She had thought…he cared about her. And needed her! But he had never said that. And she felt like a fool, a cold wind seeming to sweep around her heart. He had spoken the truth. The simple truth. He was an earl. She was a commoner. He cared for her, certainly. But surely many such a man had entertained himself with a young commoner!

"To the woods."

Corwin pulled out his pocket watch, studied the time. "An hour, Miss Camille?

She nodded, thinking. An hour! And she'd be packed off to the woods like…like an unwanted child.

Anger suddenly grew within her. So the Earl of Carlyle, whatever his motives, wanted her out of his castle. Fine.

"An hour will be fine, Corwin. What of Tristan and Ralph?"

"Sir Tristan has said that he will go where you go, and it doesn't matter where that might be."

"The cottage in the woods isn't all that large, is it, Corwin?"

"Ah, Sir Tristan and his man will be fine. There's a comfortable enough little spot in the barn, miss."

"With the animals?"

"Oh, no, there are no animals! The sisters don't need to be tending to animals, miss. They have a child to raise!"

No animals, no horses. Once she was out there, she'd be all but marooned.

"And what about Alex?" she asked.

"Miss Camille, he's doing very well. Tomorrow we'll see that he's brought back to his home."

"An hour, *then,* Corwin, thank you," she said agreeably. And she closed the door, her mind racing. She had an hour. One hour. She hesitated only briefly.

She looked around the room. There was nothing to pack, of course. Everything here had been provided for her, and anyone who knew her would know that she would take nothing with her. But she would be expected to take a few things. The earl wasn't seeing to it that she was brought home, he was having her taken to the cottage in the woods.

She threw open the door. "Corwin!"

He was only halfway down the hall and looked back.

"I…I'll have to take some clothing, I'm afraid. Would you please find me a portmanteau or something, anything in which I can pack?"

He seemed very relieved and nodded. "Yes, yes, of course, Miss Camille. Right away."

He returned quickly. And when he had done so, she washed and dressed with haste, threw a few things into the bag and scribbled a note to leave on the bed. Then she cracked the door open. She breathed a sigh of relief. The hall was empty.

BRIAN KNOCKED AT THE DOOR and waited. In a moment, he saw the eye that peered through the tiny hole, and then the door was opened.

"Well?" Sir John demanded.

"Word is out. Shelby made the announcement that you were dead, bitten by an asp. Whoever planted the snake in your flat is going to believe that you are gone. The papers are carrying the news of your demise. So we need only wait now and see what steps are taken next. Whoever is behind this might have taken a partial payment, and be growing desperate. During the dinner last evening, they were in the crypts. That's nothing new—I know that someone has been getting in, despite the wall and gate, since there is a tunnel, just as my father suspected. But the entry has now been bricked in." He paused. "And last night, someone threw Camille down the staircase."

Sir John gasped, halfway rising. "Camille! My God, is the girl—"

"She is fine, Sir John. And I'm seeing to it that she's taken somewhere safe, where whoever is up to all this will not make another attempt against her."

"You're quite certain?" He was agitated. "She's there now?"

"She will be quite soon. And there are officers at the gate to the castle, as well."

Brian had left without saying another word to her. She would have argued with him. He had instructed Corwin to see to it that she was taken to the sisters. And he'd told Corwin that she was to go—whether willingly, or bound and gagged and over his shoulder.

Sir John nodded. "What about Lacroisse?"

"I believe that the news of your death was frightening to him, but whether it was frightening enough for him to come to the police, or even to me, I don't know. Men like Lacroisse can become obsessed. And naturally, he has his status in his own country to temper his actions."

"Can't you just...threaten him?" Sir John suggested hopefully.

"Yes. But I wanted him really frightened first. John, I still believe that you can help me. And you know that every word I've said has been the truth. I know that you didn't want to believe that my parents were murdered, but if you can remember anything, anything about that day at all that you might not have said, I need to hear it."

Sir John sighed, and indicated that they should take chairs in the rented room. "There is a police officer on the other side of the door, right?" he asked nervously. "If you hadn't arrived when you did... I thought that I was prepared. I had my old war pistol in the drawer, ready, but I never saw the snake. If you hadn't shot it..."

"Sir John, that is over. I need you to talk to me."

"That day..." Sir John sat back, shaking his head. "Well, you know what happens after a discovery is made. Everything is slow, so slow and tedious! And yet everyone is excited. And there were so many treasures! Many pieces were slotted for the museum in Cairo, and your father paid a fantastic sum for those things he intended to take from the country, even more than was customary."

"He was fair in all his dealings," Brian said.

"Yes, a fine man to be a peer of England, a truly fine man. I miss him sorely."

"Thank you. So do I. But, go on. Please go on."

"Well, we had worked hard and almost everything was packed. We were to have a celebration dinner that night—late, of course, since we'd worked through the day and we were all in need of some thorough bathing, I can tell you!"

"Did you leave the site together?"

Sir John frowned, remembering. "No, Aubrey left first. He'd been doing the heavy work and he was exhausted, said he needed to lie down a bit. And then Alex. Alex has always been a bit fragile. He'd been ill, hadn't worked much during the weeks before, and he still looked like hell, so he was anxious for some rest, as well. Hunter was right behind him. Lord Wimbly—oh, wait! It was Lord Wimbly who left first. He wanted to get a letter out, said it was most important. Evelyn and I stayed behind with your parents and our Egyptian colleagues until the last box was hauled away. Then we headed back together. We parted in the center of Cairo. Evelyn, of course, left with your parents and I went back to the hotel. They had taken an old palace, you know, converted just for English visitors, such as ourselves. And Evelyn was in the little caretaker's cottage." He shook his head. "You really should be speaking with Evelyn. She found them."

"But you met in the restaurant for your celebration dinner, didn't you?"

"Yes, all the rest of us. Then…then Evelyn arrived with some men from the embassy. Poor woman, she was devastated."

"Hunter was with you, almost to the end?"

"Yes."

"But he still left before you?"

Sir John lifted a hand. "Yes, yes, I've told you all this."

"Who arrived at the restaurant first?"

"I did." He grimaced. "I was quite hungry, and didn't think that I'd be able to stay up much later!"

"And then?"

"Oh, Brian, it was a long time ago!"

"Please, Sir John."

"All right. I was there, and then, let's see…was it Aubrey who showed up first? Yes, yes, it was Aubrey. No! It was Alex. I remember now, because we were talking about his position at the museum. Then Aubrey, Hunter and Lord Wimbly. Lord Wimbly arrived last." He shook his head. "I'm not sure what good this is going to do you."

"Think again. Who did you see the day you found the newspaper clipping on the desk?"

Sir John shook his head in disgust. "Aubrey was in. I'm not sure about the others. You were there that day, you know. And Camille, of course. And I—" He paused, looking troubled, then sighed. "I had refused to believe that anyone could have caused those deaths on purpose. But once Camille had been at Carlyle and she seemed to believe you, I began to realize that I had been suspicious all along."

"But of *whom,* Sir John?"

Though his life had nearly been forfeit, Sir John hesitated. "Well, there were a couple of things," he said.

"Whatever your thoughts, I'm begging you, tell me."

"But I could be wrong!"

"Yes, but if you give me your thinking…"

"I believe that Lord Wimbly was in debt to someone. Serious debt. Yet, of course that's ridiculous! He's *Lord* Wimbly."

"Yes, he is in debt," Brian agreed.

"But Lord Wimbly loathes snakes of any kind," Sir

John said. "That's just it. There's only one man I know who can really handle them."

"Aubrey Sizemore."

Sir John nodded.

MIRACULOUSLY, CAMILLE WAS ABLE to slip along the hall, down the stairs and through the ballroom without seeing another soul. She had seriously feared a run-in with Evelyn, but the woman hadn't been about. In fact, the great castle seemed entirely deserted.

From the ballroom she entered the chapel, and from there, the crypts. The stairs were dark. Whatever work Shelby and Corwin had done, thankfully, they had completed last night. She was proud to have had the foresight to remember a lamp, and with it, she traveled down the winding steps easily. Once there, she knew that she could be caught by any member of the household at any time, so she moved quickly. And as quietly as she could. But there were so many cartons!

There was nothing else to do but start opening the lids one by one. That wasn't at all difficult; she was certain that Brian had been through everything here. At least ten of the large cartons held mummies. All she had to do then...was unwrap every single one, which would make many an Egyptologist shudder in horror. But present lives were worth more than history, she decided.

And so she began, probing, pulling and sneezing at the ancient dust and decay. She could have eliminated male mummies, but there didn't seem to be any. Instead, she had come upon most of the high priest's harem, she was certain.

She lifted her locket watch, checking the time. Her hour was nearly gone. They would be looking for her soon. Hopefully, they would believe the note.

Three mummies to go, and then it wouldn't matter. It

would mean that Hethre's mummy was at the museum, and she would somehow make someone listen to her enough that she could find the cobra—and stop the search.

She hesitated. Her discovery wouldn't expose the killer, but it would stop the attempted theft, and possibly more murders.

THE CARRIAGE RATTLED through the streets and at last arrived at Lord Wimbly's town house. Determined to accost him then and there, Brian left Shelby with the carriage, and pounded on the door.

Lord Wimbly's valet, Jacques, answered. He looked at Brian with suspicion, but he had been impeccably trained for his role as the great Lord Wimbly's man's man.

"Lord Stirling. Lord Wimbly is resting, I'm afraid. Did you have an appointment?"

"No."

Brian stepped forward, forcing the man to let him in.

"Dear me! Lord Stirling, I've told you. Lord Wimbly has not arisen from his private chambers! He has not rung for me once this morning."

Brian hesitated only a moment, then started for the stairs.

"Lord Stirling!" Jacques cried in dismay, racing after him.

"Get back!" Brian warned, throwing the door open.

As he had feared, Lord Wimbly lay on the floor. Brian strode across the room, watching his step. Behind him, Jacques let out a shrill cry.

"Stop it!" Brian commanded, stooping down to feel for a pulse. But Lord Wimbly's heart had long since ceased to beat. His eyes were open, and the bell he might have used to summon Jacques had fallen, just inches from his reach.

He had been dead for hours. Brian meticulously examined the body, then rose.

Jacques started to scream again. "The curse! Oh, my

God, the curse. An asp! He was bitten by an asp! Oh, good God, there are cobras here, snakes in the house. I've got to get out. I've got to get out, I've—"

"Jacques! Stop it!" Brian said again, and he took the man by the shoulders, shaking him. "He didn't die by an asp bite. I assure you, I would have found the marks. The way his mouth gapes open and he lies so contorted, I think we might be looking at a very different kind of poison. Get the police. Quickly. Do you hear me? Get through to a Detective Clancy with the Metropolitan police. This may appear at first to be a heart attack, brought on by his age. But there must be an autopsy. He was murdered."

"Murdered! Oh, God! Murdered. But I've been in the house all the time, ever since he returned last night! No one has come in, Lord Stirling, no one. Oh, my God! Lord Wimbly is dead! I…oh! I was here. They'll think that I… oh, I would never! What will I do now? What will the police think? What will they do? They'll arrest me! It's the curse! He should have stayed out of Egypt!"

"He was dead before he came home, he just didn't know it," Brian said. "The police are not going to arrest you. And I've got to go now. Do as I say, Jacques. Do it now!"

Brian ran down the stairs and out the door. He knew exactly who had been doing the killing and why. And he had to move fast.

ANOTHER MUMMY, crudely and heedlessly torn apart. True scholars would believe that she should be tortured for the next two hundred years, she thought. Then she began on the last one.

Even before she started, she felt a thrill of excitement. The embalming had the mark of care, with fine linen and exceptional resin. The mask that had been placed over the face was that of a boy, but the mummy was not male, no matter what the subterfuge. The wrapping had been built up in the chest area, possibly to flatten the breasts, but, Camille thought, more probably to hide the fact that something had been secreted in the wrappings.

She was so engrossed in her work that she didn't hear the footsteps on the stairs. She was totally unaware that she was being watched.

She took shears to the wrappings, carefully cutting the hardened area of resin. Then she began tearing at the ancient linen. Only when she heard the voice did she realize that she had been followed.

"You've found something!"

She looked up, startled by Hunter's arrival. He came walking across the floor to her, and she was afraid. "No…um, not really. I thought I was a scholar, that I could find something, but as you can see, I've just made quite a mess. If there were a department left, if Sir John were still alive, he would surely fire me."

Hunter's eyes widened and he shook his head. "No, Camille, you were right! I know what you were thinking. By God, yes! She was a witch. Hethre was a witch, revered, but feared, as well. And she *was* buried as she was because they wanted her soul locked in the world of the dead!" He paused. "And here…it is!"

She had found it, but it was Hunter who pulled the piece from the breast of the mummy. The years had done nothing to take away the magnificence of the piece. It wasn't the amount of gold in the sculpture, it was the jewels. The cobra was depicted with its collar flared. The eyes were huge, shimmering with the color of their gemstones. But diamonds, sapphires and rubies all made up the sparkling points on the reptile's collar.

Hunter was right next to her. She needed to get out of the crypt, away from him, as fast as possible.

"Camille!" he whispered.

He wasn't looking at her. He was staring at the magnificent piece. She walked away from him. He didn't seem to notice.

"Hunter, what are you doing here?" she asked.

"What?" He glanced back at her then. "I came to see Brian, to insist that he involve me in what was going on."

"So…you came to the crypts?"

He smiled. The smile terrified her.

"Believe it or not, there isn't a soul around. There were police at the gate. I stated my business, and they let me enter."

"There's no one upstairs?"

"I didn't go upstairs."

"You came straight here?"

"Yes?"

"Why?"

"Well, because—"

"Hey! Who is down there!"

The sound of the voice at the top of the stairs relieved Camille so much that she began shaking. Quickly she moved away from Hunter.

"Down here, Alex!" she cried. She kept backing away from Hunter. Alex came down. He had on a work suit and carried a little bag. He was ready to go home, she realized. He was well enough, and they were all being expelled from the castle.

She found herself between the two men. Alex waited curiously on the stairs. She turned from him to Hunter, who had slipped the cobra behind his back.

"Alex," she said, feeling ill, "call for Corwin, please!"

Hunter frowned.

"Alex!"

She turned to push past him and run up the stairs herself. But Alex blocked the way.

"Camille! Get away from him!" Hunter warned.

And Alex smiled. "Ah, yes! The great adventurer, the explorer, the ever charming Sir Hunter MacDonald! How convenient that you're here."

Shocked, Camille did as Hunter had suggested, she began to back away.

"Alex, I always knew that you were pathetic. I just didn't know how very sad, wretched and lethal you were!" Hunter returned.

"Lethal, my good and valiant, knighted friend!" Alex spat out. "I see you've found my treasure for me, Camille. Hunter, hand it over."

"Alex, if you don't get out of the way right now," Hunter warned, "I'll tear your heart right out of your chest."

"Will you?"

In a split second, Alex had caught Camille by the hair, wrenching her to him. At the same time, he dropped the bag he carried, spilling its living contents.

Asps, a dozen of them, slithered and hissed on the floor, right at Camille's feet. She cried as he dragged her with him, stooping down, securing one of the creatures and bringing the gaping fangs of the furious creature nearly to her throat.

"I'll take the treasure, Hunter," he said. "Toss it over! I'll throw this one down, and then leave the two of you here with a fighting chance, at least."

Hunter threw the bejeweled cobra. Alex had to drop the snake to snatch it out of the air. He shoved Camille. She screamed, plowing forward through the field of asps.

BRIAN HAD ESCHEWED the carriage, taking one of Lord Wimbly's fine riding horses instead and giving Shelby instructions. He raced the poor animal the entire distance back to Carlyle Castle. As he neared it, he damned his ancestors. Walled, gated at one time, surrounded by a trench!

Oil could have been poured down upon the heads of their enemies. But the castle had been made vulnerable.

At the gates he reined in long enough to speak to the police officer on duty there.

"Has my man left with Miss Montgomery yet?"

"No, Lord Stirling. But Sir Hunter MacDonald is at the castle. I told him you were out. He said that it was important, and he would wait."

Brian said nothing more to the man, but raced the soaked and panting steed along the path through the forest, over the drawbridge and to the house.

SOMEHOW, SHE STUMBLED past the snakes and came around the mummy cartons to stand with Hunter. Then they heard the shouting.

"Camille!"

Alex stopped where he stood on the stairs and smiled. "Stirling!" he shouted. "Stirling! Help, help us! It's Hunter. He's gone insane. He's trying to kill us!"

"No!" Camille screamed. "Brian, don't come down—"

Too late. He was at the top of the stairs, past Alex… Stopping when he saw the asps writhing on the floor.

"KILL HIM! Kill Hunter!" Alex cried out.

"Brian, watch him!" Camille screamed.

Behind him, Alex was preparing to shove him down the rest of the stairs. Her scream didn't stop Alex. Yet Brian didn't topple. He prepared for the assault that came his way. Alex had assumed that he could easily offset the balance of the larger, stronger man, but Brian was braced. He wrenched Alex from the stairs, hurtling him toward the floor. But Alex wasn't going down alone. He caught hold of Brian's lapels, and the larger man crashed down the last few steps with him.

"Dear God! Get something!" she cried to Hunter.

"What?"

She reached into the nearest carton, ripping free a mummy calf and foot. Amazingly, so far, the snakes had slithered away from the fighting men. They would be gone in seconds, hidden in cartons, beneath desks…. Or else, they would begin to attack.

Alex, weaker though he might be, was desperate. He struggled to reach into a pocket as Brian labored to subdue him. Alex produced a knife, brandished it beneath Brian's throat. They were locked in a fierce battle, Brian's fingers wired around Alex's wrist. One of the cobras slipped toward them, then rose in a defensive gesture.

"No!" Camille screamed, and she rushed forward, striking at the creature with the mummified foot.

The knife fell from Alex's hand. Brian got to his feet, dragging Alex up with him. When Alex would have lunged for the blade, Brian shoved him. Alex fell backward against the wall, slammed hard against it, sank downward. Right beside one of the cobras. It hissed and struck, catching him in the neck. He almost started to smile. But then another struck him, and another. He let out a piercing scream. And fell silent.

Camille could only watch in horror.

"Camille!"

Hunter came to her side, whacking away at something precariously close to her legs.

"Get out, *now!*" Brian shouted, drawing a gun, shooting one of the snakes, then taking aim at another.

The gunfire roared. A path was cleared. Camille started up the stairs, Hunter behind her. As she started to round the first curve, she stopped, causing Hunter to crash into her.

"Brian!" she cried.

Gunfire exploded again. A minute later, he was behind her, pushing her up the rest of the stairs. And yelling!

"When in God's name will you ever learn to listen to me!" he demanded.

"I was listening!" she shouted back. "An hour...Corwin gave me an hour. I was just using my hour, and...oh, God!" She fell into his arms.

"How the hell did you know *not* to kill me?" Hunter demanded.

"It's a long story. And I'm afraid of what we may find in the rest of the house," Brian said wearily. "We've got to find the others. Then we'll talk."

BRIAN'S SENSE OF URGENCY awakened new dread and anguish in Camille. With Hunter close behind her, she raced up the stairs to the living quarters.

She heard the thundering against the door as she neared Tristan's room. Someone was trying to break it down, apparently hammering it with a chair. And Tristan was shouting, hoarsely now, calling for help in one breath and damning Evelyn as a traitorous bitch in the next—language he would not customarily use.

Hunter pulled the ancient wooden bolt from across the door, and Tristan and Ralph tumbled out, Tristan trying to balance the chair he had used as a battering ram.

"Where is she? She locked us in, I know she locked us in!"

"I *did* not lock you in, you idiot man!" Evelyn Prior announced, coming down the hall in great disarray. She was furious, her eyes snapping. "I have spent the last hour in a linen closet, I'll have you know!"

Brian, still looking desperately worried, followed behind her. "Corwin remains missing," he said.

"The stables?" Hunter suggested.

Brian nodded grimly and started down the stairs. They

all followed. Brian began to run. The barn, too, had been latched from the outside. Brian threw it open and went in, looking around. They heard a groaning sound.

"Alive!" Evelyn breathed with gratitude. Following Brian, she ran for the bales of hay from which the groan had come.

There was Corwin, trying to sit up. He saw Brian and shook his head, seeming to be in more mental anguish than physical. "I failed you. I was in the loft…getting new tackle…and he came from behind…pushed me. I'd be dead now if it weren't for the hay. Oh, Jesu and Mary!" he cried, trying to stagger to his feet. "I failed you, the girl…"

His voice trailed as he stared at Camille. "You didn't stay in your room, did you."

"She has a very stubborn way of never listening," Brian said.

"Yes, and a lovely thing! She's quite a fitting lady for a Lord Stirling," Evelyn said, causing Camille to spin around with surprise. Evelyn smiled at Camille. "You would have truly loved Abigail, my dear. She was stubborn to a fault, too."

Camille felt a rush of guilt. She smiled in return, and almost informed Evelyn that Lord Stirling really had no intention of actually *marrying* a commoner, but it didn't seem the right time to do so. She shook her head. "I still can't…grasp this. Alex did all this? But he'd been bitten himself? He was ill, living in the house. Where did he get the asps? *How* did he do all this?"

"We may never have all the answers, but I have a few," Brian told her. "We need to get the officer at the gate to ride in to London and get Detective Clancy out here. Evy, we need to do something about poor Corwin's head."

"I'll take a ride down to the gate," Corwin said.

"No, you won't," Hunter told him. "I will. You're lucky you're in one piece, man."

"And you're lucky, as well," Brian told Hunter. It took him a moment, but then he added, "Thank you. I don't know what the hell you're doing here, but you definitely came to the defense. Thank you."

Hunter nodded. "Let me go talk to that officer. I think that I will expire myself with curiosity soon."

"Ask him to see that Sir John is brought out here, as well," Brian said.

"Sir John is dead," Camille reminded him. "I imagine you mean Lord Wimbly."

"No," Brian said, "Lord Wimbly is dead. Sir John is actually alive. And I'll explain it all soon enough. Corwin, lean on my shoulder. We'll get you to the house."

He helped Corwin to his feet. For a moment, his eyes touched Camille's. He smiled with so much tenderness and promise in his eyes. She hesitated, then reached out, pulling at the tie on his mask.

"You really don't need it anymore," she said. "I'm still completely confused, but it seems that beasts are no longer needed to keep guard at Carlyle Castle. I believe the curse has been broken."

CHAPTER TWENTY

"WHAT I DON'T UNDERSTAND is how Alex managed all this," Camille said, sipping Evelyn's delicious tea laced with brandy, feeling the warmth of the fire in the hall, and that of those gathered there. "And who was he whispering to in the crypts when he first attacked me?"

"You don't see that yet?" Sir John asked her, a wry smile curling his lips.

"Lord Wimbly?" she asked.

"We'll never know the whole truth," Brian said, standing by the hearth, an arm resting upon the mantel. "Both Lord Wimbly and Alex are now dead. And though I'd heard the story a dozen times from a dozen sources, I didn't really put the pieces together before this morning, when I was talking with Sir John."

"I helped you? This morning?"

"It was your reference to the fact that Alex had been ill. I'd seen mention of that before, in one of my mother's journal pages," he explained.

"You're not making any sense," Sir John said.

In silence, Camille agreed.

"Alex was ill, I believe, because that's when he suffered his first bite. He might even have begun experimenting with asps after that. That's why he dared allow the asp to bite him at the fund-raiser. He knew that there were enough people present who would know to slash the bite and suck out most of the venom. He might have gambled a little, but he was right on one count. Our suspicions centered on others because Alex, the poor workingman who'd tried to save the day, had nearly died for his pains."

"But *how* did he manage to bring in the asps today?" Camille asked, still at a loss.

"He procured them last night," Brian said.

"Last night! But he was here."

"Was he? There was a great deal of confusion and commotion going on. You had fled into the woods. Hunter and I were at one another's throats," Brian said.

"Alex! Who would have imagined," Hunter murmured.

"But he wasn't alone," Camille said. "He was working with Lord Wimbly. Yet why would Lord Wimbly have killed your parents when he was peer himself?"

"Titles don't keep one from falling into horrendous debt," Tristan supplied. "He was a gambler, is that it, Brian?"

Brian inclined his head toward the detective. "Detective Clancy started looking into a number of records after Green was shot in the square."

"Who was Green?" Camille demanded.

"A no-good cad and a hard-core criminal!" Tristan supplied. "Ralph and I helped in that one!" he said proudly.

A slow smile curved Brian's lips and he inclined his head toward Tristan. "Indeed, you did."

"What?" Camille demanded. She stared at Tristan. "You were too ill to leave the castle! When did you become involved in all this? And Brian! How could you risk Tristan's life—?"

"My dear lass!" Tristan interrupted. "I am a man well grown, having served in Her Majesty's forces. Ralph and I can handle ourselves quite well, thank you."

"I never realized I'd be putting him in danger," Brian

said, looking at Camille. He shrugged. "But he's a lot like you, apparently, unable to keep himself out of it!"

"Perhaps we should go back to the beginning," Aubrey said, clearing his throat. "Lord Wimbly would argue with your father now and then, Brian. Something that didn't seem to mean much, since we all argued over what should go where, how something should be excavated, how to deal with the Egyptian authorities and antiquarians, the French influence…many things. It was natural. No expedition exists without that kind of discussion going on."

"I argued with your father," Hunter admitted to Brian. "It was my belief that he was far too concerned with preserving Egyptian history for the Egyptians."

"Imagine," Camille murmured dryly.

"I believe," Sir John said, "that your father had bailed Lord Wimbly out of debt a few times. The day before they died, Lady Abigail had been excited about something she thought she'd read in one of the wall texts."

"Something about a golden cobra?" Camille asked.

"I didn't know it at the time, but now, in hindsight, of course. And Alex must have been with her when she read it. Therefore, he knew that it existed—and that it hadn't been catalogued. All he had to do was search long and hard, and he was convinced that he'd find it," Sir John said. "And the rest of us…we just didn't see any of this!" He shook his head. "Sadly, we didn't see the handwriting on the wall."

"Throughout the last year," Detective Clancy told them, "Alex has been managing to get little pieces to Monsieur Lacroisse, with the promise that an incredible find was coming. Lord Wimbly was pushing him hard. You see, Lord Wimbly was the one with the contacts in the Queen's social and international circles."

"But—"

"Right, I know what you're about to say," Detective

Clancy told her. "How would Lord Wimbly manage all this? He didn't. He made the contacts, Alex made the finds, and they'd hired the man killed in the square, Green, to be their go-between."

"Wait a minute!" Tristan protested. "Who shot Green?"

"Lord Wimbly himself," Clancy said.

"I still don't understand how Alex could have left here last night, gotten back to London and procured all those asps!" Camille said.

"He didn't have to go all the way back to London," Brian told her. "Neither of us followed the main tunnel from the crypts. It's a very long and narrow path, but I would assume, once a person has gotten accustomed to crawling its length, it is quite easily managed. We haven't sent anyone through yet, but I believe that we'll discover the tunnel leads out to a road, and that there will be cottages on that road. Alex Mittleman had most probably rented one of them and used it for his base of operations." He was quiet for a minute. "I believe he tortured my parents for any bit of information before they died."

Tristan looked at Evelyn. "So…you weren't out to smother Alex in the middle of the night!"

"No, and how dare you!" Evelyn said tartly.

"I have to admit, I grew suspicious of you myself," Camille told her.

"You were the one to discover the Stirlings, Evelyn," Hunter reminded her.

"Yes, and I suppose I did keep my secrets," Evelyn said. She looked at Brian apologetically. "They were alive when I reached them. Just barely. And there was truly nothing I could do. I was terrified, of course, afraid that the asps were still about."

"Aubrey, you were definitely under suspicion, being the one who handled the cobra at the museum," Brian said.

Aubrey groaned. "What about you! I had no idea myself that you were Arboc!"

Evelyn turned to Detective Clancy. "What about the Frenchman, Lacroisse? It's absolutely infuriating! He had to know that the objects being sold to him were obtained illegally." She was totally indignant.

Clancy sighed. "I'd like to see him rotting away in prison for the rest of his life. I believe he knew that lives were lost in all these quests. But the best I have managed is to see that every bit of information on him has been delivered to both the Queen and Lord Salisbury. He'll be expelled from the country. But that's about all we can do."

"I just can't believe it all," Evelyn said.

"An amazing conspiracy," Detective Clancy said. "And all of us working from different directions. From what I understand, Lord Stirling, the Queen did have tremendous respect for your parents. And you must have had an audience with her regarding all this, because she informed all her police agencies that they must be on guard for such illegal activities. It's just...well, we were searching for such a needle in a haystack!"

"And I'm afraid that I doubted the ability of the police to make discoveries when I was doing so poorly myself," Brian apologized.

"Excuse me!" Camille said, shaking her head. "But how did Lord Wimbly die?"

"Ah...well, my good friend will perform an autopsy, but I have a suspicion that Alex had begun to mistrust his partner. After all, Lord Wimbly was reaping all the benefits thus far while Alex was sneaking around the museum, trying to get his job done, and spending all his nights looking for the entry to the tunnel so he could comb through the cartons here as well as at the museum. There was a lot of money to be made in small pieces, and I believe we'll discover, once a thorough investigation has been done, that there are pieces missing from both the castle and the museum—catalogued pieces. But the cobra, both Lord Wimbly and Alex were certain, was the one treasure that would ease Lord Wimbly from his debt and give Alex an entirely new life," Brian said.

"But how did he die?"

"I think we'll find out that it was a massive dose of arsenic poisoning, and that Alex managed to administer it to Lord Wimbly when they were together here. I suspect Alex was afraid that Lord Wimbly might crack under pressure, and he'd also decided that his noble friend was faring far better than he from an illegal enterprise in which he was the one taking the risks."

Camille turned to Sir John. "And you! How could you let us believe that you were dead!"

Sir John cleared his throat. "Lord Stirling's idea, my dear. You'll have to take it up with him. I would have been dead, however, had he not arrived at my house, ready to question and accuse me!"

Brian's deep blue eyes settled on Sir John. "I was never more delighted, sir, to find myself able to believe in the innocence of anyone."

"You might have told me!" Camille said to Brian with a flash of anger.

He shrugged. "I'm sorry. Truly. But I wasn't taking any chances. If people believed that Sir John was dead, there would be no more attempts on his life."

"I imagine we'll be talking about this forever and ever," Hunter murmured. "Still, with Lord Wimbly, Alex, and even that man, Green, dead, we'll never know the complete story."

Evelyn stood angrily. "Perhaps this is very wrong of me, but I'm only sorry that Alex didn't suffer as Lord and Lady

Stirling did. He died in the same manner, but far more quickly, I'm certain. He was saved a date with the hangman, and true contemplation for his heinous greed and cruelty."

Tristan stood and walked over to her. "But it's over, my good Mrs. Prior. It's over now. That will have to be enough."

"It's not just enough. It's everything," Brian said quietly. He turned to Detective Clancy. "I'll ride into the city with you now. I believe we've explained everything the best we can. The body has been removed?" he asked.

"Yes," Clancy said. "Don't blame my poor fellows—they were afraid of coming upon more asps any second! They were like a group of women, afraid of mice!"

"All women are not afraid of mice!" Camille said, and she was startled when her exact words were spoken nearly in unison by Evelyn Prior.

They laughed together nervously. There was relief among them all, yet a touch of sadness remained that so much truly precious life had been lost to greed.

"I'll go in with you," Camille told Brian.

He absently fingered the scar on his cheek, and she knew that, though he wasn't a beast, it might take a bit of time to accustom himself to a life without pretense.

"Camille, it's not necessary," he told her.

"I choose to come in with you," she said firmly. Then she added, "Please. I'd really like to be with you."

She thought that he would protest again. After all, this had been his passion, his quest, for a very long time. The pain, sorrow and loss had been his. Finally it was over. Now he could allow himself to be the Earl of Carlyle in all ways, taking his place in society. And she would go back to her life as she knew it. But right now, she merely wanted to be with him.

"Brian," she murmured.

"As you wish, my love," he said.

IT WAS LATE when they left the police station, having told the story over and over again. And Brian and Clancy had prepared a release for the press together, one that would expel all rumors of curses, put blame where it belonged— and extol Queen, country and learning.

As they rode back to Carlyle Castle, they were finally alone in the back of the carriage.

"So, what will you do now?" Camille asked him.

He turned to her and grinned. "Hire a gardener? Open the grounds to the public on certain days? Bring in dozens of little orphans for picnics and games?"

She smiled. "Well, as for me, I believe I'll still have a job. Sir John will certainly remain working head of the department. I wonder who the board of trustees will find to take Lord Wimbly's place."

He was quiet for a minute. "Me."

She was startled. "And you...you will want the position?"

"Indeed. Men killed my parents, not learning or the wonders of history and the ancient world."

"Well, at least I should have work, then," she murmured.

"No."

"You would fire me?"

"Well, I don't see how you'll be able to keep your old position."

"Oh?" She was dismayed to feel bizarrely breathless, as if her heart had leaped to her throat and lodged there.

"An expedition down the Nile can take many months."

"Are you offering to hire me on for an expedition?"

"Hire you? Good God, no!"

Even in the dim light, she could see the cobalt-blue glitter in his eyes. "Well, then, Lord Stirling, just what are you suggesting?"

"As an Egyptian scholar, my love, you show me up a million times over. But as to hiring you, I don't think that one actually hires his wife for a honeymoon!"

Her heart leaped. *Honeymoon! And the Nile, an expedition, something she had only ever dared dream before.*

She looked away from him, tears stinging her eyes suddenly. "You needn't jest, you know. You stated quite clearly that you'd never marry a commoner, and solved though your riddles may be, I remain a commoner. And when the rest of the flurry dies down, some intrepid newsman will discover that my mother was an East End doxy and…"

"Camille?"

"What? I am merely speaking—"

"Don't."

"Don't what? You're the one—"

"Oh, my God you are argumentative! I shall just have to learn to live with it, or else find a way to keep you quiet. Ah! I may know one!" he said, and before she could draw away or protest, his mouth was on hers. When he finished with the tenderness and passion of the kiss, she couldn't remember a word she had intended to say.

"Good, you're quiet!" he teased. "I never meant a word of what I said. I'm truly sorry that you never met my parents, for they were blessed, yet the least class-conscious people I ever knew. My mother would have adored you. She would have had the greatest admiration in the world for you and *your* mother because you had nothing and made everything of yourself from it. Abigail, my dear, was first and foremost a mother, a fabulous parent. She would have admired and had great sympathy for all that your mother did for you and your future."

"But you don't have to marry me just because—"

His finger fell on her lips. "Good God, let me finish!" His smile eased the firm force of his words. "I am not marrying you 'just because' of anything. Ah, Camille! You're so brilliant, so fierce and yet so blind in some ways! I adore you. I am madly in love with you, with your determination, your stubborn streak, your intelligence—as well as your recklessness in following your heart. But you will have to quit putting your life at risk—that is something I will insist on in my wife! Camille, don't you see? It wasn't just a mask I wore. Everything about me was ugly, bitter and cursed. Then you stumbled into my life and stripped away the mask and the curse. Without you I fear I may find myself stumbling again, cursed for all time. You'd not allow that, would you?"

She was unable to speak.

"Now I'm asking you to talk," he said.

She smiled. And in the small confines of the carriage, she threw herself atop his lap, kissing him with the wildest abandon.

"You mean it…to marry me?" she asked incredulously.

"Well, only if you love me."

"Oh, dear God!"

"It is asking a lot, for a woman to love a wretched beast."

"I do love you!" she whispered fervently. She locked her arms around his neck. "Absolutely. And we will open the grounds to orphaned children, and we'll do what we can to help those who are born into poverty and squalor. And the Nile! Oh, Lord, we'll go down the Nile!" She grew serious suddenly. "But Brian, we must bring the child to the castle to raise!"

"What child?"

"Ally! The sisters are wonderful, but you must take responsibility."

To her amazement, he burst into laughter.

"This is not a joking matter!" she told him fiercely.

"I dare say the sisters will break both your arms, my dear, if you try to take Ally from them."

"But—"

"I'm sorry, Camille. I should have corrected you before, but I'm not sure you would have believed me. Ally is not my child."

"But—"

"I have no children, my love, though I am quite willing to make all manner of attempts to achieve the state of fatherhood. I would love a little girl like Ally."

"But then who…?"

"The sisters were great friends of my parents. My father granted them several annuities, and thus, they are like aunts to me. I know Ally's suspected parentage, but it is suspected only, and a confidence. I have to ask you to believe in me, and love us both, if you will. She isn't my child, but she does refer to me as Uncle Brian." He hesitated. "She's not my father's child, either. There is a possible royal connection, but this is something you must never repeat. Many are afraid it could cost the child her life."

"Good Lord!" Camille exclaimed.

He brought a finger now to his lips. "It must be kept forever secret," he said very seriously.

"Of course!"

He smiled. "She is a lovely child and ever dear to me. She was never frightened by the mask."

"Well, neither was I!" Camille told him.

"Never?"

"Well, only a little!"

He laughed and kissed her.

When they reached the castle, they entered hand in hand. Evelyn came anxiously from the ballroom.

"Well, the others are back to their lives or picking up the pieces thereof!" she said. "And now, finally, here you two are! Ralph has gone off to some pub with Corwin. Tristan and I waited dinner for the two of you but you didn't come. Still, we've really just begun."

"Forgive me, Evelyn. Please go ahead," Brian said. He cleared his throat and looked at Camille, unable to keep the spark of sheer vitality from his eyes. "I'm afraid I feel the need to retire immediately."

"Well," Evelyn murmured, frowning. "Camille…"

"Exhausted! Absolutely exhausted!" Camille said, and she flew for the stairs.

Seconds later, he was behind her. And she was in his arms. Clothing was strewn…and she enjoyed every single, wonderful inch of her naked beast.

IN THE GREAT BALLROOM BELOW, Evelyn sighed, taking her seat, watching Ajax nap happily before the fire. She looked at Tristan.

"Well, Sir Tristan, I do believe we'd best plan this wedding quickly!"

"Ours?" he teased.

"I never!" she protested.

"But you will," he promised.

Evelyn was shocked to silence.

"Oh, come, come, Evelyn!" Tristan said. He rose. "Good heavens, woman! You may use that superior little tilt of the nose and perhaps confuse others, but never me."

"I never!" she said again, her voice sounding a little strangled.

He walked around the table, coming up behind her. His

hands landed gently upon her shoulders and he lowered his lips to whisper against her ear.

"But don't you want to?" he asked with quite an insinuating grin.

"*Their* wedding!" she said firmly.

"Of course. And then ours," Tristan said.

"We shall talk!" she said primly.

"Ah, we shall do much, much more!" he assured her.

She turned, ready to protest once again, but he kissed her. An excellent kiss, he thought. Not pushing his luck too far, but…

And at last, when he drew away, she was silent for several moments.

"We will talk," he assured her.

At last, she cast propriety to the wind.

"And much, much more!" she whispered, whereby he determined he absolutely must kiss her once again.

Don't miss out on
SHANNON DRAKE'S
next epic tale of passion and adventure

Coming in September 2006

Reckless

*Turn the page for an exclusive extract from
this enthralling read*

Chapter 1

"DEAR LORD! HE'S GONE into the water!"

Katherine Adair—Kat to her friends and beloved family—gasped and leapt to her feet. Just seconds before, she'd been sitting on the deck of her father's vessel—sadly misnamed *The Promise*—reading and indulging in dreams. The day had been like many other Sundays she had spent throughout the years with her small family aboard the boat on the Thames. Often, as they'd watched the elite in their far more magical vessels, she had smiled as her sister, Eliza, mimicked the upper-crust accents, then joined her in singing old sea chanties—all the while looking to see if their father was about before adding a few of the more risqué lyrics.

But there were times, of course, when she did nothing but indulge in dreaming…about the very fellow whom a wave had just swept from the deck of the far finer leisure yacht *The Inner Sanctum!*

David. David Turnberry, youngest son of Baron Rothchild Turnberry, brilliant student at Oxford and avid sailor and adventurer.

"Kat! Do sit down! You'll rock this old scow and we'll be in the drink, too," Eliza chastised. "Don't worry. One of those Oxford chaps will dish him out!" she said with a sniff.

But none of them did. The river was wicked that day—fine for Kat's father, who used the turbulence in his work—but a poor time for entertainment. The young swains who had accompanied David on the sail were clinging to the rigging, looking into the water, shouting…but *not* jumping in and attempting a rescue! She recognized one—Robert Stewart, handsome, landed and charming, as well, David's best friend. Why wasn't he in the water? And there was another of his chums…she couldn't remember his name…Allan… something…

Oh, the fools! They hadn't even thrown in a life preserver, and David was so far from her own vessel that any attempt on her part to do so would be useless.

They shouldn't have been out on a day like today. They imagined themselves to be such sailors, and they were still so young, so raw. The river was far too rough, only for fishermen and fools. And, she thought ruefully, her father.

But now they'd lost David! And still, there was no one aboard heroic enough to dive in for the dear man's salvation.

Indeed, the waves were high, and she could understand their trepidation. But her heart cried otherwise. He was beautiful, magnificent. No fellow in all of England or surely even beyond had such a smile. Nor had she ever heard a fellow of his social position speak so kindly to those who were hard put to earn their meager living from the sea. She had watched him so often.

"They're not going for him!" she cried.

"They will."

"But he will drown!" Kat looked around quickly. Her father had brought in their own sails; the scow was merely riding the waves now.

In fact, her dear father was not working or paying the least attention to her. Lady Daws had come with them today; and she was laughing—the sound something like that of a sea-witch cackling, Kat thought sadly, something her father simply didn't hear—and that completely enraptured the hardworking man upon whom she had set her sights.

Kat looked back anxiously at the river. Maybe what had seemed like an eternity to her had been nothing more than a few seconds. Maybe the fellows had needed a moment to draw on their reserves of courage. But no…time ticked away, and none of those young swains aboard the richer vessel had made the slightest attempt to effect a rescue.

"Kat! Don't look so perplexed. Come, come…he can probably swim. The beaches are still all the rage with his crowd, even though the poor can now reach our beaches by train. Of course, the elite, they say, prefer to frolic in the Mediterranean."

Though Eliza spoke of the rich with disdain, in these moments with the sailing almost done for the day and the afternoon near its end, she always had her nose thrust into the pages of *Godey's Lady's Book*. She did love her fashion. And she could sew delightfully, creating fantastic designs from such bizarre materials as cast-off sails and canvas.

Kat paid her sister little attention. Her heart seemed to have lodged in her throat. She couldn't even see the young man's head bobbing in the waves.

Ah, there! And far from his own sleek vessel.

"The sea is too rough!" she exclaimed in a whisper. "He will die!"

"There is nothing *you* can do. You'll but kill yourself," Eliza warned fiercely.

"Ah, but I *would* die for him. I would sell my very soul for him!" Kat returned.

"Kat, what…?" Eliza began in horror.

Too late.

Being poor sometimes had its advantages. Kat shed her heavy, solid and sensible shoes and slid her cotton skirt down her hips to the floorboards. In seconds, she had also shed her secondhand jacket. She had no corset, no bustle, no darling little hat to discard, and so, despite her sister's protests, she leapt into the filthy water in her shift.

The chill hit her viciously.

And the waves were mercilessly rough.

But she had spent her life nearly as one with the sea. So she took a big lungful of air, plunged beneath the surface and swam hard.

She bobbed up first near the sleek yacht. She could hear the fellows on deck shouting, their voices sounding desperate.

"Can you see him?"

"His head… He's down again. Oh, God! He's going to drown… Bring her around, bring her around, we've got to find David!"

"I can't see him anymore!"

Kat took another deep breath and plunged beneath the surface again. She kept her eyes open, straining to see through the murky depths. And there…

There she saw him. To the right and a few feet below her.

Dead?

Oh, Lord, no! She prayed as fervently as she sought to reach the man. David. David the beautiful, the magnificent. Eyes closed…body sinking…

She grasped him, as her father had taught her to grasp a fisherman fallen overboard, catching him beneath the chin with the palm of her hand, allowing her to draw his head to the surface, while leaving her torso, legs and the solid strength of one arm to draw him toward shore.

Ah! The distance.

She could not make it!

But it seemed that both the luxury yacht and her father's fishing vessel were ever farther out to sea. What other vessels were at sail or anchored seemed at even greater distances. She had to make the shore.

She kicked, trying to stay calm, to remember that she mustn't lose her strength by using it to fight the rough water— that she must go with it, let the tempest take her until it drove her toward the shore.

She tried hard to keep David's head above the water, tried harder to keep breathing and moving herself against the waves, white-tipped, gray and brown, like living, breathing, beings anxious to suck her into their depths. How slender the river could seem at times, but…how great its span!

And yet, chilled and desperate as she was, it occurred to her…

He was in her arms. Oh, God! He could die in her arms.

As she would gladly die in his.

"GOOD LORD! WILL YOU LOOK at those young fools!" Hunter MacDonald stared at the young swains who raced around their yacht like simpletons. They'd lost one of their number, yet none was doing a damn thing about it.

He cursed them roundly, then called out to Ethan Grayson—his mate at sea, manservant and his friend. "Bring her in! I'm going for the boy."

"Sir Hunter!" Ethan, weathered and strong and far too sensible a fellow not to have risen far, protested strongly. "You'll but go down yourself!"

"No, Ethan, I'll not." Hastily removing shoes, jacket and trousers, he offered Ethan a grimace. "My good man, I've escaped crocodiles in the Nile. I shall be fine in this bit of English weather."

And so, stripped down to his drawers and shirt, he dove neatly overboard in the direction where he had last espied the young fellow's bobbing head. As he did, he could hear Ethan scolding him angrily: "Being a 'sir' does not give a fellow common sense, no, it does not! He survives famine, war and the evil in the hearts of men, but then drowns himself like the young idiot he would save!"

Too late! thought Hunter. The Thames closed around him as he cut through the waves, swimming with strong exertion to bring the heat of movement to his person.

The water was bitterly cold.

It had been easier to swim in the Nile with crocodiles, he ruefully admitted to himself.

AT LAST! KAT AND HER BURDEN had nearly reached the embankment.

She was far from the docks, closer to Richmond now than the City of London. A mist of rain was falling as she struggled through the remaining few yards of water, hitting mud beneath her feet at last, mud and God knew what else, some broken crockery that cut into her sole. She barely felt it, however, for she had him to land at last. Exhausted, near crawling at the end, she dragged David's dead weight up onto muddy sod and scraggly grasses, but not far from the road; homes and businesses and even ships at dock were visible nearby. She fell to his side at first, breathing, ah, doing nothing at all but breathing! Then as her lungs filled, she looked at his face and was roused to fear. She jerked up, then leaned on his chest, hard, pushing, determined to expel the water from his lungs. He choked, and water dribbled from his blue lips. Then he coughed and coughed...

And finally fell silent, other than the slow rasp of his breath.

She stared down at him, shaking. He lived. "Thank you, God!" she whispered fervently. And then, seeing his long lashes sweeping the contours of his noble face, she added, "You are so beautiful!"

His amber eyes opened. He stared up at her.

And she was horrified, for she was far from looking her best. Her hair was, as a rule, rich and long, if a bit glaringly red, but now it hung in sodden ropes. Her eyes—normally the oddest shade of green and hazel, sometimes almost the color of grass and at others almost gold—must be quite pinkened. And her lips were surely as blue as his. Her linen shift clung wetly to her body, and she was shaking uncontrollably. That he should see her so, when she still lived in a world of dreams, when society did not allow for the daughter of a humble, struggling artist, an Irish one at that, to so much as dare imagine a life among the elite, was the worst thing she could have imagined.

His hand moved. Fingers touched her face. For a moment, his own was dark and troubled, as if he sought an answer as to where he was, and why. "We were with the wind, listening...laughing...for there were songs on the air, as if the Si-

rens called to us, and then...pushed!" he murmured. "By God,
I swear I was pushed! Why..."

Then his eyes focused on her. And a smile flitted over his
lips. "Yes, yes, I felt hands against my back, pushing...but who
the devil...and then...the cold...and the darkness. Then...you!
Am I seeing things? You're an angel!" he whispered. "A sea
angel...an angel, and I love you!" Then he laughed. "No! A
mermaid, and thus I am alive!"

His fingers—on her face!

And the words he had said!

Ah, she could have died then and drifted to heaven in pure
bliss.

His eyes closed. Panic seized her. But she could see him
breathing, his chest rising and falling, and she could feel his
warmth.

Voices suddenly sounded. Looking up, she saw a group coming from the gravel road that led down to the embankment. She
jumped to her feet, aware of her near-naked state, her shift plastered to her body, providing not the least bit of modesty. And she
was very chilled, of course, making that immodesty all the more
apparent. She wrapped bare arms around herself.

"Oh, they're searching for him...but I saw...something!"
The voice was feminine, sweet and touched with the sound of
a sob.

"Now, now, our boy can swim, Margaret!" returned a male
voice. "He'll be just fine."

Kat now saw a very pretty woman, slim and elegant in a late-
summer day dress, a jaunty little hat sitting at an angle on her
head, a parasol in her hands, her bustle twitching as she walked
on dainty heels. Her hair was a soft ashen blond, and her eyes
were as blue as the sea. Beside her was an older gentleman in

a resplendent suit, cape and top hat, and they were coming closer and closer.

Kat's heart seemed to stop. In her mind's eye, she saw only the contrast between the elegant lady and herself, and she knew she had to escape. Quickly.

As she turned to run back into the water, a man rose from the waves not twenty yards away.

He was tall, lean and sinewy, his musculature quite evident, for he, too, but for an open shirt, was stripped down to his unmentionables. His dark hair was plastered to his head, and his classically sculpted face was frowning.

"Miss!" he called.

And that was it. She cried out softly, sprinted the few feet back to the muddy water's edge and plunged in, diving beneath the surface as soon as she could and swimming harder than she had ever done in her life, unaware now of the cold and the aching in her lungs and limbs.

She surfaced, she knew not where, just as the rain began.

"MARGARET!"

David blinked, staring up through the mist of rain. And there she was, Lord Avery's fair daughter, the very lovely and rich Lady Margaret, on her cheeks tears of a greater substance than the rain, staring down at him. Heedless of the mud, she sat on the embankment, his head cradled in her lap.

His heart leapt. Although she often appeared to care for him deeply, in fact, in the race for her hand, he had thought both Robert Stewart and Allan Beckensdale to be far ahead of him.

And yet now…how sweet to see her face!

For a moment, he was puzzled. There had been a fleeting moment when…he had thought he'd seen someone else. A different face. Fair and comely, with eyes a strange green fire and hair a searing flame-red. An angel? Had he come so close to death? No, then perhaps a mermaid, a sprite from the sea, or rather the river?

Had he imagined her?

And had he imagined, too, in the bluster of the day and the roll of the yacht, the hands at his back, pushing him, forcing him into the river?

"David! David, please, speak to me again, are you all right?" Margaret demanded anxiously.

"I…oh, dear, dear Margaret! Yes, I…I'm fine!" Not true. In fact, he was quite cold, but that mattered not in the least, not when this much-sought, beautiful lady was so gently tending to him.

Those eyes, so brilliantly blue, so studded with tears!

But…

"You saved me," he said, still confused.

"Well," she murmured, "I did drag you up the bank, hold you here, so dearly, in my lap."

"He will live!" These words, dry, rough and impatient. And a spray of icy water falling on him.

"Sir Hunter?" David gasped, looking toward the voice. And, indeed, he was there, the renowned sailor, soldier, excavator and all-round adventurer; the toast of London society, standing above him, furious and frowning.

And dripping.

"He's safely in your hands now, Lord Avery," Hunter said dryly to Margaret's father, who stood, David saw then, anxiously watching just a few feet away. "I must find the girl."

"The girl?" David echoed, blinking again.

"The one who saved your life," Sir Hunter said curtly, and David could hear the unspoken "You fool."

"Good God, Sir Hunter, you cannot mean to plunge back in—" Lord Avery began.

"Oh, but I do," Hunter said. "Lest she drown."

"You'll drown yourself!" Lord Avery argued. "If there is a girl out there, the boatsmen or fishermen will find her surely."

Lord Avery's protests were apparently insufficient for Hunter turned and strode back into the water.

"Father, he'll be all right!" Margaret called, adding with a touch of admiration that sent a pang through David's heart, "Sir Hunter MacDonald can withstand any hardship."

Sir Hunter, David thought, ever the hero, strong and brave and invincible. And I myself here on the muddy shore, gasping, barely alive…

But in her arms!

"I hope you're right, my dear," Lord Avery said, kneeling down beside David as well and, slipping his fine jacket from his shoulders, placed it around David. "Thank God you survived, my boy! Can you rise? We'll get you to the road and then to the town house before you catch your death of cold."

David, trying to fathom what was real and what lay in the soul of his imagination asked, "There really was a girl?" He looked at Margaret.

"Yes…that or, truly, a sea creature!" Margaret said.

"We'll see that she's rewarded for the act, assuming that Sir Hunter can indeed find her. How very odd that she ran back into the river. She must be quite mad. Or perhaps she's a lady of some fine family, afraid to be seen!" Lord Avery said gruffly. "One can only speculate, however, David. Right now, we must get you warm. That blasted river! Rarely is it anything less than wretched!"

"Yes, of course," David murmured, "Thank you. But if there was a girl…a strong girl, rich or poor, we must indeed see that she is rewarded."

Again he remembered—imagined?—being pushed into the river. It had been an act of pure malice and evil intent.

Whoever had done it had meant for him to die.

But why?

Margaret? To eliminate the competition for her hand?

Or was it something else entirely?

Suddenly he was afraid, deeply afraid, though he dared not show it. The thoughts tore through his mind. He and his friends had simply gone out for a day of sport and fun. Alfred Daws, Robert Stewart, Allan Beckensdale, Sydney Myers, all fellows he knew well. He'd studied with them, played cricket with them, trusted them….

He had to be mistaken!

And yet, if it hadn't been for the girl who'd—

"David?"

His name was said with such anxiety! And Margaret smelled of roses, so delicious, and her arms were around him as she helped him to his feet.

"The girl saved your life," Margaret agreed. "Your precious life."

He forgot Lord Avery, forgot his fear regarding his friends, everything, as he stared into the sky-blue of her eyes. He needed his future secured. As the son-in-law of Lord Avery, it would be.

"Ah, but we know the real truth! *You* saved my life," he declared. "You, with your gentle caring. You have brought me back. Even here, upon this shore, I might have died. Indeed, I would have died had I not opened my eyes to see your beautiful face!"

Her cheeks turned a delightful shade of pink, and he dared to mouth "I love you so!"

She did not reply, but the pink suffused to a darker shade as she reminded him softly, "My father, David!"

Yes, he thought, Margaret was indeed beautiful. And sweet. And very rich. For him, she would be the perfect wife.

He vowed then and there that he would be her husband.

SAVING THE OBJECT OF HER deepest desire had been difficult, but never in the long, cold struggle to bring him to shore had Kat feared for her own life.

Now, suddenly, she did so.

What a fool she had been to plunge back into the water! True, her sad state of undress might have brought about a few snickers and she'd certainly be considered rather scandalous. But what was scandalous compared to being dead!

Tired, cold and disoriented, she fought to retain her strength, to rise enough within the growing fury of the river to find either the shore or one of the vessels—fine or misbegotten—that braved the Thames no matter the weather. But though the rain had not come in heavy sheets as the sky had seemed to warn, it had formed a thick, blinding mist atop the churning waves. She was adrift in a cold sea of gray in which she seemed entirely alone.

She treaded water, turning this way and that, trying to see something through the haze. She knew she had to keep moving, lest the chill enshroud her. The euphoria she had felt after her rescue had faded completely, along with her strength. She was not sorry she had saved him—was his life not worth far

more than her own?—but only sorry that she had been so foolish to run—or swim!—away. She struggled to give herself the
impetus to go forward. She was her father's daughter, after all.
A creature of the sea, a part of this wet, murky world.

At last, she calmed herself and rolled onto her back, then
frog-kicked sideways into the current. But as she relaxed, a new
fear—that of the darkness, of knowing that the Thames was
little more than a sewer pit, seized her as she saw something
move. Ridiculous notions shot into her mind. Snakes! No,
none in the waters here, surely. Serpents—just as silly. Sharks—
in from the sea? Here? In the Thames? Heavens, no, but still...
Oh, God, there was something in the water!

She let out a scream, then choked on water from the wave
that splashed over her, gagged. Desperate, choking, barely able
to breathe, she started her frog kick again.

Something touched her!

Something...against her bare leg, and then on her hip. She
kicked harder, to propel herself away. Then she felt it again.
Something smooth, strong, slippery...

"No!" she shrieked. She would not die so—definitely not
on the day he had told her he loved her! She would not die
in the water. Water was her home, it was what she knew, and
she would not, could not, give in.

When the thing rose near her, she lashed out with a fist as
hard as she could.

"Good God, girl! What on earth ails you? I am doing my
best to save your life."

It was a man. Just a man. She could make out little of him
against the waves, but his voice was deep and rich and commanding. And then she remembered that a man had come out
of the water when she'd been at David's side, that his appear-

ance, along with that of the elegant young woman, had been the impetus to send her back into the dreadful river.

"Save my life! You're the reason that I'm threatened with the end of it!" she shouted back.

"Child, my craft is but a hundred yards south!"

A wave crested and washed over her. She had not been prepared, and she chocked in water, coughing, gasping.

And he was there, a wall of steel, an arm coming beneath her breasts, sliding most immodestly against her. She struggled.

"Damn you, be still! How on earth will I save you?"

"I don't need to be saved!"

"Indeed, you do!"

"If you'd cease trying to drown me, I'd be doing quite well!"

But she was lying, she realized. She was truly spent. Staying on the surface and fighting the waves was becoming ever more difficult.

Naturally, however, as she cried out her accusation, he released her.

And just as naturally, another wave smacked over her just as she was still recovering from the last. And she went under.

A mighty kick brought her back to the surface and into his arms.

"Be still!" he snapped. "Else I shall slap you into unconsciousness so that I can save your wretched life!" The sting of his words was far worse than a slap.

"I'm telling you—"

"Don't tell me!"

"But—"

"Dear God, woman, will you shut up!"

She had to then, for once again her mouth filled with river water, and she choked. She felt that steely power wind around her again, and despite the cold, his arms were warm, and despite her fury, exhaustion was winning. She felt a blackness creeping over the gray and brown of the day and the river, and suddenly it seemed right to close her eyes, give in....

His strength was great, for she was no longer moving on her own, yet felt as if she had been lifted, as if she were skimming over the water. Her head and nose remained above the surface.

Then there were voices, men's voices, and she realized that they had come to a sailing vessel, a very fine one.

"Ethan!"

The shout startled her and she jerked violently away. Her head slammed against the bow of the yacht, making her gasp with pain.

Stars burst brilliantly before her eyes.

And then...blackness.

"SWEET MARY!" ETHAN exclaimed, his powerful arms capturing the slender being Hunter had salvaged from the sea, lifting her as if she were no more than a toy. And holding her tenderly, he stared at Hunter for the briefest moment before hurrying with his bundle down to the cabin.

The yacht yawed, and Hunter stumbled to the helm, grasping control as the wind ripped around them. Ignoring the fact that he was soaking wet and chilled to the bone, he swore as he struggled with a wicked shift in the wind, furled the sail on his own and brought the craft around. Ah, well, he was a sportsman, was he not? Still, he had not intended such sport today.

Ethan returned topside bringing a blanket and a cup of warm brandy. With a nod of thanks, Hunter took the latter first, drained it and felt the heat seep back into his body. He took the blanket, wrapping it around his shoulders, while Ethan took the helm.

"She's all right?" Hunter asked, shouting to be heard.

"Nasty crack on her head!" Ethan shouted back. "But she opened her eyes. I've wrapped her in several blankets and given her a sip of brandy. She'll be warm enough, and well enough, I imagine, while we make for shore. Where do we take her? To hospital?"

Hunter frowned and shook his head. "They say such places are improving, but I'd not take even a dog there. We'll go to the town house. You're sure she's all right? She fought me like an insane woman…."

"Begging your pardon, Sir Hunter, but when you reached the yacht, I believe her head might have struck the hull."

Ethan had seen a number of injuries, since he'd served alongside Hunter in battle and across several continents. He was a fine man when it came to setting bones, and he was equally adept at dispensing medications. He knew a mortal injury when he saw one, and this one certainly didn't qualify.

"Who is she?" he demanded.

"I haven't the faintest notion," Hunter replied. "She apparently dived in to save young David, but from where, I do not know." He paused, thinking. Had he seen her before? She was not among last season's display of coming-of-age young society beauties, of that he was certain. He would have remembered her. Even wet and bedraggled, she was striking.

She had the abilities of a fish in water, so it seemed, and had been quite positive she didn't need rescuing. Her hair…what color! Even wet, it was like fire. And her eyes, when opened, flashed fire to match that hair.

Then, of course, only a blind man could miss the perfection of her form. She was no hothouse flower, but all lean muscle and sinew, long legs, trim hips and…beautiful breasts. Firm, full, straining against the taut fabric.

He winced at his lascivious thoughts. But he wasn't a blind man. He couldn't have missed them.

"Brave little thing!" Ethan said. "Diving in when none of his fine, hearty companions could manage to do so."

That, too, was true.

But then again, Hunter had seen the way she had looked at David on the embankment. Utterly rapt. She hadn't dived in for someone who was a stranger to her. There had been something about that look, something that any man or woman living seldom achieved, yet might crave with all the heart. Indeed, she would have gladly given her life for David.

She's in love, he thought.

"You think she's a friend of the chap?" Ethan asked now.

"I've never seen her before," Hunter said. "But then, I'm certainly not privy to all of young David's acquaintances. Indeed, I've only come to know him because he is due to take part in the upcoming excavations along the Nile. And because, of course, his father is interested in financing such work."

"Good Lord! You don't think she's a…"

"Doxy?" Hunter cocked his head, musing. "No," he said after a moment. "She hasn't the look. No hardness in her eyes. Not yet, anyway. But whoever she is, she will be a bit richer than she was, for Lord Avery is determined she be rewarded. Meanwhile, let's just see to her welfare, eh?"

In another thirty minutes, the yacht was in and duly berthed. Hunter held the girl in his arms, wrapped warmly in the blankets Ethan had provided her, while Ethan brought round the carriage. Though the area at the docks had been much busier early in the day, the fair-weather sailors had come to realize that such a day was not for sport. Now there was no one about.

Certainly not young David, or any of his party. Though Hunter knew that Lord Avery would be true to his word and reward the girl, the man would not be overly concerned about her welfare. David would be his first concern.

And, of course, Margaret.

Ethan reined in the handsome carriage horses, and the two stood still, awaiting their burden. Hunter entered the carriage with the girl in his arms, needing little assistance.

"Home then, and quickly," Ethan said, closing the doors and climbing up top to take the reins.

And as they rode, Hunter looked down at her face. It was truly beautiful. Skin, though ever so slightly tanned, as smooth as alabaster. Straight nose, lips perhaps a bit too wide and full for the current accepted state of fashion. Her cheekbones were high, her eyes large, lashes long and dark.

She stirred. Frowned.

A smile creased her lips, so sweetly.

She seemed to doze and to dream, and whatever she dreamed, it was sweet.

The dark lashes twitched and then rose.

Her eyes focused upon his, and she frowned.

"You're with us," he said softly.

Her lips moved. She seemed to have lost her voice.

"What?" he coaxed.

Something about her at that moment awoke a deep tenderness in him. He wanted to protect her. To bring all that was warm and gentle around her.

Her lips moved again.

He leaned close to catch the least whisper.

"You!" she breathed.

He heard the intense dismay. He clenched his teeth, forced a smile. And remembered the way she had looked at young David.

"Indeed, dear girl, 'tis I. And I do apologize. I should have left you in the water!"

Her eyes closed again. Apparently she still hadn't realized where she was.

He was tempted to throw her off his lap, but he held his temper. Even in his most wretched moments, he had never been that bad a scoundrel.

"All right, then, who are you? And when we return you safely to your home, just where would that be?"

Once again, her eyes flew open and assessed him with what appeared to be anger. By all the gods, they were truly magnificent eyes, blazing with their unusual color. At this close range, he could truly inspect them. Blue-green along the outer rims, fading to green, then to gold. Extraordinary. Hmm, she was definitely a redhead, but it wasn't a carrot color, rather like a deep, rich flame. And those dark lashes...

Wherever she came from, she was probably pure temper, and some poor father, brother or lover might well be glad of a holiday from her tongue!

She continued to stare at him, her expression becoming perplexed.

"Well? Who are you?" he demanded.

Her lashes fell. "I..."

"Good God, answer me!"

"I don't know!" she snapped.

And so saying, she pushed from his hold, righting herself most regally—until she realized that she'd lost her blankets. She flushed, cast him a furious glance, and dragged the blanket back up to sit in noble silence.

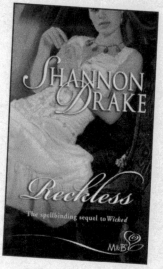